Marcus Tullius Cicero, Andrew P. Peabody

**Ethical Writings of Cicero**

De officiis, De senectute, De amicitia, Scipio's dream

Marcus Tullius Cicero, Andrew P. Peabody

**Ethical Writings of Cicero**
*De officiis, De senectute, De amicitia, Scipio's dream*

ISBN/EAN: 9783337405908

Printed in Europe, USA, Canada, Australia, Japan

Cover: Foto ©Andreas Hilbeck / pixelio.de

More available books at **www.hansebooks.com**

# ETHICAL WRITINGS

OF

# CICERO:

## DE OFFICIIS; DE SENECTUTE;

## DE AMICITIA,

### AND SCIPIO'S DREAM.

### TRANSLATED

WITH

### AN INTRODUCTION AND NOTES.

BY ANDREW P. PEABODY.

BOSTON:
LITTLE, BROWN, AND COMPANY.
1887.

# CICERO DE OFFICIIS.

TRANSLATED

WITH

AN INTRODUCTION AND NOTES.

BY

ANDREW P. PEABODY.

BOSTON:

LITTLE, BROWN, AND COMPANY.

1887.

University Press:
John Wilson and Son, Cambridge.

# SYNOPSIS.

---

## BOOK I.

## BOOK II.

## BOOK III.

# INTRODUCTION.

THERE are two systems of ethical philosophy, which in every age divide speculative moralists, and are recognized with a more or less distinct consciousness in the conduct of life by all in whom the moral sense has attained mature development. They are, indeed, in different ages and by different writers stated more or less explicitly, in widely varying terminology, and with modifications from culture, religion, national character, and individual proclivities. They are, also, sometimes blended by an eclecticism which cannot wholly transcend the lower, yet feels the intense attraction of the higher sphere. One system is that which makes virtue a means; the other, that which makes it an end. According to the one, we are to practise virtue for the good that will come of it to ourselves or our fellow-beings; according to the other, we are to practise virtue for its own sake, for its intrinsic fitness and excellence, without reference to ulterior consequences, save when, and so far as, those consequences are essential factors in determining the intrinsic quality of the action.

Of course, this general division admits of obvious subdivisions. The former system includes the selfish and the utilitarian theory of morals, — the selfish making the pursuit of our own happiness our duty, and adaptation to that end the sole standard of right; the utilitarian identifying virtue with benevolence, accounting the greatest good of the greatest number the supreme aim, and beneficent utility the ultimate standard of duty. The alternative system, according to which virtue is to be practised, not for what it does, but for what it is, includes, also, various definitions of virtue, according as its standard is deemed to be intrinsic fitness, accordance with the aesthetic nature, the verdict of the moral sense, or conformity to the will of God. These latter theories, widely as they differ, agree in representing the right as having a validity independent of circumstances and of human judgment, as unaffected by the time-and-place element, as possessed of characteristics connate, indelible, eternal; while the selfish and utilitarian schools alike represent it as mutable, dependent on circumstances, varying with time and place, and possessed of no attributes distinctively its own.

In Cicero's time the left and the right wing in ethical philosophy were represented by the Epicureans and the Stoics respectively, while the Peripatetics held a middle ground. The Epicureans regarded happiness — or, according to their founder, painlessness — as the sole aim and end of moral conduct, and thus resolved all virtue into prudence, or judicious self-love, — a doctrine which with such a disciple as Pliny the Younger identified virtue with the highest self-culture as alone conducive to the happiness of the entire selfhood, intellectual and spiritual as well as bodily; but with Horace and his like, and with Rousseau, who professed adherence to that school, afforded license and amnesty to the most debasing sensuality.

The Stoics regarded virtue as the sole aim and end of life, and virtue is, in their philosophy, the conformity of the will and conduct to universal nature, — intrinsic fitness thus being the law and the criterion of the right. Complete conformity, or perfect virtue, is, according to this school, attainable only by the truly wise; and its earlier disciples, while by no means certain that this ideal perfectness had ever been realized in human form even by Zeno, the great master, yet admitted no moral distinction between those who fell but little short of perfection and those who had made no progress toward it. The later Stoics, however, recognized degrees of goodness, and were diligent expositors and teachers of the duties within the scope of those not truly wise, by the practice of which there might be an ever nearer approach to perfection. This philosophy was, from Cicero's time till Christianity gained ascendency, the only antiseptic that preserved Roman society from utter and remediless corruption.

The Peripatetic philosophy makes virtue to consist in moderation, or the avoidance of extremes, and places each of the individual virtues midway between opposite vices, as temperance between excess and asceticism; generosity between prodigality and avarice; meekness between irascibility and pusillanimity. It admits the reality of the intrinsically right as distinguished from the merely expedient or useful; but it maintains that happiness is the supreme object and end of life, and that for this end, virtue, though essential, is not sufficient without external goods, — so that the wisely virtuous man, while he will never violate the right, will pursue by all legitimate means such outward advantages as may be within his reach.

The New Academy, whose philosophy was a blending of Platonism and Pyrrhonism, while it denied the attainableness of objective truth, maintained that on all subjects of speculative philosophy probability is attainable, and that wherever there is scope for action, the moral agent is bound to act in accordance with probability, — of two courses to pursue that for which the more and the better reasons can be given. The disciples of this school accepted provisionally the Peripatetic ethics.

Cicero professed to belong to the New Academy, and its ethical position was in close accordance with his nature. Opinion rather than belief was his mental habit, — strong opinion, indeed, yet less than certainty. His instincts as an advocate — often induced by professional exigencies, not only to cast doubt on what he had previously affirmed, but with the ardor of one who threw himself with his whole soul into the case in hand to feel such doubt before he gave it utterance — made the scepticism of this school congenial to him. At the same time, his love of elegant ease and luxury and his lack of moral enterprise — though not of courage when emergencies were forced upon him — were in closer affinity with the practical ethics of the Peripatetics than with the more rigid system of the Stoics; while his pure moral taste and his genuine reverence for the right brought him into sympathy with the Stoic school. Under no culture short of that Christian regeneration which is less a culture than a power could he have become heroically virtuous; under no conceivable influence

could he, such as he was in his early manhood,
have become grossly vicious. He believed in virtue, admired it, loved it. His aesthetic nature
was pre-eminently true and pure. His private
character indicates high-toned principle. In an
age when all things were venal, no charge of corruption was ever urged against him, even by an
enemy. He neither bought office, nor sold its
functions. Associating familiarly with well-known
convivialists, who regarded a wine-debauch as
always a welcome episode in the pursuits whether
of war or of peace, we have no vestige of a proof
that he ever transgressed the bounds of temperance, and there is not a word in his writings that
indicates any sympathy with excesses of the table.
Living at a time when licentiousness in its foulest
forms was professed without shame and practised
without rebuke, we have reason to believe that he
led a chaste life from his youth ; and though as an
advocate he was sometimes obliged to refer to subjects and transactions offensive to purity, and in
his letters there are passages which might seem
out of place in the correspondence of a Christian
scholar of the nineteenth century, it may be
doubted whether in all his extant writings there is
a single sentence inconsistent with what a purist
of his own age would have deemed a blameless
moral character.

He has been, indeed, charged by some of his biographers with motives of the lowest order in the divorce of the mother of his children after a union of thirty years, and his marriage with a young heiress, his own ward. But by the best standard that he knew, though not by the Christian standard so profligately ignored and outraged in our own section of Christendom, he was more than justified. His wife was no little of a virago, had wasted a great deal of money for him in his absence, and had willed property under her control in such a way as to give him just displeasure; and it appears from his letters that he exercised the then unquestioned right of divorce solely on these grounds, with no specific marriage in view, and that the alliance which he actually made was preceded by overtures both to and from other candidates for that honor. Moreover, the charge of mercenary views in this marriage is negatived by its speedy dissolution on his part, with the sacrifice of the entire and large fortune which it brought to him, on the sole ground that his bride had manifested unseemly satisfaction in the death of his daughter Tullia, whom she regarded as her rival in her husband's affection.

Yet there were heights of virtue beyond Cicero's scope. He was wholly destitute of the martyr-spirit. He was much of a Sybarite in his habits. His many villas, furnished with equal taste and splendor, gave him the sumptuous surroundings and the aesthetic leisure without which he could not regard even virtue as sufficient for his happiness, and times of enforced absence from wonted pursuits and enjoyments were filled with unmanly complaint and self-commiseration. He loved applause, suffered keenly from unpopularity, and vacillated in his political allegiance, sometimes with the breeze of public opinion, sometimes with his faith in the fortunes of an eminent leader. He often worshipped with manifest sincerity the ascending star, and had little sympathy with fallen greatness. He was thoroughly patriotic, would have sacrificed for his country anything and everything except his own fame, and coveted nothing so much as opportunities like that afforded by the Catilinian conspiracy for winning celebrity by signal service to the republic. He had, too, large and profound wisdom as a statesman; but his best judgment generally came too late for action, so that had he derived a surname from classic fable, it would have been Epimetheus, not Prometheus. As an advocate he was supple and many-sided, yet he always impresses his reader with his sincerity, and probably a prime element of his pre-eminent success in the courts was the capacity of making a cause his own, and throwing into it for the time genuine feeling and not its mere eloquent semblance.

His lot was cast in an age when only an iron will could have maintained, along with the conscious integrity which, as I think, characterized Cicero's whole life, the perfect self-consistency which no stress could bend or warp. When we compare him with his most illustrious contemporaries, it is impossible not to assign to him a pre-eminent place both as to private virtues and as to public services. It is only when we try him by his own standard that we have a vivid sense of his deficiencies and shortcomings.

Cicero's only son, with the heritage of his name, Marcus Tullius, seems to have inherited few of his father's distinguishing characteristics, and not improbably may have borne, in some respects, a close moral kindred to his high-spirited mother. He was impetuous, irascible, headstrong, brave as a soldier, and though indolent except when roused to action, not without ability and learning. At the age of sixteen he served with great credit in Pompey's army. After the defeat of Pharsalia he was sent to Athens to complete his education. He fell there into habits of gross dissipation, being led astray by one of his teachers. He, however, yielded to his father's earnest remonstrances, expressed great grief and shame for his misconduct,

and entered upon a regular and studious course
of life, winning high credit with Cratippus his
teacher, and receiving warm commendation from
his father's friends resident or sojourning in
Athens.   He subsequently fought with distinction
under Marcus Brutus, and after the battle of Phi-
lippi joined Sextus Pompeius in Sicily.   Returning
to Rome when peace was concluded with the
Triumvirate, he was an object of special regard
with Augustus, and after holding several offices of
lower grade, became his colleague in the consulship.   He afterward went as proconsul to Asia
Minor, where his name drops from history, which
but for his father might never have found place
for it.

When it appeared that Brutus and Cassius had
effected nothing for the republic, and Antony was
becoming all-powerful in the state, in the spring of
44 B. C., Cicero, deeming his life insecure, left Rome,
and spent the summer successively at several of
his villas in Western Italy. . He beguiled his disappointment and sorrow at the issue of public
affairs by philosophy and ethics, and this summer
seems to have been, at least for posterity, the most
fruitful season of his life, being the epoch of the
completion of his *Tusculan Disputations* and his
*De Natura Deorum*, and of the composition of
several of his smaller treatises.   In June of that

year he says, in a letter to Atticus, that he is
writing for his son's benefit an elaborate treatise
on Morals. "On what subject," he asks, "can a
father better write to a son?" In the latter part
of the summer he started on a journey to Athens
to visit his son, but was recalled by the intelligence of a probable understanding on amicable
terms between Antony and the Senate. Deceived
in this hope, he repaired to Rome, and pronounced
his first Philippic against Antony in the beginning
of September. In November he writes again about
his ethical work, tells Atticus that he has completed two books and is busy on the third, and
announces and explains the title. The work was
completed before the end of the year.

Cicero's time was a period of eclecticism in
philosophy, especially so among the cultivated
Romans, with whom philosophy was not indigenous, but a comparatively recent importation.
Cicero himself was pre-eminently a lover of philosophical thought, study, and discussion, and probably was more intimately conversant with the
history of opinions and the contents of books in
that department than any man of his time; yet
he seems to have lacked profound convictions on
the subjects at issue among the several schools.
Thus in the *De Officiis,* while he repeatedly professes his adherence to the New Academy and

the Peripatetic doctrine of morals, he bases his discussion on the Stoic theory, and intimates very clearly that he thought his son safer under the rigid discipline of the Stoic school than under the more lax though wise tuition of his Peripatetic preceptor. It is as if a Mohammedan, while recognizing the divine mission of the Arab prophet, were to write for his son a treatise on the ethics of the New Testament as better adapted than the moral system of the Koran for the training and confirming of a young man in the practice of virtue.

This treatise, then, may be regarded as an exposition of the ethical system of the Stoics of Cicero's time, yet with a special limitation, purpose, and adaptation. It is not designed for the ideally perfect philosopher, nor for a candidate for that exalted position, but for one on the lower plane of common · life. It therefore defines not the moral consciousness of the truly wise man, but the specific duties by the practice of which one may grow into the semblance of true wisdom. Nor does it purport to be a compendium even of these duties. It is simply a directory for a young Roman of high rank and promise, who is going to enter upon public life, and to be a candidate for office and honor in the state. It prescribes the self-training, the social relations, and the habits of living, by which

such a youth may both deserve and attain distinction and eminence, and the respect and confidence of his fellow-citizens. Of course, many of
the details in this treatise were of merely local and
transient import and value; but its underlying
principles are in such close harmony with the
absolute and eternal right that they can never
become obsolete. At the same time, the division
and arrangement of the treatise give it, so far as I
know, the precedence over all other ethical treatises
ancient or modern. The division is exhaustive.
The arrangement is such as to leave an open space
for the insertion and full treatment of any topic
within the scope of ethical philosophy.

The First Book treats of the Right. The right
consists in accordance with nature, with the nature
of things, with the nature of man. Hence is derived its imperative obligation upon the human
conscience. Its duties are evolved from man's
own consciousness. Man by his very nature desires knowledge, and craves materials for the active
exercise of his cognitive powers. He is by his
birth, by his instinctive cravings, by the necessity
of his daily life, a gregarious being, a member of
a family, of society, of the state, and as such cannot
but recognize justice, including benevolence, as his
imperative duty. He postulates distinction, eminence, a position from which he can look down on

earthly fortunes as beneath him, and can sacrifice all exterior good for the service of mankind and the attainment of merited fame. He has also an innate sense of order, proportion, harmony, which can satisfy itself only by practical reference to the due time, place, manner, and measure of whatever is done or said. Hence the four virtues of Prudence or Wisdom, Justice, Fortitude or Magnanimity, and Order, Temperance, or Moderation. These virtues in their broadest significance include all human obligations,[1] and form a series of divisions, under one or another of which may be classed every specific duty. Under each of these heads Cicero shows what was demanded by the highest sentiment of his time from a youth of spotless fame and of honorable ambition.

The Second Book has Expediency, or Utility, for its subject. Outside of the province of duty or of things required there is large room for choice among things permitted, — consistent with the Right, yet forming no part of it. The question that underlies this Book is, By what honorable methods, other than the discharge of express duty, can a young man secure for himself the favor, gratitude, assistance, and — in case of need — the suffrages of his fellow-citizens? This Book has its proper place in a treatise on morals, because it is

---

[1] See p. 10, note.

the author's aim throughout to discriminate between the immoral and the legitimate modes of obtaining reputation and popularity.

The Third Book deals with the alleged or seeming discrepancy between the Expedient and the Right. Cicero denies the possibility of such mutual repugnance, and maintains that whatever is expedient must of necessity be right, and that what is right cannot be otherwise than expedient.

In this translation I have attempted to give, not a word-for-word version of the Latin text, but a literal transcript in English of what I suppose that Cicero meant to write in his own tongue. I have not used his moods and tenses in the instances in which our English idiom would employ a different form of the verb. I have not infrequently omitted the connective and illative words that bind sentence to sentence, in cases in which we should use no such words.[1] In the few obscure

---

[1] I am strongly impressed with the belief that such words were largely employed as catch-words for the eye, and that they served the purpose now effected by punctuation and by the capital letters at the beginning of sentences. This opinion cannot of course be verified; yet could we have phonographic reports of Cicero's orations, I am inclined to think that we should miss some of the conjunctions that are found in their written form. As to Greek particles I have no right to an opinion; but I will hazard the conjecture that they would have been scattered with a more sparing hand, had the art of punctuation been coeval with " the letters Cadmus gave."

passages I have sought the aid of the best commentators, but have generally found them hazy or ambiguous in their interpretation where there was any room for doubt. I may have made mistakes in translating; but if so, it has not been for lack of close and careful study, with the help of the best editions which I could procure for myself or find in the Harvard College Library.

I have used Beier's text as the basis for my translation, and have preferred not to deviate from it even where a different reading seemed to me intrinsically probable; for in every such instance Beier gives satisfactory reasons for his preferred reading, and destitute as I am of the needed apparatus for textual criticism, I cannot but regard his judgment in such a case as much better than my own.

# CICERO DE OFFICIIS.

## BOOK I.

1. ALTHOUGH you, my son Marcus, having listened for a year to Cratippus, and that at Athens, ought to be well versed in the maxims and principles of philosophy, on account of the paramount authority both of the teacher and of the city, — the former being able to enrich you with knowledge; the latter, with examples, — yet, as for my own benefit I have always connected Latin with Greek, and have done so, not only in philosophy, but also in my self-training as a public speaker, I think that you, too, ought to do the same, in order that you may be equally capable of either style of discourse.[1] To this end I have, as it seems to me, been of no small service to my fellow-citizens, so that not only those ignorant of Greek literature, but highly educated men also, think that they have

[1] Either philosophical discussion or oratory.

1

gained somewhat from me, both as to public speaking and as to philosophical discussion. Therefore, while you will be the pupil of the first philosopher of our time, and will continue so as long as you please, — and that ought to be as long as you can profit by his instruction, — yet by reading my writings, which dissent very little from the Peripatetics (for both they and I regard ourselves as disciples both of Socrates and of Plato), though on the subjects of discussion I would have you freely exercise your own judgment, you will certainly acquire a fuller command of the Latin tongue. Nor in speaking thus ought I to be regarded as presumptuous. For while in the science of philosophy I may have many superiors, if I claim for myself what belongs properly to the orator, aptness, perspicuity, and elegance of diction, since I have passed my life in this pursuit, it is not without a good measure of right that I proffer the claim. Wherefore I earnestly exhort you, my Cicero, to read carefully not only my orations, but these books of mine on philosophy, which already in bulk are nearly equal to the orations. For while in oratory there is a greater force of expression, the more even and moderate style of writing that belongs to philosophy ought also to be cultivated. And indeed I do not see that it has fallen to any Greek author to exercise himself in both styles, and to pursue at once forensic eloquence and unimpassioned philosophical discussion; unless, perchance, this may be said of Demetrius Phalereus,[1] — a keen disputant, and at the same time an orator, though of no great power, yet with a winning grace by which one might recognize him as a disciple of Theophrastus. But what proficiency I have made in either style let others judge; I certainly have pursued both. Indeed, I think that Plato, too, if he had been disposed to attempt forensic eloquence, would have spoken with equal fluency and power; and that Demosthenes, if he had retained and had wished to put into writing what he had learned from Plato, would have done so in a style both graceful and magnificent. I have the same opinion of Aristotle and Isocrates, each of whom, charmed with his own department, held the other in low esteem.

2. But, having determined to write expressly for your benefit something at the present time, much hereafter, I have thought it best to begin with what is most suitable both to your age and to my parental authority. Now, among the many important and useful subjects in philosophy that have been discussed by philosophers with precision and fulness of statement, their traditions and precepts concerning the duties of life seem to have the widest scope.

---

[1] He was known chiefly as an orator; but the list of his numerous works comprises philosophy, history, and poetry. Driven from Athens, he took refuge in Alexandria; and it was owing to his influence that Ptolemy Lagi commenced the collection of books which grew into the famous Alexandrian library. No probably genuine work of Demetrius Phalereus is now extant.

Indeed, no part of life, whether in public or in private affairs, abroad or at home, in your personal conduct or your social relations, can be free from the claims of duty ; and it is in the observance of duty that lies all the honor of life, in its neglect, all the shame. This, too, is a theme common to all philosophers. For who would dare to call himself a philosopher, if he took no cognizance of duty ? Yet there are some schools of philosophy that utterly pervert duty by the view which they propose as to the supreme good, and as to the opposite extreme of evil. For he who so interprets the supreme good as to disjoin it from virtue, and measures it by his own convenience, and not by the standard of right, — he, I say, if he be consistent with himself, and be not sometimes overcome by natural goodness, can cultivate neither friendship, nor justice, nor generosity ; nor can he possibly be brave while he esteems pain as the greatest of evils, or temperate while he regards pleasure as the supreme good. These things, though too obvious to need discussion, I yet have discussed elsewhere.[1]    Those schools, therefore, can, if self-consistent, say nothing about duty; nor can any precepts of duty, decisive, immutable, in accordance with nature, be promulgated, except by those who maintain that the right is to be sought solely,[2] or chiefly,[3] for its own sake. This

---

[1] In the *De Finibus.*    [2] As was the case with the Stoics.

[3] As was the case with the Peripatetics, and, hypothetically, with the Academics.

prerogative belongs to the Stoics, the Academics, and the Peripatetics; for the opinions of Ariston, Pyrrho, and Herillus [1] were long since exploded, though they might fittingly have discussed subjects pertaining to duty, if they had left any ground for the preference of one thing over another, so that there might be a way open for the ascertainment of duty. In this treatise I shall follow the Stoics, not as a translator, but drawing from their fountains at my own discretion and judgment, as much, and in such way, as may seem good.

I think it fit, however, since duty is to be my sole subject, to define duty at the outset.[2] I am surprised that Panaetius should not have done this; for the rational treatment of any subject ought to

---

[1] Ariston, while he regarded virtue as the supreme good, maintained that among the external conditions and objects with which duty is conversant, there is no ground for preference, therefore no reason why one should be sought or pursued rather than another. Pyrrho, the founder of the school of the Sceptics, in denying the possibility of attaining any objective truth, denied the possibility of determining any condition, object, or action to be better than any other. Herillus — like Ariston, a professed Stoic — regarded knowledge as the supreme good, and external life, with all its doings and objects, though practically necessary, as of no ethical value, because not contributing to the supreme good.

[2] Yet Cicero leaves duty (*officium*) undefined. *Officium* may be abbreviated from *opificium*, i. e. work-doing; or it may be derived from *ob* and *facio*, in which case it denotes doing on account of, or for a reason, and would include all acts for which a reason, i. e. a right reason, can be given. I am inclined to think that it is in this latter sense that Cicero made choice and use of the word.

take its start from definition, that readers may understand what the author is writing about.

3. The discussion of duty is twofold. One division relates to the supreme good in itself considered ; the other, to the rules by which the conduct of life may in all its parts be brought into conformity with the supreme good. Under the first head belong such questions as these : Whether all duties are of perfect obligation; whether any one duty is greater than another; and, in general, inquiries of a similar kind. But the duties for which rules are laid down belong, indeed, to the supreme good, as means to an end ; yet this is the less obvious, because they seem rather to have reference to the ordering of common life. It is of these that I am going to treat in the present work. There is also another division of duty. Duty may be said to be either contingent or perfect. We may, I think, give the name of perfect duty to the absolute right, which the Greeks term κατόρθωμα; [1] while contingent duty is what they call καθῆκον. [2] According to their definitions, what is right in itself is perfect duty; that for the doing of which a satisfactory reason can be given is a contingent duty.

According to Panaetius, in determining what we ought to do there are three questions to be considered. It is first to be determined whether the con-

---

[1] The *direct*, i. e. the intrinsically right.

[2] The *fitting*, i. e. that which is rendered right by circumstances.

templated act is right or wrong, — a matter as to
which there often are opposite opinions. Then
there is room for inquiry or consultation whether
the act under discussion is conducive to convenience and pleasure, to affluence and free command
of outward goods, to wealth, to power, in fine, to the
means by which one can benefit himself and those
dependent on him ; and here the question turns on
expediency. The third class of cases is when what
appears to be expedient seems repugnant to the
right. For when expediency lays, as it were, violent hands upon us, and the right seems to recall us
to itself, the mind is distracted, and laden with two-
fold anxiety as to the course of action. In this distribution of the subject, while a division ought by
all means to be exhaustive, there are two omissions.
Not only is the question of right or wrong as to an
act wont to be considered, but also the question, of
two right things which is the more right; equally, of
two expedient things which is the more expedient.
Thus we see that the division which Panaetius
thought should be threefold ought to be distributed
under five heads. First, then, I am to treat of the
right, but under two heads ; then, in the same way,
of the expedient ; lastly, of their seeming conflict.

4. In the beginning, animals of every species were
endowed with the instinct that prompts them to
take care of themselves as to life and bodily well-
being, to shun whatever threatens to do them harm,
and to seek and provide whatever is necessary for

subsistence, as food, shelter, and other things of this
sort. The appetite for sexual union for the produc-
tion of offspring is, also, common to all animals,
together with a certain degree of care for their offspring.

But between man and beast there is this essential difference, that the latter, moved by sense
alone, adapts himself only to that which is present
in place and time, having very little cognizance of
the past or the future. Man, on the other hand —
because he is possessed of reason, by which he
discerns consequences, sees the causes of things,
understands the rise and progress of events, compares
similar objects, and connects and associates the future with the present — easily takes into view the
whole course of life, and provides things necessary
for it. Nature too, by virtue of reason, brings man
into relations of mutual intercourse and society with
his fellow-men; generates in him a special love for
his children; prompts him to promote and attend
social gatherings and public assemblies; and awakens in him the desire to provide what may suffice
for the support and nourishment, not of himself
alone, but of his wife, his children, and others whom
he holds dear and is bound to protect. This care
rouses men's minds, and makes them more efficient
in action. The research and investigation of truth,
also, are a special property of man. Thus, when we
are free from necessary occupations, we want to see,
or hear, or learn something, and regard the knowl-

edge of things either secret or wonderful as essential
to our living happily and well.[1]  To this desire for
seeing the truth is annexed a certain craving for precedence, insomuch that the man well endowed by
nature is willing to render obedience to no one, unless
to a preceptor, or a teacher, or one who holds a just
and legitimate sway for the general good.  Hence
are derived greatness of mind and contempt for the
vicissitudes of human fortune.  Nor does it indicate
any feeble force of nature and of reason, that of all
animals man alone has a sense of order, and decency, and moderation in action and in speech.
Thus no other animal feels the beauty, elegance,
symmetry, of the things that he sees; while by nature and reason, man, transferring these qualities
from the eyes to the mind, considers that much
more, even, are beauty, consistency, and order to be
preserved in purposes and acts, and takes heed that
he do nothing indecorous or effeminate, and still
more, that in all his thoughts and deeds he neither
do nor think anything lascivious.  From these elements the right, which is the object of our inquiry,
is composed and created ; and this, even if it be not
ennobled in title, yet is honorable, and even if no
one praise it, we truly pronounce it in its very nature worthy of all praise.

[1] It will be seen that, in the sequel, Cicero transposes the
virtues springing from man's social nature and his desire for knowledge, placing wisdom or prudence first, and assigning the second
place to justice.

5. You behold, indeed, my son Marcus, the very form and, as it were, the countenance of the right, which, were it seen by the eyes, as Plato says, would awaken the intensest love of wisdom. But whatever is right springs from one of four sources. It consists either in the perception and skilful treatment of the truth; or in maintaining good-fellowship with men, giving to every one his due, and keeping faith in contracts and promises; or in the greatness and strength of a lofty and unconquered mind; or in the order and measure that constitute moderation and temperance.[1] Although these four are connected and intertwined with one another, yet duties of certain kinds proceed from each of them; as from the division first named, including wisdom and prudence, proceed the investigation and discovery of truth, as the peculiar office of that virtue. For in proportion as one sees clearly what is the inmost and essential truth with regard to any subject, and can demonstrate it with equal acuteness and promptness, he is wont to be regarded, and justly, as of transcendent discretion and wisdom. Therefore truth is submitted to this virtue as the

---

[1] These four virtues may be easily so enlarged in their scope as to cover the whole of life, and to comprehend the entire duty of man. Thus, Prudence embraces all selfward obligations; Justice (which includes benevolence, and is not exclusive of piety), all duties to fellow-beings; Fortitude (including patience, submission, and courage), duty with reference to objects and events beyond one's control; Order (in time, place, and measure), duty with reference to objects under one's control.

material of which it treats, and with which it is
conversant. The other three virtues have for their
sphere the providing and preserving of those things
on which the conduct of life depends, so that the
fellowship and union of society may be maintained,
and that superiority and greatness of mind may shine
forth, not only in the increase of resources and the
acquisition of objects of desire for one's self, and for
those dependent on him, but much more in a position from which one can look down on these very
things. But order, and consistency, and moderation,
and similar qualities have their scope in affairs that
demand not merely the movement of the mind, but
some outward action ; for it is by bringing to the
concerns of daily life a certain method and order
that we shall maintain honor and propriety. .

6. Of the four heads into which I have divided
the nature and force of the right, the first, which
consists in the cognizance of truth, bears the closest
relation to human nature. For we are all attracted
and drawn to the desire of knowledge and wisdom,
in which we deem it admirable to excel, but both
an evil and a shame to fail, to be mistaken, to be
ignorant, to be deceived. In this quest of knowledge, both natural and right, there are two faults to
be shunned, — one, the taking of unknown things
for known, and giving our assent to them too hastily,
which fault he who wishes to escape (and all ought
so to wish) will give time and diligence to reflect on
the subjects proposed for his consideration. The

other fault is that some bestow too great zeal and too much labor on things obscure and difficult, and at the same time useless. These faults being shunned, whatever labor and care may be bestowed on subjects becoming a virtuous mind and worth knowing, will be justly commended. Thus we learn that Caius Sulpicius was versed in astronomy,[1] as I myself knew Sextius Pompeius to be in geometry,[2] as many are in logic, many in civil law, — all which sciences are concerned in the investigation of truth, but by whose pursuit duty will not suffer one to be drawn away from the active management of affairs. For the reputation of virtue consists wholly in active life, from which, however, there is often a respite, and frequent opportunities are afforded for returning to the pursuit of knowledge. At the same time mental activity, which never ceases, may retain us, without conscious effort, in meditation on the subjects of our study. But all thought and mental action ought to be occupied either in taking counsel as to the things that are right and that appertain to a good

[1] When serving in the Macedonian war, as military tribune under Aemilius Paulus, he predicted an eclipse of the moon, and obtained liberty to announce his prediction to the assembled army, thus precluding the else inevitable terror and foreboding which pervaded the Macedonian army, and very probably turning the scale in favor of the Romans in the then imminent battle in which Perseus, the Macedonian king, was utterly overthrown.

[2] Uncle of Cneius Pompeius Magnus, not in political life, but celebrated for his proficiency in geometry, jurisprudence, and philosophy. He was a Stoic.

and happy life, or in the pursuit of wisdom and knowledge. I have thus spoken of the first source of duty.

7. Of the remaining three heads, the principle which constitutes the bond of human society and of a virtual community of life has the widest scope. Of this there are two divisions, — justice, in which consists the greatest lustre of virtue, and which those who possess are termed good ; and in close alliance with justice, beneficence, which may also be called benignity or liberality. · The first demand of justice is, that no one do harm to another, unless provoked by injury ;[1] the next, that one use common possessions as common, private, as belonging to their owners. Private possessions, indeed, are not so by nature, but by ancient occupancy, as in the case of settlers in a previously uninhabited region; or by conquest, as in the territory acquired in war; or by law, treaty, agreement, or lot.[2] Thus it comes to pass that the territory of Arpinas is said to belong to the Arpinates, that of Tusculum to the Tuscans, and a similar account is to be given of the possessions of individual owners. Because each person thus has for his own a portion of those

[1] This exception is one of the few points of discrepancy between the Ciceronian ethics and the moral precepts of Christianity.

[2] The veterans who settled on the public lands (*coloni*) received their portions of land by lot, and when a limited number from a particular corps were to be colonized, the persons to be colonized were determined by lot.

things which were common by nature, let each hold
undisturbed what has fallen to his possession.  If
any one endeavors to obtain more for himself, he
will violate the law of human society.  But since,
as it has been well said by Plato, we are not born
for ourselves alone; since our country claims a part
in us, our parents a part, our friends a part; and
since, according to the Stoics, whatever the earth
bears is created for the use of men, while men were
brought into being for the sake of men, that they
might do good to one another, — in this matter we
ought to follow nature as a guide, to contribute our
part to the common good, and by the interchange of
kind offices, both in giving and receiving, alike by
skill, by labor, and by the resources at our command, to strengthen the social union of men among
men.  But the foundation of justice is good faith,
that is, steadfastness and truth in promises and
agreements.  Hence, though it may seem to some
too far-fetched, I may venture to imitate the Stoics
in their painstaking inquiry into the origin of words,
and to derive *faith* [1] from the *fact* corresponding to
the promise.

Of injustice there are two kinds, — one, that of
those who inflict injury; the other, that of those who
do not, if they can, repel injury from those on whom

---

[1] *Fides*, from *fit* quod *dictum* est, a derivation certainly very
improbable, but hardly more so than the derivation from πίστις,
or, in the Aeolic dialect, πίττις, which most lexicographers assign
to *fides*.

it is inflicted. Moreover, he who, moved by anger
or by some disturbance of mind, makes an unjust
assault on any person, is as one who lays violent
hands on a casual companion; while he who does
not, if he can, ward off or resist the injury offered
to another, is as much in fault as if he were to desert
his parents, or his friends, or his country. Indeed,
those injuries which are purposely inflicted for the
sake of doing harm, often proceed from fear, he who
meditates harm to another apprehending that, if he
refrains, he himself may suffer harm. But for the
most part men are induced to injure others in order
to obtain what they covet; and here avarice is the
most frequent motive.

8. Wealth is sought sometimes for the necessary
uses of life, sometimes for indulgence in luxury. In
those possessed of a higher order of mind the desire
for money is entertained with a view to the increase
of the means of influence and the power of generous
giving. Thus, not long ago, Marcus Crassus [1] pro-

[1] Surnamed Dives. He inherited this *cognomen*, and belonged
to the fifth generation of the *gens* Licinius that had borne it. His
prime ambition seems to have been to verify his name. Pliny
says that the estates which he owned outside of Rome amounted in
value to two hundred millions of sesterces, equivalent to little less
than eight millions of dollars, no account being taken of the
much greater value of money then than now. He was a man of
respectable ability, of no mean reputation as an orator, and of considerable executive capacity; but it was probably his wealth that
gave him his place in the triumvirate with Caesar and Pompey,
and that thus procured for him the command in the Parthian war,
in which he lost his army and his life.

nounced no property sufficient for one who meant
to hold a foremost place in the republic, unless its
income would enable him to support an army.
Others, again, delight in magnificent furniture, and
in an elegant and profuse style of living. In all
these ways there has come to be an unbounded
desire for money. Nor, indeed, is the increase of
property, without harm to any one, to be blamed;
but wrong-doing for the sake of gain is never to be
tolerated. Most of all, however, large numbers of
persons are led to lose sight of justice by the craving for military commands, civic honors, and fame.
The saying of Ennius,

> " Where kingship is concerned,
> No social bond or covenant is sacred,"

has a much broader application ; for, as to whatever
is of such a nature that but few can be foremost in it,
there is generally so keen a rivalry that it is exceedingly difficult to keep social duty inviolate. This
was recently illustrated by the audacity of Caius
Caesar, who overturned all laws, human and divine,
to obtain the sovereignty which he had shaped for
himself in the vagaries of his fancy. In this respect it is indeed unfortunate that it is, for the
most part, in the greatest minds and in men of
transcendent genius that the desire for offices civil
and military, for power and for fame, is rife. The
more heed, therefore, is to be taken against criminal
conduct in this matter.

But in every form of injustice it makes a very essential difference whether the wrong be committed in some disturbance of mind, which is generally brief and temporary, or whether it be done advisedly, and with premeditation. For those things which are done from some sudden impulse are more venial than what is done with plan and forethought. Enough has now been said with regard to the infliction of injury.

9. For omitting to defend the injured, and thus abandoning duty, there are many reasons in current force. Men are sometimes unwilling to incur the enmity, or the labor, or the cost involved in such defence; or by mere carelessness, indolence, sloth, or engrossment in pursuits or employments of their own, they are so retarded in their movements as to leave undefended those whom they ought to protect. It will thus be seen that Plato is not entirely in the right when he says of philosophers, that because they are engaged in the investigation of truth, and because they despise and count as naught what most persons eagerly seek and are always ready to fight with each other for, they are therefore just men.[1] They indeed attain one part of justice, in injuring no one: they fail as to the other part; for, kept inactive by their zeal for learning, they forsake those whom they ought to defend. Plato thinks, too, that they will take no part in pub-

[1] This is the substance of a discussion in the 6th Book of Plato's Republic.

lic affairs, unless by compulsion. But it were more
fitting that they should do this of their own accord;
for the very thing which it is right to do, can be
termed virtuous only if it be voluntary. There are,
also, those who, either from the over-anxious care of
their property or from misanthropic feeling, profess
to confine their attention to their own affairs, so as
to avoid even the appearance of doing injury to any
one. They are free from one kind of injustice:
they fall into the other; for they forsake social
duty, inasmuch as they bestow upon it neither care,
nor labor, nor cost. Since, then, we have assigned
to each of the two kinds of injustice its inducing
causes, having previously determined the constituent elements of justice, we shall easily ascertain the
specific duty of any particular occasion, unless we
be blinded by inordinate self-love. However, the
care of other men's concerns is difficult. Although
Chremes, in Terence's play, thinks nothing human
indifferent to him, yet because we perceive and feel
the things, prosperous or adverse, which happen to
ourselves more keenly than those that happen to
others, which we see, as it were, at a great distance,
we decide concerning them otherwise than we
should concerning ourselves in like case. Therefore those give good counsel who forbid our doing
that as to the equity of which we have any doubt.
For equity is self-evident; doubt implies a suspicion of wrong.

10. But there are frequent occasions when those

things which are generally regarded as worthy of a just man, and one of good report, such as the restoring of a trust or the fulfilment of a promise, are reversed, and become the opposite of right, and what belongs to truth and good faith seems to change its bearing, so that justice demands its violation. Here reference is fittingly made to what I have laid down as the fundamental principles of justice, first, that injury should be done to no one, and in the next place, that service should be rendered to the common good. When these principles are modified by circumstances, duty is also modified, and is not always the same. There may perchance be some promise or agreement, the fulfilment of which is harmful to him to whom the promise was made or to him who made it. Thus, to take an instance from the popular mythology, if Neptune had not kept his promise to Theseus,[1] Theseus would not have been bereft of his son, Hippolytus; for, of the

---

[1] Among the myths as to the parentage of Theseus, there is one which makes him the son of Poseidon, or Neptune, who was said to have promised to grant him three wishes, two of which had already been granted, when Phaedra, his wife, accused her step-son Hippolytus of an attempted criminal intrigue with her. Theseus claimed of Poseidon his son's destruction, and Poseidon accordingly sent a bull from the water to frighten the horses of Hippolytus, as he was driving in his chariot by the sea-shore. The horses upset the chariot, and dragged Hippolytus till he died. Theseus too late ascertained that his son was innocent, and that his wife had falsely accused him because he had repulsed her advances toward a criminal intimacy.

three wishes which Neptune had promised to grant
him, the third, as the story runs, was his demand in
anger for the death of Hippolytus, the granting of
which plunged him into the deepest sorrow. Promises, then, are not to be kept, when by keeping them
you do harm to those to whom they are made; nor
yet if they injure you more than they benefit him
to whom you made them, is it contrary to duty that
the greater good should be preferred to the less.[1]
For instance, if you engaged to appear as an advocate in an impending lawsuit, and meanwhile your
child became severely ill, you would not fail in your
duty to your client by breaking your promise; on the
other hand, he to whom you made the promise would
be false to his duty, if he complained of your deserting him. Again, who does not perceive that promises
extorted by fear,[2] or obtained by fraud, are not to
be kept? Indeed, such promises are made void, in

---

[1] The Hebrew conception of righteousness, "He that sweareth
to his own hurt and changeth not," is certainly in closer accordance with the absolute right than this maxim of Cicero. Yet
Cicero's example under this head really belongs to another cate-
gory, that of circumstances so altered as in the very nature of the
case to make a promise void.

[2] A promise wrong in itself cannot be rightfully made, even
under stress of fear; and if made, should not be kept; for two
wrongs cannot make a right. But a promise which one has a
right to make, as that of a ransom for one's life, is sacred in the
forum of conscience, if not binding in law. If a man regards his
life as worth a certain price, and offers that price, there is no
rightful reason why he should not pay it.

most cases by praetorian edict,[1] in some by express statutes.

There are, also, wrongs committed by a sort of chicanery, which consists in a too subtle, and thus fraudulent, interpretation of the right. Hence comes the saying : The extreme of right is the extreme of wrong. Under this head, there have been many violations of the right in the administration of public affairs, as in the case of him who, during a thirty days' truce with an enemy, ravaged the enemy's territory by night, on the pretext that the truce had been agreed upon for so many days, not nights.[2] Nor can we approve of our fellow-citizen, if the story is true, that Quintus Fabius Labeo, or some one else, — I know of the matter only by hearsay, — being appointed by the Senate as an umpire between the people of Nola and those of Neapolis about their boundaries, when he came to the spot, argued with each party separately that they should not be greedy or covetous, but should rather recede than advance in their demands of each other. When they had

[1] The *praetor urbanus* was virtually the chief justice of Rome. On entering upon the duties of his office he published a manifesto, or *edictum*, stating the principles to be recognized by him in the interpretation and application of the laws. The principles laid down in these successive edicts, and those involved in praetorian decisions under them, unless abrogated or nullified by express legislation, were regarded as having the force of law, and corresponded to what we familiarly term judge-made law.

[2] There are two transactions of this kind on record, — one of Cleomenes, the Spartan king, in a war with Argos ; the other, of the Thracians, when at war with the Boeotians.

both complied with his advice, there remained some territory between these previously contiguous states; and so he fixed their bounds in accordance with their respective claims, and adjudged the intermediate territory to the Roman people.[1] This, indeed, is swindling, not arbitration. Shrewdness like this is to be shunned in transactions of every kind.

11. There are also certain duties to be observed toward those who may have injured you. For there is a limit to revenge and punishment, — nay, I know not whether it may not be enough for him who gave the provocation to repent of his wrong-doing, so that he may not do the like again, and that others may be the less disposed to do as he has done. In the public administration, also, the rights of war are to be held sacred. While there are two ways of contending, one by discussion, the other by force, the former belonging properly to man, the latter to beasts, recourse must be had to the latter if there be no opportunity for employing the former. Wars, then, are to be waged in order to render it possible to live in peace without injury; but, victory once gained, those are to be spared who have not been cruel and inhuman in war, as our ancestors even admitted to citizenship

---

[1] Quintus Fabius Labeo lived more than a century before Cicero. Valerius Maximus tells the same story, but without expressing any doubt as to the name of the umpire. He adds that the same Labeo, after a victory over Antiochus, King of Macedonia, having made peace on condition of the surrender of half of the king's fleet, cut all the vessels into halves, so as utterly to destroy the fleet.

the Tuscans, the Aequi, the Volsci, the Sabines, the Hernici; while they utterly destroyed Carthage and Numantia. I could wish that they had not destroyed Corinth; but I believe that they had some motive, especially the convenience of the place for hostile movements, — the fear that the very situation might be an inducement to rebellion.[1] In my opinion, peace is always to be sought when it can be made on perfectly fair and honest conditions. In this matter had my opinion been followed, we should now have, not indeed the best republic possible, but a republic of some sort, which is no longer ours. Still further, while those whom you conquer are to be kindly treated, those who, laying down their arms, take refuge in the good faith of the commander of the assailing army, ought to be received to quarter, even though the battering-ram have already shaken their walls.[2] In this respect justice used to be so carefully observed by our people, that by the custom of our ancestors those who received into allegiance states or nations subdued in war were their patrons. Indeed, the rights of war are prescribed with the most sacred care by the fecial law[3] of the Roman people, from which it may be

---

[1] Corinth had two ports, — one commanding the Ionian, the other the Aegean sea.

[2] It was the established custom of the Romans to admit to quarter enemies who surrendered before the application of the battering-ram to their walls.

[3] So called from the *fetiales*, — priests whose duty it was, as heralds, to perform all the ceremonies connected with the declara-

understood that no war is just unless after a formal
demand of satisfaction for injury, or after an express
declaration and proclamation of hostilities. Popilius, as commander, held control of a province. A
son of Cato served his first campaign in his army.
When Popilius saw fit to discharge one of the
legions, he discharged also Cato's son, who served
in that same legion. But when the youth remained
in the army for love of military service, Cato wrote
to Popilius that if he permitted his son to stay, he
must make him take a second oath of military duty,
else, the term of the first oath having expired, he
could not lawfully fight with the enemy. Thus
there used to be the most scrupulous observance of
the right in the conduct of war. There is, indeed,
extant a letter of Marcus Cato the elder to his son
Marcus, in which he writes that he has heard of his
son's discharge by the consul, after service in Macedonia in the war with Perseus, and warns him not
to go into battle, inasmuch as it is not right for
one who is no longer a soldier to fight with the
enemy.[1]

tion of war, the ratifying of peace, and the making of treaties.
These forms were regarded as religious solemnities.

[1] Commentators in general see here two versions of the same
story, and suppose one of the two to be spurious. Yet there is no
reason other than the internal evidence for rejecting either, and
they may both be true of the same Cato and the same son. The
Ligurian war in which Popilius was commander occurred four
years before the war with Perseus. In the former, Marcus Cato
the younger may have made his first campaign, and in the latter,

12. In this connection it occurs to my mind that
in the early time the name denoting an enemy engaged in actual war was the word employed to denote a foreigner, the unpleasantness of the fact being
thus relieved by the mildness of the term; for he
whom we call a foreigner bore with our ancestors
the appellation which we now give to an enemy.
The laws of the Twelve Tables show this, as, for
instance, " A day assigned for trial with a foreigner,"
" Perpetual right of ownership as against a foreigner." [1]　What can more truly indicate gentleness

---

though no longer a *tiro* or novice in the art of war, he may have
been discharged as before, and his father have repeated his legal
objection to the son's continuous service.

[1] This passage can be literally rendered only by retaining the
Latin terms employed, as thus: " He who by our present usage
would be called *perduellis* was in former time called *hostis,* the
unpleasantness of the fact being thus relieved by the mildness of
the term; for him whom we now term *peregrinus* our ancestors
called *hostis*. The laws of the Twelve Tables show this, as, for
instance, ' A day assigned for trial *cum hoste,*' ' Perpetual. right
of ownership *adversus hostem*.' "

In extant Latin literature the use of *hostis* in the sense of
*enemy* seems to have been nearly, if not quite, universal.　There
is, indeed, a passage in Plautus in which the word is evidently
used in the sense of *foreigner;* but this appears to be a reference
to the title in the law of the Twelve Tables cited above, *status
dies cum hoste*.　It seems by no means unlikely that the two
meanings of *hostis* may have co-existed in early use.　*Hostis*
probably is derived from the same root with ἑστία (whence comes
Vesta), a *hearth*, or — what was the same thing as to the rites
of domestic worship — an altar; and if so, *hostis* might mean
either a *stranger* to be received to the hospitality of the hearth,
or an *enemy* to be made a victim at the altar.　*Hostia,* an ani-

of spirit than calling him with whom you are at
war by so mild a name? Yet time has made that
word harsher; for it has ceased to denote a foreigner,
and has retained, as properly belonging to it, its
application to an adversary in arms. Even when
there is a contest for power, and fame is sought in
war, there ought still to underlie the conflict the
same grounds that I have named above as just
causes for war. But the wars waged for superiority
in honor or in dominion should be conducted with
less bitterness of feeling than where there are actual
wrongs to be redressed. For as we contend with
a fellow-citizen in one way if he is an enemy, in a
very different way if he is a rival, — the contest with
the latter being for honor and promotion, with the
former for life and reputation, — so our wars with
the Celtiberi and the Cimbri were waged as with
enemies, to determine not which should come off
conqueror, but which should survive; while with
the Latins, the Sabines, the Samnites, the Carthaginians, Pyrrhus, the contest was for superiority. The
Carthaginians, indeed, violated their treaties; Hannibal was cruel; the others were more worthy of

mal sacrificed, and *hostire*, to strike, throw light upon this last
meaning.

Some of the old lexicographers, including no less a man than
Scaliger, derive *hostis* from the pronoun ὅστις, *whoever*, i. e. any
person whatsoever outside of one's own family, neighborhood, or
nation, a stranger, and therefore, *prima facie* an enemy. With
this derivation — which I do not regard as valid — the two meanings of *hostis* might have been coeval and concurrent.

confidence. Indeed, what Pyrrhus said about restoring the captives of war is admirable:—

> "I ask that you should give no gold, ro price;
> In war I ply no trade but sword with sword ;
> With steel, and not with gold, stake we our lives.
> Wills queenly Fortune you or I should rule,
> Try we by might. And bear this message with you, —
> For those whose prowess Fortune spared in battle
> Freedom is also spared by my decree.
> Lead them away, — I grant, — the gods approve." [1]

A sentiment truly royal, and worthy of the race of the Aeacidae.[2]

13. Still further, if any person, induced by stress of circumstances, makes a promise to a public enemy, good faith must be observed in keeping such a promise. Thus Regulus, in the first Punic war, taken captive by the Carthaginians, sent to Rome to negotiate an exchange of prisoners, and bound by an oath to return, in the first place, on his arrival, gave his opinion in the Senate that the prisoners should not be sent back, and then, when his kindred and friends tried to retain him, preferred returning to punishment to breaking his faith with the enemy.

[1] These verses are from the "Annales" of Ennius, and are supposed to be addressed to the deputies sent with a large sum of money to treat with Pyrrhus for the release of prisoners after the battle of Heraclea, B. c. 280.

[2] The kings of Epeirus claimed to be lineal descendants of Aeacus, the son of Zeus, who for the righteousness of his rule on earth was made judge in the under-world.

But in the second Punic war, after the battle of
Cannae, the ten men whom Hannibal sent to Rome
bound by an oath that they would return unless
they obtained the redemption of the prisoners of
war, were all disfranchised for life [1] by the censors,
because they had perjured themselves. Nor did
that one of the ten escape who had incurred guilt
by the fraudulent performance of his oath. He,
having been suffered by Hannibal to leave the
camp, returned shortly afterward, saying that he
had forgotten something. Then going out again
from the camp, he imagined himself acquitted of
his oath, and he was so in words alone, not in fact.
But in a promise, what you mean, not what you
say, is always to be taken into account. The most
illustrious example of justice toward an enemy was
presented by our ancestors, when the Senate and
Caius Fabricius sent back to Pyrrhus a deserter
who promised the Senate to kill the king by poison.
Thus they refused to sanction the murder of an
enemy, and a powerful one, and one who was making war on them without provocation.

Enough has now been said about duties connected
with war.

We should also bear it in mind that justice is
to be maintained even toward those of the lowest
condition. But the lowest condition and fortune
is that of slaves, who, it has been well said, ought

---

[1] Literally, left among the *aerarii*, i. e. liable to taxation, but
without the rights of citizenship.

to be treated as hired servants, to have their daily tasks assigned them, and to receive a just compensation for their labor.[1] In fine, while wrong may be done in two ways, either by force or by fraud, the latter seems to belong, as it were, to the fox, the former to the lion, and neither to be congenial with man. Yet of the two, fraud is the most detestable. But of all forms of injustice, none is more heinous than that of the men who, while they practise fraud to the utmost of their ability, do it in such a way that they appear to be good men. Enough has been said about justice.

14. In the next place, as was proposed, let us speak of beneficence and liberality, than which, indeed, nothing is more in harmony with human nature; yet at many points it demands circumspection. In the first place, care must be taken lest our kindness be of disadvantage to those whom we seem to benefit, or to others; in the next place, lest our generosity exceed our means; still further, that our benefactions be apportioned to the merit of our beneficiaries, — a fundamental principle of justice to which reference should be had in whatever we do for others. Now, those who bestow on any person what is likely to be of disadvantage to

---

[1] The Stoics deduced the obligation to treat slaves humanely from their doctrine of human equality, and the indifference of outward conditions to the truly philosophic mind. Seneca goes in this direction to as great length as that of modern anti-slavery reformers. Cicero was an eminently humane master.

him to whom they seem to be kind, are to be regarded not as beneficent and liberal, but as harmful flatterers; and those who injure some that they may be generous to others, are as much in the wrong as if they directly converted what belongs to others into their own property. Yet there are many, especially those greedy for show and fame, who take from some what they mean to lavish on others, and these persons think that they shall seem beneficent toward their friends if they enrich them, no matter how. But this is so remote from duty, that nothing can be more contrary to duty. We must, then, take care that in our generosity, while we do good to our friends, we injure no one. Therefore the transfer of property by Lucius Sulla and Caius Caesar[1] from its rightful owners to those to whom it did not belong ought not to be deemed generous; for nothing is generous that is not at the same time just. The second caution is that our generosity should not exceed our means; for those who want to be more generous than their property authorizes them to be, in the first place are blameworthy because they are unjust toward their nearest kindred, giving to strangers what ought to be employed for the needs of their own families or

---

[1] Reference is here made to the vast amount of property confiscated by Sulla from the victims of his proscription, and bestowed with lavish prodigality on his partisans, and to the rich spoils of the provinces which Caesar largely employed to purchase and reward adherents, and to win the popular favor.

bequeathed for their future use. There is, too, connected with generosity of this type, in almost every instance, a disposition to seize and appropriate wrongfully the property of other men, in order to furnish means for prodigal giving. We can see, also, that a large number of persons, less from a liberal nature than for the reputation of generosity, do many things that evidently proceed from ostentation rather than from good will. It was said, in the third place, that in beneficence regard should be had to merit, in which matter we should take into consideration the character of the candidate for our favor, his disposition toward us, the degree of his familiarity and intimacy with us, and the good offices which he may have previously rendered for our benefit. That all these reasons for our kindness should be combined, is desirable; if some of them are wanting, preponderant weight must be given to the more numerous and more important reasons.

15. But since we pass our lives, not among perfect and faultlessly wise men,[1] but among those in whom it is well if there be found the semblance of virtue, it ought, as I think, to be our purpose to leave none unbefriended in whom there is any trace of virtue; but at the same time those have the highest claim to our kind offices who are most richly endowed with the gentler virtues, moderation, self-control, and this very justice about which I

---

[1] The Stoics maintained that the truly wise man lived only in theory, but had had no actual being in this world.

have said so much.   For in a man not perfect or
wise, a bold and ambitious mind is generally too impetuous; while the virtues that I have just named
seem to be more in accordance with the character
of a truly good man.   Thus far I have spoken only
of the character of those to whom our kind offices
are to be rendered.   In the next place, as to the
good will borne to us, our first duty is to bestow
the most on those who hold us in the dearest
regard.   We ought, however, to judge of their good
will not, as young people often do, by ardent
expressions of love, but rather by the firmness and
constancy of their attachment.   But if there are
obligations on our part, so that kindness is not to
begin with us, but to be returned by us, there is all
the greater responsibility laid upon us; for there is
no more essential duty than that of returning kindness received.   If Hesiod bids us to restore what
we have borrowed for use in a greater measure, if
we can, what ought we to do when appealed to by
unsolicited beneficence?   Ought we not to imitate
fertile fields, which bring forth much more than they
received?   If we do not hesitate to confer favors
on those who, we hope, will be of service to us,
what ought we to be toward those who have already
done us service?   For while there are two kinds of
generosity, one that of bestowing, the other that
of returning good offices, — whether we bestow or
not, it is for us to choose; but to omit the returning of kindness is impossible for a good man, if he

can do so without wronging any one. But there is room for discrimination as to the benefits received; nor can it be denied that the greater the benefit, the greater is the obligation. In this matter the first thing to be considered is, with what degree of earnestness, zeal, and true benevolence one has shown us kindness. For many bestow benefits at haphazard, without judgment or method, or roused to action by some sudden impulse of mind, as if by a blast of wind; and their kindnesses are not to be esteemed so great as those which are conferred with judgment, deliberately and continuously. But alike in bestowing benefit and in returning kindness, other things being equal, it is in the highest degree incumbent upon us to do the most for those who need the most. The contrary is the common habit. Him from whom men hope the most, even if he has no need, they are the most ready to serve.

16. Still further, human society and fellowship will be best maintained, if where there is the most intimate relation, the greatest amount of kindness be bestowed. Here it may be well to trace back the social relations of men to their principles in nature. The first of these principles is that which is seen in the social union of the entire race of man. Its bond is reason as expressed in language,[1] which by teaching, learning, imparting, discussing, deciding, conciliates mutual regard, and unites men by

[1] In the Latin, *ratio et oratio*, — a verbal assonance which our language affords us no means of translating.

a certain natural fellowship; nor in any respect are we farther removed from the nature of beasts, in which, we often say, there is courage, as in the horse and the lion, but not justice, equity, goodness, inasmuch as they have neither reason nor language. Indeed, it is through this society, so broadly open to men with one another, to all with all, that common possession is to be maintained as to whatever nature has produced for the common use of men; so that while those things that are specially designated by the statutes and the civil law are held as thus decreed, according to these very laws other things may be regarded in the sense of the Greek proverb, "All things are common among friends." Indeed, all those things seem to be common among men, which are of the kind designated by Ennius in a single example, but comprehending many others:—

> "Who kindly shows a wanderer his way,
>    Lights, as it were, a torch from his own torch,—
>  In kindling others' light, no less he shines."

This one instance suffices to illustrate the rule, that whatever one can give without suffering detriment should be given even to an entire stranger. Thus among common obligations we may reckon, to prohibit no one from drinking at a stream of running water; to permit any one who wishes to light fire from fire; to give faithful advice to one who is in doubt,—which things are useful to the receiver, and

do no harm to the giver. But since the resources
of individuals are small, while the multitude of
those who need them is unbounded, this indis-
criminate giving should have the limit suggested
by Ennius, "No less he shines," so that we may
have the means of generosity to those peculiarly
our own.

17. But there are several degrees of relationship
among men. To take our departure from the tie
of common humanity, of which I have spoken,
there is a nearer relation of race, nation, and language, which brings men into very close community
of feeling. It is a still more intimate bond to
belong to the same city; for the inhabitants of
a city have in common among themselves forum,
temples, public walks, streets, laws, rights, courts,
modes and places of voting, beside companionships
and intimacies, engagements and contracts, of many
with many. Closer still is the tie of kindred; for
by this from the vast society of the human race
one is shut up into a small and narrow circle.
Indeed, since the desire of producing offspring is
common by nature to all living creatures, the nearest association consists in the union of the sexes;[1]
the next, in the relation with children; then, that
of a common home and a community of such goods
as appertain to the home. Then the home is the

---

[1] Latin, *conjugium*, which is often employed to denote marriage without religious ceremonies, and not necessarily permanent,
and is used equally as to men and the lower animals.

germ of the city, and, so to speak, the nursery of
the state. The union of brothers comes next in
order, then that of cousins less or more remote,
who, when one house can no longer hold them all,
emigrate to other houses as if to colonies. Then
follow marriages[1] and affinities by marriage, thus increasing the number of kindred. From this propa-
gation and fresh growth of successive generations
states have their beginning. But the union of
blood, especially, binds men in mutual kindness
and affection; for it is a great thing to have the
same statues of ancestors, the same rites of domestic
worship, the same sepulchres. But of all associations none is more excellent, none more enduring,
than when good men, of like character, are united
in intimacy. For the moral rectitude of which
I have so often spoken, even if we see it in a
stranger, yet moves us, and calls out our friendship
for him in whom it dwells. Moreover, while every
virtue attracts us to itself, and makes us love those
in whom it seems to exist, this is emphatically true
of justice and generosity. At the same time, nothing is more lovable, and nothing brings men into
more intimate relations, than the common possession
of these moral excellences; for those who have
the same virtuous desires and purposes love one another as they love themselves, and they realize what
Pythagoras would have in friendship, the unifying

---

[1] Latin, *connubia*, which denotes legal marriages, deemed
sacred and permanent as compared with *conjugia*.

of plurality. That also is an intimate fellowship which is created by benefits mutually bestowed and received, which, while they give pleasure on both sides, produce a lasting attachment between those who thus live in reciprocal good offices. But when you survey with reason and judgment the entire field of human society, of all associations none is closer, none dearer, than that which unites each of us with our country. Parents are dear, children are dear, so are kindred and friends; but the country alone takes into her embrace all our loves for all, in whose behalf what good man would hesitate to encounter death, if he might thus do her service? The more detestable is the savageness of those who by every form of guilt have inflicted grievous wounds on their country, and are and have been employed in her utter subversion. Now, if you make an estimate and comparison[1] of the degree of service to be rendered in each relation, the first place must be given to our country and our parents, bound as we are to them by paramount benefits; next come our children, and the entire family which looks to us alone, nor in stress of need can have any other refuge; then, afterward, the kindred with whom we are on pleasant terms, and with whom, for the most part, we are in the same condition of

[1] Latin, *contentio et comparatio*, literally, a stretching of two or more objects side by side, and measuring their equality or non-equality in length, — a figure which can hardly be represented in translation.

life. For the reasons indicated we owe chiefly to these that I have named the necessary protection of daily life; but companionship, conviviality, counsel, conversation, advice, consolation, sometimes reproof also, have their most fruitful soil in friendship, and that is the most pleasant friendship which is cemented by resemblance in character.

18. In discharging all these duties, we ought to consider what is most needful for each person, and what each person either can or cannot obtain without our aid. Thus the degrees of relationship will not correspond with those of the occasions for our kind offices; and there are duties which we owe to some rather than to others, on grounds independent of their connection with us. Thus you would help a neighbor rather than a brother or an intimate friend in harvesting his crops; while in a case in court you would appear as an advocate for your kinsman or friend rather than for your neighbor. These and similar points are to be carefully considered in every department of duty, and we should practise and exercise ourselves so that we may be good calculators of duty, and by adding and subtracting may ascertain the remainder, and thus know how much is due to each person. Indeed, as neither physicians, nor commanders, nor orators, though they understand the rules of their art, can accomplish anything worthy of high commendation without practice and exercise; so, though the precepts for the faithful discharge of duty be delivered,

as I am delivering them now, the very greatness of
the work which they prescribe demands practice
and exercise. I have now shown, with nearly
sufficient fulness of detail, how the right, on which
duty depends, is derived from the constituent elements of human society.

It is to be observed that of the four sources from
which right and duty flow, the greatest admiration
attends that consisting in a large and lofty mind,
which looks down on human fortunes. Thus, when
reproach is intended, nothing occurs more readily
than utterances like this, —

> "Ye, youths, indeed show but a woman's soul;
> That heroine, a man's;"—

or this, —

> "Give, Salmacis,[1] spoils without sweat and blood."[2]

On the other hand, in panegyrics, our speech rolls
on with a fuller flow when we praise deeds that
have been wrought with a large mind, bravely and
grandly. Hence the field for eloquent discourse
about Marathon, Salamis, Plataea, Thermopylae,
Leuctrae; hence the fame of our own fellow-coun-

---

[1] Salmacis was the name of a fountain in Caria, so called from
a not very virtuous nymph of that name. The waters of the
fountain were said to enervate those who bathed in it, and it was
fabled to have been the resort of eager pleasure-seekers of both
sexes. Trophies were, of course, won there by wanton dalliance,
and not by deeds of prowess.

[2] Some commentators say that these scraps of verse are from
Ennius; others say that it is not known whence they come.
The latter are probably in the right.

trymen, Cocles, the Decii, Cneius and Publius
Scipio; hence the glory of Marcus Marcellus, and
of others more than can be numbered; and the
Roman people, as a nation, excels other nations
chiefly in this very greatness of souL In particular, the prevailing love for glory in war is manifested in the almost uniform clothing of statues in
military attire.[1]

19. But this loftiness of spirit, manifested in
peril and in toil, if devoid of justice, and contending
for selfish ends, not for the public good, is to be
condemned; for not only does it not appertain to
virtue, — it belongs rather to a savageness that
spurns all human feeling.[2] Therefore courage is
well defined by the Stoics as the virtue that contends for the right. No one, then, who has sought
a reputation for courage by treachery and fraud,
has won the fame he sought. Nothing that is
devoid of justice can be honorable. It was well
said by Plato: "Not only is knowledge, when
divorced from justice, to be termed subtlety rather
than wisdom; but also the soul prompt to encounter
danger, if moved thereto by self-interest, and not
by the common good, should have the reputation

---

[1] There were hardly any distinguished Romans that had not
held some military command, so that even for those best known
as civilians a military costume might not have been inappropriate.

[2] Latin, *inmanitatis* omnem *humanitatem* repellentis, — one
of those untranslatable assonances in which Cicero delights, and
which contribute largely to the euphony of his diction.

of audacity rather than of courage." Therefore I would have brave and high-spirited men also good and simple, friends of truth, remote from guile,— traits of character which belong to the very heart of justice. But the mischief is, that in this exaltation and largeness of soul obstinacy and an excessive lust of power very easily have birth. For as, according to Plato, the entire character of the Lacedaemonians was set on fire by the desire for victory, so now, in proportion as one surpasses others in grandeur of soul, he is ambitious to hold the foremost place among those in power, or rather, to rule alone. Now it is hard, when you covet pre-eminence, to maintain the equity which is the most essential property of justice. Hence it is that such men suffer themselves to be overcome neither in debate nor by any legal or constitutional hindrance, and in the state they, for the most part, employ bribery and intrigue that they may acquire the greatest influence possible, and may rise by force, rather than maintain equality with their fellow-citizens by justice. But the greater the difficulty, the greater the glory. Nor is there any occasion that ought to be devoid of justice. Therefore not those who inflict, but those who repel wrong ought to be deemed brave and magnanimous. A soul truly and wisely great regards the right to which the nature of man aspires as consisting in deeds, not in fame; it chooses to be chief rather than to seem so. On the other hand, he who depends

on the waywardness of the undiscerning multitude
does not deserve to be reckoned among great men.
But in proportion to a man's towering ambition,
he is easily urged by the greed of fame to deeds
averse from justice.　His is a slippery standing-
ground;[1] for we seldom find a man, who, for labors
undertaken and dangers encountered, does not demand fame as the price of his exploits.

20. A brave and great soul is, in fine, chiefly
characterized by two things. One of these is the
contempt of outward circumstances in the persuasion that a man ought not to admire or wish
or seek aught that is not right and becoming, or
to yield to human influence, or to passion, or to
calamity. The other is that, with this disposition
of mind, one should undertake the conduct of
affairs great, indeed, and, especially, beneficial, but
at the same time arduous in the highest degree,
demanding severe toil, and fraught with peril
not only of the means of comfortable living, but
of life itself. Of these two things, all the lustre
and renown, and the utility too, belong to the
latter: but their cause and the habit of mind that
makes men great lie in the former; for in this is
inherent that which renders souls truly great, and
lifts them above the vicissitudes of human fortune.
Moreover, this first constituent of greatness consists
in two things, in accounting the right alone as
good, and in freedom from all disturbing passions:

[1] On which it is hard to maintain one's moral equipoise.

for to hold in light esteem, and on fixed and firm
principles to despise, objects which to most persons
seem excellent and splendid, is the token of a
brave and great soul; and to bear those reputedly
bitter experiences which are so many and various
in human life and fortunes, in such a way as to
depart in no wise from the deportment that is
natural to you, in no wise from the dignity befitting
a wise man, is the index of a strong mind and of
great steadfastness of character. But it is incon-
gruous for one who is not broken down by fear
to be broken down by the love of gain, or for him
who has shown himself unconquered by labor, to
be conquered by sensuality. These failures must be
provided against, and the desire for money must
especially be shunned. For nothing shows so narrow and small a mind as the love of riches; nothing is more honorable and magnificent than to
despise money if you have it not, — if you have
it, to expend it for purposes of beneficence and
generosity. The greed of fame, also, as I have
already said, must be shunned; for it deprives one
of liberty, which every high-minded man will strive
to the utmost to maintain. Indeed, posts of command[1] ought not to be eagerly sought, nay, they
should sometimes rather be refused, sometimes re-
signed. One should also be free from all disturbing emotions, not only from desire and fear, but

---

[1] *Imperia*, by which Cicero, oftener than not, denotes high
military office.

equally from solicitude, and sensuality, and anger, that there may be serenity of mind, and that freedom from care which brings with it both evenness of temper and dignity of character. But there are and have been many who, in quest of the serenity of which I am speaking, have withdrawn from public affairs, and taken refuge in a life of leisure. Among these are the most eminent philosophers, including those of the very first rank, and also some stern and grave men, who could not endure the conduct either of the people or of their rulers. Some, too, have taken up their abode in the country, engrossed in the care of their own property. Their design is the same as that of kings, to lack nothing, to obey no one, to enjoy liberty, the essence of which is to live as one pleases.

21. While the purpose of living as one pleases is common to those greedy of power and to the men of leisure of whom I have spoken, the former think that they can realize it if they have large resources; the latter, if they are content with what they have, and with little. Nor is either opinion to be despised. But the life of the men of leisure is easier, and safer, and less liable to give trouble or annoyance to others; while that of those who have fitted themselves for the public service and for the management of large affairs, is more fruitful of benefit to mankind, and more conducive to their own eminence and renown. All things considered, we ought, perhaps, to excuse from bearing part in public

affairs those who devote themselves to learning
with superior ability, and those who, from impaired
health, or for some sufficiently weighty reason, have
sought retirement, abandoning to others the power
and the praise of civic service. But as for those
who have no such reason, yet say that they despise
what most persons admire, places of trust and
honor in the military or civil service,[1] this, I think,
is to be reckoned to their discredit, not to their
praise. They, indeed, deserve approval for despising fame and thinking it of no account. But they
seem to dread not only toil and trouble, but a
certain imagined shame and disgrace from the dis-
appointments and repulses which they must encounter. For there are those who in opposite
circumstances fail to act consistently, — who have
the utmost contempt for pleasure, yet are unmanned
by pain, — who scorn fame, yet are broken down
by unpopularity; and these are, indeed, manifest
incongruities in a man's character. But those
whom nature has endowed with qualities that fit
them for the management of public affairs ought,
without needless delay, to become candidates for
office and to take the interests of the state in charge;
for only thus can the state be well governed, and
only thus can commanding power of mind be made
manifest. At the same time, for those who undertake public trusts, perhaps even more than for
philosophers, there is need of elevation of mind,

---

[1] Latin, *imperia et magistratus.*

and contempt of the vicissitudes of human fortune, and that serene and unruffled spirit of which I often speak, in order that they may be free from solicitude, and may lead dignified and self-consistent lives. This is easier for philosophers, inasmuch as their condition in life is less open to the assaults of fortune, their wants are fewer, and in case of adverse events they encounter a less heavy fall. On the other hand, those who hold public trusts are obviously liable to stronger mental excitement, and are more heavily burdened with care than those who live in retirement; and they should therefore bring to their duty a corresponding strength of mind, and independence of the ordinary causes of vexation. But let him who meditates entering on any important undertaking, carefully consider, not only whether the undertaking is right, but also whether he has the ability to carry it through ; and here he must beware, on the one hand, lest he too readily despair of success from mere want of spirit, or, on the other hand, lest he be over-confident from excessive eagerness. In fine, in all transactions, before you enter upon them, you should make diligent preparation.

22. Moreover, since military achievements are very commonly regarded as outranking civil service, this opinion needs to be refuted; for wars have often been encouraged from the desire of fame, especially by men of superior intellect and genius, when they have the requisite ability for the

service of arms, and are ambitious of the places of command which it offers. Yet if we will only look at facts, there have been many civic transactions that have surpassed feats of arms in importance and in renown.[1] Thus, although Themistocles be rightly held in honor, and his name be more illustrious than that of Solon, and Salamis be cited as witness of a most splendid victory which may have a higher place in the popular esteem than Solon's establishing the Areopagus,[2] yet this last must be regarded as no less glorious than the victory. For this was once of benefit; that will always be of benefit to the state, as preserving inviolate the laws of the Athenians and the institutions of their ancestors. And Themistocles could have named no particular in which he could have given help to the Areopagus; while the Areopagus rendered substantial aid[3] to Themistocles, the war having been conducted by the counsel of that same Senate established by Solon. The like may be said of Pausa-

---

[1] " Peace hath her victories
No less renowned than war."
MILTON, *Sonnet* XVI.

[2] Solon did not establish the Areopagus, which was of even prehistoric origin ; but before his time it was merely a criminal court, while he gave it censorial jurisdiction, advisory authority in public affairs, and, in fine, functions that rendered it a council of state, and a strongly conservative force against else unchecked democracy.

[3] The Areopagus, in a time of great dearth, furnished funds for the payment of the seamen who were going to fight at Salamis.

nias[1] and Lysander.[2] Although the common idea
is that the Lacedaemonian empire owed its enlarge-
ment to their prowess, yet their achievements bear
no comparison with the laws and discipline of
Lycurgus. For was it not these very institutions
that made their armies both more obedient and
more courageous? Nor, indeed, when I was a boy,
did I regard Marcus Scaurus[3] as inferior to Caius
Marius; nor, when I was in public life, did I think
Quintus Catulus[4] inferior to Cneius Pompeius.

"Valor abroad is naught, unless at home be wisdom."[5]

Nor yet did Africanus, of rare worth both as a man
and as a commander, do greater service to the
republic in exterminating Numantia, than at the
same time did Publius Nasica, a private citizen,
in killing Tiberius Gracchus. This last transac-

---

[1] Pausanias overthrew the Persian general, Mardonius, in the
battle of Plataea.

[2] Lysander took Athens, and destroyed the Long Walls.

[3] Marcus Aemilius Scaurus was a strong conservative and a
zealous supporter of the aristocratic party. His deportment, too,
was remarkable for its gravity and its general respectability. He
may have been a better man than Marius; but he was charged
with receiving a heavy bribe from Jugurtha for securing a peace
on terms favorable to the king, and he saved himself from penal
accountability only by procuring his own appointment as one of
the judges for the trial of his accomplices.

[4] Quintus Catulus supported Cicero at the time of the Catilinian conspiracy, and was the first in the Senate to hail him as
Father of the Country (*pater patriae*).

[5] A verse, quoted probably from some lost comedy, the measure being one employed by the comic poets.

tion, indeed, is not wholly of a civil character, —
as it was performed by force and arms, it borders
on the military; yet it was effected by civic policy
without military array. That verse of mine, against
which, as I hear, unprincipled and envious men are
wont to rail, —

" Let arms yield to the robe, the laurel to the tongue," [1]

is by no means devoid of excellence. Not to mention others, when I was at the helm of the republic,
did not arms yield to the gown? For there was
never in the republic greater danger, and never a
more profound peace. Thus by my counsels and
my assiduity their very weapons fell speedily from
the hands of the most audacious citizens. What
equally great achievement was ever performed in
war? What triumph is to be compared with it?
I may take the liberty of boasting to you, my son
Marcus, to whom belong both the heritage of this
fame and the imitation of my deeds. Forsooth,
Cneius Pompeius, a man rich in military renown,
in the hearing of many did me the honor of saying
that he would in vain have obtained his third
triumph, unless by my service to the state he
would have had a place for the celebration of his
triumph. There are, then, cases of civic courage

---

[1] This verse is from a poem of Cicero on his own times, and
mainly to his own glory as carried to its climax in his suppression
of the Catilinian conspiracy. It was laughed at for the patent
self-conceit which it exhibited. ·

not inferior to those in war, nay, demanding even a
larger amount of labor and of zeal.

23. Of a certainty, the virtue which we demand
of a lofty and large mind is generated by strength
of mind, not of body. Yet the body must be dis-
ciplined, and brought into a condition in which it
can obey counsel and reason in following out affairs
to their issue, and in enduring toil. But the virtue which we demand consists in mental care
and thought, in which those who preside over
the state in the robe of peace, perform no less
service than those who take the lead in war.
Indeed, by the counsel of the former, wars have
been often prevented or terminated, sometimes,
also, begun, as the third Punic war, by the counsel
of Marcus Cato,[1] then dead, whose authority outlived him. Therefore skill in the settlement of
controversies is more desirable than courage in
disputing them by arms; but care must be taken
lest we resort to peaceful measures rather to avoid
fighting than for the public good.

But war should be undertaken in such a way
that it may seem nothing else than a quest of
peace. Moreover, it belongs to a brave and firm
man not to be disturbed in misfortune, nor to be
so thrown off his balance as to be, in the trite

---

[1] As is well known, Cato never gave his vote in the Senate,
no matter what the subject, without repeating the words, *Delenda
est Carthago*, Carthage must be destroyed. Its destruction took
place three years after his death.

phrase, hustled down from his position, but to take prompt thought and counsel, and not to be betrayed into unreason. While as much as this belongs to a great mind, it is also the part of a man of transcendent ability to anticipate the future in thought, and somewhat beforehand to consider what is liable to happen on either side, and what is to be done in case of any possible event, so as not to be compelled at any time to say, "I had not thought of this." Such is the work of a mind large, and lofty, and trusting in discretion and good counsel. But to make rash manoeuvres in battle, and to come to close quarters with the enemy, is something savage and beastlike. Yet when occasion and need demand, there must be hand-to-hand fighting, and death is to be preferred to slavery or poltroonery.

24. As to the destruction and plundering of conquered cities, care must be taken that nothing be done precipitately, nothing cruelly; and it is the part of a truly great man, in times of disorder, to punish the guilty, to spare the many, and, whatever takes place, to keep rectitude and honor inviolate. For as there are those, as I have already said, who prefer military to civil service, so you may find many to whom perilous and hot-headed counsels seem more splendid and imposing than calm and deliberate measures. Never, certainly, are we by shunning danger to make ourselves seem tame and timid; but equally are we to avoid encountering needless perils, than which nothing can be more

foolish. Therefore, in impending danger, we should
imitate the custom of physicians, who employ mild
treatment for those but slightly ill, but are compelled to use dangerous and doubtful remedies for
severer diseases. Thus it is the part of a madman,
in a calm sea to desire a storm with a head-wind;
but that of a wise man, to withstand the storm as
best he may, especially if the benefits obtained
by carrying the matter through successfully are
greater than the evil that may be incurred in the
conflict. But public transactions are perilous, sometimes to those who undertake them, sometimes to
the state; and, again, some run the risk of life,
others of fame, and of the good-will of their fellow-
citizens. We ought to be more ready to encounter
danger for ourselves than for the state, and to contend more promptly for honor and fame than for
anything else that concerns ourselves personally.

Yet there have been found many who were ready
to pour out not only their money, but even their
blood for their country, who would not make the
least sacrifice of reputation, even when the well-
being of the state demanded it; as, for instance,
Callicratidas, who, after having been at the head of
the Lacedaemonian forces in the Peloponnesian war,
and having repeatedly rendered excellent service,
at last reversed everything by rejecting the advice
of those who thought it best to remove the fleet
from the Arginusae and not to fight with the
Athenians. He answered them that the Lacedae-

monians, if they lost that fleet, could equip another, while he could not retreat without disgracing himself.[1] This was, indeed, to the Lacedaemonians a blow of moderate severity; that, a ruinous one, by which, when Cleombrotus,[2] for fear of unpopularity, fought rashly with Epamiuondas, the power of the Lacedaemonians utterly collapsed. What a contrast here to the advantage of Quintus Maximus,[3] of whom Ennius writes: —

> "One man by slow delays restored our fortunes,
>   Preferring not the people's praise to safety,
>   And thus his after-glory shines the more."

This same kind of error is also to be shunned in civil affairs; for there are those who, for fear of unpopularity, dare not say what they think, even if it be the very best that could be said.

25. In fine, let those who are to preside over the state obey two precepts of Plato, — one, that they so watch for the well-being of their fellow-citizens that they have reference to it in whatever they do, forgetting their own private interests; the other,

[1] Callicratidas himself perished in the battle.

[2] Cleombrotus was taunted for excess of caution, and was thus induced to risk the battle with the Thebans, against his own judgment. There seems to have been as much hesitation on the Theban side, so that, prior to the battle, the scales would probably have seemed equipoised.

[3] Quintus Fabius Maximus, who from his repeatedly avoiding direct conflict with Hannibal in the determination to weary him out by delay, acquired the surname of Cunctator, and has bequeathed the enduring epithet of *Fabian* to a policy like his own.

that they care for the whole body politic, and not, while they watch over a portion of it, neglect other portions. For, as the guardianship of a minor, so the administration of the state is to be conducted for the benefit, not of those to whom it is intrusted, but of those who are intrusted to their care. But those who take counsel for a part of the citizens, and neglect a part, bring into the state an element of the greatest mischief, and stir up sedition and discord, some siding with the people, some with the aristocracy, and few being equally the friends of all. From this cause arose great dissensions among the Athenians, and in our republic it has led not only to seditions, but also to destructive civil wars. Partiality of this kind, a citizen who is substantial and brave, and worthy of a chief place in the state, will shun and abhor, and will give himself wholly up to the state, pursuing neither wealth nor power; and he will so watch over the entire state as to consult the well-being of all its citizens. Nor will he expose any one to hatred or envy by false accusation, and he will in every respect so adhere to justice and right as in their behalf to submit to any loss however severe, and to face death itself rather than surrender the principles which I have indicated. Most pitiful in every aspect is the canvassing and scrambling for preferment, of which it is well said by the same Plato, that those who strive among themselves which shall be foremost in the administration of the state, act like sailors who should quarrel for a place at the helm. The same writer exhorts us to regard as enemies those who bear arms against us, not those who desire to care for the interests of the state in accordance with their own judgment, as in the case of the disagreement without bitterness between Publius Africanus and Quintus Metellus.[1]

Nor are they to be listened to who think that anger is to be cherished toward those who are unfriendly to us on political grounds, and imagine that this betokens a large-minded and brave man ; for nothing is more praiseworthy, nothing more befitting a great and eminent man, than placability and clemency. Moreover, in free states and where all have equal rights, there is a demand for courtesy, and for a soul superior to petty causes of vexation, lest if we suffer ourselves to be angry with those who intrude upon us inopportunely, we fall into irritable habits equally harmful and hateful. Yet an easy and accommodating temper is to be approved only so far as may be consistent with the strictness demanded in public business, without

[1] They were often on opposite sides in the politics of the city, and sometimes on non-friendly, if not unfriendly terms ; but when Africanus was found dead in his bed, and supposed to have been assassinated, Metellus exclaimed, "Come, citizens, to the rescue ; the walls of our city are thrown down ; " and he ordered his sons to put their shoulders under the bier, saying that they would never have the opportunity to perform that office for a greater man.

which the state cannot be administered. But all punishment and correction ought to be free from personal insult, and should have reference, not to the pleasure of him who administers punishment or reproof, but to the public good. Care also must be taken lest the punishment be greater than the fault, and lest for the same cause some be made penally responsible, and others not even called to account. Most of all is anger to be eliminated in punishment; for he who enters on the office of punishment in anger will never preserve that mean between too much and too little, of which the Peripatetics make so great account,[1] and rightly too, if they only would not commend anger, and say that it is implanted by nature for useful ends. On the other hand, it is under all circumstances to be shunned, and it is desirable that those who preside over the state should be like the laws, which are led to inflict punishment, not by anger, but by justice.

26. Again, in prosperity, and when affairs flow on as we would have them, we should with the utmost care avoid pride, fastidiousness, and arrogance; for it is the token of a frivolous mind to bear either prosperity or adversity otherwise than

---

[1] The Peripatetics, after Aristotle, defined virtue as always consisting of the mean between two extremes. Thus, courage is the mean between rashness and cowardice. The New Academy, to which Cicero belonged, accepted hypothetically the ethics of the Peripatetic school.

moderately, and pre-eminently praiseworthy is an
equable temperament in one's whole life, the same
countenance and the same mien always, as we
learn was the case with Socrates, and equally
with Caius Laelius.[1] I regard Philip, king of
the Macedonians, though surpassed by his son in
achievements and in fame, as having been his superior in affability and kindness. Thus the one was
always great, the other often very mean, — so as
to give good ground for the rule of those who
say that the higher our position is, the more meekly
we should carry ourselves. Panaetius, indeed, tells
us that Africanus, his pupil and friend, used to say,
that as it is common to give horses that, from having been often in battle, rear and prance danger-
ously, into the hands of professional tamers, that
they may be ridden more easily, so men, when at
loose reins in prosperity, and over self-confident,
should be brought, as it were, to the ring[2] of reason
and instruction, that they may fully see the· frailty
of man's estate, and the fickleness of fortune. Still
further, in the extreme of prosperity, especially,

---

[1] Caius Laelius Sapiens, who died before Cicero was born, was
a man of but moderate, though not mean reputation as a general,
a statesman, and an orator; but had a strong hold on Cicero's
veneration as second to no man of his time in elegant culture,
especially in Greek literature and philosophy, and also as a stanch
advocate of the aristocracy as opposed to the *plebs*. Cicero makes
him the chief interlocutor in the *De·Amicitia*, and one of the
speakers in the *De Senectute* and the·*De Republica*.

[2] Latin, *gyrum*, the ring or circle, round which horses are
ridden to break or tame them.

resort is to be had to the counsel of friends, and
even greater authority to be given to them than
under ordinary circumstances.  In such a condition we must also take heed lest we open our ears
to flatterers, and suffer ourselves to be cajoled.  In
yielding to sycophancy, we are always liable to be
deceived, thinking that we deserve the praise bestowed upon us, whence proceed numberless mistakes, men who are inflated by self-conceit becoming the objects of coarse derision, and committing
the most egregious eccentricities in conduct.  But
enough on this point.

From what has been said, it is to be inferred
that the most important affairs, and those indicative
of the highest tone of spirit, come under the direction of men in public life, their official duty having
the widest scope, and extending to the largest number of persons ; but that there are and have been
many men of great mind in private life, engaged in
important investigations or enterprises, yet attending to no affairs but their own; while others, no
less great, midway between philosophers and statesmen, are occupied with the care of their property,
not, indeed, increasing it by every means in their
power, nor yet depriving their friends of the benefit
of it, but rather, whenever there is need, giving
freely to their friends and to the state.  Property
thus held should, in the first place, have been fairly
obtained, and not by any mean or offensive calling;
then it should show itself of service to as many

as possible, if they only be worthy; then, too, it
should be increased by industry and frugality, and
should not lie open to the demands of sensuality
and luxury rather than to those of generosity and
beneficence. He who observes these rules may
live in splendor, dignity, and independence, and at
the same time with simplicity, with integrity, and
in friendly relations with mankind.

27. I have now to speak of the only remaining
division of the right, embracing modesty, which
gives a certain lustre to life, temperance, discretion,
serenity of soul, and moderation in all things.
Under this head is included what we may fitly
call decorum, or becomingness;[1] the Greeks call
it πρέπον.[2] The property of this is that it cannot
be separated from the right; for whatever is becoming is right, and whatever is right is becoming.
In what way the right and the becoming differ is
more easily felt than told; for whatever it is that
constitutes becomingness, it makes its appearance
when the right has gone before; and thus the
becoming is not confined to the division of the
right now under discussion, but is equally manifest
in the three other divisions. For it is becoming to
employ both reason and speech with discretion, and

---

[1] Literally, what may be called in Latin *decorum*. In what
follows I have translated *decorum* by the awkward, yet legitimate
word, becomingness, which corresponds in sense very closely to
the Latin word, while in making *decorum* an English word we
have dropped a part of its native meaning.

[2] That which is becoming, or decorous.

to do what you do deliberately, and on every subject to perceive and discern the truth; and, on the
other hand, it is as unbecoming to be deceived, to
misjudge, to commit grave mistakes, to be deluded
into unwise conduct, as it is to be delirious or
insane. Then, too, whatever is just is becoming;
on the other hand, whatever is unjust, as it is base,
is also unbecoming. The case is the same with
courage; for whatever is done manfully and high-
spiritedly seems worthy of a man, and becoming;
whatever is the opposite of this, as it is base, is
also unbecoming. Thus this becomingness of which
I speak belongs, indeed, to all virtue, and so belongs
to it that it is not discerned by any abstruse process of reasoning, but is perfectly obvious. For
there is, in truth, a certain something which is
becoming — and it is understood to be contained
in every form of virtue — which can be separated
from virtue in thought rather than in fact. As
grace and beauty of body cannot be separated from
health, so this becomingness of which I am speaking is entirely blended with virtue, yet is distinguished from it in conception and thought. It has
a twofold definition; for there is a certain general
becomingness which has its place in every kind of
virtue; and another, subordinate to this and included
within it, which belongs to single departments of
virtue. The former is usually defined somewhat
in this way: That is becoming which is in accordance with the superiority of man in those respects

in which his nature differs from that of other animals. The special type included under this general
head may be defined as designating that as becoming which is so in accordance with nature as to
present the aspect of moderation and self-restraint,
together with the air and manner that befit ingenuous breeding.

28. That these things are so understood, we may
infer from that becomingness which is the poet's
aim, about which I speak more at large in another
treatise.[1] We say that poets observe what is
becoming, when they represent that which befits
each individual character as both done and said.
Thus were Aeacus or Minos[2] to say, —

> "No matter how they hate me while they fear me,"

or,

> "The very father is his children's tomb,"[3]

it would seem unbecoming; for the tradition is that
they were just men. But when Atreus[4] so speaks,
the audience applaud; for the speech befits the
character. Now, the poets will determine from the
type of the character in hand, what befits each
character. To us, however, Nature has assigned

---

[1] In the *Orator*.

[2] Sons of Jupiter, said to have led such righteous lives that
they were made judges in the underworld.

[3] These passages are probably from the lost tragedy of Atreus,
by Attius.

[4] He, in Greek fable, killed the children of his brother
Thyestes, and feasted him on their flesh.

a character endowed with great excellence and superiority over other animals. The poets, on their part, in a great diversity of characters, will determine what is suitable and becoming to each, even to the very worst. But since the parts of consistency, moderation, self-restraint, modesty, are assigned to us by Nature, and since the same Nature teaches us not to be indifferent as to the manner of our conduct toward men, we may thus see how broad is the scope, both of that becomingness which belongs to all virtue, and of this which is made manifest in each several kind of virtue. For as the beauty of the body attracts notice by the symmetry of the limbs, and gives delight by the very fact that all its parts harmonize with a certain graceful effect, so this becomingness which shines in the life calls forth the esteem of society by the order, consistency, and moderation of all that is said and done. A certain measure of respect should indeed be shown toward all men, whether in superior position or on the common level; for indifference to the opinion of others is the token, not only of self-sufficiency, but of utter recklessness. But in the treatment of men there is a difference between justice and courtesy.[1] It is the part of justice not to injure men; of courtesy, not to give them offence, and it is in this last that the influence of becoming-

---

[1] Latin, *verecundia*, which commonly denotes modesty, but here evidently means that courtesy which is a part or a consequence of modesty.

ness is most clearly seen. With this exposition, I think that the nature of what we term becoming may be sufficiently understood.

The duty derived from it first leads to conformity with Nature and observance of her fitnesses, whom if we follow as a leader, we shall never err, and shall attain equally that which is in its essence keen and clear-sighted, that which is adapted to human society, and that which is strong and brave.[1] But the chief province of becomingness is in the division of virtue now under discussion; for not only movements of the body fitted to nature, but much more those movements of the mind which are in harmony with nature, claim approval. The natural constitution of the human mind is two-fold. One part consists in impulse, ὁρμὴ [2] in Greek, which hurries a man hither and thither; the other, in reason, which teaches and explains what is to be done and what to be avoided. Thus it is that reason fitly presides, and impulse obeys.

29. Every purpose ought to be free alike from rashness and from negligence, nor ought anything to be done for which a reason worthy of approval cannot be given. This, indeed, is almost a complete definition of duty.[3] Moreover, the impulses

---

[1] The first three cardinal virtues are thus enumerated. ⟨Prudence, Just.⟩

[2] Literally, *impulse*. The Latin word here is *appetitus*, which ⟨fortiu⟩ I have rendered impulse, because anger and fear are included under it.

[3] *Officium*, from *facere ob*, to do on account of, or for a sufficient reason.

must be made obedient to reason, and neither get
the advance of it, nor yet from stupidity or indolence lag behind it, and they must be quiet and
free from all excitement, — a state of things which
will show consistency and moderation in their full
lustre. For impulses which rove too far, prancing,
as it were, either in the pursuit or avoidance of
objects within their scope, and not sufficiently held
in by reason, evidently transcend bound and measure; for they desert and repudiate obedience, nor
do they submit themselves to reason, to which they
are subject by the law of nature. By such impulses
not only minds, but bodies are thrown into disturbance. You can discriminate at sight the very coun-
tenances of the angry, of those who are excited
by sensual passion or by fear, or of those who are
beside themselves through excess of pleasure, in all
of whom face, voice, gait, and posture are changed.
Hence, — to return to the delineation of duty, — it
is inferred that all the appetites must be checked
and calmed, and that watchfulness and care must
be on the alert to prevent us from doing anything
rashly and at haphazard, inconsiderately and care-
lessly. For we are not so constituted by nature
as to seem made for sport and jest, but rather for
sobriety and for certain more weighty and important pursuits. It is, indeed, right to indulge in sport
and jest, but only as in sleep and other relaxations,
when we have done full justice to grave and serious
concerns. Still further, the very style of jesting

ought not to be extravagant or immoderate, but in pure taste and with genuine humor. For as we do not give boys the unlimited liberty of play, but only that degree of freedom which is consistent with good conduct, so in jest itself there ought to shine forth something of the radiance of a pure character. There are, in truth, two kinds of jokes, — the one vulgar, impertinent, vicious, obscene; the other, elegant, refined, witty, humorous. This last kind fills not only our own Plautus and the old comedy of the Athenians, but also the books of the Socratic philosophers; and many things of this sort have been wittily said by many persons, as, for instance, those sayings collected by the elder Cato [1] which they call ἀποφθέγματα.[2] The distinction between a refined and a vulgar joke is easily made. The one, if not untimely, is worthy of any man at leisure; the other, unworthy of any man above the condition of a slave, if polluted by vile images or filthy words. A certain limit is to be observed

---

[1] Marcus Porcius Cato, the Censor. This collection is lost; but there are some specimens of its contents in Cicero's *Orator.* Collections of this kind, probably, were not unusual among the ancients, though, so far as I know, but one has been preserved in either of the classic tongues, namely, the 'Αστεία of Hierocles, the work, probably, of a compiler of whom no other vestige remains.

[2] Apophthegms, terse, pithy sayings, including jokes. Lord Bacon's "Apophthegms New and Old" are, all of them, anecdotes comprising smart, pointed sayings, and many of them jokes.

in sport, also, lest we run into excess, and, carried away by pleasure, lapse into some kind of disgraceful conduct. Our field[1] for athletic exercises, and the amusement of the chase, furnish proper examples of sport.

30. It is appropriate to every discussion of duty, always to bear in mind how far the nature of man excels that of cattle and other beasts. They feel nothing save sensual pleasure, and toward that they are borne by every instinct; but the mind of man is nourished by learning and reflection, is constantly thinking or doing something, and is led by the pleasure and profit derived from what is seen and heard. And even if one is unduly inclined to sensual pleasure, if he only be not on a level with brute beasts, — for there are some who are men, not in fact, but in name, — if he be ever so little above them, although captivated with the mere delight of the senses, he hides and dissembles the appetite for such pleasure from very shame. Hence it is inferred that bodily pleasure is unworthy of man's superior endowments, and ought to be despised and spurned; and if there be any one who sets some value on sensual gratification, he should carefully keep it within due limits. Thus food and the care of the body should be ordered with reference to health and strength, not to sensual pleasure.

---

[1] The Campus Martius, used by the Roman youth for riding, driving, swimming, and various athletic sports.

Indeed, if we will only bear in mind what excellence and dignity belong to human nature, we shall understand how base it is to give one's self up to luxury, and to live voluptuously and wantonly, and how honorable it is to live frugally, chastely, circumspectly, soberly.

But it is to be borne in mind that we are endowed by nature as it were with two characters, one of which is common to us with other men, inasmuch as we all partake of reason, and of the traits which raise us above the brutes, from which all that is right and becoming is derived, and from which we seek the method of ascertaining our duty; while the other is that which is assigned to each of us individually. For as in bodies there are great dissimilarities, — we see some excelling in speed for the race, others in strength for wrestling; also in personal appearance, some have dignity, others grace, — so in minds there are even greater diversities. Lucius Crassus and Lucius Philippus had a great deal of pleasantry; Caius Caesar, the son of Lucius, even more and more elaborate; while in their contemporaries, Marcus Scaurus and Marcus Drusus the younger, there was an unusual severity of manner; in Caius Laelius, much mirthfulness; in his friend Scipio, greater ambition, a more austere type of character. Among the Greeks, too, we have learned that Socrates was pleasant and facetious, and had a jocose way of talking, and meant more than he said, one whom the Greeks call εἴρωνα;[1] on the other hand, that Pythagoras and Pericles obtained the highest authority in their intercourse with men without any seasoning of mirthfulness. We are informed that, of the Carthaginians, Hannibal was crafty, and of our own commanders, that Quintus Maximus readily practised concealment, kept silence, dissembled, laid snares, anticipated the plans of his enemies. In these traits the Greeks assign the foremost place to Themistocles and Jason of Pherae, and accord pre-eminent praise to the cunning and crafty procedure of Solon, who, for his own safety, and that he might render additional service to the state, feigned insanity.[2] There are others of very unlike character, simple and open, who think that nothing should be done covertly or insidiously, votaries of truth, enemies of fraud; others still, who will endure anything whatever, and will be subservient to any one whomsoever, till they attain what they desire, as we saw in the case of Sulla and of Marcus Crassus. Of this class of men we learn that Lysander, the Lacedaemonian, was unsurpassed in crafty

---

[1] The accusative of εἴρων, which literally means a dissembler. Hence our word *irony*, which always involves the idea of a double meaning, and especially of a secondary meaning which shall be latent to the person addressed or satirized, patent to every one else.

[2] When Athens had failed in a contest with Megara for the possession of Salamis, a law was passed rendering it criminal to advocate the renewal of the contest. Solon evaded the law by feigning insanity, and recited a poem of his own, calling upon the people to reconquer the "lovely island." The law was repealed, the war renewed, and the island won.

plotting and in his power of endurance, while
Callicratidas, who succeeded Lysander in the command of the fleet, was of the opposite character.
Also in speech, we sometimes see a man of
surpassing ability contrive to appear like one of
the multitude, as we witnessed in Catulus, both
father and son, and in Quintus Mucius Mancia.
We have heard from those of an earlier generation
that this was the habit of Publius Scipio Nasica,
and, on the other hand, that his father, the man
who avenged the nefarious enterprises of Tiberius
Gracchus, had nothing genial in his address. We
learn, too, that Xenocrates, indeed the sternest of
philosophers, was on this very score eminent and
renowned.[1] There are other innumerable diversities of nature and of manners, which yet give no
good ground for obloquy.

31. Every one ought to hold fast, not his faults,
but his peculiarities, so as to retain more easily the
becomingness which is the subject of our inquiry.
We ought, indeed, to act in such a way as shall
be in no respect repugnant to our common human
nature; yet, holding this sacred, let us follow our
individual nature, so that, if there are other pursuits in themselves more important and excellent,

---

[1] Of the traits of personal character described in this section,
some are known only on Cicero's authority; while others, attached
to well-known names, are matters of history. I have not thought
it necessary to give, as I easily might, under the successive names,
a series of extracts from a dictionary of classical biography.

we yet may measure our own pursuits by the standard of our own nature. For it is of no avail to
resist nature, or to pursue anything which we cannot reach. It is the more apparent of what quality
is the becomingness under discussion, when we
consider that nothing is becoming that is done, as
the phrase is, without Minerva's sanction, that is,
with the opposition and repugnancy of nature. In
truth, if anything is becoming, nothing surely is
more so than uniform consistency in the whole
course of life and in each separate action, which
you cannot preserve if, imitating the nature of
others, you abandon your own. For as we ought
to use our native tongue, and not, like some who
are perpetually foisting in Greek words, incur well-
deserved ridicule, so we ought not to introduce any
discordance into our conduct and our general way
of living. This difference of natures, indeed, has
so much force that sometimes one person ought,
and another under the same circumstances ought
not, to commit suicide.[1] For was the case of Marcus Cato different from that of the others who
surrendered to Caesar in Africa? Yet had they
killed themselves, they might perhaps have been
worthy of censure, because their mode of life was

---

[1] It is well known that from Zeno, who committed suicide
when he thought his life no longer serviceable, down to Seneca,
the Stoics maintained the right of suicide as a mode of relief
from irretrievable evil, whether bodily disease or untoward circumstances.

less severe, and their characters were more pliant; while, since Nature had given Cato an incredible massiveness of character, and he himself had strengthened it by undeviating self-consistency, and had always been steadfast in the purpose once conceived and the design once undertaken, it seemed fit for him to die rather than to look upon the face of a tyrant. How many things did Ulysses endure in his long wandering, while he submitted to the service of women, — if Circe and Calypso are to be called women, — and while he strove to be affable and pleasant to all in his whole social intercourse! At home, also, he bore the jeers of slaves and maid-servants, that he might attain the object of his desire. But Ajax, with the temper which he is said to have had, would have faced death a thousand times rather than have borne such insults. In view of these things, it will be each man's duty to weigh well what are his own peculiar traits of character, and to keep them in serviceable condition, and not to desire to try how far another man's peculiarities may be becoming to him; for that is most becoming to each man which is most peculiarly his own. Let each of us, then, know his own capacities and proclivities, and show himself a discriminating judge of his own excellences and defects, lest performers on the stage may evince more discretion than we do. For they choose, not the best plays, but those the best adapted to their respective abilities, — those who rely on voice, the

Epigoni and Medus; those who depend on action, Menalippa or Clytaemnestra; Rutilius, whom I remember, Antiopa always; Aesopus, not often Ajax.[1] An actor, then, will look to this fitness on the stage; shall not the wise man have equal regard to it in life? Let us therefore bestow our diligence chiefly on those concerns for which we are the best fitted. But if at any time necessity shall have forced us to undertake things outside of our specialty, we must employ all possible care, thought, and diligence, that we may be able to dispose of them, if not becomingly, yet with the least degree of unbecomingness; nor ought we in that case to endeavor to attain capacities not our own, so much as to avoid mistake or failure.

32. To the two characters which, as I have said, every man must sustain, is added a third, imposed upon us by chance, or by circumstances beyond our power; a fourth, also, which we assume at our own discretion. Posts of authority, military commands, high rank, honors, wealth, and their opposites, at the disposal of chance, are controlled by circumstance. But it depends on our own choice what character we will assume as to a favorite pursuit or profession. Thus some apply themselves to

[1] None of the tragedies here named are extant. It would appear that on the Roman as on the modern stage, actors not only had parts assigned them according to their peculiar types of ability, but that the genius of a leading actor determined the choice of the play in which he should appear.

philosophy; some, to the civil law; some, to oratory; and of the several virtues some prefer to
excel in one, some in another. Those, indeed,
whose fathers or ancestors have held any special
distinction, generally aim at eminence in the same
department, as Quintus Mucius, the son of Publius,
in the civil law; Africanus, the son of Paulus, in
military service. But some add to the honors
inherited from their fathers a special reputation
of their own, as this very Africanus crowned his
military renown by eloquence. Timotheus, the
son of Conon, also did the like, being fully his
father's equal in military reputation, and adding
to it the praise of learning and genius. It is, however, now and then the case that young men, for-
saking the example of their ancestors, pursue some
plan of their own; and this is the course, almost
always, of those who, of obscure origin, set before
themselves large aims. All these things ought to
be taken into careful consideration when we inquire
what is becoming.

At the outset, we should determine in what condition we wish to be, in what kind of pursuits, and
whether in private or public life, — a decision the
most difficult of all; for it is in early youth, when
judgment is the weakest, that one chooses some
mode of life with which he has become enamored,
and thus is involved in a fixed avocation and course
before he is capable of judging what is best for
him. For as to what they say of the Hercules of

Prodicus, as quoted by Xenophon,[1] that when he was just approaching maturity — the time given by nature to every one to choose what course of life he will enter — he went into a solitary place, and sitting there, hesitated long and seriously within himself, which of the two paths before him, one of pleasure, the other of virtue, it was better for him to take, — this might perchance happen to Hercules, the son of Jupiter, but not in like manner to us, who imitate whomsoever we see fit, and feel impelled toward their pursuits and modes of life, yet still oftener, imbued with the advice of our parents, are drawn into their manners and habits; while others, still, are carried away by popular opinion, and make choice of those things that seem most charming to the multitude. Yet some, whether by happy fortune, or by goodness of nature, or by parental discipline, enter upon the right way of living.

33. But the rarest description is of those who, endowed either with the prestige of surpassing genius, or with pre-eminent culture and learning, or with both, have time to deliberate what course of life they would prefer to follow, — in which deliberation the issue should be made to conform to one's own natural bias. For while in the details of conduct we determine what is becoming from a man's native disposition, so in ordering the entire

---

[1] Xenophon, in the *Memorabilia*, gives this story by Prodicus, as cited by Socrates.

course of life much greater care should be taken
that we may be consistent with ourselves so long as
we live, and may not falter in the discharge of any
one duty. But while in determining our course nature has the greatest influence, fortune comes next
in controlling power, and account must be taken
of both in choosing a mode of life, — yet most,
of nature. For Nature is far the more stable and
consistent of the two, so that Fortune — herself
mortal — sometimes seems to be in conflict with
Nature, the immortal. Let him, then, who refers
his entire plan of life to his nature so far as it is
unvitiated, go on as he has begun (for this is in the
highest degree becoming), unless he be made aware
that he was mistaken in his choice. If this take
place (and it may), a change of habits and of plans
is requisite. If circumstances favor this change,
we can make it with a good measure of ease and
convenience; otherwise, it must be made gradually
and step by step, just as it is more becoming, in the
opinion of the wise, to unknit gradually friendships
which no longer please or satisfy us, than to cut [1]
them in sunder with a single stroke. But when
our mode of life is changed, we ought by all means
to take heed that we present some show of sufficient
reason. To return to what I said awhile ago as to
the fitness of imitating parents and ancestors, an
exception is to be made, in the first place, as to
their faults, which we are not to reproduce; and, in

---

[1] Latin, *dissuere — praccidere;* to unsew — to cut.

the next place, if nature will not permit this imitation in certain particulars, — as the son of the elder Africanus[1] (who adopted the younger Africanus, the son of Paulus) on account of feeble health could not resemble his father as his father had resembled his grandfather, — if, for instance, one cannot frequent the courts as an advocate, or hold the ear of the people in their assemblies, or conduct military enterprises, he ought at least to exhibit the qualities which are at his own command, justice, good faith, generosity, moderation, temperance, so that public opinion may not require of him those things in which he is inevitably deficient. But the best inheritance that fathers can give their children, more precious than any patrimony however large, is reputation for virtue and for worthy deeds, which if the child disgraces, his conduct should be branded as infamous and impious.

34. Since the same duties are not assigned to different periods of life, some belonging to the

---

[1] Publius Cornelius Scipio Africanus, bearing the same name with his father, the conqueror of Hannibal, whose father was Publius Cornelius Scipio, alternately victor and vanquished in the first Punic war. This second Africanus was regarded as superior in ability, no less than in learning and elegant culture, to all the other members of the Scipio *gens*, but was too feeble in health to take any part in public affairs, except in the peaceful offices of Augur and Flamen Dialis. He had no children, but adopted a son of Lucius Aemilius Paulus, Publius Cornelius Scipio Aemilianus Africanus, under whose generalship Carthage was finally subdued, and the city destroyed.

young, others to those more advanced in years,
this distinction needs to be spoken of. It is, then,
the part of the young man to revere his elders, and
to choose from among them the best and the most
approved, on whose advice and authority he may
rely; for the inexperience of early life demands the
wisdom of older men for its stability and its right
direction. But most of all is this early age to be
guarded against sensuality, and to be trained in
labor and endurance, both of mind and of body,
that the capacity of persistent diligence may be
developed alike for military service and for civic
duty. Moreover, when the young wish to relax
their minds and to give themselves up to enjoyment, let them beware of excess, let them keep
modesty in mind, which they will do the more if
their elders will interest themselves also in matters
of this sort. But for old men it would seem that
bodily labor ought to be slackened, while mental
efforts are to be even increased. At the same time
they should take pains to aid their friends, and the
young men, and, above all, the state, as much as
possible by their counsel and experience. But
nothing is to be more shunned by old age than
self-surrender to listlessness and indolence. Luxurious living, too, unbecoming at any period of life,
is most shameful for old age; and if to this licentiousness be added, the evil is double; for thus old
age at once disgraces itself, and makes the excess of
youth still more shameless.

Still further, it is not irrelevant to treat of the duties of magistrates and of those in private life, of citizens [1] and of foreigners. It is, then, the special function of the magistrate to regard himself as representing the person of the state, and bound to maintain its dignity and honor, to enforce the laws, to define conflicting rights, and to bear in mind whatever is committed to his good faith. The private citizen ought to live on fair and equal terms with his fellow-citizens, neither cringing and grovelling, nor yet assuming supercilious airs. Then too, in the state he ought to choose those things which are peaceful and honorable; for we are wont to feel and to say that such a man is a good citizen. It is the duty of a foreigner and a temporary resident to do nothing beyond his own business, not to pry into the concerns of other people, and, least of all, to be meddlesome in the affairs of the state in which he is an alien. Thus, for the most part, duties can be ascertained, when the inquiry is raised what is becoming and what is fitting for different persons, occasions, and ages. But there is nothing which is so becoming as to maintain consistency in all that we do and undertake.

35. Since becomingness in all that is done and said has its place also in the movement and atti-

---

[1] Latin, *privatorum — civium*, referring to the same persons, in contradistinction, first to magistrates, and secondly to foreigners.

tude of the body, and consists in three things, beauty, order, and attire fitted for the work in hand, difficult to express in words, — but it will be enough if they are felt, — and since in these is included our care to win the approval of those among whom we live, a few things ought to be said as to these particulars. In the beginning Nature seems to have made great account of our bodies, having placed in plain sight our frame and such parts of our structure as have a comely appearance, while she has covered and concealed those parts of the body bestowed for the needs of nature, which might have an unshapely and ugly aspect. This so careful construction of Nature the modesty of men has followed; for the very things which Nature has hidden all persons of sound mind keep out of sight, and are at pains to obey the necessities connected with them as secretly as possible. Moreover, as to these same parts of the body, whose uses are necessary, they call neither them nor their uses by their proper names, and what it is not disgraceful to do, if it be only in secret, it is obscene to name. Thus the open doing of these things and the obscene mention of them are equally liable to the charge of immodesty. Nor is any heed to be given to the Cynics, or to those Stoics who are almost Cynics,[1] who make it a matter of reproach

---

[1] The Cynics undoubtedly took their name from the κυνόσαρ-γες, — one of the Athenian gymnasia in which their founder, Antisthenes, a pupil of Socrates, held his school ; but some by no

and ridicule that we deem things that are not shameful in fact unfit to be called by their right names, while we apply their proper names to things that are really shameful. Thus theft, fraud, and adultery are shameful in fact, but it is not obscene to call them by their names; while to perpetuate one's family is right in fact, yet obscene in name. On this notion those same philosophers hold prolix arguments at the expense of modesty. But let us follow Nature, and refrain from whatever lacks the approval of eye and ear. Let attitude, gait, mode of sitting, posture at table, countenance, eyes, movement of the hands, preserve the becomingness of which I speak. In these matters there are two extremes to be especially shunned, — on the one hand, effeminacy or daintiness, on the other, coarseness or rusticity. Nor ought it to be admitted that these rules, though proper for actors and public speakers, are matters of indifference to us. The custom of actors, from ancient tradition, carries modesty so far that no one is permitted to go upon

means contemptible authorities derive the name from κύων, *a dog*, and ascribe it to the snarling habit of the early disciples of the school, who were wont to sneer and scoff at what the rest of the world admired and prized. Diogenes of Sinope represented this type of character. Stoicism, in the person of Zeno, sprang out of the bosom of Cynicism, and embodied in its philosophy and ethics the fundamental principle of Antisthenes, that virtue is not the supreme, but the sole good. The later Cynics were characterized mainly by insolence, gratuitous indecency, and aimless asceticism.

the stage without drawers, in the fear that in case
of the accidental exposure of certain parts of the
body they may present an unbecoming spectacle.
Our usage also forbids sons of ripe age from bath-
ing with their fathers, sons-in-law with their fathers-
in-law. This kind of modesty is to be adhered
to, especially as Nature herself is mistress and
guide.

36. While there are two kinds of beauty, in one
of which grace, in the other dignity, predominates,
we ought to regard grace as belonging to woman,
dignity to man. Let then every species of apparel
or adornment unworthy of a man be removed from
his person, and let him guard against similar faults
in attitude and gesture. For the manners of the
wrestling ground [1] are apt to be somewhat disagree-
able, and the affected attitudes of actors frequently
give offence; while in the entire carriage of the
body whatever is direct and simple receives commendation. Dignity of person is to be made sure
by healthiness of complexion, and the complexion
is to be maintained by bodily exercise. There
should be rendered, with reference to neatness, a
regard not offensively remiss, nor yet over-punctil-
ious, just sufficient to avoid rustic and ill-bred
slovenliness. The same rule is to be observed in
dress, in which, as in most things, that which is

---

[1] *Palaestrici motus*, literally, palaestric movements. The *pa-
laestra* was the resort of the young men of wealth and fashion, and
thus a nursery of foppish manners no less than of bodily vigor.

6

becoming lies between the two extremes. Care must also be taken lest in our gait we accustom ourselves to effeminate slowness, like the litters that carry in procession the images of the gods, or when time presses attempt excessive speed, in consequence of which panting ensues, the countenance is changed, the features are distorted, from all which the obvious inference is that there is a lack of steadfastness in the character. But much greater pains should be taken lest the movements of the mind should transcend their natural equipoise; and this we shall effect if we guard against violent emotions and fits of despondency, and if we keep our minds intent on the observance of what is becoming. But the operations of the mind are of two kinds, — the one of thought, the other of impulse. Thought is occupied chiefly in seeking the truth; impulse urges to action. Care, then, is to be taken that we employ thought on the best subjects possible, and that we make impulse obedient to reason.

37. To pass to another subject, the power of speech being great, and of two kinds, the one of oratory, the other of conversation, let oratory find place in the arguments of courts, popular assemblies, and the Senate; let conversation have its scope in smaller circles, in the discussion of ordinary affairs, in the gatherings of friends, — let it also follow [1]

---

[1] *Sequatur*, which I have translated literally; for so far as I have been able to trace the festal habits of the ancients, from Homer's heroes downward, they ate in silence, and talked after-

convivial entertainments. The rhetoricians give
rules for oratory; there are none for conversation.
Yet I know not but that conversation might also
have its rules. Masters are found when learners
want them; but there are none who make conversation a study, while the rhetoricians have crowds
of pupils. Yet the rules given about words and
sentences apply to conversation no less than to
oratory. And since we have the voice as the organ
of speech, let us at least attempt two things as to
the voice, — to have it distinct, and to have it
pleasing to the ear. For both we must of course
look to nature; but the one may be improved by
practice, the other by imitating those who pronounce
neither too broadly nor too rapidly. There was
nothing in the Catuli [1] that would make you think
them of exquisite taste in literature, — though they
were men of letters, but only as others are, — yet
they were thought to speak the Latin language
as perfectly as it could be spoken. Their pronun-
ciation was sweet to the ear; the separate letters
were neither drawled nor clipped, so as to avoid
equally indistinctness and affectation; they spoke
without effort, in a voice neither languid nor shrill.

ward. This is implied in the uses of the term συμπόσιον, *sympo-*
*sium*, a drinking together after the more solid portions of the feast
have been disposed of.

[1] Both of them men who held high places in the republic, and
were worthy of its better days. The father was distinguished as
an orator, and both father and son were among the foremost of
their respective times in solid learning and in elegant culture.

Lucius Crassus[1] had a more copious flow of language, with no less humor; yet the reputation of the Catuli as good talkers was fully equal to his. Caesar, the brother[2] of the elder Catulus, surpassed them all in wit and humor, so that when he spoke in the courts in his conversational way he was more efficient than other advocates with their set speeches. On all these matters we must bestow labor, if we aim at what is becoming in every detail of conduct.

Let then conversation, in which the followers of Socrates are pre-eminent, be easy, and by no means prolix; let politeness be always observed, nor must one debar others from their part, as if he had sole right to be heard; but, as in all things else, so in social intercouse, let him regard alternation as not unfair. Then, too, let him at the outset consider on what sort of subjects he is talking; if on serious things, let him show due gravity; on amusing, grace. Especially let him take heed lest his conversation betray some defect in his moral character, which is most frequently the case when the absent are expressly ridiculed or spoken of slanderously and malignly, with the purpose of injuring their reputation. For the most part, conver-

---

[1] The greatest orator of his age. He was in his prime in Cicero's boyhood.

[2] They had the same mother; their fathers were of different *gentes*, — Catulus being of a plebeian, Caesar of a patrician *gens.*

sation relates to private affairs, or politics, or the
theory and practice of the arts. Pains must then
be taken that, if the conversation begins to wander
off to other subjects, it be recalled to these. Yet
reference must be had to the persons present; for
we are not all interested in the same things, at all
times, and in a similar degree. We should always
observe, also, the length of time to which the pleasure of conversation extends, and as there was reason
for beginning, so let there be a limit at which there
shall be an ending.

38. But as it is a most fitting rule for the entire
life, that we shun passion, by which I mean emotions that transcend the control of reason, so conversation ought to be free from emotions of this kind,
that thus no anger or inordinate desire may show
itself, and that at the same time there be no appearance of listlessness, or indifference, or anything of the
kind. We must also take special care to preserve
the bearing of respect and esteem for those with
whom we converse. There is sometimes occasion
for administering reproof, in which we must perhaps use a greater stress of voice and a keener
severity of diction; indeed, this may need to be
carried so far as to make us seem under the influence of anger. But we shall have recourse to this
kind of oral castigation, as to the cautery and the
knife, rarely and reluctantly, nor ever, unless it
be necessary in the absence of any other remedy.
And at all events let anger be kept far away; for

with anger nothing can be done rightly, nothing judiciously. But in most cases we can administer mild reproof, yet combined with earnestness, so that at once due severity may be employed and invective avoided. Moreover, the very bitterness which our reproof carries with it should be made to appear as designed for the benefit of the person reproved. It is right, also, even in our disputes with those the most hostile to us, and even though we receive from them unmerited reproach, to maintain a serious bearing indeed, but to exclude irritation. For what is done under some degree of excitement cannot be done with self-respect or with the approval of bystanders. Still further, it is in bad taste to talk about one's self, especially to lie about one's self, and with the derision of the audience to play the part of the Braggart Soldier.[1]

39. Since I want to make a thorough discussion of everything involving the question of duty, — for such is my purpose, — I ought to say also what sort of a house, in my opinion, should belong to a man in high office and conspicuous station. The ultimate end, of course, is convenience, and to this the plan of the building should be adapted, while at the same time care should be taken as regards

---

[1] *Militem gloriosum. Miles Gloriosus* is the title of a comedy of Plautus, in which Pyrgopolineces, a military braggadocio, is the principal personage. The character was a favorite one with the Roman comedians and stage-lovers. Thraso, in Terence's *Eunuchus*, plays this part so well, as to have enriched the English language with the adjective *thrasonical.*

stateliness of appearance and amplitude of accom-
modation. We are told that it redounded to the
honor of Cneius Octavius, the first of his family
that was made consul, that he had built a splendid
house, one in all respects magnificent, on the Palatine Hill,[1] which, being seen by the people at large,
was thought to have procured for the owner, belonging to a family that had before held no high office,
the votes that raised him to the consulship. This
house Scaurus demolished, and built where it
stood an addition to his own house. And so the
former of the two, first of his race, brought the
consulship into his house; the latter, the son of a
man of distinguished eminence and renown, bore
home to his enlarged house on the same spot not
only failure as a candidate for the consulship, but
disgrace and disaster.[2] In truth, high standing in
the community should be adorned by a house, not
sought wholly from a house; nor should the owner
be honored by the house, but the house by the
owner. Moreover, as in matters of various kinds
one must take account not of himself alone, but of
others also, so in the house of a distinguished man,

[1] *In Palatio,* — the Palatium was the most fashionable quarter
on the Palatine Hill.

[2] Marcus Aemilius Scaurus, son of the Scaurus named in § 22,
when candidate for the consulship, was accused of extortion in
the government of Sardinia, and though undoubtedly guilty, was
defended by Cicero, and was acquitted, but failed of election.
Two years afterward he was accused of bribery, condemned, and
banished.

into which many guests are to be received, and a multitude of men of all kinds are to be admitted, care must be taken to have it roomy. Under other circumstances a very large house is apt to bring discredit to its owner if it have the air of loneliness, especially if under some former owner it used to be thronged. For it is offensive to have it said by those who pass by, —

> " O ancient house ! Ah, how unlike a lord
> Now lords it over thee ! " [1]

which in these times may be said about many a house. But special care should be taken, if you build yourself, not to go beyond reasonable limits in costliness and splendor. In such extravagance great mischief is done by mere example; for very many are anxious, especially in this direction, to follow the example of distinguished men. Thus who imitates the virtue of Lucius Lucullus, a man of the highest character? But how many have imitated the magnificence of his villas! [2] Here there certainly is need of a limit, and of a return to a moderate standard. This same standard ought

---

[1] From an unknown poet.

[2] Lucullus would have transmitted to coming time a great name as the conqueror of Mithridates, had he not become still more famous by magnificence, ostentation, and extravagance in his villas, gardens, fish-ponds, and entertainments. A single supper is said to have cost him a sum equivalent in silver to about ten thousand dollars, in value to at least five times as much. From him is derived the word *lucullite,* both French and English, denoting a devotee of luxury.

· to be applied to the entire habit and style of living. But enough on this head.

In whatever we do there are three things to be endeavored. The first is that impulse be subservient to reason, than which there is no more fitting rule for the observance of duty. In the next place, we should make ourselves acquainted with the magnitude of the object in hand, so that we may take upon ourselves neither more nor less care and labor than the case demands. The third rule is that the outlay for show and parade be brought within moderate limits; and those limits are best kept when we maintain the becomingness of which I have already spoken, and suffer ourselves not to go beyond it. Yet of these three the most excellent is that impulse should be subservient to reason.

40. In the next place, I am to speak of the order of our doings and the fit arrangement of time, which are comprehended in the science which the Greeks term εὐταξίαν, yet not in its sense of moderation (which involves the idea of measure or quantity), but in that sense of εὐταξία[1] which implies the observance of order in time and place. Yet in favor of our calling this moderation, we might cite the definition of the Stoics, who say that moderation is the art of putting in the right place whatever is done or said. Thus the import of order and that of collocation seem identical with

[1] This word is used by Xenophon in the sense of *order;* by Thucydides, in that of *moderation.*

it; for they define order to be the putting of things in fit and suitable places, and say that the fit time is the place of an action, — the fit time for an action, which we call occasion, being called in Greek εὐκαιρία.[1] Thus it is that moderation, which I interpret as I have said, comes to denote skill in determining the fitness of times for specific acts. But the same definition may be given of prudence, of which I treated in the earlier part of this essay.[2] Here, however, our subject is regularity, self-control, and virtues of that kind. What belongs peculiarly to prudence has been spoken of in its proper place; but of the class of virtues which has of late occupied our attention, it remains for me to

---

[1] *Opportuneness.*

[2] This passage, as it treats of the definition of words, can hardly be understood without the use of the specific Latin words, both defining and defined. I therefore give here a more literal translation: "I am to speak of the order of our doings and the fit arrangement of time, which are comprehended in the science which the Greeks term εὐταξία, — not in that meaning of the word which we term *modestia* in which *modus* is implied, but in that sense which denotes the order of time and place. Yet in favor of our translating the word (εὐταξία) *modestia*, it may be said that the Stoics define *modestia* as the art of putting whatever is done or said in the right place. Thus *ordo* and *collocatio* seem to have the same import with it. For they define *ordo* as the putting of things in fit and suitable places; but they say that the fit time is the place of an action, — the fit time being called in Greek εὐκαιρία, in Latin, *occasio*. Thus it is that *modestia*, interpreted as I have said, comes to denote skill in determining the fitness of time for specific acts. But the same definition may be given of *prudentia*, of which I treated in the early part of this essay."

speak of what may fall under the head of modesty and of regard for the approval of those among whom we live.

Such, then, should be the order applied to whatever we do, that, as in a coherent speech, so in the life, all things should be fitted to one another, and in harmony with one another. For it is disgraceful and exceedingly blameworthy, on a serious subject to introduce the kind of talk that belongs to a festive occasion, or any wanton strain of utterance. When Pericles had Sophocles for a colleague in military command, and they had met on their common official duty, and, a handsome boy happening to pass by, Sophocles said, "Oh, Pericles, what a beautiful boy!" Pericles very fittingly answered, "It becomes a commander, Sophocles, to have his eyes as abstinent [1] as his hands." [2] Yet had Sophocles said the same at a trial of skill among athletes, he would have incurred no just censure. So great is the significance of both place and time. Thus, if one who is going to plead a cause should, on a journey or in walking, be self-absorbed in meditation, or if at such a time he be wrapt in earnest thought on any other subject, he cannot be blamed; but if he present this appearance on a festive occasion, he would be regarded as ill-bred, because unmindful of the fitness of time. Such things, indeed, as are at a very great remove from propriety, like singing in the forum, or any

[1] From lust.          [2] From bribes.

other gross misconduct, are readily perceived, nor do they stand in special need of admonition and direction. But one should avoid with peculiar care offences that seem small, and cannot be appreciated by the many. As in stringed instruments or flutes an expert detects discord, however slight, so we should in our lives be on the watch for even the least discord, and all the more so, inasmuch as the harmony of actions is greater and better than that of musical notes.

41. Therefore, as in stringed instruments the ears of musicians detect the slightest falsity of tone, so shall we, if we are willing to be keen and careful observers of faults, often learn great things from small. From the glance of the eyes, from the expansion or contraction of the brows, from depression, from cheerfulness, from laughter, from the tone of the voice, from silence, from a higher or lower key of utterance, and other similar tokens, we may easily determine which of the greater things that they typify are fittingly done and which of them are at variance with duty and nature. Nor is it unsuitable in matters of this sort to judge of the character of our actions by looking at others, so that we may ourselves avoid whatever is unbecoming in them; for it is the case — I know not how — that we perceive any delinquency more readily in others than in ourselves. Therefore those pupils whose faults their masters mimic in order to cure them are most easily corrected. Nor yet is it out

of place, before forming our judgment in doubtful
cases, to consult men of superior natural intelligence or those who have become wise by experience, and to ask them what they think as to any
matters in which the question of duty is involved.
Indeed, most persons are wont to be drawn in
nearly the direction in which their nature leads
them, and we want to learn of men, not merely
what they say, but what they think, and also why.[1]
As painters, and sculptors, and poets, too, like to
have their work pass under review by the people,
that if any fault is found by a considerable number
of persons it may be corrected, and as they earnestly inquire both of themselves and of others
wherein the fault consists, so for us there are many
things to be done and left undone, and changed
and corrected by the opinion of others. Concerning things done by established custom or in order
to obey the laws of the state, there are no rules to
be given; for custom and law are themselves rules.
Nor ought any one to be led into the error of supposing that, if Socrates or Aristippus[2] did or said

---

[1] Which we may learn by consulting men of sound discretion
and practical experience.

[2] Aristippus maintained that the pleasure that lies nearest,
whatever it be, is to be sought and enjoyed, and that man has no
other end of being. The records that remain of his life give
reason for believing that his personal morality was not so bad as
his philosophy; yet he was luxurious in his habits, boasted of
his freedom from moral restraints, and boasted also of his ability
to forego without a sense of loss the indulgences which he had

anything contrary to custom and to legal usage, he may regard the like as lawful for himself. They obtained this liberty by superior and divine endowments. The entire system of the Cynics also is to be shunned; for it is opposed to modesty, without which there can be neither right nor honor. But we ought to respect and revere those whose life has been passed in the transaction of honorable and important affairs, who have a right feeling toward the state, and have rendered or are still rendering it service, no less than those in civil office or military command; to pay great deference to old age; to yield precedence to the magistrates; to make a distinction between citizens and foreigners, and in the case of foreigners, between those who come in a private and those who come in a public capacity. In short, not to treat of particulars, we ought to cherish, defend, preserve, the common harmony and fellowship of the whole human race.

42. Now as to the trades and modes of getting gain that are to be regarded as respectable,[1] and those that are to be deemed mean and vulgar, the general opinion is as follows: In the first place, those callings are held in disesteem that come into collision with the ill will of men, as that of tax-gatherers, as that of usurers. The callings of hired

---

made habitual. He was a hearer, not to say a pupil, of Socrates, whose eccentricities were abnormal in the direction of a severer type of virtue.

[1] *Liberales*, worthy of a free man.

laborers, and of all who are paid for their mere work and not for skill, are ungenteel [1] and vulgar; for their wages are given for menial service. Those who buy to sell again as soon as they can are to be accounted as vulgar; for they can make no profit except by a certain amount of falsehood, and nothing is meaner than falsehood. All mechanics are engaged in vulgar business; for a workshop can have nothing respectable about it. Least of all can we speak well of the trades that minister to sensual pleasures, —

"Fishmongers, butchers, cooks, poulterers, and fishermen,"

as Terence says. Add, if you please, to this list perfumers, ballet-dancers, and the whole tribe of dice-players. The professions which require greater skill and are of no small benefit to the community, such as medicine, architecture, the instruction of youth in liberal studies, are respectable for those whose rank they suit.[2] Commerce,[3] if on a

[1] *Illiberales*, unworthy of a free man.

[2] For men of senatorial, or even equestrian rank, these employments, if practised for gain, were regarded as derogating from respectability.

[3] The Romans in general, till near the last days of the republic, despised commerce, and though they depended for grain in great part on Sicily and remoter provinces, it was long before they brought grain in their own ships. In Cicero's time, however, it was the reproach of the equestrian order that many members of it, tired of genteel poverty, were enriching themselves by commerce; and Cicero, as a *parvenu* in the Senate, was weak enough to fall in with this foolish prejudice.

small scale, is to be regarded as vulgar; but if large and rich, importing much from all quarters, and making extensive sales without fraud, it is not so very discreditable. Nay, it may justly claim the highest regard, if the merchant, satiated, or rather contented with his profits, instead of any longer leaving the sea for a port,[1] betakes himself from the port itself to an estate in the country. But of all means of acquiring gain nothing is better than agriculture, nothing more productive, nothing more pleasant, nothing more worthy of a man of liberal mind. Since I have said enough of this in my Cato Major, you will find there what belongs to the subject.

43. I think that I have sufficiently expounded the way in which specific duties are derived under the several divisions of the right. But as to the very things that are right there may be sometimes a question as to alternatives,[2] of two right things which is the more imperatively right, — a subject omitted by Panaetius. Since all that is right is deduced from four divisions of virtue, the first, knowledge; the second, social obligation; the third, elevation of mind; the fourth, moderation, — these must of necessity be often brought into comparison with one another in determining a specific duty.

---

[1] Merchants, engaged in traffic from port to port, owned and commanded the ships that carried their goods.

[2] Latin, *contentio et comparatio,* — stretching two objects side by side, and determining their comparative length. See § 17.

In my opinion the duties derived from the relations of society have a closer adaptation to nature[1]
than those which are derived from knowledge, as
may be established by this argument, — that should
such a life fall to the lot of a wise man that in the
full abundance of all things and in entire leisure
he could consider and contemplate within his own
mind whatever is worth knowing, yet, were his solitude such that he could never see a human face, he
would rather die. Then, too, the chief of all the
virtues, that wisdom which the Greeks term σοφίαν[2]
(for prudence, which the Greeks call φρόνησιν,[3] has
another, narrower meaning, namely, the knowledge
of things to be sought and shunned), — the wisdom
which I have designated as chief of the virtues is
the knowledge of things divine and human, which
comprises the mutual fellowship and communion
of gods and men. But if wisdom is the greatest of
the virtues, as it undoubtedly is, it follows of necessity that the duty derived from this fellowship and
communion is the greatest of duties. Moreover,
the knowledge and contemplation of nature are

---

[1] A Stoic idea. The Stoics derived all duty from nature, —
the nature of things, the nature of man. They therefore made
nature the sole test of duty, and (if I may so express what in
less awkward phrase would be less clear) regarded the greater
or less naturalness of a duty as the criterion of its relative
importance.

[2] Σοφία primarily meant *sagacity*, but is commonly employed
to denote *wisdom* in its broadest sense.

[3] Φρόνησις means *prudence*, in the sense of practical wisdom.

somehow defective and imperfect, unless they lead
to some result in action; and this appropriate action
is best recognized in care for the well-being of mankind. The virtue from which it springs belongs,
then, to the sodality of the human race, and is
therefore to be preferred to knowledge. That this
is so, every excellently good man shows and indicates in very deed. For who is there so deeply
interested in penetrating and understanding the
nature of things, that if, while he is handling and
contemplating subjects most worthy of being understood, there is suddenly announced to him some
danger and peril of his country in which he can
render aid and succor, will not abandon and fling
away his learned pursuits, even though he imagines
that he can number the stars and find out the
dimensions of the universe? And he would do the
same thing in the business or in the peril of a father
or a friend. It is thus seen that the duties of justice which concern the interests of our fellow-men,
than which nothing ought to be more sacred to man,
are to have precedence over the pursuits and duties
of knowledge.

44. Now those whose pursuits and whose entire
life have been devoted to the acquisition of knowledge, have nevertheless not withdrawn from the
obligation of contributing to the advantage and
benefit of mankind; for they have so instructed
many as to make them better citizens and more
useful to their respective states. Thus Lysis, the

Pythagorean, taught Epaminondas of Thebes, and Plato was the preceptor of Dion of Syracuse, and many others have had numerous pupils. I myself, in whatever I have contributed to the well-being of the state (if I have indeed contributed anything), entered upon the public service well furnished in point of teachers and teaching. Nor is it only when these men are living and present that they instruct and teach those desirous of learning; but they follow up this same work even after death by the records of their knowledge and wisdom. For there is no topic omitted by them that could relate to laws, to morals, to the government of the state; so that they seem to have bestowed their leisure on our business.[1] Thus the very men who are devoted to the pursuit of learning and wisdom employ their intelligence and practical discretion chiefly for the benefit of mankind. Therefore it is better to speak fluently, if wisely, than to think, no matter with what acuteness of comprehension, if the power of expression be wanting; for thought begins and ends in itself, while fluent speech extends its benefit to those with whom we are united in fellowship. Moreover, as swarms of bees are not gathered for the purpose of making honeycombs, but make honeycombs because they are gregarious by nature, so, and even much more, men, sociable by nature,

---

[1] *Otium*, leisure; *negotium = nec otium*, business, — a favorite play upon words with Cicero, which we have not the means of rendering into English.

bring to their union skill in joint and associate action. Therefore, unless the virtue which consists in caring for the well-being of men, that is, in the maintenance of human society, accompany the knowledge of things, that knowledge must seem isolated and meagre ; and equally loftiness of mind, if divorced from human society and fellowship, becomes mere brutality and savageness. Thus it is that the society and fellowship of men transcend in importance the pursuit of knowledge. Nor is it true, as some say, that it is on account of the necessities of life — because we could not obtain and accomplish what nature demands without the aid of others — that fellowship and society were initiated among men, but that if everything appertaining to subsistence and comfortable living were supplied for us, so to speak, as by a magic wand, every person of excelling genius, giving up all other concerns, would occupy himself wholly in knowledge and science. It is not so ; for man in that case would shun solitude, and seek companionship in his pursuits, — would want now to teach, then to learn ; now to hear, then to speak. Therefore every form of duty which is of avail for the union of men and the defence of society is to be regarded as of higher obligation than the duty which is dependent on abstract study and science.

45. It may perchance be asked whether this human fellowship which is most closely allied to nature is also always to have the precedence over

modesty and decency. I think not. For there are certain things, some so repulsive, some so scandalous, that a wise man would not do them even to save his country. Posidonius[1] has brought together a great many of these things, some of them so foul, so indecent, that it would be offensive even to name them. These things, then, one will not do for the sake of the state, nor yet will the state demand that they should be done for its sake. But the question is the more easily settled, inasmuch as there cannot come any crisis in which it can be for the interest of the state that a wise man should do any of these things.

This, then, may be regarded as settled, that in choosing between conflicting duties preference must be given to the class of duties essential to the maintenance of human society. Moreover, considerate action is the result of knowledge and prudence. It therefore follows that to act considerately is of more worth than to think wisely.[2] But I have said enough on this point; for this division of the subject has been so laid open that it cannot be difficult in an inquiry as to duty to see in any particular case which duty is to be regarded as of prime and which of secondary obligation.

[1] Posidonius was a Stoic, a disciple of Panaetius, a voluminous writer on an encyclopedic range of subjects. Of his works only fragments are preserved, and happily the catalogue of things not fit to be done has left no traces of itself. His works are known chiefly by copious extracts made by Athenaeus.

[2] An inference so illogical as to seem an oversight.

But in society itself there are gradations of duties, from which it may be determined what one owes in any individual relation. Thus we are bound in obligation, first to the immortal gods, secondly to our country, thirdly to our parents, then by successive degrees to other persons more or less nearly related to us.

From this brief discussion light may be thrown, not only on the question whether certain specific acts are right or wrong, but also, when the choice lies between two right things, on the question which of the two is of the highest obligation. This last head, as I said above, is omitted by Panaetius. Let us go on now to what remains of the subject.

# BOOK II.

1. I THINK, my son Marcus, that it has been sufficiently explained in my first book how duties are to be derived from the right, and from each of the four virtues which I named as divisions of the right. It comes next in order, to treat of those kinds of duties that belong to the adornment of life and the command of its utilities, to influence and resources of every description. Under this head I have said that the inquiry is, first, what is expedient and what inexpedient, and then, of expedient things which is the more expedient, which the most expedient. I shall proceed to the discussion of these things, after saying a few words concerning my design and method in writing on philosophical subjects.

Although, indeed, my books have roused not a few to the desire not only of reading, but of writing, still I sometimes fear that the mere name of philosophy may be offensive to certain worthy men, and that they may marvel that I spend so much labor and time upon it. In truth, so long as the state was administered by men of its own choice, I bestowed upon it all my care and thought. But

when all things were held under the absolute sway
of one man, and there was no longer room for
advice or influence, while at the same time I had
lost my associates in the guardianship of the state,
men of the highest eminence, I did not abandon
myself to melancholy, which would have consumed
me had I not resisted it, nor yet, on the other hand,
to sensual pleasures unworthy of a philosopher.
And oh that the state had continued in the condition in which it recommenced its life,[1] and had
not fallen into the hands of men desirous not so
much of reforming as of revolutionizing its constitution! In that case, in the first place, as I used to
do when the state stood on a firm basis, I should
expend more labor in pleading than in writing; and
in the next place, I should commit to writing not
the subjects now in hand, but my arguments before
the courts, as I have often done. But when the
state, on which all my care, thought, labor, used to
be expended, had utterly ceased to be, my forensic
and senatorial literature was of course silenced.
Yet since my mind could not be unemployed, having been conversant with these studies from my
early days, I thought that my chagrin could be
most honorably laid aside if I betook myself to
philosophy, to which I devoted a large part of my
youth as a learner, while after I began to hold

---

[1] After the assassination of Caesar, when for a very little while
there seemed some hope of a return to republican institutions in
fact as well as in name.

important offices and gave myself wholly to the
service of the state, philosophy had as much of my
time as was not taken up by the claims of my
friends and the public. Yet this time was all consumed in reading; I had no leisure for writing.

2. I seem, then, in the severest calamities to
have attained at least this good fortune, that I am
able to commit to writing subjects not sufficiently
familiar to my fellow-countrymen, and yet pre-
eminently worthy of their cognizance. For what,
in the name of the gods, is more desirable than
wisdom? What more to be prized? What better?
What more worthy of man? It is the seekers of this,
then, who are called philosophers; nor is philosophy,
if you undertake to translate it, anything else than
the love of wisdom. But wisdom, as defined by
the ancients, is the knowledge of things divine and
human, and of the causes by which these things are
kept in harmony. I cannot well understand what
he who blames the pursuit of this knowledge can
regard as commendable. For if gratification of the
mind and repose from care be sought, what pleasure can be compared with the pursuits of those who
are always searching out what may look and tend
toward a good and happy life? Or if regard is
paid to consistency of character and to virtue,
either this is the science [1] by which we may attain
them, or there is none at all. To say that there
is no science of these greatest of human interests

---

[1] Latin, *ars;* but *art* is here an inadequate rendering.

when there are none of the smallest concerns that have not their science, is the language of men who talk without thinking, and who deceive themselves in matters of the highest moment. Then, too, if there is any instruction in virtue, where should it be sought, when you turn away from this department of learning? But these things are usually discussed with greater precision in urging readers to the study of philosophy, as I have done in another treatise.[1] My present purpose was simply to say why, deprived of opportunities for the service of the state, I chose this department of study above all others.

It is objected to me, and that too by educated and learned men, that I seem not to act consistently, when I say that nothing can be known with certainty, and yet am accustomed to give my opinion on other subjects, and am now setting forth the rules of duty. I could wish that these persons had an adequate understanding of my philosophical doctrine.[2] For I am not one of those whose minds drift about in uncertainty, and never have any definite aim. Indeed, what sort of an intellect, or rather of a life, would remain, if fixed principles not only of reasoning, but of conduct, were abolished? This is not my case; but while others say that some things are certain, some doubtful, so I, differing from them, call some things probable, some improbable. What is there, then, that can

---

[1] In *Hortensius.*        [2] That of the New Academy.

hinder me from pursuing those things that seem to
me probable, rejecting those things that seem improbable, and, while I shun the arrogance of positive
assertion, escaping the recklessness which is at the
farthest remove from wisdom? All opinions are
controverted by our school, on the ground that this
very probability cannot be brought to light unless
by a comparison of the arguments on both sides.
These things, however, are, as I think, expounded
with sufficient care in my Academics. But though
you, my Cicero, are becoming versed in the most
ancient [1] and noble of philosophies, under the
guidance of Cratippus, who bears the closest resemblance to the illustrious founders of the school,
I am unwilling that these speculations of mine,
nearly allied to those of your school, should be
unknown to you. But let us now take up the
plan proposed for our discussion.

3. At the outset I proposed for the full discussion of duty five divisions, two relating to what is
becoming and right; two to the conveniences of
life, resources, influence, wealth; the fifth to the
determination of our choice, whenever the right and
the expedient might seem mutually repugnant.
The divisions relating to the right, which I would
have you thoroughly understand, are finished. This

---

[1] Cratippus was a Peripatetic, and thus regarded Aristotle as
his master; but as Aristotle derived much of his philosophy from
Plato, and Plato, much or all of his from Socrates, Cicero, with
more rhetorical aptness than literal truth, antedates the school of
which his son was the pupil.

of which I am now going to treat is what is termed
expediency, with reference to which custom has
turned out of the right way, and has been gradually
brought to the point of separating the right from
the expedient, and of maintaining that what is not
expedient may be right, and what is not right,
expedient, than which there could be no doctrine
more pernicious to human well-being. There are,
indeed, philosophers of the very highest authority
who on strict and tenable grounds make a distinction in theory between three several kinds of excellence, which yet, as they admit, are inseparable in
their nature; for whatever is just they regard as
expedient, and likewise what is right as just.
Hence it follows that whatever is right is also
expedient.[1] Those who imagine that the distinction is not in mere theory, but in fact, often
admiring adroit and crafty men, take roguery for
wisdom. Their mistake ought to be eliminated, and
the universal opinion brought over to the hope that
men may learn to expect the attainment of what
they desire by right purposes and honest deeds, not
by fraud and roguery.

The means of sustaining human life are in part
inanimate, as gold, silver, the products of the earth,
and other things of that sort; in part, living beings
that have their own instincts and appetites. Of these
last some are destitute of reason, others are rational.
Those destitute of reason are horses, oxen, other

---

[1] A syllogism in *Barbara.*

cattle, bees, by whose labor contribution is made to the service and subsistence of men. Of the rational there are named two classes, — the one of gods, the other of men. Reverence and purity will make the gods propitious. But next to and close after the gods, men can be of the greatest service to men. The same division applies to those things that cause injury and obstruction. But because it is thought that the gods do no injury, these being out of the question, men are regarded as most of all interfering injuriously with men.

Indeed, the very things that I have called inanimate are produced for the most part by the labor of men, nor could we have them unless handicraft and skill had given their aid, nor could we utilize them except under the management of men. Nor without the labor of man could there be any care of health, or cultivation of the soil, or harvesting and preservation of grain and other products of the ground. Nor could there be the exportation of our superfluous commodities, nor the importation of those in which we are lacking, unless men performed these offices. By parity of reason the stones that we need for our use could not be quarried from the earth,

"Nor iron, brass, silver, gold, be dug from their deep caverns,"[1]

without the labor and handicraft of men.

[1] A verse from some lost poem, probably the *Prometheus* of Attius.

4. Whence, indeed, could houses, to dispel the severity of the cold and to allay the discomfort of the heat, have been furnished for mankind in the beginning, or how could they have been repaired, when made ruinous by storm, or earthquake, or age, unless society had learned to seek aid in these things from men? Take into the account also aqueducts, canals, works for the irrigation of fields, breakwaters, artificial harbors. Whence could we have these without the labor of men? From these and many other things it is obvious that we could in no wise have received the revenues and uses derived from inanimate objects without the skill and labor of men. Then, again, what revenue or what convenience could be derived from beasts, unless by the aid of men? For it was men certainly who were foremost in discovering what use we might make of the several beasts in our service; nor could we now without the labor of men either feed them, or tame them, or keep them, or receive returns from them in their season.[1] By men also those beasts that do harm are killed, and those that can be of use are captured. Why should I enumerate the multitude of arts without which life could not have been at all? How would the sick be cured, what would be the enjoyment of the healthy, what would be our food or our mode of living, did not so many arts give us their ministries? It is by these things

---

[1] For instance, wool, at the proper time of shearing.

that the civilized life of men is so far removed
from the subsistence and mode of living of the
beasts. Cities, too, could not have been built and
peopled but for the association of men, in consequence of which laws and rules of moral conduct
have been established, as also an equitable distribution of rights, and a systematic training for
the work of life. These things have been followed by mildness of disposition and by modesty,
and the consequence is that human life is better
furnished with what it needs, and that by giving, receiving, and interchanging commodities and
conveniences we may have all our wants supplied.

5. I am dwelling on this subject longer than
is necessary; for who is there to whom what
Panaetius says with no little prolixity is not perfectly obvious, that no one, either as a military
commander or as a civil magistrate, could ever have
carried into effect important and serviceable measures without the zealous co-operation of men?
He names Themistocles, Pericles, Cyrus, Agesilaus,
Alexander, who, he says, could not have accomplished such great things without the aid of men.
He cites witnesses that are unnecessary in a matter
beyond doubt.

Still further, as we obtain great benefits by the
sympathy and co-operation of men, so there is no
degree of evil, however execrable, which may not
spring from man for man. There is extant a book

about the destruction of men,[1] by Dicaearchus, a distinguished and eloquent Peripatetic, who, after enumerating other causes, — such as inundation, pestilence, perils of the desert, the sudden inrush of destructive beasts[2] (by whose assaults, he says, whole races of men have been consumed), — then shows by comparison how many more men have been exterminated by the violence of men, that is, by wars or seditions, than by all other forms of calamity.

Since, then, there is no doubt on this point, that men transcend all other causes both of benefit and of injury to men, I maintain that it is a special property of virtue to conciliate the minds of men, and to make them availing for its own uses. Thus, while whatever in inanimate objects and in the use and management of beasts redounds to human benefit is to be ascribed to the mechanic arts, the

---

[1] This work has entirely perished. Dicaearchus, a contemporary and follower of Aristotle, was a copious writer in the departments of geography and history, as well as of philosophy. One of his books on "The Life of Greece," if we may judge by the fragments of it that remain, would have been worth more than all other extant records of Athenian life in his age.

[2] I do not know that there is any ancient record of the extensive destruction of human life by wild beasts, except that in the Old Testament (2 Kings xvii. 25), of the slaughter of people by lions in some of the Samaritan cities. But there are several traditions of instances in which the inhabitants of cities or towns were compelled to change their abodes, and hardly without some loss of life, by devastating, tormenting, or perilous incursions of mice, frogs, scorpions, serpents, moles, rabbits, and locusts.

good will of men, prompt and ready for the improvement of our condition, is elicited only by the wisdom and virtue which belong to men of superior excellence.

Indeed, all virtue may be said to consist in three things,[1] one of which lies in the clear discernment of what is true and real in every subject, of the correspondences of things, of their consequences, sources, and causes; the second, in the restraining of those troubled movements of mind which the Greeks call πάθη,[2] and in making the impulses which they call ὁρμάς[3] obedient to reason; the third, in the considerate and wise treatment of those with whom we are associated, by whose good will we may have in full and overflowing measure whatever nature craves, and by whose agency we may ward off impending evil, may exact retribution of those who attempt to do us harm, and visit them with such punishment as justice and humanity will permit.

6. By what means we can attain this capacity of winning and holding men's affections, I will shortly expound; but there are a few things to be said first. Who does not know that Fortune has great power on either side, whether toward prosperous or adverse

---

[1] We have here the first, fourth, and second of the cardinal virtues portrayed in Book I. The third is omitted, as peculiarly non-utilitarian; the second has the third place, as a text to be enlarged upon, — as the prime means of securing such utilities as men can bestow.

[2] Passions.　　　　　　　　　　　　　[3] Impulses.

events ? For when we sail under her propitious breath, we reach our desired port, and when she sends a contrary wind, we founder. Fortune herself, then, occasions some calamities — though comparatively rare — independently of human agency : in the first place, from inanimate things, as by gales, tempests, shipwrecks, falling buildings, conflagrations; then from beasts, by stings, bites, assaults. These, as I have said, are comparatively infrequent. But the destruction of armies, as of three very recently,[1] and of many others in former times; the murder of commanders, as lately that of an eminent and remarkable man ;[2] the enmity, also, of the multitude, and by its means the exile,[3] ruin, flight, often of well-deserving citizens ; and, on the other hand, prosperous events, civic honors, military commands, victories, — these, although they are partly dependent on fortune, cannot be brought to pass on either side without the aid and endeavor of men. This, then, being understood, I am to explain how we can elicit and call forth the good will of men for our own benefit. If the discussion shall seem too long, let it be compared with the advantage to be derived from it. It will then, perhaps, seem too brief.

[1] The army of Pompey the Great, in Pharsalia ; that of his son, at Munda ; and that of Scipio, at Thapsus, — all defeated by Julius Caesar.

[2] The murder of Pompey the Great, in Egypt.

[3] Cicero undoubtedly has in mind, here, his own exile by the machinations of Clodius.

Whatever, then, men bestow upon a man to enrich and ennoble him, they do it, either from kind feeling to a person whom for some reason they hold dear; or from respect for one to whose virtue they look up, and whom they think worthy of as ample good fortune as can accrue to him; or for one in whom they have confidence, and whose counsel and aid for their own benefit they hope in return; or for one whom they hold in dread for his capacity to injure them; or, on the other hand, for those from whom they have expectations, as when kings and demagogues distribute largesses; or, finally, when they are moved by price and bribe, which is the meanest and vilest way, both for those whose favor is held by it and for those who endeavor to resort to it; for it is a bad case when what ought to be effected by virtue is attempted by money. Yet since subsidies of this kind are sometimes necessary,[1] I will define their proper use, when I shall have first spoken of things which bear a closer relation to virtue. Moreover, men put themselves under the command and power of others for several reasons. They are led to this either by kind feeling, or by the greatness of favors received, or by the high social position of him to whom they yield deference, or by hope that such a course will be of use to them, or by fear of being forcibly compelled to render obedience; or they are attracted by the

---

[1] Cicero here refers, not to bribery, but to such liberal uses of money as he designates with approval in the sequel.

prospect of generous gifts and by promises; or, lastly, as we often see in our state, they are hired for wages.

7. But of all things nothing tends so much to the guarding and keeping of resources as to be the object of affection; nor is anything more foreign to that end than to be the object of fear. Ennius says most fittingly : —

> "Hate follows fear; and plotted ruin, hate."

It has been lately demonstrated, if it was before unknown, that no resources can resist the hatred of a numerous body. It is not merely the destruction of this tyrant, whom the state, subdued by armed force, endured so long as he lived and obeys most implicitly now that he is dead,[1] that shows how far the hatred of men may prove fatal; but similar deaths of other tyrants, hardly one of whom has escaped a like fate, teach this lesson. For fear is but a poor guardian for permanent possession, and, on the other hand, good will is faithful so long as there can be need of its loyalty. Those who hold under their command subjects forcibly kept down must indeed resort to severity, as masters toward their slaves when they cannot otherwise be restrained. But nothing can be more mad than the policy of those who in a free state conduct themselves in such a way as to be feared. For though

[1] The Senate were induced by Antony to pass sundry laws, the drafts of which he professed — in part, no doubt, falsely — to have found among Caesar's papers.

the laws be submerged by some one man's power, though liberty be panic-stricken, yet in time they rise to the surface, either by opinions circulated, though unuttered, or by the quiet mustering of votes that shall dispose of the high offices of state. Men indeed feel more keenly the suppression of liberty than any evils incident to its preservation. Let us then embrace the policy which has the widest scope, and is most conducive, not to safety alone, but to affluence and power, namely, that by which fear may be suppressed, love retained. Thus shall we most easily obtain what we desire both in private and in public life. For it is inevitable that those who wish to be feared should themselves fear the very persons by whom they are feared. What, for instance, must have been the case with the elder Dionysius?[1] With what tormenting fear must he have been racked, when, dreading the barber's razor, he used to singe off his own beard with burning coals? What are we to think of Alexander of Pherae?[2] In what state of mind must we suppose

---

[1] Of Syracuse, — a sovereign of signal ability, energy, magnificence, and public spirit, a liberal patron of literature and philosophy, but at the same time jealous, suspicious, arbitrary, and cruel, — leaving at once vestiges of true greatness as a king, and records, undoubtedly in large part authentic, of acts that disgrace humanity. The story is that while his daughters were very young, he made them shave him and cut his hair; when they were old enough for him to fear them, he used shoots of the walnut (*juglans*) to burn off his beard. He had a ditch round his bed, with a drawbridge commanded by himself.

[2] He came to the throne by the murder of his uncle and predecessor.

him to have lived, who, as we read the record, though somewhat fond of his wife Thebe, yet when he came from supper to her chamber, ordered a barbarian attendant, and indeed one, as we are told, branded with the marks of a Thracian,[1] to precede him with a drawn sword, and sent in advance some of his body-guards to search the woman's boxes, and see whether there were not some weapon concealed among the clothes? O wretch, to think a tattooed savage more to be trusted than his own wife! Yet he was in the right; for he was slain by that very wife,[2] because she suspected him of adultery. Nor indeed is there any ruling power strong enough to be enduring, when it makes itself the object of dread. Of this we may find an example in Phalaris[3] whose cruelty was notorious beyond that of any other tyrant, who perished, not by treachery, like that Alexander of whom I have just spoken, — not

---

[1] The Thracians, who were accounted as barbarians, were employed as body-guards by some of the petty tyrants of the Grecian cities, as the Swiss have been employed in Paris and in Rome, and as Scythians were employed in a similar capacity at Athens.

[2] Alexander's chamber was at the top of a ladder, and a fierce dog was chained at the door. His wife concealed her three brothers in the house during the day, removed the dog after Alexander was asleep, covered the steps of the ladder with wool, and led the young men up to murder her husband.

[3] Phalaris is almost a mythical personage. Different authorities assign dates nearly a century apart for the beginning of his reign, the latest date being 570 B. C. There are also opposite traditions as to his character, some authorities representing him as mild and humane.

by the hands of a few, like this tyrant of ours, but who was assailed by the whole mass of the people of Agrigentum. What ? Did not the Macedonians desert Demetrius,[1] and in a body betake themselves to Pyrrhus ? What ? When the Lacedaemonians usurped power that was not rightfully theirs, did not almost all their allies leave them, and show themselves idle spectators of the disaster at Leuctra ? [2]

8. I prefer on such a subject to draw my examples from foreign states rather than from our own. Yet so long as the sway of the Roman people was maintained by the bestowal of benefits, not by injustice, wars were waged either in defence of our allies or of our own government ; the issues of our successful wars were either merciful or no more severe than necessity demanded ; our Senate was the harbor and refuge of kings, tribes, nations ; while our magistrates and military commanders sought to obtain the highest praise from this one thing, — the guarding of the interests of our provinces and our

[1] Demetrius Poliorcetes. Pyrrhus, King of Epeirus, had invaded Macedonia, and when Demetrius marched to meet him, the Macedonian army *en masse* passed over to the invader. Demetrius was a ruler of marvellous vigor, and though sometimes truculent and cruel, and always grossly sensual, was not wholly devoid of humane and generous feeling.

[2] The campaign against Thebes, closed by the battle of Leuctra, was opposed to the wishes of all the allies of Sparta, and their soldiers were accused by the Spartans of utter inefficiency in the field, to be accounted for only by their reluctance to engage in the conflict.

allies by equity and good faith. Our sovereignty
might then have been termed the patronage, rather
than the government, of the world. We previously
had encroached by degrees on this habit and policy;
after Sulla's victory we entirely departed from it;
for nothing any longer appeared inequitable toward
our allies, after so much cruelty had been exercised
upon our own citizens. In his case a worthy cause[1]
was crowned by a disgraceful victory; for he dared
to say, when under the auctioneer's spear[2] he sold
in the market-place the property of good men and
rich men who were undoubtedly citizens, that he
was selling his booty. He was succeeded by one
who in an impious cause, after even a more disgraceful victory, not merely offered for public sale
the goods of individual citizens, but embraced whole
provinces and countries in one destructive ban.
And so, foreign nations being thus oppressed and
ruined, in token of our forfeited empire, we saw
Massilia borne in effigy in a triumphal procession,
and a triumph celebrated over that city without
whose aid our commanders never gained a Trans-
alpine triumph.[3] I might mention many other

---

[1] Sulla was the champion of the aristocracy, and thus far his
position had Cicero's approval and sympathy.

[2] A spear stuck in the ground was in Rome, as a red flag is
with us, the sign of a sale at auction.

[3] Massilia (*Marseilles*), a city settled by Grecian colonists, and
in Caesar's time second to no other city in the world as a seat of
extensive commerce, was from the first a faithful ally of Rome,
and, when the region of Gaul in which it is situated became a

abominable things done to our allies, if the sun had ever beheld anything more shameful than this very transaction. We therefore are justly punished; for unless we had so often had impunity from guilt, so great liberty of sinning would never have come into the hands of one man, whose heritage of property falls to few, that of depraved desire to many bad men. Nor indeed will there ever be wanting seed and pretext for civil wars, so long as abandoned men remember and hope to see again that bloody spear which Publius Sulla[1] brandished in the dictatorship of his kinsman, not refusing to be salesman under a more atrociously guilty spear thirty-six years afterward; while another Sulla,[2] who in the former dictatorship was secretary, in this last was city-quaestor. Hence it ought to be inferred that while such prizes are held in view, civil wars will never cease to be. And so only the walls of the city stand and remain, and even they already fear the extremity of crime; the state itself we have utterly lost. Moreover (for I must return to the point

Roman province, that city was suffered to retain its independence. In the civil war the Massilians espoused the cause of Pompey, and shut their gates against Caesar, who besieged and took the city, and had a model of it borne in procession in his triumph.

[1] Publius Cornelius Sulla, the nephew of the dictator, and, about midway between his dictatorship and Caesar's, found guilty of bribery when a candidate for the consulship.

[2] Cornelius Sulla, a freedman of the dictator, who, as Sulla's secretary, could secure large profits from confiscated property, and as quaestor under Caesar had access to the city treasury.

under discussion), we have fallen into these calamities because we preferred to be feared rather than
to be loved and esteemed.  If these things could
befall the Roman people exercising an unrighteous
sway, what ought individuals to think as to their
own conduct and fortune ?  Since it is manifest that
the power of good will is great, that of fear feeble, it
follows that we should inquire by what means we
can most easily obtain, together with respect and
confidence, that love of others which we crave.  We
do not all, indeed, need this love in an equal degree ;
for it must be determined by each person's plan
of life, whether he requires the love of many, or
whether it is enough for him to be held in dear
regard by a few.  This, however, may be accounted
as certain, that it is a prime and most essential
requisite, to have the enduring intimacy of friends
who love us and hold us in high esteem.  This one
thing, precious above all others, if attained, leaves
but little difference between persons of the loftiest rank and those in moderate condition, and
it is almost equally attainable by those of either
class.  All, perhaps, do not alike need promotion,
and fame, and the good will of the citizens at
large ; but yet, if one has these, they render some
help, as to other ends, so to the obtaining of friendships.

9. But I have treated of friendship in another
book, under the title of Laelius.  Let me now speak
of fame.  Though on that subject also I have written

two books,[1] let me touch briefly upon it here, since
it is of the utmost service in the administration of
important affairs.

The highest fame, and that to which there are no
drawbacks, consists of these three things, — the
affection of the multitude, their confidence, and
their regarding a person as worthy of honor because
they hold him in admiration.[2] Moreover, these
requisites to fame — to speak plainly and concisely
— are obtained from the multitude by nearly the
same means by which they are obtained from individuals. But there is also a certain other avenue
to the popular favor, by which we may, as it were,
steal into the affections of all.

Of the three things just named, let us consider,
first, the rules for winning good will. It is, indeed,
best secured by conferring benefits. But, in the
second place, favor is elicited by the will to do
good, even if the means of beneficence chance to be
insufficient. The love of the multitude, indeed, is
strongly excited by the very report and reputation
of liberality, beneficence, honesty, good faith, and
all those virtues which are included in gentleness
of manners and affability. For since that very
style of character which we call right and becoming,
in itself, gives us pleasure, and by its nature and

---

[1] They are both lost. Cicero mentions one of them in *Letters
to Atticus*, xvi. 27. "Librum tibi celerrime mittam de gloria."

[2] This is evidently meant to exclude the meaner ways by which
men insinuate themselves into popular favor.

aspect captivates the minds of all, and shines forth
with the greatest lustre from the virtues that I have
named, we are therefore compelled by Nature herself to love the persons in whom we think that
these virtues are found. These, however, are only
the most efficient causes of good will; for there
may be some others, though of less weight.

Of the confidence which may be reposed in us
there are two efficient causes, our having a reputation for discretion and, at the same time, for honesty.
For we have confidence in those whom we think
our superiors in intelligence, who, as we believe,
look into the future, and who, when an affair is in
agitation and a crisis is reached, can clear it of difficulty, and take counsel according to circumstances
(for this men regard as true and serviceable discretion); while the confidence reposed in honest and
faithful men, that is, in good men, is such that
there can rest upon them no suspicion of fraud and
wrong. And so we think that our personal security,
our fortunes, our children, can be most fittingly
intrusted to their care. Of these two qualities,
then, honesty has the greater power to create confidence; for while without discretion honesty has
sufficient prestige, discretion without honesty can
be of no avail in inspiring confidence. For the
more skilful and adroit one is, for this very reason
is he the more odious and the more open to suspicion, if he has no reputation for honesty. Intelligence, then, combined with honesty, will have all

the power that it can desire in creating confidence; honesty without discretion will have much influence toward that end; discretion without honesty will be of no avail whatever.

10. But if any one may have wondered, why, while all philosophers alike maintain, and I myself have often asserted, that whoever has one virtue has all, I now separate them as if a man could be honest without being wise also, my answer is that the nicety of expression employed when the inmost truth is under discussion is one thing; the language used when what we say is entirely adapted to popular opinion is another. Therefore, on this head I am speaking as people in general do, when I call some men brave, others good, others wise; for I ought to employ common and usual terms when I am speaking of public opinion, and Panaetius employed them in the same way. But let us return to our subject.

Of the three requisites for fame, the third that I named was this, — that men should so hold us in admiration as to regard us worthy of honor. Men generally admire all things that they see to be great and beyond their expectation, and specially in individual objects such unexpected good qualities as they discern. Therefore they admire and extol with the highest praise those men in whom they think that they perceive certain rare and surpassing virtues; while they look down with contempt on those in whom they imagine that there is no manliness, no spirit, no energy. For they do not despise all of whom they think ill. They do not despise, indeed, those whom they regard as villanous, malicious, fraudulent, capable of doing mischief, — by no means; of persons of this sort they think ill. But, as I have said, those are despised who, as the saying is, are of no good to themselves or to any one else, in whom there is no work, no industry, no forethought. On the other hand, those are regarded with a certain measure of admiration, who are thought to excel others in virtue, and to be free not only from all disgrace, but also from those vices which their fellow-men cannot easily resist. For sensual pleasures, the most alluring of mistresses, turn away the minds of the greater part of mankind from virtue, and equally when the fiery trial of affliction [1] comes most persons are beyond measure terrified. Life, death, riches, poverty, most violently agitate the great mass of mankind. When men with a lofty and large soul look down on these experiences, whether prosperous or adverse, while any great and honorable object of endeavor proposed to them converges and concentrates their whole being in its pursuit, who can fail to admire in them the splendor and beauty of virtue?

11. This contempt of the mind for outward fortunes thus excites great admiration; and most of all, justice, for which one virtue men are called good, seems to the multitude a quality of marvellous

---

[1] Latin, *dolorum faces*, — the torches, or cautery, of sorrows.

excellence, — and not without good reason; for no one can be just, who dreads death, pain, exile, or poverty, or who prefers their opposites to honesty. Men have, especially, the highest admiration for one who is not influenced by money; for they think that the man in whom this trait is made thoroughly manifest has been tested by fire.

Thus justice constitutes all three of the requisites to fame which I have named, — affection, because it aims to do good to the greatest number, and for the same reason, confidence and admiration, because it spurns and neglects those things to which most men are drawn with burning greediness. Moreover, in my opinion, every mode and plan of life demands the aid of men, and craves especially those with whom there may be friendly conversational intercourse, which is not easy, unless you are looked upon as a good man. Therefore, even to a recluse, or to one who passes his life in the country, the reputation of honesty is essential, and the more so because, if he do not have it, in his defenceless condition, he will be assailed by many wrongs. Those, too, who sell and buy, hire and lease, and are involved in business affairs, need honesty for the management of their concerns. The force of this virtue is such that those who obtain their subsistence by crime and guilt cannot live entirely without honesty. For he who takes anything by stealth or force from a fellow-robber cannot maintain his place in a band of robbers;

and even the man who is called captain of a crew
of pirates, if he were not impartial in the division
of their plunder, would be either killed or deserted
by his crew.    Indeed, it is said that even among
robbers there are laws which they obey, which they
hold sacred.    Thus by fairness in the distribution
of booty, Bardylis, an Illyrian robber, of whom
Theopompus makes mention, obtained great wealth,
and Viriathus, the Lusitanian,[1] much greater, to
whom indeed some of our armies and commanders
gave way in battle, whom Caius Laelius, commonly
called the Wise, when he was praetor, crippled and
reduced, and so subdued his ferocity that he transmitted an easy conflict with him to his successors.
Since, then, the force of justice is such that it
strengthens and augments the resources even of
robbers, how great shall we account its efficacy
among laws and courts, and in a well ordered
state ?

12. I am inclined to think, indeed, that not only
among the Medes, as Herodotus relates,[2] but also

---

[1] These men were hardly robbers in the ordinary sense of the
word ; but they carried on for many years guerilla warfare, and,
as is generally the case in such warfare, their forays were fully as
much predatory as murderous.    They were called robbers because
they were barbarians.    But Bardylis is termed by Diodorus king
of the Illyrians, having Pyrrhus, king of Epeirus, for his son-in-
law ; and Viriathus seems to have been a patriotic chieftain,
whose prime aim was to resist the Roman supremacy.

[2] According to Herodotus, Deioces, ambitious of sovereignty,
commenced as arbitrator in his own village, and on account of the
reputation thus obtained for justice was chosen king.    His admin-

among our ancestors, men who had borne a high
moral character were in early times appointed
kings, in order to the administration of justice;
for when the poor commonalty were oppressed by
those of greater wealth, they had recourse to some
one man pre-eminent in virtue, who, while he
defended the poorer classes from wrong, by establishing equitable jurisdiction kept the highest under
the same legal obligations with the lowest. There
was like reason for making laws as for choosing
kings; for equality of right was always sought, nor
without equality can right exist. If this could be
obtained through the ministry of one just and good
man, the people were contented under his rule.
But when this ceased to be the case, laws were
invented which should speak with all, at all times,
in one and the same voice. This, then, is manifest,
that those of whose justice the mass of the people
had an exalted opinion used to be chosen as rulers.
If in addition these same persons were thought
wise, there was nothing that men did not expect
to obtain under their administration. Justice is,

istration is represented as having been, though impartial, annoy-
ingly inquisitorial and relentlessly severe. But as his reign began
more than seven centuries before the Christian era, he may be
regarded as a semi-mythical personage, and a like doubt may
be thrown on the origin of the Median sovereignty. The theory
of the origin of kingly power here given seems to have been a
favorite notion with Cicero, and is found in other works of his.
It perhaps defines what ought to have been; but in fact the
kingly office was probably at the outset but an extension of patri-
archal sovereignty.

therefore, by all means to be cherished and held fast, at once for its own sake — else it would not be justice — and for the increase of one's honor and fame.

But as there is a method, not only of acquiring money, but also of investing it, so that it may supply constant demands for generous giving no less than for necessary uses, so is fame to be properly invested as well as sought. There is great truth, however, in the saying of Socrates, that this is the nearest way, and, as it were, a short road to fame, — for one to endeavor to be such as he would wish to be regarded. If there be those who think to obtain enduring fame by dissembling and empty show, and by hypocrisy, not only of speech, but of countenance also, they are utterly mistaken. True fame strikes its roots downward, and sends out fresh shoots;[1] all figments fall speedily, like blossoms, nor can anything feigned be lasting. Very many cases might be cited in attestation on either side; but for the sake of brevity I will name but a single family. Tiberius Gracchus, the son of Publius, will be praised as long as the memory of Roman affairs shall last; but his sons were not approved by good men while they were living, and in death they have their position among those whose murder was justifiable.[2]

[1] The allusion here seems to be to trees like the banyan, whose branches, as they bend to the ground, take root, and send up fresh shoots.

[2] All the surviving records of the father's life entirely justify Cicero's encomium; it is an open question whether the sons may

13. Let him, then, who would obtain genuine fame discharge the duties of justice. What these are I have shown in the First Book.

But in order that we may be taken for what we really are, though there is the greatest efficacy in our being what we would be taken for, yet some additional rules are to be given. If, indeed, one from early youth finds himself in a position of celebrity and reputation, either inherited from his father (as I think is the case with you, my Cicero,) or by some chance or happy combination of circumstances, the eyes of all are turned to him; inquiry is made about him, what he is doing, how he is living, and, as if he were moving in the clearest light, nothing that he says or does can be concealed. But those whose first years, on account of their lowly and obscure condition, are passed out of the knowledge of men, as soon as they emerge from childhood, ought to hold great aims in view, and to strive after them with unswerving diligence, which they will do with the greater confidence, since that age is not only exempt from envious regard, but is even looked upon with favor.

not have fully inherited his high moral worth and devoted patriotism. The family was plebeian, and it may not be otherwise than natural, that while the father — allied by marriage to the patrician family of the Scipios — was identified with the aristocracy, the sons should with honest and disinterested zeal have devoted themselves to the relief, elevation, and well-being of the plebeians, who in their time might justly complain of disabilities and oppression.

A youth, then, has the first title to fame, if he have the opportunity of obtaining it by military service, in which many in the days of our ancestors won early distinction; for wars were almost perpetual. But your time of service fell upon the epoch of that war in which one party was exceedingly guilty, the other unsuccessful. Yet in this war, when Pompey had made you commander of the left wing of his army,[1] you won great praise both from that illustrious man and from your fellow-soldiers for your horsemanship, your skill in the use of weapons, and your endurance of all the hardships of the camp and the field. This reputation of yours sank, indeed, simultaneously with the state. I have undertaken this discussion, however, not with reference to you alone, but with reference to young men as a class. Let us then pass on to the remaining subjects.

As in all other respects mental are much greater than bodily achievements, so those things which we accomplish by intellect and reason win greater

---

[1] Latin, *alae alteri*. *Ala* may mean either one of the wings of an army or one of the squadrons of cavalry usually attached to every legion of foot-soldiers in service. Without the *alteri*, as young Cicero was only sixteen years of age, *alae* should undoubtedly be rendered *a squadron*, and many of the commentators suspect *alteri* to be a spurious interpolation. But as Pompey was to the last degree solicitous to secure and retain the moral support of Cicero, he may have sought to flatter the father by appointing the son to a nominal command, delegating its more important duties to officers of maturer years and experience.

favor than those which we perform by mere physical strength. The first claim that can be proffered for the general esteem proceeds from regularity of conduct, with filial piety and kindness to those of one's own family. Then, too, young men become most favorably known when they seek the society of eminent, wise, and patriotic citizens, with whom if they are intimate, they inspire the people with the expectation that they are going to resemble those whom they have chosen as models for imitation. His frequenting the house of Publius Mucius [1] gave the youth of Publius Rutilius [2] the reputation both of moral purity and of legal knowledge. On the other hand, however, Lucius Crassus, while yet a mere boy, sought no countenance from his elders, yet won for himself the highest reputation from that splendid and famous accusation; [3] and (as we learn

[1] Publius Mucius Scaevola, of the highest reputation as a jurist, and a copious writer on the Roman law. While vehemently opposed to the Gracchi, and approving of the murder of Tiberius Gracchus, he gave a legal opinion in favor of compensation from the public treasury for the value of the effects constituting the dowry of the wife of Caius Gracchus, lost in the popular disturbance caused by her husband.

[2] A man of rigid integrity and probity, and eminent for ability and learning as a jurisconsult and a forensic orator.

[3] Lucius Licinius Crassus. He was undoubtedly the greatest orator of his time. Cicero may have heard him, having been sixteen years of age at his death. When a mere stripling, — Tacitus says, of nineteen years, — he accused Caius Papirius Carbo, of what crime we do not know, probably of bribery or extortion, and met with such signal success that Carbo committed suicide to escape condemnation.

was the case with Demosthenes),[1] at the very age
when young men are wont to be applauded for their
exercises in declamation, Lucius Crassus showed
that he could already do to perfection before the
judges what it would have been to his . credit
to have merely rehearsed by way of practice at
home.

14. But while there are two kinds of speech, to
one of which conversation belongs, to the other
public debate,[2] there is no doubt that the latter is
most conducive to the acquisition of fame (for it is
that which we dignify by the name of eloquence) ;
yet it is hard to say to what a degree agreeableness
and affability of conversation win favor.   There are
extant letters of Philip to Alexander, of Antipater
to Cassander, and of Antigonus to Philip, — all three,
as we learn, men of the greatest practical wisdom, —
in which they advise their sons to allure the minds
of the multitude in their favor by kindliness of
address, and to charm the soldiers by accosting
them in a genial way.

But the speech that is uttered with energy in
a great assembly often awakens the enthusiasm

[1] Demosthenes, at the age of eighteen, brought a successful
suit against his guardians, to compel them to render account of
his property in their hands.

[2] Latin, *contentio.*  The only occasions for the practice of
oratory in Rome were such as might be designated by this term,
which means *contention.*  They were the advocacy of disputed
measures in the Senate or before the people and the pleading of
cases in the courts of law.

of the entire audience; for great is the admiration bestowed on him who speaks fluently and wisely, and those who hear him think that he also has more intelligence and good sense than other men. And if there is in the speech substantial merit united with moderation, there can be nothing more worthy to be admired, especially if these properties are found in a young man. But while there are many kinds of occasions that demand eloquence, and many young men in our state have obtained praise by speaking both before judges and in the Senate, the highest admiration attends the eloquence of the courts,[1] before which there are two descriptions of oratory, that of accusation, and that of defence, of which, although the latter is more worthy of praise, yet the former is very frequently regarded with favor. I spoke just now of Crassus. Marcus Antonius[2] did the same when he was a

---

[1] There was in Rome no profession corresponding to that of the modern advocate. There were jurisconsults, men learned in the law, many of whom were also eloquent advocates, while others were chamber-counsel, to whom advocates, as well as the immediate parties in a suit, resorted for legal opinions and advice. But any man who had the will and the ability might take charge of a case in court; and for young Romans who aspired to distinction, after military ambition began to wane, the bar was the favorite avenue to the popular favor. There were no public prosecutors; but any person who was ready to make and sustain a criminal charge had only to present himself before the *praetor urbanus*, and to swear that he was acting not from malicious motives, but in good faith, and in the interest of the state.

[2] Grandfather of the triumvir, — a contemporary of Crassus, and of nearly equal reputation as an orator.

young man. A public accusation also brought into
favorable notice the eloquence of Publius Sulpicius,[1]
when he arraigned for trial that seditious and worthless citizen, Caius Norbanus. Yet this ought not
to be done often, nor ever except in the interest
of the state, as in the cases that I have named, or
to avenge wrongs, as the two Luculli did,[2] or for
those under one's special patronage, as when I
appeared in behalf of the Sicilians,[3] and Julius[4]
in behalf of the Sardinians in the accusation of
Albucius the propraetor. The painstaking fidelity
of Lucius Fufius in the accusation of Manius
Aquillius[5] is also well known. One may, then,
venture upon accusation once, or, at any rate, not
often. Or if there be reason for doing so more
frequently, let it be done as a service to the state,
whose enemies one is not to be blamed for punish-

[1] He was twenty-eight years old when he accused Caius
Norbanus of *majestas*, or treason, for turbulent and seditious
conduct as tribune of the people.

[2] The augur Servilius had prosecuted their father for bribery
and malversation in Sicily, and procured his condemnation and
exile. Though the elder Lucullus was undoubtedly guilty, his
sons may have supposed him innocent, and at any rate they
avenged themselves by the unsuccessful impeachment of Servilius.

[3] In the impeachment of Verres.

[4] Caius Julius Caesar, who commenced public life by the accusation of Titus Albucius of extortion as praetor in Sicily, and
procured his condemnation.

[5] He was accused by Fufius of extortion in Sicily; but, not-
withstanding strong proofs of guilt, was acquitted on the ground
of signal courage and ability in military command.

ing repeatedly. But even then let there be a limit; for it is the part of a hard man, or, I should rather say, scarcely of a man, to prefer a capital charge against any considerable number of persons.[1] While it is fraught with personal danger, it is also damaging to one's reputation, to allow himself to be called an accuser, which was the fortune of Marcus Brutus,[2] born of an illustrious race, the son of the Brutus who was eminent for his skill in the civil law. Moreover, this maxim of duty is to be carefully observed, that you never bring an innocent person to a capital trial; for this cannot possibly be done without guilt. Nay, what is so inhuman as to pervert eloquence, bestowed by Nature for the security and preservation of men, to the destruction and ruin of good citizens? On the other hand, we are not to be so scrupulous as to decline defending on some occasions a guilty man, if he be not utterly depraved and false to all human relations. This the people demand, custom permits, even humanity endures. It belongs to the judge in the cases before him always to seek the truth; to the advocate, sometimes to defend the probable, even if it be not abso-

---

[1] *Judicium capitis*, or a capital trial, was a phrase used, not only where life was put in jeopardy, but with reference to all cases in which one's standing and privileges as a citizen were imperilled, and the danger of degradation or exile was incurred.

[2] Marcus Junius Brutus. His father was eminent for his legal learning. Of the son we know little except from Cicero, who may have been prejudiced against him as belonging to the opposite political party.

lutely true, — which I should not dare to write, especially in a philosophical treatise, unless that strictest of the Stoics, Panaetius, were of the same opinion. But fame and favor are best secured by the defence of accused persons, especially if it so happens that this service is rendered in aid of one who seems to be circumvented and put in peril by the influence of some man in power, — a service which I have performed on many other occasions, and especially — when I was still a young man — in defending Sextus Roscius[1] against the power of Lucius Sulla, then playing the tyrant, — a speech which, as you know, is published.

15. Having explained the ways in which, consistently with duty, young men may obtain fame, I must speak, in the next place, of beneficence and liberality, of which there are two sorts, kindness to those needing it being shown either by personal service or by money. The latter is more easy, especially for

---

[1] There is nothing in the entire record of Cicero's life more honorable to him than his conduct on this trial, in which he was for the first time engaged in a criminal cause. Sextus Roscius was accused of the murder of his father, on no valid or probable evidence, and undoubtedly with the view of securing permanent legality to the seizure of the father's property on the false pretence of unpaid debts. The principal in the fraud and the instigator of the criminal pursuit was Chrysogonus, a freed man of Sulla. With every possible obstacle thrown in his way, and with the whole influence of the dictator pressed into the opposite scale, Cicero procured, by the masterly management of the case, no less than by his eloquent defence, the acquittal of his client, but undoubtedly incurred imminent peril.

one who is rich; but the former is more noble, more
magnificent, and more worthy of a strong and eminent man. For although in both modes there is the
generous desire of bestowing benefit, yet in the one
case the kindness is drawn from the purse, in the
other from the giver's own ability and worth. The
bounty which proceeds from one's property drains
the very source of liberality. Thus generosity is
made impossible by generosity, which you can
extend to the fewer in time to come, the more
numerous its beneficiaries have been in the time
past. But those who will be beneficent and generous in personal service, that is, by influence and
effort, the more persons they have already benefited,
will have the more helpers in doing good. Then,
too, by the habit of beneficent action, they will be
better prepared, and, as it were, better trained, to
merit the gratitude of the larger number. Philip,
in a certain letter of his, very justly blames his son
Alexander for seeking the good will of the Macedonians by distributing gifts among them. "What,
the mischief!" says he, "ever induced you to enter-
tain a hope like this, that those whom you had
corrupted by money would be faithful to you? Are
you doing this that the Macedonians may hope to
have you not for their king, but for their lackey
and caterer?" "Lackey and caterer" is well said,
since such conduct is mean for a king; and still
better was it that he termed lavish giving "corruption." For he who receives such gifts grows worse,

and more ready to expect the like in all time to come. He said this to his son; let us regard his advice as given to all. It is, then, beyond doubt that the kindness which consists in personal service and effort is more honorable, and extends farther, and can benefit a larger number. Yet gifts must be sometimes bestowed, nor is this form of kindness to be wholly repudiated; and aid should be often given to the deserving poor from one's own property, but thriftily and moderately. Many, indeed, have squandered their property in inconsiderate generosity. But what is more foolish than to disable yourself from continuing to do what you take pleasure in doing? Moreover, rapine follows extravagance in giving; for when men in consequence of their lavish generosity have begun to be in want, they are constrained to lay hands on the property of others. Thus, while they desire to be generous in order to win favor, they obtain not so much the attachment of those to whom they have been liberal as the hatred of those whom they have robbed. Therefore private property should neither be so shut up that kindness cannot open it, nor so thrown wide as to lie open to all. Let a limit be observed, and let this be determined by our means. We ought always to remember what has been so often repeated by our people as to have come into use as a proverb, that prodigal giving has no bottom.[1] For what

[1] The allusion here is, undoubtedly, to the cask with a perforated bottom which the Danaides are eternally attempting to fill.

bound can there be to such giving, when those who
have been accustomed to receive, crave what they
have been wont to get, and others also crave the
same ?

16. Of bountiful givers there are, in fine, two
kinds, the one class prodigal, the other liberal, —
the prodigal, those who, in public banquets, distri-
butions of flesh, gladiatorial shows, and the preparation of games and wild-beast fights, pour out money
on the kinds of things of which they will leave but a
brief remembrance, or none at all ; the liberal, those
who by their wealth redeem persons captured by
robbers, or take upon themselves the debts of their
friends, or render them aid in marriage-portions for
their daughters, or help them in acquiring or increasing property. I therefore wonder what came
into the mind of Theophrastus in the book that he
wrote about Riches,[1] in which he said many things
admirably well, but that to which I now refer,
absurdly. For he is prolix in praise of the magnificence and elaborateness of popular entertainments,
and regards the means of meeting such expenses as
the chief advantage of wealth. But in my mind the
advantage derived from the liberality of which I
have given a few examples seems much greater and
more certain. How much more soberly and justly
does Aristo of Ceos [2] reprove us for not being sur-

---

[1] A lost book.

[2] Latin (in many of the best editions), *Aristo Ceus;* (in all
extant manuscripts and early editions) *Aristoteles.* Aristotle not

prised at these outpourings of money which are made
to propitiate the multitude! "If those besieged
by an enemy," he says, "are forced to pay a pound[1]
for a pint[2] of water, at the first hearing it seems
incredible and all are amazed; yet when they consider the case they excuse it on the plea of necessity; but in this immense waste and these boundless
expenditures we feel no great astonishment, and
that too, though neither is want thus relieved nor
respectability enhanced, and the very delight of the
multitude is transient and lasts but a little while,
and, withal, is felt only by the most fickle, whose
memory of the enjoyment expires as soon as they
are satiated." He fittingly concludes that "these
things are gratifying to boys, and weak women, and
slaves, and to free men who bear the nearest resemblance to slaves; but that they cannot by any
means be approved by a serious man and one who
weighs what is done by fixed principles." Yet I am
aware that in our city it is an old tradition, and one
that has come down from good times, that lavish-

only has no sentiment like this in his extant writings, but can
hardly have had in his time the material for such a description
of senseless extravagance. The public entertainments of his age,
especially in Athens, while redolent of superior culture, were comparatively inexpensive. Aristo of Ceos wrote a treatise (now lost)
on Vain Glory (περὶ κενοδοξίας), from which this passage may
very probably have been quoted. But the reading which gives
his name is at best an ingenious and not unlikely conjecture.

[1] *Mina*, in value a little more than four pounds sterling.

[2] *Sextarius*, about a pint.

ness in the aedileship may be expected even from
the best men.[1]  Thus Publius Crassus, rich equally
in his surname and in his estate, gave the most
costly public entertainments in his aedileship, and
shortly afterward Lucius Crassus, with Quintus
Mucius, the most moderate of all men, for his colleague, served through a most magnificent aedileship; and in like manner Caius Claudius, the son of
Appius, and many afterward, the Luculli, Hortensius, Silanus.  Publius Lentulus, when I was consul,
surpassed all that went before him.  Scaurus imitated him.  But the entertainments given by my
friend Pompey in his second consulship were the
most magnificent.  With reference to all these
matters you see what my opinion is.

17. Yet the suspicion of penuriousness must be
avoided.  Mamercus, a very rich man, by declining
to be a candidate for the aedileship, lost his election
as consul.  If such expenditure, then, is demanded
by the people, and though not desired, at least
approved by good citizens, it is to be incurred, yet

---

[1] Of course, popularity in an aedileship contributed largely to
one's success as a candidate for higher offices, and in the best days
of the republic an aspirant for the popular favor may, as aedile,
have made for the entertainment of the public an expenditure
fully level with his ability.  But before Cicero's time it had become common for an aedile to incur in that office heavy debts, to
be liquidated, if ever, when as propraetor or proconsul he should
be able to fill his exchequer with provincial spoils.  Debts thus
contracted were regarded as an obligatory mortgage on the popular suffrage, by which the debtor should have the opportunity of
reimbursing himself for his outlay to please the people.

in proportion to one's ability, as in my own case;[1] and if at any time some end of great importance and value can be gained by largesses to the people, they may be bestowed, as in the recent instance in which Orestes gained great honor by a public dinner in the streets under the name of a tithe-offering.[2] Nor did any one find fault with Marcus Seius, because in a time of dearth he gave the people corn for a penny[3] a peck;[4] for he thus freed himself from great and inveterate odium by a lavishness not unbecoming inasmuch as he was an aedile, and not very extravagant. But it was to the highest honor of my friend Milo when, not so very long ago, by gladiators bought for the sake of the state which was dependent on my safety, he suppressed all the plots and mad endeavors of Publius Clodius.[5] There is, therefore, sufficient reason for profuseness, if it is

---

[1] Cicero, as aedile, gave three public games.

[2] The Romans frequently offered to some god, generally to Hercules, a tithe of their property on the eve of any great enterprise, or of their gains, in case of any signal success. But a small part of such an offering was consumed in sacrifice, and the rest was commonly utilized for a magnificent public festival. The words *polluceo* and *polluctura* as applied to such feasts may authorize the supposition (though I know of no other ground for it) that Pollux may have had in earlier time the honor which was subsequently paid to Hercules.

[3] *As,* about half an English penny.

[4] *Modius,* a little less than a peck.

[5] Clodius was undoubtedly the greater ruffian and the worse man of the two; but it is only by shutting out all testimony save that of Cicero's magnificent defence of Milo, that we can regard him as a pre-eminently law-abiding and patriotic citizen.

either necessary or useful. Yet in expenditures of this sort the rule of moderation is the best. Lucius Philippus, indeed, the son of Quintus, a man of great genius and of the highest eminence, used to boast that, without giving any public entertainment, he had been elected to all the offices that were regarded as the most honorable. Cotta said the same; so did Curio. I can also to a certain extent[1] make the same boast; for, as compared with the importance of the offices which I obtained without any opposing votes[2] in the years at which I became eligible[3] to them respectively, — which was not the case with either of those whom I have named, — the expense of my aedileship was very small. At the same time, the more desirable expenditures in connection with public office are for moles, docks, harbors, aqueducts, and whatever may be of service to the community. Although what is given personally, as it were, into men's hands, confers more immediate gratification, the expense incurred in public works is more thankworthy. I blame the cost bestowed on theatres, porticos, new temples,

---

[1] Cicero never attained the censorship, to which, by custom tantamount to constitutional law, and seldom departed from, ex-consuls alone were eligible.

[2] The vote was taken by centuries, so that a large opposing minority might be consistent with a nominally unanimous suffrage.

[3] The normal age at which one was eligible to the quaestorship was thirty; to the aedileship, thirty-seven; to the praetorship, forty; to the consulship, forty-three. These rules had sometimes been disregarded, but were generally adhered to.

with diffidence on account of my regard for Pompey's memory;[1] but the wisest authorities disapprove of such expenditures, as did this very Panaetius whom in my present treatise I have followed, not translated; as did also Demetrius Phalereus, who finds fault with Pericles for throwing away so much money on that famous vestibule of the Parthenon.[2] But this entire subject is carefully discussed in my book on the Republic.[3] The whole system of such extravagant largesses, in general worthy of censure, is under certain circumstances necessary, — yet, when it becomes necessary, the expense must be apportioned to one's means, and kept within moderate limits.

18. In the other style of free expenditure which proceeds from liberality, we ought not to be equally ready to give where the cases are unlike. The case of him who is laboring under misfortune differs from that of him who, without any actual stress of adverse circumstances, seeks to improve his condition. Generosity ought to be more readily bestowed on the unfortunate, unless perchance they deserve what they suffer. Yet with regard to those who desire assistance, not to be saved from utter ruin, but to reach a higher position, we ought to

[1] Pompey erected the most splendid of the then existing theatres, and temples to Venus and Victoria.

[2] The Propylaea, said to have cost a sum equivalent to two millions of our money.

[3] This discussion is not found in any of the portions of the *De Re Publica* that have been recovered.

be by no means niggardly, but to be judicious and careful in selecting suitable subjects for our bounty. For Ennius says very fittingly : —

"Good done amiss I count as evil done."

But what is given to a good and grateful man yields us in return a revenue both from him and from others. For when one does not give at haphazard, generosity confers the highest pleasure, and most persons bestow upon it the greater applause, because the kindheartedness of any one who holds a conspicuous station is the common refuge for all. Care must be taken, therefore, that we confer on as many as possible benefits of such a nature that their memory may be transmitted to children and posterity, so that they too cannot be ungrateful. All, indeed, hate him who is unmindful of a benefit received, and think themselves wronged when generosity is thus discouraged; and he who is thus ungrateful becomes the common enemy of persons of slender fortunes.[1] Moreover, the liberality of which I now speak is of service also to the state in redeeming captives from slavery, and in provid-

---

[1] Injustice is done to Cicero when these interested motives to beneficence are regarded as standing alone. It must be remembered that in the First Book the duty of beneficence is urged on grounds of intrinsic right; while expediency is the express and sole subject of the Second Book, in which it is his aim to show that interest and duty point in the same direction, — that the selfish man sins against himself no less than against his neighbor.

ing needy persons with the comforts of life, which used to be very commonly done by men of senatorial rank,[1] as .we find written out in full in the speech of Crassus.[2] This habitual practice of charity I regard as far preferable to the giving of public shows. The former is the part of substantial and prominent citizens; the latter seems to belong to those who fawn on the people, and tickle, so to speak, the fickleness of the multitude by low pleasure. But it will be becoming for one, while munificent in giving, to be also not severe in exacting, and in all contracts, in selling and buying, in hiring and leasing, in questions arising out of adjoining houses and estates,[3] to be fair and accommodating, freely making concessions from his own right, avoiding litigation as much as he can

[1] So long as there was a wide distinction between the orders of the Roman state, the patricians, in general, took a generous care of the interests of their respective clients and dependents. Indeed, the very term *patrician* is an enduring record of kindly relations between the higher and the lower orders.

[2] Lucius Licinius Crassus (§ 13). The reference is undoubtedly to his speech in favor of the restoration of judicial functions from the *equites* to the Senate.

[3] There were subtleties in the Roman law as to the falling of water from the eaves of houses (*stillicidium*), the preservation or obstruction of light, and various matters of dispute that might arise and in all time do arise between owners of contiguous houses. Between estates outside of the city there was legally a space of five or six feet in which each owner had a right of way, and neither a right of occupancy for his own uses. Rights of way and other easements were attached, also, to many private estates. Hence a fruitful field for litigation.

without excessive sacrifice, and perhaps even beyond what might seem the proper limit. For .it
is not only generous, but sometimes profitable also,
to abate a little from one's rightful claims. Yet
reference must be had to one's own estate, which
cannot be suffered to go to ruin without disgrace
to the owner; but private property must be so
cared for as to leave no suspicion of penuriousness
and avarice. Indeed, the ability of being generous
without robbing one's self of his patrimony is the
greatest revenue that money can yield. Theophrastus also rightly commends hospitality; for it
is, as it seems to me, very becoming that the houses
of distinguished men should be open to distinguished guests; and it is even for the honor of the
state that foreigners should not lack this kind of
liberality in our city. It is also in the highest
degree expedient for those who desire to obtain
great influence by honorable means to avail themselves of help and favor among foreign nations
through their guests. Theophrastus, indeed, says
that Cimon, at Athens, was hospitable not to
strangers only, but to all of his own district of
Laciadae,[1] making such arrangements ·and giving
such orders to his farm-servants, that every attention should be shown to any citizen of that district
who might turn aside to his country residence.

---

[1] The territory of Attica (including Athens) was divided into
one hundred and seventy-four δῆμοι, or districts. The *demos* of
Laciadae was outside of the city.

19. But the benefits which are bestowed, not by
gift, but by personal service, are conferred, sometimes on the whole state, sometimes on individual
citizens.  To protect the rights of others, to aid
them by legal advice, and by this sort of knowledge
and skill to be of service to as many as possible,
tends very largely to the increase of one's influence
and popularity.  Thus among many things to be
commended in the days of our ancestors, it is
worthy of note that the knowledge and the interpretation of our admirably constituted civil law
were always held in the highest honor.  This science, until the present unsettled times, the leading
men of the state retained as one of their special
prerogatives.  Now, as is the case with civil offices
and with all grades of rank, its prestige is destroyed,
and this the more shamefully, as it took place in
the lifetime of him who would have transcended
in legal learning all his predecessors whom he
equalled in rank.[1]  This kind of service, then, is
gratifying to many, and is adapted to bind men
by the ties of benefit.  Closely allied to skill in
interpreting the law is oratory, which even surpasses it both as a grave pursuit and as a personal
accomplishment.  For what stands before eloquence,
whether in the admiration of its hearers, the hope

[1] Servius Sulpicius, after the death of Mucius Scaevola the
most learned and celebrated jurisconsult.  He died but a year
before this treatise was written, and Cicero pronounced a eulogy
on him in the Senate.

of those who need its aid, or the gratitude of those
defended by it ? To this, therefore, our ancestors
assigned the first rank among civil professions.
There is, then, an extended range of beneficial
services and of patronage open to the eloquent
man, who willingly appears in the courts, and, as
was the custom in the time of our fathers, without
reluctance and without compensation [1] defends the
causes of the many who seek his aid. The subject
was reminding me to deplore here, as elsewhere in
my writings, the discontinuance, not to say the
extinction, of eloquence, — only I should dread
the appearance of making complaint in my own
behalf. But yet we see how many orators have
passed away, in how few is there good promise,
in how much fewer ability, in how many nothing
save presumption. Yet while not all, indeed only
a few can be either skilled in the law or eloquent,
still one may render service to many, by canvassing in their behalf for appointments, by appear-
ing in their interest before judges and magistrates,
by watching the progress of their cases in court,
and soliciting for them the aid of legal counsellors
and of advocates. Those who do thus, obtain the
largest amount of good will, and their labor has

---

[1] The Roman law prohibited advocates from taking fee or
reward. There is no proof that Cicero was ever paid directly
or indirectly for his services as an advocate, though undoubtedly
presents and legacies from those who had enjoyed the benefit
of his services may have been among the sources of his wealth.

a most widely extended influence. Nor need they here to be admonished (for it is obvious), that they take heed lest while they desire to assist some, they disoblige others. For under such circumstances they are liable to hurt the feelings of those whom it is either morally wrong or inexpedient for them to wound. If they do this unwittingly, it is the result of carelessness; if knowingly, of recklessness. You must even resort to apology wherever you can, to those to whom you unwillingly give offence, showing them why what you did was necessary, so that you could not have done otherwise, and promising them that the omission shall be compensated by other services and kind offices.

20. But while in giving assistance to men reference is usually had either to character or to condition, it is easy to say, and men commonly do say, that in conferring[1] favors they are influenced by the character, not by the outward condition of their beneficiaries. This mode of speaking sounds well. Yet who is there, who in rendering his service does not prefer the cause of a rich and influential man to that of a man without influence, though of signal excellence? Our will, for the most part, inclines the more strongly toward him from whom we may expect the more prompt and speedy remuneration. Yet we ought to look more carefully at the nature

---

[1] Latin, *collocandis*, investing, i. e. conferring favors with a view to the revenue in influence and popularity which they may bring in return.

of things. Undoubtedly that poor man, if he is
a good man, even if he cannot return the favor,
can bear it faithfully in mind; and it is well said,
whoever he be that first said it, "He who has
money has not repaid it; he who has repaid it
has it not: but he who has returned kindness has
it, and he who has it has returned it." Now those
who think themselves rich, respectable, fortunate,
are unwilling to be placed under obligation by
kindness rendered, nay, they even think that they
have bestowed a favor when they have received
one however great, and they imagine that something is also demanded or expected of them,—
still more, it seems to them as bad as death to
have it said that they are indebted to any one's
patronage, or to be called any one's clients. On
the other hand, the man of slender means just
spoken of, thinking that whatever is done for him
is done from regard to himself, not to his outward
condition, endeavors to appear grateful, not only
to him who has deserved his thanks, but also,—
for he needs many helpers,— to those from whom
he expects similar favors. Nor, if perchance he
can render some good office in return, does he mag-
nify it, but rather underrates it in what he says
about it. This also is to be observed, that if you
defend a rich and successful man, the favor does
not extend further than to the man himself, or,
peradventure, to his children; while if you defend
a poor, yet upright and self-respecting man, all men

of humble condition who are not bad — and there
is a great proportion of these among the people —
see in you a defence prepared for their exigencies.
Therefore I think a kindness better invested with
good men than with men of fortune.    In fine, we
should endeavor to meet the claims of those of every
class; but if it come to a competition between rival
claimants for our service, Themistocles may be well
quoted as an authority, who, when asked whether
he would marry his daughter to a good poor man,
or to a rich man of less respectable character,
replied, "I, indeed, prefer the man who lacks
money to the money that lacks a man." But the
moral sense is corrupted and depraved by the
admiration of wealth.    Yet of what concern to any .
one of us is another man's great fortune ?    Perhaps
it is of benefit to him who has it, — not always,
however.    But suppose it to be of benefit to him, —
he may, indeed, have more to spend ; but how is he
made any better ?    If, however, he be really a good
man, let not his wealth be a hindrance, only let
it not be a motive for your serving him.    The
decisive question must be, not how rich one is, but
what sort of a man he is.    But the ultimate rule
in conferring favors and rendering service is, never
to make any effort against the right, or in behalf of
the wrong; for the basis of enduring praise and
reputation is justice, without which there can be
nothing worthy of commendation.

21. Having now spoken of the kinds of good offices

that concern individuals, I must next discuss those which have reference to a body of men and to the state. Of these a part are such as accrue to the benefit of the whole community; a part, such as affect individuals, though in the form of public service. Both interests ought certainly to be cared for, that of individuals no less than of the community at large, yet in such a way that what is done may be of benefit, or at all events, not of injury to the state. The distribution of corn by Caius Gracchus [1] was excessive, and tended to drain the public treasury; that of Marcus Octavius [2] was moderate, and both within the easy ability of the state and necessary to the people, — therefore a beneficial measure both to the individual citizens who received the public bounty and to the state. He who administers the affairs of the state must take special care that every man be defended in the possession of what rightfully belongs to him, and that there be no encroachment on private property by public

[1] Caius Gracchus, as tribune of the people, procured the passage of a law by which every resident of the city who should personally appear at the Capitol might buy five *modii* (or pecks) of corn each month, at less than half the average price, therefore at much less than cost. The tendency, and of course a prime object, of this measure was to bring into the city, and under the influence of the popular leaders, large numbers of the poorer population in the rural districts.

[2] Tribune of the people not long after Caius Gracchus. He procured the passage of a law raising the price of corn from the public granaries to a rate which arrested the depletion of the treasury.

authority. Philippus, during his tribunate, when he proposed the agrarian law (which he readily suffered to be rejected, behaving in the matter with great moderation), while in defending the measure he said many things adapted to cajole the people, did mischief by the ill-meant statement that there were not in the city two thousand men that had any property. It was a criminal utterance, tending to an equal division of property, than which what more ruinous policy can there be? Indeed, states and municipalities were established chiefly to insure the undisturbed possession of private property; for though under the guidance of Nature men were brought together, still it was with the hope of guardianship for their property that they sought the defence of cities. Pains should also be taken that there may be no need of levying a tax on property,[1] which in the time of our ancestors was often done on account of the poverty of the treasury and the frequency of wars. Against such a contingency provision should be made long beforehand. But in case such a tax should be necessary for any state — for I would rather speak thus than forebode evil for our own state, and I am treating not of our own, but of states in general — pains must be taken to make

---

[1] For one hundred and four years, from the close of the Macedonian war (B. C. 147), which brought an immense amount of treasure into the public coffers, till the very year succeeding Cicero's death, no property-tax was levied, the spoils of war and the tribute from the provinces sufficing for the public expenditure.

all the citizens understand that in order to remain
secure they must yield to this necessity. Moreover, it will be the duty of those who govern the
state to take care that there be a full supply of
everything requisite for the public service. How
this provision is commonly made and how it ought
to be made, there is no need of discussing, — it is a
perfectly plain matter; the subject required to be
merely alluded to.

But the chief thing in every department of public
business and official administration is that even the
least suspicion of greediness for money be put at
rest. Caius Pontius,[1] the Samnite, said, "Oh that
Fortune had reserved me and delayed my birth till
the time, should it ever come, when the Romans
had begun to take bribes! I would not then have
suffered them to hold their supremacy any longer."
Many generations must, indeed, have been waited
for; for only of late this evil has invaded our state.
Therefore I am glad that Pontius lived then rather
than now, if indeed he was so much of a man. It
is not yet a hundred and twenty years [2] since
Lucius Piso's law about extortion was passed,
whereas there had been no such law before. But
there have since been so many laws each more

---

[1] The Samnite general who defeated the Roman army at the
Caudine Pass, and many years later was himself defeated by
Quintus Fabius Maximus, taken prisoner, led in triumph, and
beheaded.

[2] About a century and a half after the death of Pontius.

severe than the preceding, so many accused, so many penally sentenced, so great an Italian war[1] caused by fear of judicial proceedings, such a pillaging and plundering of our allies[2] when laws and courts were suspended, that we owe what strength we have to the weakness of others, not to our own virtue.

22. Panaetius praises Africanus because he abstained from all illicit gain. Why should he not praise him? There were in him other greater qualities; the merit of abstaining from illicit gain belongs not only to the man, but to those times. Paulus obtained all the immense treasure of Macedonia. He brought so much money into the public treasury, that the booty acquired by that one commander put an end to the property-tax. But to his own house he brought nothing save the eternal

[1] Commonly called the Social War. Marcus Livius Drusus had, while tribune of the people, procured the passage of a law providing for inquiry into the corrupt practices of the courts, which had in many instances acquitted persons justly charged with bribery and extortion. He had also procured the passage of laws conferring certain privileges — with a view to ultimate citizenship — on the Italian allies. The Senate, under the influence of those who feared an honest judiciary, annulled all the laws that had been enacted under the auspices of Drusus, on the pretext that they had been carried against the auspices, and in defiance of certain provisions by statute requiring a seventeen days' promulgation of laws before they could be passed, and forbidding the massing of several distinct clauses in the same vote. The allies were, of course, thwarted of their expectations, and hence the Social War.

[2] During the dictatorships of Sulla and Caesar.

memory of his name. Africanus imitated his father, being none the richer for the overthrow of Carthage. What think you ? Was Lucius Mummius, his colleague in the censorship, any the richer when he had destroyed to its foundations a city of vast wealth ? [1] He chose to embellish Italy rather than his own house ; [2] though indeed in the embellishment of Italy his house also seems to me more truly embellished. There is, then, — to return to the point whence I made this digression, — no fouler vice than the greed of money, especially in the case of the leading citizens who govern the state; for to turn the state into a source of profit is not only vile, but even outrageous and execrable. Thus the oracle which the Pythian Apollo pronounced,

" By naught but greed of gain will Sparta perish,"

he seems to have proclaimed not to the Lacedaemonians alone, but to all rich nations. But by no means can those who preside over public affairs more readily conciliate the favor of the multitude than by abstinence from the acquisition of wealth and the moderate use of what they have.

Those, therefore, who desire to be popular, and

---

[1] Corinth.

[2] He flooded Rome with the richest spoils of Grecian art ; but though by no means a man of pure life, he rigidly abstained from participating in the booty or gain of his conquest. Pliny says of him, that he filled the city with trophies of conquered Achaia, yet left not a dowry for his daughter.

with that view either attempt agrarian measures,[1] that the occupants of the public domains may be driven from their homes, or advocate the remission of debts,[2] are undermining the foundations of the state, — in the first place, harmony, which cannot exist when money is taken from some and debts are cancelled for others ; in the next place, equity,

[1] The agrarian laws that have so large a place in Roman history are often misunderstood in consequence of a misapprehension of the Latin terms *possessor* and *possessio*. These laws proposed the eviction, in many instances, of possessors, but not of owners: *Possessio* means not ownership, but occupancy. The lands obtained by conquest were for the most part leased on what were understood to be and what we should call perpetual leases, on condition of the payment of one tenth or one fifth of the annual revenue of the estate into the public treasury, — a condition which after a time lapsed into disuse and oblivion, so that the lands thus acquired were transmitted, bequeathed, and sold, as freeholds would have been, and with no expectation that the possession would ever be disturbed. The possessors thus had the consciousness of ownership, and the sympathy of the aristocracy and the rich men, on their side ; and though the state, having never ceded the fee of its domain, had, no doubt, a right to take its lands from defaulting tenants and give them to the veterans or the landless plebeians, still this could not be done without the commission of virtual wrong to a large extent, and perhaps reducing to utter penury some who had felt as secure in the possession of their property as if it had come down to them in an unbroken line of inheritance from the beginning of time. We thus can reconcile the by no means delusive show of right and humanity on the face of the agrarian laws with the virtuous detestation expressed for them by not a few law-abiding Romans.

[2] *Novae tabulae*, or the general remission or scaling down of debts, was, in the latter days of the Roman republic, a frequent demand of demagogues and of their followers and dupes.

which is utterly destroyed, if hindrances are laid in the way of men's keeping their own property. For, as I said above, this belongs to the very idea of a state and a city, that the protection of every man's property should be certain and not a subject of solicitude. Moreover, by measures thus ruinous to the state men do not gain the favor that they anticipate. He from whom property is taken becomes their enemy. He to whom it is given conceals his desire to receive it, and especially in the case of debt cancelled, hides his joy, lest he may be suspected of having been insolvent. On the other hand, he who is wronged remembers it, and keeps his grievance in full sight.[1] Nor if those to whom property is wrongfully given are more numerous than those

---

[1] These words of Cicero describe with wonderful accuracy the result of an experiment with *novae tabulae* in the United States of America. A profligacy at which Rome in her worst days might have blushed found expression in a national bankrupt law passed by Congress in 1841, repealed in 1843. By this law fraudulent insolvency had every possible facility and inducement. There were in every community notorious instances in which men who had paid little or nothing except the required legal fees showed openly and shamelessly the property of which they had cheated their creditors. In fine, any man who chose to do so, whatever his pecuniary ability, could repudiate his debts. The law resulted in the collapse and defeat of the very party that had hoped by means of it to consolidate its power. Those who had taken the benefit of the law were ashamed of it when they needed it no longer ; while those whom it had wronged had no tolerance for the authors of their wrong, — thus verifying to the letter what Cicero says about the effect of such measures on the popularity of their authors and abettors.

11

from whom it has been unjustly taken, are they therefore possessed of more influence; for these matters are determined, not by number, but by weight. But what justice is there in a proceeding by which he who had no landed estate obtains an estate that has been in the possession of the same family for many years, or even generations, while he who has had the estate loses it ?

23. It was for wrongs of this sort that the Spartans banished Lysander the ephor, and put to death Agis the king,[1] the first instance of the kind; and from that time such dissensions ensued that tyrants sprang up, and men of high rank were expatriated, and that most admirably constituted state fell to pieces. Nor did it fall alone, but overthrew also the remainder of Greece by the contagion of evils which, starting from the Lacedaemonians, spread from state to state. What more ? Did not agrarian agitations destroy our citizens the Gracchi, sons of that most eminent man Tiberius Gracchus, grandsons of Africanus ? On the other hand, praise is most justly bestowed on Aratus of Sicyon, who, when his state had been kept under oppression by tyrants for fifty years,[2] going from Argos to Sicyon,

---

[1] Agis, the fourth Spartan king of the name, under whose government the Lysander here referred to was ephor. Their endeavor was to procure the entire cancelling of debts, and the re-distribution of the Spartan territory.

[2] With only a brief interval, during which the father of Aratus had served as one of two chief magistrates chosen by the people. He probably was not in power long enough, or had not sufficient

obtained possession of the city by entering it secretly, and after suddenly crushing the tyrant Nicocles, restored six hundred exiles who had been the
richest men in the state, and freed the people by his
advent. Then when he came to reflect on the difficulty about property and its occupancy, thinking it
very unjust that those whom he had restored and
whose estates were in the possession of others
should remain poor, and at the same time deeming
it hardly fair that possessions of fifty years' standing should be disturbed, because after so long a time
many estates were innocently held by inheritance,
many by purchase, many by dowry, he determined
that neither ought the property to be taken from
those in possession, nor ought the former owners to
be left without compensation. Having come to the
conclusion that there was need of money to set this
matter right, he said that he wanted to go to Alexandria, and ordered everything to remain as it was
till his return. So he hastened to Ptolemy, who
had been his host, the second king after the building of Alexandria. Having explained to him his
purpose to restore freedom to his country, and informed him of the posture of affairs, this man most
worthy of celebrity easily obtained from the rich

authority, to right the wrongs committed by a series of tyrants.
He was killed by a usurper when Aratus was seven years old, and
in the interval of thirteen years before the successful expedition of
Aratus, that usurper and his successor had been slain, so that
Nicocles was the third in this latter series of tyrants.

king the aid of a large amount of money. Carrying
this to Sicyon, he took into his counsel fifteen of
the principal men, with whom he considered carefully the cases both of those who held the property
of others, and of those who had lost their own property, and managed by a valuation of the estates to
persuade some of the present occupants to resign
their estates and accept money instead, and others
to account it more to their advantage to have the
value of their estates paid to them than to recover
possession of them. Thus it was brought about that
all went their ways perfectly satisfied, without any
ground of mutual complaint. O truly great man,
well worthy to have been a native of our own commonwealth! Thus it is fitting to deal with citizens;
not, as we have twice seen, to plant the spear in the
market-place, and to submit the property of citizens
to sale by the auctioneer. That Greek, indeed, as
was to have been expected of a wise and excellent
man, thought that the welfare of all should be consulted; and this is the consummate reason and
wisdom of a good citizen, not to create separate interests among those of the same state, but to hold
all together by the same principles of equity. May
men live without compensation on the estates of
others? Why so? That when I have bought,
built, keep the estate in good order, spend money
upon it, you without my consent may have the use
of what is mine? What else is this but to take
from some what is their own, and to give to others

what is not their own ? Then too, what does the
cancelling of debts mean, but that you may buy an
estate with my money, and keep it, while I go without the money ?

24. Therefore the care should be to check such
excessive indebtedness as will be of injury to the
state (which may be prevented in many ways),[1]
and not, if there are debts, to deprive the rich
of their money, and to let the debtors gain what
is not theirs. For nothing holds the state more
firmly together than good faith, which cannot possibly exist unless the payment of debts is obligatory.
Never was there a more earnest endeavor against
the payment of debts than in my consulship. The
attempt was made by arms and military operations,
and by men of every kind and order, which I
resisted with such energy that so dire a calamity
was averted from the state. Never was there a
larger amount of debt, nor was it ever discharged
more fully or more easily; for when the hope
of successful fraud was removed, the necessity of
paying was the consequence. He indeed, of late
conqueror, but at that time conquered,[2] carried

[1] Cicero would undoubtedly have said, by sumptuary laws,
which were sanctioned by the imperfect political economy of that
day.

[2] Cicero undoubtedly suspected, and with good reason, that
Caesar had covertly abetted the Catilinian plot, and Caesar's
speech in the Senate, if its tone and spirit are fairly represented
in Sallust's report of it, shows that he was solicitous to save the
lives of the conspirators.

out what he had then planned after he had ceased to have any personal interest in it.[1] So great was his appetite for evil-doing, that the very doing of evil gave him delight, even when there was no special reason for it. From this kind of generosity, then, — the giving to some what is taken from others, — those who mean to be guardians of the state will refrain, and will especially bestow their efforts, that through the equity of the laws and of their administration every man may have his own property made secure, and that neither the poorer may be defrauded on account of their lowly condition, nor any odium may stand in the way of the rich in holding or recovering what belongs to them; while they will also aid the growth of the state in power, territory, and revenue, by whatever means, military or domestic, may be at their command. Such are the aims of truly great men; these things were wont to be done in the times of our ancestors; and those who perform faithfully duties of this class will with the greatest benefit to the state secure for themselves distinguished favor and reputation.

[1] At the time of Catiline's conspiracy Caesar was very deeply in debt. He, in the first year of his dictatorship, was the author of a law by which debts were liquidated by payment of seventy-five per cent of their amount, the pretext being the increased value of money occasioned by the expenditure and loss of treasure during the civil war. Caesar himself had by that time become, not only free from debt, but absolutely rich, in great part, no doubt, from the perquisites of his Gallic campaigns.

Among these precepts relating to expediency, Antipater of Tyre, a Stoic, who recently died at Athens, thinks that two subjects were omitted by Panaetius,—the care of health and that of money, —which, I suppose, were passed over by that illustrious philosopher, because they presented no difficulty. They certainly belong under the head of expediency. I would say, then, that good health is maintained by the knowledge of one's own constitution, by observing what things are wont to be salutary or injurious, by self-restraint in the whole manner and habit of living, by abstaining from sensual indulgences, and, lastly, by the skill of those to whose profession these matters belong. Property ought to be obtained in ways not dishonorable, to be preserved by diligence and frugality, to be increased also by the same means. These things Xenophon, the disciple of Socrates, has thoroughly discussed in his book on Domestic Economy,[1] which, when I was about of your present age, I translated into Latin.

25. But the comparison of things that are expedient — this being the fourth division, omitted by Panaetius — is often necessary. For bodily endowments are wont to be compared with outward advantages, and outward advantages with bodily endowments, bodily endowments themselves, too, with one another, and outward advantages, some

---

[1] *Oeconomicus* (Οἰκονομικός), a work wholly devoted to the administration of the household and private property.

with others.   Thus in comparing bodily endowments with outward advantages, you would rather
be in good health than rich ; in comparing outward
advantages with bodily endowments, you would
choose to be rich rather than to possess extraordinary strength of body.   In comparing bodily
endowments among themselves, good health would
be preferred to sensual gratification, strength to
swiftness of foot; and of outward advantages, fame
to wealth, city revenues [1] to country revenues.[2]
Of this last kind of comparisons is that quoted
from the elder Cato, who, when asked what was
the most profitable thing to be done on an estate,
replied, " To feed cattle well."    " What second
best ? "  " To feed cattle moderately well."   " What
third best ? "  " To feed cattle, though but poorly."
" What fourth best ? "  " To plough the land."    And
when he who had made these inquiries asked,
" What is to be said of making profit by usury ? "
Cato replied, " What is to be said of making profit
by murder ? " [3]   From this and from many things
beside it may be inferred that comparisons of things

---

[1] From rents, and from the wages of slaves, — this last a very
lucrative and therefore a favorite source of income, though not
deemed entirely respectable.

[2] Returns at a lower percentage than city investments, and
more precarious, as contingent on the character of the season and
the abundance or scantiness of the crops.  Agriculture, though
not the most gainful, was regarded as the most respectable source
of income.

[3] Usury was held in abhorrence even more than in contempt.

expedient are not infrequently made, and that this
is rightly added as a fourth head to our discussion
of duty. But in everything appertaining to this last
topic, the acquisition and investment of money, — I
could wish, as to its use, too, — the discussions that
might be held by certain very good men sitting
among the bankers in the Exchange [1] are worth more
than those by any philosophers of any school. Yet
these matters ought to be taken notice of; for they
belong under the head of expediency, — the subject
of this book. Let us, in the next place, pass on
to what remains of the proposed plan.

[1] Latin, *ad Janum medium.* Janus was the name of a street
in or near the forum, in which were to be found almost all the
brokers' and bankers' offices in the city; and *Janus summus,
medius,* and *imus* meant, respectively, the top, middle, and bottom
of Janus Street.

# BOOK III.

1. My son Marcus, Cato, who was nearly of the same age [1] with Publius Scipio, the first of the family that bore the name of Africanus, represents him as in the habit of saying that he was never less at leisure than when he was at leisure, or less alone than when he was alone, — a truly magnificent utterance and worthy of a great and wise man, indicating that in leisure he was wont to think of business [2] and in solitude to commune with himself,[3] so that he was never idle, and had no need betweenwhile [4] of another person's conversation. Thus the two things, leisure and solitude, which with others occasion languor, quickened his energies. I could wish that I were able to say the same; but if I cannot by imitation attain such transcendent excellence of temperament, I at any rate in my inclination make as near an approach to it as I can; for, debarred from political and forensic employments by sacrilegious arms and vio-

---

[1] About ten years younger.
[2] Latin, *otio* de *negotiis* = *nec-otiis*.
[3] Latin, in *solitudine* secum loqui *solitum.*
[4] Latin, *interdum*, literally, betweenwhile.

lence, I am abandoning myself to leisure, and therefore, leaving the city and wandering from one place in the country to another, I am often alone. But neither is this leisure of mine to be compared with the leisure of Africanus, nor this solitude with his. He, indeed, reposing from the most honorable public trusts, upon certain occasions snatched leisure for himself, and from the company and concourse of men betweenwhile betook himself to solitude as to a harbor. But my leisure proceeds from lack of employment, not from desire for repose. For, the Senate being silenced[1] and the courts suspended,[2] what is there worthy of myself that I can do either in the senate-house or in the forum? Thus, after having lived in the greatest publicity and in the presence of my fellow-citizens, I now hide myself to escape the sight of bad men who swarm everywhere, and I am often alone. Yet since philosophers say that one ought not only of evils to choose the least, but from even these least evils to extract whatever of good there may be in them, I therefore am utilizing my leisure, though it be not that to which I was entitled after having obtained leisure[3] for the state, nor am I

---

[1] Antony had surrounded the Senate in its sessions with armed followers of his, and of course the purpose, as well as the effect of so doing, was to repress freedom of utterance.

[2] Brutus and Cassius, both praetors, could not safely remain in or return to the city, and as they were legally at the head of the judiciary, the courts were suspended.

[3] Latin, *otium.* *Repose* would be a better rendering, were it

suffering this solitude — which necessity, not choice, imposes upon me — to remain idle. Africanus, indeed, as I think, attained a higher merit; for no monuments of his genius were committed to writing, there remains no work of his leisure, no fruit of his solitude, — whence it should be inferred that it was in consequence of mental activity and the investigation of those things to which he directed his thoughts, that he was never at leisure or alone. But I who have not such strength of mind that I can abstract myself from the weariness of solitude by silent meditation, am directing all my study and care to this labor of writing, and thus in the short time that has elapsed since the overthrow of the state, I have written more than in many years while it stood.[1]

2. But while all philosophy, my Cicero, is fertile and fruitful, nor is any part of it untilled or unoccupied, there is no department within its pale more productive or more prolific than that relating to the duties whence are derived rules for living consistently and virtuously. Therefore, although I trust that you are diligently hearing and receiving instruction on this subject from Cratippus, the foremost philosopher of the present age, yet I think

not that we should lose Cicero's play upon *otium*, which is broad enough in its meaning to apply to the repose of the state from the plots of conspirators no less than to the rest of a worker from his labor.

[1] Almost all Cicero's philosophical and rhetorical works were written in the last three or four years of his life.

that it will be for your benefit that your ears should
constantly ring with such themes, and, were it possible, should hear nothing else. While this should
be the case with all who mean to enter on a virtuous
life, I am inclined to think that there is no one for
whom it is more fitting than for you, — liable as you
are to no small anticipation of imitating my diligence, to the confident expectation that you will
succeed me in public trusts, and to some hope, perhaps, of rivalling my reputation. You have, beside,
taken upon yourself the heavy responsibility of both
Athens and Cratippus, to which and to whom, after
resorting as to a mart of good culture, it would be
in the last degree shameful for you to return empty-
minded, thus disgracing the reputation of both the
city and the master. Look to it, then, that you
accomplish as much as you can aim after in purpose, and strive for by labor, — if learning be labor
rather than pleasure, — nor suffer it so to be, that
when I have given you the most liberal supplies,[1] you
may appear to have been false to your own interest.
But enough of this; for I have written to you
much and often by way of exhortation. Let us
now return to the remaining head of my proposed
division.

Panaetius, then, who without doubt discussed
the subject of duty with the utmost precision, and
whom I have thus far followed for the most part,

---

[1] Young Cicero's annual allowance would amount in our money
to a little more than four thousand dollars.

with an occasional correction, having laid down
three heads under which men were wont to reason
and deliberate concerning duty, — one, the inquiry
whether the act under discussion is right or wrong,
the second, whether it is expedient or inexpedient,
the third, the mode of settling the discrepancy in
case what has the appearance of right is repugnant
to what seems expedient, — treated of the first two
heads in three books, and said that he would speak
of the third head in its turn, but failed to keep his
promise. I am the more surprised at this, because
Posidonius, his pupil, says that he lived thirty years
after writing those first three books. I am surprised, too, to find this head but slightly touched
upon in certain essays of Posidonius, especially as
he says that there is no subject of so essential importance in all philosophy. 'I by no means agree
with those who maintain that this subject was not
overlooked by Panaetius, but purposely omitted, and
that it ought not to have been written upon at all,
inasmuch as expediency can never be in conflict
with the right. With regard to this assertion one
thing admits of doubt, whether this third head of
Panaetius ought to have been taken into consideration or entirely omitted ; the other thing admits of
no doubt, that it was undertaken by Panaetius, but
left unwritten ; for to him who has finished two
heads of a threefold division the third of necessity
remains. Besides, at the close of his third book he
promises to treat of this division in its turn. We

have further the testimony of Posidonius, a credible witness, who also writes in one of his letters that Publius Rutilius Rufus, a pupil of Panaetius, used to say that as no painter could be found who would finish the part of the Venus of Cos [1] which Apelles had left imperfect — the beauty of the countenance putting it beyond hope that the rest of the body could be finished so as to bear comparison with it — so no one had attempted what Panaetius had left incomplete, on account of the surpassing excellence of the things that he had completed.

3. There can, then, be no doubt about the intention of Panaetius; but whether he was right or not in annexing this third head to his discussion of duty may, perhaps, admit of doubt. For whether the right is the sole good, as the Stoics think, or whether, as your Peripatetics maintain, the right is the supreme good in such a sense that all things else placed in the opposite scale are of insignificant moment, it is beyond question that expediency can never clash with the right. Thus we learn that Socrates used to denounce as worthy of execration those who regarded as separable the expedient and

[1] The most admired of all the pictures of Apelles. He completed one picture of Venus *Anadyomene* (or rising out of the sea) for the temple of Aesculapius at Cos, which was afterward placed by Augustus in the temple which he built to Julius Caesar. This was injured, and no one dared to repair it. The painter commenced another picture of Venus, for the Coans, intending to surpass the previous one, but died before it was completed, and it remained unfinished. It is probably to this that Cicero refers.

the right, which are conjoined by nature. The Stoics have agreed with him in maintaining that whatever is right must be expedient, and that nothing can be expedient which is not right. Now if Panaetius were the sort of man to say that virtue ought to be cultivated because it is productive of utility, as those do who measure the desirableness of objects by the pleasure or the freedom from pain that they may afford, he might in that case have said that expediency is sometimes repugnant to the right. But since he belongs to the class of men who regard what is right as alone good, and consider life as made neither better by the acquisition nor worse by the loss of those things which with a certain show of expediency are in conflict with the right, it does not seem as if he ought to have introduced a discussion in which what appears to be expedient should be compared with what is right. For what the Stoics term the supreme good, to live in conformity with nature, means, as I think, to be always in harmony with virtue, yet to make free choice among things in general that are in accordance with nature, only on condition of their not being repugnant to virtue. Such being the case, some think that this comparison is not properly brought forward, and that no practical lessons ought to have been given under this head. Indeed, that which is properly and with literal truth called the right is found in the wise alone, nor can it ever be separated from virtue; while in those not possessed of perfect wisdom, the perfect right itself cannot possibly be, but only semblances of the right. For all these duties discussed in the present treatise — contingent,[1] as the Stoics call them — are common, and are largely practised, and many attain to them by excellence of natural disposition and by advancement in knowledge. But that duty which the Stoics term the right is perfect and absolute, and, in the phrase of those same philosophers, has all the numbers,[2] nor can it come into the possession of any one except the wise man. But when anything is done in which contingent duties are manifest, it seems to be abundantly perfect, because people in general do not understand what in it is wanting to perfection, while so far as they do understand, they think nothing omitted. The like is of ordinary occurrence in poems, pictures, and many other matters, namely,

[1] Latin, *media*, which, literally translated, conveys no meaning. *Contingent* expresses, perhaps, as well as any single word the Stoic conception of the ordinary duties performed by persons not philosophers. The truly wise or ideal man (for the extreme Stoics denied that he had ever existed) discerned the absolute right in its very essence, by direct intuition. Other men performed duties, not because they were intrinsically right, but because each specific act of duty had for them its rule or law in external circumstances.

[2] Most commentators say that the allusion here is to the rhythmical movements in dancing and gymnastic exercises, in which he who was perfect was said to have or to keep all the numbers. It seems to me more probable that Cicero refers to the Pythagorean doctrine of numbers, specific numbers denoting perfection of specific kinds, and "all the numbers" designating absolute perfection.

that the unskilled view with delight and commendation things that do not deserve praise, because, I suppose, there is in them something good of a kind to take the fancy of the ignorant, who are incapable of determining what defect there may be in the several objects thus placed before them ; while after they have been taught by experts, they readily change their opinion.

4. These duties which I am discussing in the present treatise the Stoics call a sort of second-grade duties, not belonging to the wise alone, but common to them with the whole human race. Thus all in whom there is a virtuous disposition are favorably inclined to them. Nor, indeed, when the two Decii or the two Scipios are commemorated as brave men, or when Fabricius is called just, is the example of fortitude sought from them, or of justice from him, as from men in the strict sense of the term "wise ;" for neither of them was wise as we would have the word " wise " understood. Nor yet were the men who were esteemed and surnamed Wise, Marcus Cato and Caius Laelius, wise in this sense, nor yet those famous seven ;[1] but from their constant practice of common duties they bore to a certain degree the semblance and aspect of wise men.[2] Therefore,

---

[1] The seven sages of Greece, — Bias, Chilo, Cleobulus, Pittacus, Periander, Solon, and Thales.

[2] There is a striking analogy between the ideal man of the Stoics whom man never saw, and the Christian ideal of humanity but once realized in human form, and with reference to which as

while it is an error to compare the right properly so called with expediency when repugnant to it, at the same time that which is commonly called right, and is held sacred by those who want to be regarded as good men, should never be compared with external goods; and it is as incumbent on us to defend and preserve that right which is on a level with our apprehension, as it is on the wise to cherish the right properly and truly so called. Otherwise, if any progress toward virtue has been made, it cannot be maintained. Enough has now been said about those who are reputed as good men on account of the discharge of common duties. But those who measure everything by the standard of gain and personal convenience, nor are willing that these goods should be outweighed by virtue, are accustomed, in their plans of life, to compare the right with what they deem expedient; good men are not so accustomed. I therefore think that when Panaetius said that men are wont to hesitate in this comparison, he meant precisely what he said; for he said only that they were wont, not that they ought, to hesitate. And, indeed, it is in the utmost degree base not only to prize what seems expedient above what is right, but even to compare them with each other and to incline to doubt with regard to them. What is it, then, that is wont sometimes to occasion doubt and may seem worthy of consideration? I

incarnate the best Christians hold the same position that was held by the warriors, patriots, and sages here named with reference to the Stoic ideal.

believe that if doubt ever occurs, it is as to the
actual character of that which is under consideration; for it often happens, under special circumstances, that what is wont for the most part to be
accounted as wrong is found not to be wrong.   Let
a case which admits of a wider application be taken
by way of example.   What greater crime can there
be than to kill not only a man, but an intimate
friend ?   Has one, then, involved himself in guilt
by killing a tyrant, however intimate with him ?[1]
This is not the opinion of the Roman people, who
of all deeds worthy of renown regard this as the
most noble.   Has expediency, then, got the advantage over the right ?   Nay, but expediency has followed in the direction of the right.

Therefore, that we may be able to discriminate
without mistake, if at any time what we call expedient shall seem repugnant to what we conceive of
as right, there must be established some general
rule,[2] which if we recognize in the comparison of
things, we shall never be false to our duty.   But
this rule shall be in close accordance with the
method and system of the Stoics, whom I am following in this treatise, because though by the early
Academics and by the Peripatetics who were for-
merly identical with them those things that are
right are preferred to those that seem expedient,

[1] The reference here is, obviously, to the friendly relation in
which Brutus stood to Caesar.

[2] Latin, *formula.*

yet these themes are discussed in a loftier tone by
those to whom both whatever is right is also expedient, and there is nothing expedient that is not
right, than by those to whom anything right can be
otherwise than expedient, or anything expedient
otherwise than right. Moreover, my sect of the
Academy gives me broad liberty, so that I have a
right to defend whatever seems to me probable.
But I return to the general rule.

5. For a man to take anything wrongfully from
another, and to increase his own means of comfort
by his fellow-man's discomfort, is more contrary to
nature than death, than poverty, than pain, than
anything else that can happen to one's body or his
external condition.[1] In the first place, it destroys
human intercourse and society; for if we are so
disposed that every one for his own gain is ready to
rob or outrage another, that fellowship of the human
race which is in the closest accordance with nature
must of necessity be broken in sunder. As if each
member of the body were so affected as to suppose
itself capable of getting strength by appropriating
the strength of the adjacent member, the whole body
must needs be enfeebled and destroyed, so if each
of us seizes for himself the goods of others, and

---

[1] This is the general rule, or *formula*, referred to in § 4. It
embraces all forms of wrong-doing from man to man, and thus
extends to all offences under the second and third of Cicero's divisions of duty, but would not include sins under the first and
fourth.

takes what he can from every one for his own emolument, the society and intercourse of men must necessarily be subverted. It is, indeed, permitted, with no repugnancy of nature, that each person may prefer to acquire for himself, rather than for another, whatever belongs to the means of living; this, however, nature does not suffer, — that we should increase our means, resources, wealth, by the spoils of others. Nor is this so merely by the law of nature and of nations; but also by those statutes of particular communities on which the body politic in each state depends for its safety, it is in like manner enacted that no one can be permitted to injure another for his own benefit. It is to this that the laws look, it is this that they mean, that the union of citizens shall be secure; and those who dissever it they restrain by death, exile, imprisonment, fine. Moreover, much more is this end effected by the reason inherent in nature, which is the law of gods and of men, which he who wills to obey — and all will obey it who desire to live according to nature — will never so act as to seek what belongs to another and to appropriate to himself what he has taken from another. For loftiness and largeness of soul, and therewith affability, justice, kindness, are more in accordance with nature than pleasure, than life, than wealth, to despise which and to count them as naught when compared with the common good is the token of a great and lofty mind. To take aught from another for one's own benefit is, then, more opposed to nature than death, or pain, or any other adverse experience. At the same time, it is more in accordance with nature to assume the greatest labors and discomforts for the preservation and succor of all nations, were it possible, imitating that Hercules whom human gratitude, commemorative of his services, exalted to a seat among the gods, than to live in isolation, not only free from all causes of disturbance, but even in the fulness of sensual gratification, abounding in resources of every kind, nay, even surpassing all others in beauty and in strength. Therefore every man endowed with a mind of superior excellence and brilliancy prefers the former to the latter mode of life, whence it may be inferred that man, when obedient to nature, cannot injure man. Still further, he who maltreats another that he himself may obtain some benefit, either is unaware that he is acting contrary to nature, or else thinks that poverty, pain, loss of children, of kindred, of friends, is to be avoided rather than wrong-doing to a fellow-man. If he is unaware that he is acting contrary to nature in maltreating men, how are you to reason with one who takes away from man all that makes him man? But if he thinks that wrong-doing ought indeed to be shunned, but that death, poverty, or pain is much more to be shunned, he errs in imagining any evil affecting the bodily condition or property to be of greater consequence than moral evil.

6. This, then, above all, ought to be regarded by

every one as an established principle, that the interest of each individual and that of the entire body of citizens are identical, which interest if any one appropriate to himself alone, he does it to the sundering of all human intercourse. And further, if nature prescribes this, that man shall desire the promotion of man's good for the very reason that he is man, it follows in accordance with that same nature that there are interests common to all. The antecedent is true; therefore the consequent is true. For this is absurd indeed which some say, that they would take nothing from a parent or a brother for their own benefit, but that it is quite another thing with persons outside of one's own family. These men disclaim all mutual right and partnership with their fellow-citizens for the common benefit, — a state of feeling which dismembers the fellowship of the community. Those, too, who say that account is to be taken of citizens, but not of foreigners, destroy the common sodality of the human race, which abrogated, beneficence, liberality, kindness, justice, are removed from their very foundations. And those who remove them are to be regarded as impious toward the immortal gods; for they overturn the fellowship established among men by the gods, the closest bond of which fellowship is the opinion that it is more contrary to nature for man to take anything from man for his own benefit than to endure all forms of discomfort, whether external, or bodily, or even mental, which leave room for the exercise of justice. For this one virtue is mistress and queen of all the virtues. One may perhaps say, "Should not then a wise man who is perishing with hunger take away food from another man who is good for nothing?" No, indeed, by no means; for my life is not of greater service to me than is such a disposition of mind as would preclude my injuring any one for my own benefit. What if a good man, to save himself from perishing with the cold, should rob of his clothes the cruel and savage tyrant Phalaris? May he do it? These matters are very easy of determination. If, indeed, you were to take anything from a perfectly worthless man merely for your own benefit, you would perform an inhuman act and one contrary to nature. If, however, you are a person capable, by prolonging your life, of rendering great service to the state and to human society, and for that reason you take something from another person, you would not be blameworthy. But except in such a case, each man must bear his own privations rather than take what belongs to another. Sickness, or poverty, or anything of this kind is not, indeed, more opposed to nature than is the appropriation or coveting of what belongs to another. But at the same time the dereliction of the common good is opposed to nature, for it is unjust; and therefore the very law of nature, which preserves and maintains the good of man, undoubtedly prescribes that the necessaries of life should be transferred from an inefficient and useless man to a

wise, good, brave man, whose death would make a
large deduction from the common good, — provided
he effect the transfer in such a way that his self-
esteem and self-love may not furnish a pretext for
wrong-doing.  In this way he will perform his duty
with reference to the good of mankind and to the
human fellowship of which I have so often spoken.
Now as regards Phalaris the decision is very easy;
for we [1] have no fellowship with tyrants, but rather
the broadest dissiliency from them, and this whole
pestiferous and impious class of men ought to be
exterminated from human society.  Indeed, as limbs
are amputated when they are bloodless and virtually lifeless, and injure the rest of the body, so this
beastly savageness and cruelty in human form ought
to be cut off from what may be called the common
body of humanity.  Of this sort are all the questions in which duty is to be determined from circumstances.

7. Panaetius would, I think, have followed up
topics of this kind, had not some accident or some
other occupation frustrated his intention.  Toward
these very inquiries there may be drawn from his
first three books many maxims, from which it can
be clearly seen what is to be avoided on account
of its immorality, and what is not to be avoided
because not absolutely immoral.

But since I am, as it were, putting the topstone

[1] We, i. e. the Roman people.  Cicero evidently has the death
of Caesar in his mind.

on a work incomplete, yet almost finished, as mathe-
maticians are wont, instead of demonstrating everything, to ask that some things be admitted [1] in order
to explain more easily what they want to prove, so
I ask of you, my Cicero, to admit, if you can, that
nothing except what is right is to be sought for its
own sake.  If, however, you cannot grant this without hindrance from the teachings of Cratippus, you
can certainly admit that what is right is to be
sought chiefly for its own sake.  Either proposition
is sufficient for my purpose ; and now this, now
that, seems the more probable, while no other proposition relating to this subject is in any degree probable.  At the same time, Panaetius ought in the
first place to be defended on this point; inasmuch
as he said, not that expediency could ever be in
conflict with the right, — for this he could not consistently say, — but that things that seemed expedient might be thus in conflict.  Indeed, he often
affirms that nothing is expedient which is not also
right, and nothing right which is not also expedient;
and he maintains that no more prolific source of evil
has ever found its way into human society than the
opinion of those who have divorced the expedient
and the right.  Therefore, it was not in order that
on certain occasions we should prefer expediency to
the right, but that we might discriminate without
mistake between appearance and reality, if at any

---

[1] Axioms, which in their very nature do not admit of proof.

time there were a seeming conflict, that he introduced into the plan of his work a seeming, not an actual, collision between the expedient and the right. This division, then, which he left unwritten, I propose to fill out, relying on no authority, from my own resources;[1] for since the time of Panaetius there has been nothing written on this head of a nature to satisfy me, among the works that have come into my hands.

8. When any specious appearance of expediency is presented, one cannot help being impressed by it. But if, when you give it closer attention, you see that there is something morally wrong connected with what thus seems expedient, in that case you are not to sacrifice expediency, but you are to understand that where there is moral wrong expediency cannot be. For if nothing is so contrary to nature as immorality (inasmuch as nature craves things right, and fitting, and consistent), and nothing so in unison with nature as expediency, then it is certain that expediency and immorality cannot exist in the same thing.[2] Still further, if we were born for

---

[1] Latin, *sed, ut dicitur, Marte nostro,* literally, "But, as the saying is, by my own Mars," i. e. fighting my own battle, depending on myself alone.

[2] This was undoubtedly intended as a syllogism, — a favorite mode of statement or argument among the Stoics. It would admit of several logical forms, among others, of the following : —

Expediency is in harmony with nature;

Immorality is not in harmony with nature;

Therefore, what is immoral is not expedient. — A syllogism in Camestres.

virtue, and the right either is alone worthy to be sought (as Zeno maintained), or is assuredly to be regarded as immeasurably outweighing all things else (as is Aristotle's doctrine), then, of necessity, what is right must be either the sole or the supreme good. But what is good is certainly expedient. Consequently whatever is right is expedient.[1] It is then the misapprehension of bad men which, when it lays hold on anything that seems expedient, considers it independently of the question of right. This is the origin of assassinations, poisonings, forgeries of wills. Hence come thefts, embezzlements of public money, plunderings and pillagings of allies and of citizens. Hence, too, proceed the intolerable usurpations of excessive wealth, and, lastly, even in free states, the yearning for sovereign authority, than which nothing can be imagined more foul or more offensive. Men, indeed, in their false appreciation, see the profit of the wrong they do; they see not the punishment, I do not say, of the laws which they often evade, but of the guilt itself, of which the punishment is intensely bitter. Therefore let no quarter be given to this class of doubters, utterly wicked and impious, who deliberate whether they shall pursue what they see to be right, or shall knowingly defile themselves with guilt; for there is

---

[1] Another syllogism, in Barbara:—
Whatever is good is expedient;
Whatever is right is good (either the sole or the supreme good);
Therefore, whatever is right is expedient.

crime in the mere hesitation, even if they do not go so far as the outward act. Therefore those things in which the very deliberation is criminal ought not to be deliberated at all. Moreover, the hope and expectation of concealment, whether of the act or of the actor, ought to be excluded from every deliberation on the conduct to be pursued. If we have made even the least proficiency in philosophy, we ought to be thoroughly persuaded that, even though we could escape the view of all gods and men, still nothing ought to be done by us avariciously, nothing unjustly, nothing lustfully, nothing extravagantly.

9. For this reason Plato introduces the well-known story of Gyges,[1] who, when the ground had caved away on account of heavy rains, passed down into the opening, and saw, as the story goes, a brazen horse with doors in his sides. Opening these doors, he saw a man of unusual size, with a gold ring on his finger, which drawing off, he put it on his own finger (he was a shepherd in the king's service), and then repaired to the company of the shepherds. There, as often as he turned the part of the ring where the stone was set to the palm of his hand, he became invisible, yet himself saw everything; and was again visible when he restored the ring to its

---

[1] Herodotus makes Gyges, not a shepherd, but the prime minister of Candaules, King of Lydia, and writes that he killed Candaules and succeeded to the kingdom by the queen's connivance and aid. The story of the ring Plato quotes as a tradition, and makes the same use of it in the Second Book of the Republic that Cicero makes of it here.

proper place. Then, availing himself of the advantage which the ring gave him, he committed adultery with the queen, and by her assistance killed
the king his master, and removed by death those
whom he thought in his way. Nor could any one
see him in connection with these crimes. By means
of the ring he in a short time became king of Lydia.
Now if a wise man had this ring, he would not
think himself any more at liberty to do wrong than
if he had it not; for it is right things, not hidden
things, that are sought by good men. Here, however, certain philosophers, by no means ill-disposed,
yet somewhat deficient in acuteness, say that this is
only a fictitious and imaginary story that Plato has
told, — as though, forsooth, he asserted that such a
thing took place or could have taken place. The
meaning of this ring and of this example is as follows: If no one would ever know, if no one would
ever suspect, when you performed some act for the
sake of wealth, power, ascendency, lust, — if it would
remain forever unknown to gods and men, would
you do it? They say that it is impossible. Yet it
is not utterly impossible. But I ask, If that were
possible which they say is impossible, what would
they do? They persist, awkwardly indeed; they
maintain that such a thing could not be, and they
stand firm in this assertion; they do not take in
the meaning of the phrase, "If it were possible."
For when we ask what they would do if they could
conceal what they did, we do not ask whether they

can hide it; but we put them, as it were, on the rack, that if they answer that they would do what seemed expedient if assured of impunity, they may confess themselves atrociously guilty; and if they make the contrary answer, that they may grant that whatever is wrong in itself ought to be shunned. Let us now return to the subject under discussion.

10. There occur many cases of a nature to perplex the mind under the aspect of expediency,— cases in which the real question is not whether the right is to be sacrificed on account of the greatness of the benefit to be gained (for that is unquestionably wrong), but whether that which seems expedient can be done without guilt. When Brutus deposed his colleague Collatinus from the consulship, he might seem to have done this unjustly; for Collatinus had been the associate of Brutus, and his assistant in measures for the expulsion of the royal family. But when the chief men of the state had come to the determination that the kindred of Superbus, and the name of the Tarquins, and the remembrance of kingly government must be put out of the way, what was expedient—that is, care for the well-being of the country — was so entirely right that it ought to have satisfied Collatinus himself. Thus expediency became valid on account of the right that was in it, without which, indeed, there could not have been any expediency. Not so, however, in the case of the king who founded the city; for a bare show of expediency struck his mind. When it

seemed to him better to reign alone than with a colleague, he killed his brother. He set aside both brotherly affection and humanity, in order to attain what seemed expedient, yet was not so; and then offered in defence the pretext of the wall, — a mere show of right, improbable in itself, and insufficient even if true. He was therefore entirely in the wrong. With his leave I would say it, whether he be Quirinus or Romulus.[1] Nevertheless, advantages that are properly our own we are not to abandon, or to yield up to others, if we ourselves need them; but each one must minister to his own advantage only so far as it may be done without wrong to others. Chrysippus,[2] who has written many sensible things, wisely says: "He who is running a race ought to endeavor and strive to the utmost of his ability to come off victor; but it is utterly wrong for him to trip up his competitor, or to push him aside. So in life it is not unfair for one to seek for himself what may accrue to his benefit; but it is not right to take it from another."

But in the case of friendships there is the greatest perplexity as to duty, it being equally opposed to duty to withhold what you can rightfully concede to a friend, and to concede what is not right. Office, wealth, pleasure, other things of that sort, are

---

[1] Whether he be god or man. Romulus was deified and worshipped under the name of Quirinus.

[2] A Stoic, and the most logical interpreter of the doctrines of the Stoic school.

certainly never to be preferred to friendship. At
the same time a good man will do nothing against
the state, or in violation of his oath or of good faith,
for the sake of his friend, not even if he were a
judge in his friend's case. For

"He drops the friend, when he puts on the judge." [1]

He will yield so far to friendship as to wish his
friend's case to be worthy of succeeding, and to
accommodate him as to the time of trial within
legal limits. But inasmuch as he must pass sentence upon his oath, he will bear it in mind that he
has God for a witness, that is, as I think, his own
conscience, than which God himself has given man
nothing more divine. In this view, it is an admirable custom derived from our ancestors — if we
would only adhere to it — that when a favor is
asked of a judge, it is in the words, " So far as it
can be done without a breach of good faith." A
request proffered in such terms applies to things
which, as I just said, can be granted by a friend who
is acting as a judge. On the other hand, were one
to feel bound to do all that friends might desire,
such connections ought to be considered as not
friendships, but conspiracies. I am speaking of
ordinary friendships; for in the case of wise and
perfect men there can be nothing of the kind. It
is related that Damon and Phintias,[2] Pythagoreans,

---

[1] A verse from an unknown poet.
[2] Valerius Maximus writes this name Pythias.

were so disposed toward each other, that when Dionysius the tyrant had fixed for one of them the day of
execution, and he that was condemned to death asked
for a few days' respite to make arrangements for the
care of his family, the other became surety for his
appearance, to die in his stead if he did not return.
When he returned on the day appointed, the tyrant,
admiring their mutual good faith, begged them to
admit him to their friendship as a third person. In
fine, whenever what seems expedient in friendship
comes into competition with what is right, let the
apparent expediency be disregarded; let the right
prevail. Moreover, when in friendship things that
are not right are demanded, religion and good faith
are to take precedence of friendship. Thus will the
choice of duty, which is the subject of our inquiry,
be determined.

11. But it is in affairs of state that wrong is the
most frequently committed under the show of expediency. Our own people were thus guilty with
reference to the demolition of Corinth. The Athenians acted with still greater severity in decreeing
that the men of Aegina,[1] who were able seamen,
should have their thumbs cut off. This seemed expedient; for Aegina was too threatening on account

---

[1] This, if authentic, must have taken place in the fifth century
before the Christian era. It is mentioned in no extant work of
any Greek historian. It is related by Aelian, who, indeed, wrote
in Greek, but was an Italian, lived as late as the reign of Ha-
drian, and embodied in his work floating traditions with authentic
history.

of its proximity to the Piraeus. But nothing that is cruel is expedient; for cruelty is in the utmost degree hostile to human nature, which ought to be our guide. Those also are to be blamed who prohibit foreigners from living in their cities, and expel them, as Fannius did in the time of our fathers, and Papius more recently.[1] It is indeed right that one who is not a citizen should lack the full privileges of citizenship, as is enacted by the law passed under the consulship of those very wise men Crassus and Scaevola; but it is clearly inhumane to prohibit foreigners from living in the city. On the other hand, a worthy renown rests upon the instances in which the show of public benefit is despised in comparison with the right. Our history is full of examples of this kind, while often at other times, especially in the second Punic war, when, after the disaster of Cannae, the people manifested greater spirit than ever in prosperity. There was no symptom of fear, no intimation of peace. Such is the power of the right, that it eclipses the show of expediency. When the Athenians were utterly unable to sustain the assault of the Persians, and determined that, deserting the city and leaving their wives and children at Troezen, they would go on board of their ships and defend the liberty of Greece by their fleet, they stoned to death a certain Cyr-

---

[1] Both of these men, in their respective tribunates, procured the passage of laws by which foreigners, temporarily resident in Rome, were compelled to leave the city.

silus who pressed upon them the advice to stay in
the city and receive Xerxes. He, indeed, seemed
to advocate expediency; but expediency did not
exist, when the right was on the other side. Themistocles, after the victory in the Persian war, said in
a popular assembly that he had a plan conducive to
the public good, but that it was not desirable that
it should be generally known. He asked that the
people should name some one with whom he might
confer. Aristides was named. Themistocles said to
him that the fleet of the Lacedaemonians, which
was drawn ashore at Gytheum, could be burned
clandestinely, and if that were done, the power of
the Lacedaemonians would be inevitably broken.
Aristides, having heard this, returned to the assembly amidst the anxious expectation of all, and said
that the measure proposed by Themistocles was very
advantageous, but utterly devoid of right. There-
upon the Athenians concluded that what was not
right was not expedient, and they repudiated the
entire plan which they had not heard, on the authority of Aristides. Better this than our conduct in
holding pirates free from all exactions,[1] our allies
tributary.[2]

[1] After Pompey had suppressed piracy, the Cilician pirates
whom he had subdued were formed into a flourishing colony, and
subsequently entered into friendly and helpful relations with
Antony.

[2] The people of Marseilles, king Deiotarus, and, in fine, all the
allies that had adhered to the Pompeian faction, were burdened
with heavy tribute under Caesar's government.

12. Let it be settled, then, that what is wrong is never expedient, not even when you obtain by it what you think to be of advantage to you. Nay, the mere thinking that what is wrong is expedient is in itself a misfortune. But, as I have already said, there often occur cases of such a nature that expediency seems in conflict with the right, so that it must be ascertained by close examination whether it is really thus in conflict, or whether it can be brought into harmony with the right. Of this class are questions like the following: If, for example, a good man has brought from Alexandria to Rhodes a large cargo of corn, when there is a great scarcity and dearth at Rhodes and corn is at the highest price, — in case this man knows that a considerable number of merchants have set sail from Alexandria, and on his passage he has seen ships laden with corn bound for Rhodes, shall he give this information to the Rhodians, or shall he keep silence and sell his cargo for the most that it will bring? We are imagining the case of a wise and good man. We want to know about the thought and feeling of such a man as would not leave the Rhodians uninformed if he thinks it wrong, but who doubts whether it is wrong or not. In cases of this kind Diogenes of Babylon,[1] an eminent Stoic of high

---

[1] Diogenes was one of the three philosophers sent on an embassy from Athens to Rome (B. C. 155), to deprecate the payment of a heavy fine imposed on the Athenians. Aulus Gellius characterizes his eloquence as moderate and sober (*modesta et sobria*).

authority, is wont to express one opinion, Antipater[1] his pupil, a man of superior acuteness,
another. According to Antipater, all things ought
to be laid open, so that the buyer may be left in
ignorance of nothing at all that the seller knows.
According to Diogenes, the seller is bound to dis-
close defects in his goods so far as the law of the
land requires, to transact the rest of the business
without fraud, and then, since he is the seller, to
sell for as much as he can get. " I have brought
my cargo ; I have offered it for sale; I am selling
my corn for no more than others ask, perhaps even
for less than they would ask, since my arrival has
increased the supply. Whom do I wrong?" On the
other side comes the reasoning of Antipater: " What
say you ? While you ought to consult the welfare
of mankind and to render service to human society,
and by the very condition of your being have such
innate natural principles which you are bound to
obey and follow, that the common good should be
your good, and reciprocally yours the common good,
will you conceal from men what comfort and plenty
are nigh at hand for them ? " Diogenes, perhaps, will
reply as follows : " It is one thing to conceal,
another not to tell. Nor am I now concealing

---

[1] Little is known of Antipater, and of his works nothing
remains ; but from the incidental notices of his character and
opinions, and of the reverence in which he and his memory were
held, we have reason to believe that his opinions both in ethics
and in theology were in advance of his age. He was the teacher
of Panaetius.

anything from you, by not telling you what is the
nature of the gods, or what is the supreme good, —
things which it would profit you much more to
know than to know the cheapness of wheat. But
am I under the necessity of telling you all that it
would do you good to hear?" "Yes, indeed, you
are under that necessity, if you bear it in mind that
nature establishes a community of interest among
men." "I do bear this in mind. But is this community of interest such that one can have nothing
of his own? If it be so, everything ought, indeed,
to be given, not sold."

13. You see that in this whole discussion it is
not said, "Although this be wrong, yet, because it
is expedient I will do it;" but that it is expedient
without being morally wrong, and, on the other side,
that because it is wrong it ought not to be done. A
good man sells a house on account of some defects,
of which he himself is aware and others ignorant.
Perhaps it is unhealthy, and is supposed to be
healthy, — it is not generally known that snakes
make their appearance in all the bedrooms, — it is
built of bad materials, and is in a ruinous condition;
but nobody knows this except the owner. I ask, if
the seller should have failed to tell these things to
the buyer, and should thus have sold his house
for a higher price than he could have reasonably
expected, whether he would have acted unjustly or
unfairly? "Yes, he would," says Antipater; "for
what is meant by not putting into the right way

one who has lost his way (which at Athens exposed a man to public execration), if it does not include the case in which a buyer is permitted to rush blindly on, and through his mistake to fall into a heavy loss by fraudulent means ? It is even worse than not showing the right way ; it is knowingly leading another into the wrong way." Diogenes, on the other hand, says : "Did he who did not even advise you to buy, force you to buy ? He advertised for sale what he did not like ; you bought what you did like. Certainly, if those who advertise a good and well-built house are not regarded as swindlers, even though it is neither good nor properly built, much less should those be so regarded who have said nothing in praise of their house. For in a case in which the buyer can exercise his own judgment, what fraud can there be on the part of the seller ? And if all that is said is not to be guaranteed, do you think that what is not said ought to be guaranteed ? What could be more foolish than for the seller to tell the defects of the article that he is selling ? Nay, what so absurd as for an auctioneer, by the owner's direction, to proclaim, 'I am selling an unhealthy house'?" Thus, then, in certain doubtful cases the right is defended on the one side; on the other, expediency is urged on the ground that it is not only right to do what seems expedient, but even wrong not to do it. This is the discrepancy which seems often to exist between the expedient and the right. But I must state my decision in these cases; for I introduced them, not to raise the inquiry concerning them, but to give their solution. It seems to me, then, that neither that Rhodian corn-merchant nor this seller of the house ought to have practised concealment with the buyers. In truth, reticence with regard to any matter whatever does not constitute concealment; but concealment consists in willingly hiding from others for your own advantage something that you know. Who does not see what sort of an act such concealment is, and what sort of a man he must be who practises it? Certainly this is not the conduct of an open, frank, honest, good man, but rather of a wily, dark, crafty, deceitful, ill-meaning, cunning man, an old rogue, a swindler. Is it not inexpedient to become liable to these so numerous and to many more bad names?[1]

14. But if those who keep silence deserve censure, what is to be thought of those who employ absolute falsehood? Caius Canius, a Roman knight, a man not without wit and of respectable literary culture, having gone to Syracuse, for rest, as he used to say, not for business, wanted to buy a small estate, to which he could invite his friends, and where he could take his own pleasure without intruders. When his wish had become generally known, a certain Pythius, who was doing a banker's business at Syracuse, told him that he had a country-seat, not,

---

[1] Latin, *vitiorum nomina*, literally, names of vices.

indeed, for sale, but which Canius was at liberty to use as his own if he wished to do so; and at the same time he invited the man to supper at the country-seat for the next day. He having accepted the invitation, Pythius, who, as being a banker, was popular among all classes, called the fishermen together, asked them to fish the next day in front of his villa, and told them what he wanted them to do. Canius came to supper at the right time; a magnificent entertainment was prepared by Pythius ; a multitude of little boats were in full sight ; every fisherman brought what he had taken ; the fish were laid down at the feet of Pythius. Then Canius says, "Prithee, what does this mean ? So many fish here ? So many boats ?" And he answered, "What wonder ? All the fish for the Syracuse market are here ; they come here to be in fresh water. The fishermen cannot dispense with this villa." Canius, inflamed with longing, begs Pythius to sell the place. He hesitates at first. To cut the story short, Canius over-persuades him. The greedy and rich man buys the villa for as high a price as Pythius chooses to ask, and buys the furniture too. He gives security ; he finishes the business. Canius the next day invites his friends. He comes early ; he sees not a thole-pin. He asks his next neighbor whether it is a fishermen's holiday, as he sees none of them. "Not so far as I know," was the reply. "No fishermen are in the habit of fishing here. I therefore yesterday could not think what had occurred to bring them." Canius was enraged. But what was he to do? My colleague and friend, Aquillius,[1] had not then published his forms of legal procedure in the case of criminal fraud, as to which when he was asked for a definition of criminal fraud, he replied, "When one thing is pretended, another done." This is perfectly clear, as might be expected from a man skilled in defining. Pythius, then, and all who do one thing while they pretend another, are treacherous, wicked, villanous. Therefore nothing that they do can be expedient, when defiled by so' many vices.

15. But if the definition of Aquillius is correct, pretence and concealment should be entirely done away with. Thus a good man will neither pretend nor conceal anything for the sake of buying or selling on better terms. Indeed, this offence of criminal fraud had been previously punished both by the laws, as in the case of guardianship, by the Twelve Tables, and in the defrauding of minors, by the Plaetorian law,[2] and also, without express statute,

---

[1] Caius Aquillius Gallus was Cicero's colleague in the praetorship, and as the head of the judiciary introduced into his official edict, and thus into the body of the Roman law, important improvements in the legal remedies against criminal fraud (*dolus malus*).

[2] This law (B. C. 192) first discriminated between minors (*minores*) under twenty-five years and those of age (*majores*). By this law fraud on minors was punished by a heavy fine and public infamy. It provided also that contracts with minors should be voidable, unless made with the consent of a guardian appointed by the praetor.

by legal decisions in which the phrase "As good faith requires" is employed.[1] In other decisions the following words hold a prominent place : — in the case of arbitration about a wife's property, "The better, the more equitable ;"[2] in the case of trust-property, "Fair dealing between good men."[3] What then? Can there be any admixture of deceit in "The better, the more equitable?" Or when "Fair dealing between good men" is specified, can anything be done craftily or fraudulently? But, as Aquillius says, criminal fraud consists in misrepresentation. All falsehood, then, must be removed from contracts. The seller must not employ a sham purchaser, nor the buyer one to depreciate the article on sale by too low a bid. Let either party, if it comes to naming the price, say once for all what he will give or take. Quintus Scaevola, the son of Publius, when he asked to have the price of an

[1] The text is slightly ambiguous, at least to a modern translator. Some commentators render the sentence as referring to decisions as to contracts in which the words *ex fide bona* are used ; others, as referring to decisions in which these words are employed.

[2] *Melius aequius*, prescribing, as I understand, a leaning in the wife's favor in any questions about the dowry to be restored · in case of the wife's death, or, in that age more frequently, in case of her divorce.

[3] *Inter bonos bene agier*, in the case of property conveyed to a trustee on condition of its being restored, — a condition sometimes to be inferred from the circumstances under which the conveyance was made rather than from the express terms of the contract.

estate that he was buying named once for all, and
the seller had complied with his request, said that
he thought it worth more, and added a hundred
thousand sesterces.[1] There is no one who would
say that this was not the act of a good man; but
men in general would not regard it as the act of a
wise man, any more than if he had sold an estate
for less than it would bring. This, then, is the mis-
chievous doctrine, — regarding some men as good,
others as wise, according to which notion Ennius
writes that the wise man who cannot provide for
his own advantage is wise in vain. I would readily
account this saying true, if I were agreed with
Ennius as to what one's advantage is. I see, indeed,
that Hecato of Rhodes, a disciple of Panaetius, says,
in the books on Duties which he dedicated to Quintus Tubero: "It is a wise man's duty, while he
does nothing contrary to morals, laws, and customs,
to have regard to his private fortune. For we desire
to be rich, not for ourselves alone, but for children,
kindred, friends, and most of all for the state, —
considering that the means and resources of individual citizens are the wealth of the state." The act
of Scaevola just named cannot, then, be in any way
pleasing to Hecato. Nor is any great praise or favor
to be rendered to a man who merely says that he
will not do for his own benefit what is unlawful.
But if pretence and concealment constitute criminal

---

[1] *Sestertii*, or one hundred *sestertia*, equivalent to between four
and five thousand dollars of our money.

fraud, there are very few transactions entirely free from criminal fraud; or if he is a good man who does good to those to whom he can and injures no one, of a certainty we shall not easily find that good man. We conclude, then, that it is never expedient to do wrong, because wrong-doing is always disgraceful; and because to be a good man is always right, it is always expedient.

16. As to landed property, the law of the state enacts that defects known to the seller must be made known in selling it; and while by the law of the Twelve Tables it was enough for such things as were guaranteed to be made good, and for the seller who made false statements with regard to them to pay double damages, the jurisconsults have determined that the legal penalty applies also to reticence.[1] Their doctrine is, that whatever defect there may be in an estate, if the seller knows it, he is bound to make it good. Thus when the augurs were going to take an augury on the Capitol,[2] and had ordered Tiberius Claudius Centumalus, who had a house on the Coelian hill, to pull down those parts of it which were so high as to obstruct their view of the heavens, Claudius advertised the detached house,

[1] This statement refers not to praetorian edicts or to judicial decisions, but to the interpretation of the statute by men learned in the law.

[2] The augurs faced the east in taking their observations, so that a high house on the Coelian hill might obstruct their view, all the more so, if one of the augurs had any private grudge against the owner of the house.

and sold it. The purchaser was Publius Calpurnius
Lanarius. The same notice was given to him by
the augurs. So when Calpurnius had complied with
the order, and had ascertained that Claudius advertised the house for sale after being notified of the
decree of the augurs, he procured the appearance of
Claudius before a legally appointed arbitrator, suing
him for damages for his breach of good faith. Marcus Cato pronounced the decision, the father of my
friend Cato — for as other men are named from their
fathers, so is the father of that illustrious man to be
named from his son — he, I say, as judge, pronounced
the decision : "Forasmuch as the seller knew of
that decree when he sold the house, and did not
make it known, the damage ought to be made good
to the buyer." He thus decided that in good faith a
defect known by the seller ought to be known by
the buyer. If this was a right decision, then neither
that corn-merchant, nor the seller of the unhealthy
house, had a right to keep silence. But all such
cases of reticence cannot be comprised in the law of
the land, though those which can be so comprised
are carefully repressed. Marcus Marius Gratidianus,
my kinsman, had sold to Caius Sergius Orata the
house which he had bought from that same Orata a
few years before. The estate was subject to certain
rights of way, which Marius had omitted to name
in the contract of sale. The case was brought into
court. Crassus was advocate for Orata, Antonius
for Gratidianus. Crassus laid stress on the law that

any defect known by the seller and not mentioned ought to be made good. Antonius rested his plea on the equity of the case, that inasmuch as the defect was not unknown to Sergius, who had previously sold the house, there was no need of its being specified, nor had the purchaser been imposed upon, since he knew perfectly well to what the estate purchased was liable. To what purpose do I name these things? That you may understand that our ancestors did not approve of chicanery.[1]

17. But the laws remove chicanery in one way, philosophers in another, — the laws, so far as they can lay hold on overt acts; philosophers, so far as they can reach such cases by reason and understanding. Reason, then, demands that nothing be done ensnaringly, nothing under false pretence, nothing deceitfully. Yet is it not ensnaring to spread nets, even if you do not start and hunt your victims? For beasts themselves often fall into nets without being pursued. Is it not thus that you advertise a house, — put up a notice of sale as a net; sell the house on account of its defects; and some unwary person runs into the net? Yet such is the degenerate state of feeling, that I find this neither accounted as morally wrong, nor yet forbidden by statute or by the civil law, though it is forbidden by the law of nature. For there is — though I have

---

[1] Cicero here means to say: "Cases of this kind are comparatively recent. The records of the earlier and better times contain no such instances of chicanery."

often said it, there is need of its being said still oftener — a fellowship of men with men, which has, indeed, the broadest possible extent ; a more intimate union, of those who belong to the same race ; one closer still, of those who belong to the same state. Therefore our ancestors recognized a distinction between the law of nations and the law of the state. What is the law of the state is not necessarily also the law of nations ; but whatever is the law of nations ought also to be the law of the state. But of true law and genuine justice we have no real and lifelike representation ; their shadow and semblances alone are ours. Yet would that we might follow even these ! For they are drawn from excellent models presented by nature and truth. How precious are these words : "That I be not taken in and defrauded through you or on account of my confidence in you !" What a golden formula is this : "As ought to be done between good men, fairly and without fraud !"[1] But the great question is, Who are the "good men," and what is it to be "fairly done"? Quintus Scaevola, the head of the pontifical college, said that there was the greatest force in all decisions to which the phrase "in good faith" was annexed, and he thought that as the term "good faith" had the broadest application as employed in guardianships, partnerships, trusts, commissions, purchases, sales, hiring, leases, which

---

[1] These were forms used in deeds of trust.

make up the whole system of social transactions, it required a judge of superior capacity to determine — especially as there are often cross-suits — what each party is bound to render, and to whom, in the satisfaction of just claims.

There should, then, be an end of chicanery and of that cunning which means indeed to pass for prudence, but is an entirely different thing and at the widest distance from it; for prudence has its proper place in the choice between good and evil, while cunning,— if whatever is immoral is evil — prefers evil things to good.

Nor is it only with reference to landed estate that the civil law, derived from nature, punishes cunning and fraud; but in the sale of slaves also all fraud on the part of the seller is prohibited. By the edict of the aediles,[1] the seller who may rightly be supposed to know about the health, the truant habits, the dishonesty of the slave, is bound to guarantee the purchaser against damage. The case of persons who sell slaves that have recently come to them by inheritance is different.[2] From these instances it is clear, since nature is the fountain of law, that it is in accordance with nature that no one should act so as to prey upon another's ignorance. Nor can there be found any greater source of mischief to

[1] The regulation of the markets was among the functions of the aediles.

[2] One who had just come into an inheritance of human chattels could not be expected to know their characters and habits.

human society than the false show of intelligence in the practice of cunning. Hence spring those countless cases in which expediency seems to be in conflict with the right. For how few will be found who, if impunity and absolute secrecy were offered, could refrain from wrong-doing!

18. Let us, if you please, try the principle that I have laid down, with reference to cases in which the generality of mankind do not think that any wrong is committed. For I am not going to speak here of assassins, poisoners, forgers of wills, thieves, peculators, who are to be repressed, not by words and philosophical discussion, but by chains and imprisonment. Let us consider the things that are done by those who are accounted as good men. Certain persons brought from Greece to Rome a forged will of Lucius Minucius Basilus, a rich man. That they might more easily maintain its validity, they made joint-heirs with themselves Marcus Crassus and Quintus Hortensius, the most influential men of that time, who, while they suspected the forgery, yet being conscious of no guilt of their own in the case, did not spurn the paltry present that came to them through the crime of others. What then? Is their freedom from the positive offence of forgery sufficient for their acquittal? I think not, though I loved one of them while he lived,[1] and am not an

---

[1] Hortensius. As rival orators, Cicero and Hortensius might have been on other than friendly terms, had they not both been intimate friends of Atticus.

enemy of the other now that he is dead.[1]  But when
Basilus meant that his sister's son, Marcus Satrius,
should take his name, and had made him his heir, —
I mean this patron of the Picene and Sabine territory, to the disgrace of our time,[2] — was it right
that those distinguished citizens should have the
property, and that nothing save the name should
descend to Satrius?  Forsooth, if he who does not,
when he can, ward off or repel wrong is guilty of
injustice (as I showed in the First Book), what is to
be thought of him who, so far from repelling, abets
the wrong?  To me, indeed, genuine inheritances
do not seem right, if sought by knavish blandish-
ments, — by attentions rendered not from sincere
but simulated kindness.[3]  In such affairs, one thing
sometimes appears expedient, another right.  But it
is a deceptive appearance; for the standard of expediency is the same as that of right.  He who does

---

[1] Cicero charged Crassus with complicity in Catiline's conspiracy, and Crassus was a friend of Clodius, Cicero's bitterest enemy.
After Cicero's return from exile, Crassus sought a formal recon-
ciliation with Cicero, and there was no subsequent manifestation
of hostility on his part.

[2] It was shameful, as Cicero could not but think, that states
whose citizens nominally enjoyed the rights of Roman citizenship
should need official patrons, and equally so, in his esteem, that
those patrons should be, like Satrius, selected from among Antony's adherents and satellites.

[3] It is a singular feature of Roman society in and after Cicero's
time that the legacy-hunters (*heredipetæ*) should have been
numerous enough and should have found dupes enough to form
a distinct class, and almost a recognized profession.

not clearly see this is capable of any kind of fraud, of any crime. For he who thinks, "That is indeed right, but this is expedient," will dare in his ignorance to divorce things united by nature, — a state of feeling which is the source of all frauds, wrongs, crimes.

19. Therefore, if a good man could by snapping his fingers make his name creep surreptitiously into rich men's wills, he would not use this power, no, not even though he were absolutely certain that no one would ever have the least suspicion of it. But had you given this power to Marcus Crassus, that by snapping his fingers he could get his name inserted in a will though he were not really the heir, I warrant you he would have danced in the forum. A just man, however, and one whom we feel to be a good man, will take nothing from any one to transfer it to himself. Let him who marvels at this confess that he knows not what a good man is. But if one would only develop the idea of a good man wrapped up in his own mind, he would then at once tell himself that he is a good man who benefits all that he can, and does harm to no one unless provoked by injury.[1] What then ? Must not he do harm, who, as if by enchantment, displaces the true heirs, to put himself in their stead ? "Is he not, then," some one may say, "to do what is serviceable, what is expedient ?" Yes, but let him understand that nothing unjust can be either expedient

[1] See Book I. § 7.

or serviceable. He who has not learned this cannot be a good man. In my boyhood I heard from my father that Fimbria, who had been consul, was appointed judge in the case of Marcus Lutatius Pinthias, a Roman knight, not otherwise than respectable, who had laid a wager, to be forfeited if he did not prove himself to be a good man. Fimbria said that he would never act as judge in the case, lest, if he decided against Pinthias, he might deprive a worthy man of his reputation, or if he decided in his favor, he might seem to have pronounced some ordinary person to be a good man, while such a character was made up of innumerable duties and merits. To a good man, then, even in the conception of Fimbria, not to say of Socrates,[1] nothing can by any possibility seem expedient that is not right. Therefore such a man will not dare, not only to do, but even to think anything which he may not venture to proclaim publicly. Is it not shameful that philosophers should be in doubt about these matters as to which even peasants have no doubt? From the peasants sprang the old saying that has become proverbial. When they commend any one's honesty and goodness, they say that you might trust him to play odd and even[2] with you in

[1] Of a man of the world, not of a philosopher.

[2] Latin, *mices. Micare,* or *micare digitis* (to flash with the fingers), denotes the game of *mora,* which is still a favorite recreation, or rather mode of gambling, with the Roman populace, and may be often seen in the streets. Story, in his *Roba di Roma,* describes it as follows: "Two persons place themselves opposite

the dark. What does this mean, unless that what
is unbecoming is not expedient, even if you could
obtain it without any one being able to prove it
against you? Do you not see that according to
this proverb there could be no apology either for
that Gyges of whom I have spoken, or for this man
whom I just now supposed by way of illustration,
who by snapping his fingers could convert the
inheritances of a whole community to his own use?
For as what is immoral, though concealed, cannot
be in any way made right, so it cannot be brought
about that, in spite of the opposition and repugnancy of nature, what is not right should in any
case be expedient.

20. Yet it may be said that when the gain is very
great, there is justifying cause for wrong-doing.
When Caius Marius had no near prospect of the
consulship, and still remained in obscurity the
seventh year after he had been praetor, nor gave
any token that he was ever going to offer himself
as a candidate for the consulship, having been sent
to Rome by his commander Quintus Metellus, a
man and citizen of the highest eminence, whose

---

each other, holding their right hands closed before them. They
then simultaneously and with a sudden gesture throw out their
hands, some of the fingers being extended, and others shut up on
the palm, — each calling out in a loud voice, at the same moment,
the number he guesses the fingers extended by himself and his
adversary to make. If neither cry out aright, or if both cry out
aright, nothing is gained or lost ; but if only one guess the true
number, he wins a point."

lieutenant he was, he charged Metellus before the
Roman people with needlessly protracting the war,
intimating that if they had made him consul, he
would in a short time have given Jugurtha either
living or dead into the power of the Roman people.
And so he was indeed made consul; but in bringing into odium by a false accusation a citizen of the
highest worth and eminence, whose lieutenant he
was [1] and by whom he had been sent home, he
made a wide departure from good faith and honesty.
My kinsman Gratidianus [2] did not play the part of
a good man on the occasion when he was praetor,
and the tribunes of the people had called into
counsel the college of praetors, that the currency
might have its standard fixed by a joint resolution;
for the value of money was then so fluctuating that
no one could know how much or how little property
he had.   The tribunes and praetors jointly framed a
decree, specifying the penalty and the judicial proceedings for its violation, and agreed to mount the
rostrum together in the afternoon.   The others went
their several ways; while Marius from the seats of
the tribunes directly mounted the rostrum, and
alone announced the decree which had resulted
from their combined action.   This affair, if you want

[1] The relation of a *legatus*, or lieutenant, to his commander
was, in Roman ethics, not unlike that of a son to his father, so
that Marius in his conduct toward Metellus might have been pronounced *impius*.

[2] Marcus *Marius* Gratidianus, son of an adopted son of the
brother of Caius Marius.

to know, brought him great popularity. Statues
were erected in his honor in all the streets; incense
and wax tapers were burned before them. To cut
the story short, no man was ever more cherished by
the multitude. These are the cases which sometimes perplex one in the discussion, — cases where
the matter in which honesty is transgressed is not
so very great, while that which is obtained by means
of it is of the very highest value; as, for Marius, it
was not so irredeemably shameful to forestall the
popular favor from his colleagues and the tribunes
of the people, while by this means to become consul,
the end which he then had in view,[1] seemed in the
highest degree desirable. But there is one rule for
all cases, which I would have profoundly impressed
on your mind, — either that what seems expedient
must not be wrong, or if it be wrong, that it must
not seem to be expedient. Can we deem either that
Marius or this a good man? Unfold and examine[2]
your own consciousness, that you may see what within
it is the aspect, shape, and conception of a good man.
Does it fall in with the character of a good man
to lie, to slander, to forestall, to deceive? Nothing
certainly can be less in harmony with it. Is there,
then, any object of so much value, or any advantage
so worthy of your quest, that you should forfeit for

---

[1] He never obtained the consulship; but the very popularity
won by his agency in settling the fluctuating currency was in
Sulla's eyes a crime which made him one of the dictator's earliest
victims.

[2] Latin, *explica atque excute*, literally, unfold and shake out.

it the glory and reputation of a good man? What is there that so-called expediency can bring to you of equal worth with what it takes from you, if it robs you of the reputation of a good man, and deprives you of truth and honesty? For what difference does it make, whether one turns himself from a man into a beast, or in the form of a man carries the moral obduracy of a beast?

21. What? Do not those who violate all that is right and virtuous if they can only obtain power, do the same thing with him who chose to have even for a father-in-law the man by whose audacity he himself might become powerful?[1] It seemed expedient to him to avail himself of the other's unpopularity for his own great advancement. He did not perceive how unjust this was to the country, how base, and how harmful. The father-in-law himself had always on his lips the Greek verses from the Phoenissae, which I will render as I can, awkwardly it may be, but still so as to be intelligible:—

> "Transcend the right in quest of power alone;
> In all things else hold fast the bond of kindred."

It was criminal in Eteocles,[2] or rather in Euripides, to except that one thing which was the most

---

[1] Pompey married Caesar's daughter, and hoped to gain ascendency by throwing upon Caesar the unpopularity of whatever was offensive in the measures of the triumvirate.

[2] Words put into the mouth of Eteocles when, having agreed to hold the sovereignty of Thebes with his brother on alternate years, he refused to resign the throne at the end of the first year.

wicked of all. Why, then, do we gather up crimes
on a small scale, fraudulent heirships, bargains,
sales? Here you have a man who desired to be
king of the Roman people, and who accomplished
his purpose. Whoever says that this desire was
right, is mad ; for he approves of the destruction of
laws and of liberty, and deems their foul and detestable suppression glorious. But as for him who
acknowledges that it is not right to usurp sovereign
power in a state which was and which ought to be
free, yet that it is expedient for him who can do so,
by what remonstrance, or rather by what reproach,
can I strive to draw him back from so grave an
error ? For (ye immortal gods !) can the basest and
foulest parricide [1] committed upon his country be
expedient for any man, even though he who has
made himself thus guilty be called parent by the
citizens whom he has brought under the yoke ?
Expediency, then, ought to be measured by the
right, and so indeed, that the two, though expressed
by different names, may have to the ear the same
sound. I do not accord with the opinion of the
multitude who ask what can be more expedient
than the possession of sovereign power; on the
other hand, I find nothing more inexpedient for him
who has obtained this power unjustly, when I begin
to recall reason to things as they really are. For

[1] The term parricide (*parricidium*) was always employed with
reference to heinous crimes against the country (*patria*) as well as
to the murder of a father.

can anxieties, solicitudes, terrors by day and by night, a life crowded full of snares and of perils, be expedient for any one ? Attius says,

"The throne has many faithless, loyal few."

But of what throne does he say this ? Of one that was held by right, transmitted from Tantalus and Pelops. How much more, think you, must those words apply to that king who by the army of the Roman people subdued that very Roman people, and forced to servile obedience a state not only free, but ruling over whole races of men ? What misgivings of conscience must he have had on his mind, think you ? What inward wounds ? Whose life can be serviceable to himself if he holds it on condition that whoever deprives him of it will rise to the summit of favor and glory ? But if these things which seem in the highest degree expedient are yet inexpedient because full of disgrace and wickedness, we ought to be thoroughly convinced that there is nothing expedient that is not right.

22. This, while often indeed at other times, was expressly decreed by Caius Fabricius in his second consulate and by our Senate, in the war with Pyrrhus. For Pyrrhus having made war with the Roman people without provocation, and there being a contest for supremacy with that high-minded and powerful king, a deserter came from him to the camp of Fabricius, and promised that, if he would give him his price, as he had come secretly, so he

would return secretly to the camp of Pyrrhus, and
kill him by poison. Fabricius sent the man back
to Pyrrhus, and that act of his was commended by
the Senate. Yet if we look to the appearance and
the popular opinion of expediency, a single deserter
would have put an end to that great war and to a
dangerous enemy of the empire. But it would have
been a great disgrace and scandal for one with whom
the contest was for glory to have been overcome by
crime, not by valor. Which, then, was the more
expedient, for Fabricius, who was in this city what
Aristides was in Athens, or for the Senate, which
never divorced expediency from honor, to contend
 with the enemy by arms, or by poison ? If empire
is to be sought for the sake of glory, let crime, in
which there can be no glory, be excluded ; but if
power be sought by any means whatsoever, it can
be of no service conjoined with infamy. Therefore
the proposal of Lucius Philippus, the son of Quintus, was not expedient, namely, that the states
which by a decree of the Senate Lucius Sulla, for
money received from them,[1] had freed from tribute
should be taxed again, without our returning to them
the money that they had paid for their exemption.
The Senate assented to the proposal, to the disgrace
of the empire. Pirates keep better faith. But it
may be said that the revenues were increased, and

---

[1] Probably some of the petty states that had been obtained by
the conquest of Mithridates, and to which Sulla had sold this
exemption for the money needed to pay his army.

it was therefore expedient. How long will men dare to call anything expedient that is not right? Can odium and infamy be of service to any empire, which ought to be supported by glory and by the good-will of its allies? I was often at variance even with my friend Cato. He seemed to me to guard the treasury and the revenues too obstinately, to refuse everything to the farmers of the revenue,[1] and many things to our allies; while we ought to be generous to our allies, and to deal with the farmers of the revenue as leniently as we individually do with our own tenants, especially as the union of orders [2] to which such a course would conduce is for the well-being of the state. Curio, too, was entirely in the wrong, when he said that the cause of the colonies north of the Po [3] was just, but always added, "Let expediency prevail." He should have said that it was not just because it was not expedient for the state, rather than have acknowledged it as just while saying that it was not expedient.

[1] They were sometimes in the position of rural tenants when the crops failed. There were times when the under-farmers (*portitores*) could not make their collections of taxes in full and in due season; but Cato was in favor of the most rigid treatment of the farmers-general (*publicani*), however they might fare with their subordinates.

[2] The farmers of the revenue were of equestrian rank, and it was deemed desirable that the *equites* should be on good terms with the Senate.

[3] They had claimed the full rights of citizenship in common with the colonies south of the Po, — a claim which Caesar granted.

23. The Sixth Book of Hecato's treatise on Duties is full of such questions as these. "Ought a good man in a time of extreme dearth to continue to furnish food to his slaves?" He discusses both sides of the question, yet at the last makes expediency rather than humanity the standard of duty. He asks, "If in a storm at sea something must be thrown overboard, shall it be a valuable horse, or a slave of no value?" In this case interest inclines in one direction, humanity in the other. "If in case of shipwreck a fool gets possession of a plank, shall a wise man wrest it from him if he can?" He answers in the negative, because it would be unjust. "What may the master of the ship do in such a case? May he not take possession of the plank as his own property?" Not by any means. He has no more right to do this than to throw a passenger from the ship into the sea because the ship is his own. Until it arrives at the port to which passage has been taken, the ship belongs not to the master, but to the passengers. · "What if there be but one plank for two shipwrecked passengers, both wise men? Shall they both try to get possession of it, or shall one yield to the other?" One should give it up to the other; but let that other be the one whose life is the more valuable, either for his own sake or for that of the state. "What if their claims are equal?" There must be no quarrel between them, but one must yield to the other, as if he had come off second-best in drawing lots or at odd and even.

"What if a father pillages temples, or makes an underground passage to the public treasury? Shall the son give information to the magistrates?" That indeed would be wrong. Nay, he may even defend his father if he should be publicly accused. "Does not then duty to the country take precedence of all other duties?" Yes, indeed; but it is for the welfare of the country to have citizens dutiful toward their parents. "What if the father should attempt to usurp supreme authority, or to betray the country? Shall the son keep silence?" Yes, but he will implore his father not to do so. If that is of no avail, he will take him earnestly to task; will even threaten him; yet at the last, if there is danger of great harm to the country, he will prefer the country's safety to his father's safety. He asks also, "If a wise man by an oversight takes counterfeit coins for good, when he ascertains what they are, shall he pay them for good money to his creditors?" Diogenes says, Yes; Antipater, No, and I agree with him. "Ought the seller of wine that he knows will not keep, to tell his purchasers?" Diogenes says that there is no need of it; Antipater thinks that a good man would tell. These questions are like mooted points of law, among the Stoics. "In selling a slave, are his faults to be told? Not such faults as, if not mentioned, would by the civil law throw the slave back upon the vender's hands, but such as his being a liar, a gambler, thievish, a drunkard?" Antipater says that they are to be told; Diogenes, that they

15

are not. "If any one selling gold thinks that it is brass that he is selling, will a good man tell him that it is gold, or will he buy for a shilling [1] what is worth a thousand shillings?" It is plain enough by this time what I think of these things, and what a difference of opinion there is among the philosophers that I have named.[2]

24. It is asked whether agreements and promises are always to be kept, if made — to borrow the language of the praetorian edict — neither by force nor by criminal fraud. If one had given to a person a remedy for the dropsy, and had stipulated that he should never afterward use the medicine, — in case that person, having been cured by the medicine, were to contract the same disease some years afterward, and could not obtain from him with whom he had made the agreement leave to use the remedy again, what ought he to do? Since he who would refuse such a request would be inhuman, and no harm can be done to him by using the remedy, regard should be paid to life and health. What, if

---

[1] Latin, *denarius.* The *denarius* was about equivalent to our New England shilling.

[2] Though Cicero seems to have thought rightly on these questions, the very fact that they could be mooted among members of the school of philosophy most noted for its high ethical standard, gives us a not very favorable impression of pre-Christian ethics; and the contrast between these Stoics and certain of the post-Christian, though non-Christian moralists, gives color to the belief that Christianity had somehow penetrated where it was not recognized.

*Does Christianity share all the cut it*

a wise man were asked by one who wants to make
him his heir to the amount of a million of sesterces,[1]
to promise that before taking possession of his
legacy he will dance in the forum publicly by daylight, and if without this promise the testator would
not have given the legacy? Shall he keep his
promise, or not? I should prefer that he had not
made the promise, and this I think would have
befitted his dignity. But since he has made the
promise, if he thinks it disgraceful to dance in the
forum, the least immoral falsehood of the two will
be for him to break his promise and decline the
legacy, unless, perchance, he can expend that money
for the state in some great emergency of need, so
that even dancing in the forum for the country's
benefit would not be disgraceful.

25. Nor yet are those promises to be kept which
are not for the advantage of those to whom you
have made them. To go back to myths, Phoebus
having promised his son Phaethon that he would do
whatever he wished, the son wished to be taken up
into his father's chariot. He was taken up, and
before he was fairly seated, he was consumed by a
thunderbolt. How much better would it have been
if in this case the father's promise had not been
kept! What shall be said of the promise that Theseus exacted of Neptune? Neptune having promised to grant him three wishes, he asked for the
death of his son Hippolytus, whom he suspected of

[1] Nearly half a million of our money.

intrigue with his stepmother; but when Theseus had obtained his wish he was plunged into the deepest sorrow.[1] What shall we say of Agamemnon, who, having vowed to Diana the most beautiful creature that should be born that year in his kingdom, immolated Iphigenia, because no creature more beautiful was born that year in the kingdom? It would have been better not to keep the promise than to commit so foul a crime. Therefore promises are sometimes not to be kept, nor are deposits always to be returned. If one had deposited a sword with you when he was of sound mind, and were to ask for it in a fit of insanity, to restore it would be wrong; not to restore it, your duty. What if he who had deposited money with you were to levy war against the country? Should you deliver up the trust? I think not; for you would act against the state, which ought to be nearest to your affection. Thus many things which seem to be right by nature become wrong by circumstances. To keep promises, to abide by agreements, to restore trusts, by a change of expediency becomes wrong. I think that I have now said all that is necessary about those things that seem to be expedient under the pretext of prudence, yet are really opposed to justice.

---

[1] In Book I. § 10, this example is used to substantially the same purpose, — the object there being to show, under the head of justice, that the literal keeping of a promise may, under some peculiar stress of circumstances, be virtually wrong; while here the proposition is that the intense stress of expediency may make that right which has the *prima facie* aspect of wrong.

But since in the First Book I derived duties from four sources of right, I will adopt the same division in showing how hostile to virtue are those things that seem to be expedient, yet are not so. I have already, indeed, treated of prudence which cunning would fain imitate, and of justice which is always expedient. There remain two divisions of the right, one of which is witnessed in the greatness and superiority of a lofty mind; the other, in the shaping and government of the life by self-restraint and temperance.

26. It seemed expedient to Ulysses,[1] — as the story has come to us through some of the trage-dians;[2] Homer throws no such suspicion on him, but there are tragedies that charge him with having

[1] I leave the ellipsis as it stands in the original.

[2] Notably, Euripides and Sophocles, as also some of the Roman tragedians. The story is that he, as one of Helen's suitors, was the first to propose the oath by which they bound themselves, in case the marital rights of the successful suitor should be invaded, to join in defending or avenging him. But when he was called upon to fulfil his part of the covenant, he feigned insanity, yoked an ox and an ass together, ploughed a field with them, and sowed it with salt. Palamedes took Telemachus, and placed him where his father's plough would go over him, and Ulysses, by stopping his plough so as to avoid doing harm to the child, showed that he was not demented, and was thus compelled to keep his agreement and to bear his illustrious part in the Trojan war.

Palamedes, even a more decidedly mythical personage than Ulysses, is fabled to have been the inventor of light-houses, meas-ures, scales, the discus, dice, the alphabet, and the mode of regulating sentries, — in fine, an impersonation of nearly all the practical wisdom of the old world.

purposed to escape service in the war by feigning insanity. The purpose was not right. "Yet it was expedient," some one perchance will say, "to reign in Ithaca, and to live at his ease with his parents, with his wife, with his son. Do you think any honor won in daily labors and perils to be compared with this quiet life?" I, indeed, think that this quiet life was to be despised and spurned; for the repose which was not right I cannot regard as expedient. What, think you, would Ulysses have heard, had he persevered in his pretended insanity? when, after his greatest achievements in the war, he hears from Ajax:—

> " He who first took the oath, and he alone,
> As you all know, forswore his plighted faith.
> Madness he feigned, the compact to evade,
> And had not Palamedes, with keen vision
> And wise device, unmasked his craft and cunning,
> He still had been a perjured recreant." [1]

It was, indeed, better for him to fight, not only with the enemy, but with the waves, as he did, than to desert Greece confederated with one mind to carry war into the country of the barbarians.[2] But let us leave myths and foreign instances. Let us come to fact and to our own history. Marcus Atilius Regulus, when in his second consulship[3] he was captured by troops in ambush under Xanthippus the Lace-

[1] These verses are from the *Armorum Judicium* of Pacuvius.

[2] The Greeks called all except themselves barbarians.

[3] He was proconsul in Africa, his second consulship having expired the previous year.

daemonian, — Hamilcar, Hannibal's father, being
commander-in-chief, — was sent to the Senate under
oath that, unless certain prisoners of high rank were
restored to the Carthaginians, he would himself
return to Carthage. He on his arrival at Rome saw
the semblance of expediency — but, as fact shows,
regarded it as delusive — to be in his own home,
with his wife, with his children ; to maintain unimpaired his consular dignity, regarding the calamity
which he had incurred in battle as but a common
incident in the fortunes of war. Who can deny that
this was expedient ? Who, think you ? Magnanimity and Fortitude deny this.

27. Do you ask for better authorities ? It is the
property of these virtues to fear nothing, to despise
all human vicissitudes, to think nothing that can
happen to man intolerable. And so what did he
do ? He came to the Senate; he stated his mission;
he refused to give his own vote in the case, because
so long as he was bound by his oath to the enemy
he was not a senator. He, however, denied the
expediency of sending back the prisoners of war
("O foolish man," some one may have said, "to
contend against his own interest ") ; for the prisoners were young men and good leaders, while his
vigor was already impaired by age. By virtue of
his influence the prisoners were retained. He himself returned to Carthage, nor did his love for his
country or his kindred retain him. Yet he then
well knew that he was returning to an implacably

cruel enemy and to excruciating punishment; but he considered his oath as binding. Thus when he was killed by being deprived of sleep [1] he was in a better condition than if he had remained at home, a captive old man, a perjurer of consular dignity. "Yet he acted foolishly, in not only declining to vote in favor of sending the prisoners back, but in also giving his advice against their release." How, foolishly? Did he act foolishly, if it was for the good of the state? Can what is harmful to the state be expedient for any citizen?

28. Men subvert the very foundations of nature when they separate expediency from the right. For we all seek what is expedient, and are drawn toward it, nor can we anyhow resist its attraction. Forsooth, who is there that shuns the things that are expedient? Or rather, who is there that does not pursue them with the utmost earnestness? But because we never can find what is expedient, save in good report, honor, right, we therefore esteem these first and highest; we regard expediency thus

[1] Accounts as to the death of Regulus vary, — some saying that he was put into a chest studded in the inside with nails; others, that his eyebrows were cut off, and his face then exposed to the full glare of an African sun; while it would seem that Cicero had a still different account, that he died from enforced wakefulness. Niebuhr sees no reason to suppose that he was tortured or killed, indeed, has very little faith in any part of his story, and it is maintained by some of the writers of his school that the report of his being so tortured was circulated in Rome to excuse the cruelties perpetrated by the family of Regulus on Carthaginian captives committed to their charge.

defined as not so much respectable as indispensable.
" What is there in an oath ? " some one may say.
" Do we fear the anger of Jupiter ? It is indeed
an opinion common to all philosophers, not only to
those who believe that the Deity neither does anything nor makes manifestation of himself to any
other being,[1] but equally to those who suppose him
always active in the government and direction of
events,[2] that the Deity is never angry and never
does harm. But what more harm could an angry
Jupiter have done than Regulus did to himself?
There was then no power of religion that could
supersede expediency so weighty. Was his motive
to avoid acting basely ? In the first place, the least
of evils are to be chosen. Was then the evil in the
baseness of which you speak so great as that of the
torture which he had to bear ? Then again, this
sentiment from Attius, —

> ' Faith hast thou broken ? '
> ' I neither gave nor give faith to the faithless,'[3]

although put into the mouth of an impious king,
yet is admirably well said." They add also that as
we say that some things seem expedient that are
not so, in like manner they say that some things
seem right that are not so, — as, for instance, this
very thing, returning to torture for the sake of pre-

---

[1] The Epicureans.   [2] The Stoics.

[3] This is from the *Atreus* of Attius. Thyestes asks Atreus,
*Fregistin fidem ?* and Atreus replies that he denies the obligation
of keeping good faith with treacherous men.

serving an oath inviolate seems right, yet becomes
wrong, because a promise extorted by force ought not
to be ratified.    They still further say that whatever
is highly expedient becomes right, even if it did not
seem so before.

29. This is the substance of the case against
Regulus.  Let us now examine the first count. " He
had no need to fear any harm from Jupiter's anger ;
for Jupiter is not wont either to be angry or to do
harm."   This argument is of no more force against
Regulus than against any oath.   But in an oath the
point to be considered is not what it threatens, but
what it means.   For an oath is a religious affirma-
tion.   Therefore what you positively promise as in
the presence of God ought to be performed.   The
question, then, no longer concerns the anger of the
gods (for there is no such thing), but it is a question
of honesty and good faith.   Ennius well says : —

"Oh genial, bright-winged Faith, and oath of Jove !"

He, then, who profanes an oath, profanes Faith,
whom — as it is said in Cato's speech — our ancestors chose to have in the Capitol,[1] hard by the
shrine of Jupiter Best and Greatest.   "Then, too,
Jupiter, if he had been angry, could not have done
more harm to Regulus than Regulus did to himself."
Undoubtedly, if pain were the only evil.   But philosophers of the highest authority affirm, not only
that pain is not the greatest evil, but that it is not

---

[1] Numa was said to have built a temple to Fides on the Capi-
toline Hill.

even an evil. For the truth of this do not, I beg
you, cast reproach on the testimony of Regulus, a
witness not of moderate, but, so far as I know, of
the very highest credibility; for what more trustworthy witness can you ask than the chief man of
the Roman people, who of his own accord endured
torture that he might keep duty inviolate? Then,
as to what they say about "the least of evils," —
namely, that meanness is to be preferred to calamity,
— is there any evil greater than meanness? If such
meanness as there is in the case of bodily deformity
has in it something offensive, in what vile esteem
ought the depravation and foulness of soul to be
held! Therefore those who take the strongest
ground on these matters dare to affirm that meanness of soul is the only evil; those who speak with
more laxity do not hesitate to call it the greatest of
evils. As to the saying,

> "I neither gave nor give faith to the faithless,"

the poet had a right to say this; for in bringing
Atreus upon the stage, he had to support the character. But if those who are reasoning against Regulus assume that the faith pledged to a faithless
person is null, let them look to it lest there be
found here a subterfuge for perjury. Even belligerents have rights, and an oath is often to be kept
sacred with an enemy. For what was so sworn that
the mind of him who took the oath at the time confessed the obligation, ought to be fulfilled; what was

not so sworn may be left unfulfilled without perjury.[1] Thus you would not pay robbers a price that
you had agreed to pay for your life; it is no wrong
if you fail to do this after having promised with
an oath.  For a robber [2] is not included in the list
of belligerents, but is the common enemy of all.
Between him and other men there ought to be
neither mutual confidence nor binding oath.  For
it is not simply swearing what is false that constitutes perjury; but it is perjury not to perform what
you have sworn, as it is expressed in our legal form,
in the purpose of your own mind.  Euripides makes
a proper distinction when he says :—

> " I swore in words; my mind I keep unsworn." [3]

But Regulus was bound in duty not to violate
conditions and agreements made in war and with
an enemy; for his concern was with a rightful

[1] The most patent sophistry.  If the sincerity with which an
oath is taken be the sole ground of its sacredness, free license is
opened for unnumbered forms of perjury, — certainly for the pro-
verbially untrustworthy custom-house oaths, than which the civilization of our time has had no fouler opprobrium.

[2] Latin, *pirata*, which commonly means a robber by sea, yet is
sometimes used, as here, in the same sense with *praedo*, a robber
by land.

[3] From the Hippolytus.  Unfortunately for Cicero's use of
these words, which Euripides puts into the mouth of Hippolytus,
the oath is regarded as sacred.  He had sworn that he would not
divulge Phaedra's guilty secret to his father, and in the scene
from which this verse is taken he says that but for the oath into
which he had been entrapped unawares, nothing could have prevented him from telling his father the whole truth.

and legitimate enemy, and as to such enemies our whole fecial law and many mutual rights were valid between them and us. If it were not so, the Senate would never have surrendered to enemies men of renown as prisoners.

30. This they did in the case of Titus Veturius and Spurius Postumius, who, in their second consulship, after the defeat at Caudium when our soldiers passed under the yoke, having concluded a peace with the Samnites without the consent of the people and the Senate,[1] were delivered up to the Samnites. At the same time Tiberius Numicius and Quintus Maelius, then tribunes of the people, because the peace had been concluded by their authority, were also surrendered, to consummate the repudiation of the treaty with the Samnites. Moreover, Postumius himself, who was among those surrendered, advised and supported the measure. Many years afterward the same thing was done by Caius Mancinus, who, having made a treaty with the Numantians without authority from the Senate, was surrendered to them, he himself advising the passage by the people of the decree to that effect, reported from the Senate by Publius Furius and

---

[1] The commanders, even were they the consuls, could not lawfully make a treaty. The most that they had a right to do was to make a truce or an armistice, or to name terms of peace to be ratified by the Senate and people. The principle thus recognized is so obvious that if war be not, in Cicero's phrase, "opposed to nature," it might seem to belong to the law of nature no less than to the law of nations.

Sextus Atilius. `He acted more honorably than Quintus Pompeius, who when he was in the same case begged to be let off, and the decree of surrender was not passed. Here what seemed expedient preponderated over the right; in the former instances the false show of expediency was outweighed by the authority of the right. "But a promise exacted by force ought not to be performed." As if force could be brought to bear upon a brave man. " Still, why did he go to the Senate for the special purpose of dissuading them from surrendering the prisoners?" In asking this question, you cast reproach on what was greatest in Regulus. For he did not make himself judge in his own case; he undertook the management of the case that the Senate might decide upon it, and unless he had led the way to the decision by his authority, the prisoners would have been returned. Thus Regulus would have remained safe in his own country. Because he thought that this was not expedient for the country, he believed it right for himself to express his opinion and to suffer. Still further, as to their saying that whatever is highly expedient becomes right, the truth is that it is right, not that it becomes right. For nothing is expedient which is not also right, nor is anything right because it is expedient, but expedient because it is right. Therefore from many remarkable examples it would be difficult to name one more praiseworthy or illustrious than this.

31. Of all that is thus praiseworthy in the conduct of Regulus the one thing specially worthy of
admiration is that he gave his advice in favor of
retaining the prisoners. That, having thus advised,
he returned, now seems to us admirable; in those
times he could not have done otherwise. This
merit therefore belongs to the times, not to the man;
for our ancestors considered no bond more stringent
than an oath in securing good faith. This is declared by the Sacred Laws;[1] it is declared by treaties
in which good faith even with an enemy is made
binding; it is declared by the examinations and
sentences of the censors, who used to take no more
diligent cognizance of any other subject than they
took of oaths. Marcus Pomponius, tribune of the
people, gave notice of an impeachment to Lucius
Manlius, son of Aulus, after his dictatorship, because
he had illegally added a few days to the term of his
dictatorship. He also reproached him with having
banished his son Titus from society and ordered

---

[1] Latin, *leges sacratae.* They were, probably, laws for the
violation of which the criminal and his property were nominally
consecrated to some god, i. e. he execrated and his property confiscated, — laws which had in Cicero's time become obsolete, as had
the strict exercise of the censorial animadversion in the case of
perjury. Of this class were the laws passed on Mons Sacer on the
occasion of the first secession of the plebeians from Rome. Some
commentators say that these laws were the only ones known as
*leges sacratae.* Yet another opinion is that the *leges sacratae* corresponded to the canon law of Christendom, — that there were
certain offences, perjury among the rest, the legal cognizance of
which belonged to the priests.

him to live in the country. When the young man, the son of Manlius, heard that legal proceedings were instituted against his father, he is said to have hastened to Rome, and to have come to the house of Pomponius at early dawn. On his being announced, Pomponius, supposing that he had come in anger to bring some charge against his father, rose from his bed, and suffering none others to be present, gave orders for the young man to come to him. He, on entering, at once drew his sword, and swore that he would kill Pomponius instantly unless he gave his oath to drop the prosecution. Pomponius, constrained by imminent peril, took the oath ; did not lay the accusation before the people ; told why he had been compelled to drop the case ; discharged Manlius. Such was the importance attached to an oath in those times. This Titus Manlius is the one who obtained his surname[1] near the Anio from a collar taken from a Gaul who had challenged him and was killed by him, in whose third consulship the Latin army was scattered and put to flight near the Veseris, — a very distinguished man, as bitterly severe toward his son[2] as he had been excessively kind to his father.

[1] Torquatus.

[2] Shortly before this very battle of Veseris the consuls gave orders that no Roman should engage in single combat with any soldier of the opposing army. The son of Torquatus, driven almost to madness by the taunts and insults of a Tuscan soldier, accepted his challenge, killed him, and brought the trophies of the successful conflict to his father, who immediately ordered the youth to be beheaded.

32. But as Regulus merits renown for keeping
his oath inviolate, so are those ten whom, after the
battle of Cannae, Hannibal sent to the Senate under
oath that they would return to the camp that had
fallen into the possession of the Carthaginians,
unless they obtained the redemption of the prisoners
of war, to be held in the vilest esteem, if they really
did not return. As to these men accounts vary.[1]
Polybius, a fully trustworthy authority, says that
of ten men of the highest rank who were sent, nine
returned, not having obtained from the Senate the
release of the prisoners, but that one who had gone
back to the camp shortly after leaving it on the pretence of having forgotten something, remained in
Rome. By his return to the camp he maintained

---

[1] This story, it will be remembered, is told in a slightly different form in Book I. § 13. The passage in which that version
of it occurs is wanting in some manuscripts, and omitted in some
editions ; but the critical evidence is in its favor. It is appropriately told in each connection, and Cicero is never unwilling
to tell the same story twice, if it will in each instance serve the
purpose in hand. There seems to have been about the Punic
wars, as about many passages of Roman history, a strange min-
gling of authentic narrative and popular tradition, so that of
events that undoubtedly took place there are often several versions. The science of historical criticism had not been even
conceived of, and we find that writers, Plutarch included, always
select the version of a story that will best point a moral or illustrate a character.

Aulus Gellius says that of the ten Romans sent home by Hannibal eight returned, and two who had evaded their oath by
fraud remained in Rome, branded with ignominy by the censors,
and the objects of universal contempt and scorn.

that he was acquitted of his oath; but wrongly, for deceit aggravates perjury instead of annulling it. This was, then, a foolish cunning perversely assuming the aspect of prudence. The Senate, therefore, decreed that the rogue and cheat should be sent in chains to Hannibal. But there was something still greater on the part of the Roman people. Hannibal held as prisoners eight thousand men, who had not been taken in battle or escaped when in peril of death, but who had been left in camp by Paulus and Varro. The Senate refused to have them redeemed, though it might have been done for a small sum of money, that it might be ingrafted in the minds of our soldiers that they must either conquer or die. Polybius writes that when Hannibal heard this his spirit was broken, because the Senate and the Roman people had borne their reverses with so lofty a mind. Thus does what seems expedient sink out of account when brought into comparison with the right. I ought to add that Acilius, who wrote a history in Greek, says that there were several who returned to the camp to free themselves from their oath by the same equivocation, and that they were branded with every token of ignominy by the censors. We may close this head; for it is perfectly clear that whatever is done with a timid, sordid, abject mind — such as the action of Regulus would have been, had he either given his opinion concerning the prisoners in his own interest and not in that of the state, or consented to remain at home

— is not expedient, because it is infamous, foul, base.

33. There remains the fourth division, comprehending becomingness, moderation, discretion, self-restraint, temperance. Can anything be expedient which is opposed to this choir[1] of such virtues? However, those of the Cyrenaic school[2] and the disciples of Anniceris,[3] philosophers only in name, followed Aristippus in making all good to consist in pleasure, and regarded virtue as commendable only in its pleasure-giving capacity. They having passed almost out of notice, Epicurus holds his ground as an advocate and teacher of nearly the same doctrine. With these I must contend, as the phrase is, with infantry and cavalry,[4] if I mean to guard and main-

---

[1] This figure is used in another instance by Cicero, in the *Tusculanae Disputationes,* Book V. It is also used once in the New Testament, where our English version gives no intimation of it, in 2 Peter i. 5. "With all diligence bring up and lead on in the choir [or dance] (ἐπιχορηγήσατε) on [or next to] faith, virtue," &c.

[2] The Cyrenaic school was founded by Aristippus. See Book I. § 41, note.

[3] Anniceris is regarded as having been of the Cyrenaic school, and differed from Aristippus chiefly in admitting that the social virtues are good in themselves, yet good because, though they sometimes give trouble, their pleasure-yielding capacity transcends the labor, inconvenience, and sorrow that may incidentally result from them.

[4] Latin, *viris equisque,* literally, with men and horses, i. e. in full military array, with all the strength that I can muster, with might and main.

tain the right.   For if not only expediency but
everything appertaining to a happy life consists
in a strong constitution of body and in a reasonable expectation of preserving that constitution, as
Metrodorus [1] writes, certainly this expediency — the
highest expediency in the opinion of those who
thus reason — will be in conflict with the right.
For where, in the first place, shall room be found for
prudence ?   In raking together from every quarter
objects to delight the senses ?   How wretched this
slavery of virtue in bondage to pleasure !   What,
then, is the function of prudence ?   To choose pleasures intelligently ?   Grant that nothing can be more
delightful than this, what can be imagined meaner ?
Then, again, what room is there for fortitude, which
is the contempt of pain and labor, with him who
calls pain the greatest of evils ?   For although Epicurus may in many places, as he does, speak bravely
enough about pain, we are to look, not at what he
says, but at what it is consistent for him to say,
who acknowledged no good except pleasure, no evil
except pain.   Thus also, if I listen to him about
self-restraint and temperance, he says indeed much
in many places ; but, as the phrase is, the water

---

[1] The disciple, inseparable companion, and intimate friend of
Epicurus, and his destined successor, though Epicurus outlived
him by seven years.   He gave his master's philosophy its fullest
development in the direction of sensuality, expressly and seriously
maintaining that the organs of digestion furnish the true test and
measure for everything appertaining to a happy life.

does not run.[1] For how can he commend temperance, who places the greatest good in pleasure? Temperance is inimical to the sensual appetites; but those appetites are the handmaids of pleasure. Yet as to these three virtues they shift and turn as they can, and with no little ingenuity. They bring in prudence as knowledge employed to supply pleasures, to drive away pain. They also explain fortitude after some fashion, calling it the method of taking no account of death and putting up with pain. Temperance, too, they drag in, not very easily indeed, but as well as they can, saying that the highest pleasure amounts to no more than the absence of pain. Justice totters, or rather lies prostrate, and so do all those virtues which belong to social life and the fellowship of the human race. Nor can there be goodness, or generosity, or courtesy, any more than friendship, if they are not to be sought on their own account, but only with reference to pleasure. To sum up the whole in brief, as I have maintained that there is no expediency which is opposed to the right, so I affirm that all sensual pleasure is opposed to the right. All the more do I find fault with Calliphon and Dinomachus,[2] who

---

[1] A figure derived from a watercourse whose flow is obstructed. The idea is : What he says about these virtues does not flow easily, as if he were sincere and thoroughly in earnest.

[2] Their doctrine was that for man pleasure and virtue are both ends of being, — pleasure by nature and from the beginning, virtue after experience of the good that there is in it.

thought that they were going to put an end to the controversy by uniting pleasure with the right, as they might yoke a beast with a man. The right does not accept this union, spurns it, repels it. Nor can the supreme good, which ought to be simple, be mingled and compounded of widely unlike ingredients. But of this — for it is a great theme — I treat more at length elsewhere.[1] As to the subject now in hand, I have sufficiently shown how the matter is to be decided, if at any time what seems to be expedient is repugnant to the right. But if sensual pleasure shall be said even to have the appearance of expediency, it cannot have any union with the right. To make such concession as we can in favor of pleasure, the most that we can say of it is that it may perhaps give some seasoning to life; it certainly is of no benefit.

You have from your father, my son Marcus, a gift, in my opinion, great; but that will be according to the use that you make of it. Although you are to take in these three books as guests among the lectures of Cratippus, yet as if, in case I had come to Athens — which I should indeed have done had not the country with a loud voice recalled me midway — you would sometimes have listened to me as well as to Cratippus, so since my voice reaches you by means of these volumes, you will give them as much time as you can, and you can give them as

---

[1] In the Second Book of *De Finibus Bonorum et Malorum.*

much time as you please. When I shall have become fully aware that you take pleasure in science of
this type, while I shall, as I hope, at no great distance of time, talk with you face to face, I shall none
the less, while we are apart, converse with you
though absent from you. Farewell, then, my Cicero,
and believe that you are very dear to me, and will
be much more dear if you shall find your happiness
in writings like these and in such precepts as they
contain.

# INDEX.

# CICERO DE SENECTUTE

## (ON OLD AGE).

TRANSLATED

WITH

AN INTRODUCTION AND NOTES.

By ANDREW P. PEABODY.

BOSTON:
LITTLE, BROWN, AND COMPANY.
1887.

University Press:
John Wilson and Son, Cambridge.

# SYNOPSIS.

# INTRODUCTION.

AFTER the death of Julius Caesar, and before the conflict with Antony, Cicero spent two years in retirement, principally at his Tusculan villa. It was the most fruitful season of his life, as regards philosophy. To this period (B. C. 45 or 44) the authorship of the *De Senectute* is commonly assigned. In his *De Divinatione*, in enumerating his philosophical works, he speaks of this treatise on Old Age as "lately thrown in among them,"[1] and

---

[1] *Interjectus est etiam nuper.* The chief ground for doubt as to the time of its composition is that Cicero seems to speak of this book as "thrown in among" the six Books of the *De Republica*, written during his consulate ; while he sometimes gives a very broad sense to *nuper*, as when he writes, *nuper, id est paucis ante sæculis.* But between his mention of the *De Republica* and that of the *De Senectute* he names the *Consolatio*, which was written in B. C. 45, after the death of his daughter. *Interjectus*, as I suppose, refers, not to the date, but to the brevity of the treatise, and by virtue of the *etiam* applies equally to the *Consolatio.* "While I have written, earlier or later, the longer works that I have named, I have thrown in among them these smaller treatises."

as meriting a place in the list.   In the *De Amicitia*,
dedicated also to Atticus, he says: " In the *Cato
Major*, the book on Old Age inscribed to you, I introduced the aged Cato as leading in the discussion,
because no person seemed better fitted to speak on
the subject than one who both had been an old man
so long, and in old age had still maintained his pre-
eminence. . . . .  In reading that book of mine, I
am sometimes so moved that it seems to me as if,
not I, but Cato were talking. . . . .  I then wrote
about old age, as an old man to an old man." [1]
Again, Laelius, who is the chief speaker in the
*De Amicitia*, is introduced as saying, " Old age is
not burdensome, as I remember hearing Cato say in
a conversation with me and Scipio, the year before
he died."   Cicero repeatedly refers to this book in
his Letters to Atticus.   In the stress of apprehension about Antony's plans and movements he
writes : " I ought to read very often the *Cato Major*
which I sent to you ; for old age is making me more
bitter.   Everything puts me out of temper."   At a
later time he writes, " By saying that *O Tite, si quid
ego*,[2] delights you more and more, you increase my
readiness to write."   And again, " I rejoice that
*O Tite* [2] is doing you good."

In his philosophical and ethical writings, Cicero
lays no claim to originality ; nor, indeed, did the

---

[1] Cicero and Atticus were not old men when the *De Republica*
was written.

[2] The first words of the *De Senectute.*

Romans of his age, or even of a much later time, regard themes of this kind as properly their own. Philosophy was an exotic which it was glory enough for them to prize and cultivate. This fame appertains pre-eminently to Cicero, equally for his comprehensive scholarship, for his keenness of critical discernment, and for his generous eclecticism. Were it not for his explicit statement, we might not learn from his writings to what sect he accounted himself as belonging. Though he disclaimed the Stoic school, he evidently felt a strong gravitation toward it, and we could ask for no better expositor of its doctrines than we find in him. Indeed, I can discover no reason for his adherence to the New Academy, except the liberty which it left to its disciples to doubt its own dogmas, and to acknowledge a certain measure of probability in the dogmas of other schools.

In this treatise Cicero doubtless borrowed something from Aristo of Chios, a Stoic, to whose work on Old Age — no longer extant — he refers, and he quotes largely from Xenophon and Plato. At the same time, thick-sown tokens of profound conviction and deep feeling show that the work, if not shaped from his experience, was the genuine utterance of his aspirations. What had been his life was forever closed.[1] He was weary and sad. His home was desolate, and could never again be other-

---

[1] *Mihi quidem* βεβίωται, — "Life is indeed over with me." Letters to Atticus, XIV. 21.

wise. His daughter — dearer to him than any other human being had ever been — had recently died, and he had still more recently repudiated her young step-mother for lack of sympathy with him in his sorrow. His only son was giving him great solicitude and grief by his waywardness and profligacy. The republic to which he had consecrated his warm devotion and loyal service had ceased to be, and gave faint hope of renewed vitality. The Senate-house, the popular assembly, and the courts were closed for him, and might never be reopened. He had courted publicity, and had delighted in office, leadership, and influence; but there was now little likelihood that any party that might come into power would replace him, where he felt that he had a right to be, among the guiding and controlling spirits of his time.

Old age with him is just beginning, and it may last long. He is conscious of no failure in bodily or mental vigor, — in the capacity of work or of enjoyment. Yet in all that had contributed to his fame and his happiness, he has passed the culminating point; he is on the westward declivity of his life-way; decrease and decline are inevitable. But shall he succumb to the inevitable in sullen despondency, or shall he explore its resources for a contented and enjoyable life, and put them to the test of experience? He chooses the latter alternative, and it is not as the mere rehearsal of what he has read in Greek books, but with the glow of fresh discovery, and in the spirit of one who is mapping out the ground of which he means to take possession, that he describes what old age has been, what it may still be, and what he yearns to make it for himself. He grows strong, cheerful, and hopeful as he writes, and in coming times of distress and peril he unrolls this little volume for his own support and consolation.

In imitation of the Platonic pattern, followed by him in several previous treatises, he adopts the form of dialogue ; but after the interchange of a few sentences the dialogue becomes monologue, and Cato talks on without interruption to the end. Cato is chosen as the principal interlocutor, because he was the typical old man of Roman history, having probably retained his foremost place in the public eye, and his oratorical power in the Senate and at the bar, to a later age than any other person on record. In his part in this dialogue there is a singular commingling of fact, truth, and myth. The actual details of his life are gracefully interwreathed with the discussion, and the incidental notices of his elders and coevals are precisely such as might have fallen from his lips had he been of a more genial temperament. There is dramatic truth, too, in Cato's senile way of talking, with the garrulity, repetition, prolixity, and occasional confusion of names, to which old men are liable, and in which Cicero merges his own precision and accuracy in the character which for the time he assumes. But as regards the kindly, the aesthetic, and the spiritual traits that make this work so very charming, its Cato is a mythical creation, utterly unlike the coarse, hard, stern, crabbed ex-Censor, who was guiltless equally of taste and of sentiment.

Cicero's reasoning in this treatise is based, in great part, on what old age may be, rather than on what it generally is ; and yet I cannot but believe that, were its cautions heeded, its advice followed, and its spirit inbreathed, the number of those who find in the weight of many years no heavy burden would be largely multiplied. Yet there would remain not a few cases of hopeless inanity and helpless suffering. We are here told, and with truth, that it is often the follies and sins of early life that embitter the declining years ; yet infirmity sometimes overtakes lives that have been blameless and exemplary, nor does the strictest hygienic regimen always arrest the failure of body and of mind. Undoubtedly the worst thing that an old man can do is to cease from labor and to cast off responsibility. The powers suffered to repose lapse from inaction into inability ; while they will in most cases continue to meet the drafts made upon them, if those drafts recur with wonted frequency and urgency. Yet there is always danger that, as in the case of the Archbishop in Gil Blas, the old man who insists on doing his full tale of work will be mistaken in thinking that undiminished quantity implies unimpaired quality.

But apart from the continued life-work, Cicero indicates resources of old age which are as genuine and as precious now as they were two thousand years ago. While the zest of highly seasoned convivial enjoyment, especially of such as abuts upon the disputed border-ground between sobriety and excess, is exhaled, there is fully as much to be enjoyed in society as in earlier years. Perhaps even more; for as friends grow few, those that remain are all the dearer, and in the company of those in early or middle life, the old man finds himself an eager learner as to the rapidly fleeting present, and imagines himself a not unwelcome teacher as to what deserves commemoration in the obsolescent and outgrown past. The tokens of deference and honor uniformly rendered in society to old age that has not forfeited its title to respect are a source of pleasure. They are, indeed, in great part, conventional; but for this very reason they only mean and express the more, inasmuch as they betoken, not individual feeling, but the general sentiment of regard and reverence for those whose long life-record is unblotted.

Rural pursuits and recreations, also, as Cicero says, are of incalculable worth to the aged. The love of nature increases with added years. In the outward universe there is an infinity of beauty and of loveliness. The Creator englobes his own attributes in all his works. What we get from them is finite, solely because the taste and feeling that apprehend

them are finite. But our receptivity grows with
the growth of character, and our revenue of delight
from field and garden, orchard and forest, brook and
stream, sunset clouds and star-gemmed skies, is in
full proportion to our receptivity, and is never so
rich and so gladdening as in the later years of life.
Cicero evidently felt this. There is hardly anything in all his works so beautiful as the sections
of this treatise in which he describes the growth of
the corn and the vine, and the simple joys of a
country home. Indeed, this is almost a unique
passage. The literature of nature is, for the most
part, of modern birth. The classic writers give
now and then, in a single phrase or sentence, a
vivid word-picture of scenery or of some phenome-
non in the outward world; but they seldom dwell
on such themes. Even pastoral poetry sings of the
flocks and their keepers, rather than of their material surroundings. But here we have proof that
Cicero had grown into an appreciation of the wealth
of beauty lying around his villa, far beyond what
would have been possible for him when he sought
its quiet as a refuge from the turmoil and conflicts
of his more active days.

Cicero is right, too, in regarding the presence
of old men in the state as essential to its safety
and well-being. True, their office is, for the most
part, that of brakemen; but on a roadway never
smooth, and passing over frequent declivities, this
duty often demands more strength and skill than are

required to light the fires and run the engine. It is only by a conservatism both wise and firm that progress can be made continuous and reform permanent. Nor is there any imminent probability that old age will furnish a larger array of conservative force than the world needs. If in the advancement of physical and moral hygiene the time should come when the hoary head shall be in due season the normal crown of every man, and, according to the Hebrew hyperbole, "the child shall die an hundred years old," society will have attained a summit-level at which there will be need neither of engineers nor of brakemen.

Meanwhile, it is well for mankind that old men are so few. Were they more numerous, and at the same time worthy to retain the confidence of their fellow-men, the young would lack the exercise and discipline of their powers which alone could fit them for an honorable and useful old age. Death oils all the wheels of life. It is always throwing heavy responsibility on those who do not seek it, but accept it as a necessity, and gird themselves to bear it faithfully and nobly. As in a well-trained army the reserved forces rush in to fill the places of the fallen, so in the battle of life the ranks of the dying are recruited by those who are biding their time. Death is the ripener of manly force and efficient virtue, which would droop under the dense shadow of thoroughly matured and still active service, but are stimulated into full vitality and work-

ing power as the spaces around them are made void.
The very bereavements which are most dreaded and
deplored as utterly irreparable, are the most certain
to be repaired, and often by those who before neither
knew themselves nor were known to be capable of
such momentous charge and duty. Elijah wears his
mantle till he goes to heaven, and there is no other
on earth like it; but when he ascends he drops the
mantle, and his spirit enters into the man who picks
it up. Death is, indeed, looked upon as a calamity
by many whose faith should have taught them better.
The death which closes an undevout and worthless
life may well be dreaded; yet even in such a case
continued life is perhaps to be still more dreaded.
But in the order designed by Infinite Wisdom, and
destined to progressive and ultimate establishment,
death bears a supremely beneficent part, and is an
event only to be welcomed in its appointed season
by him who has brought his own life into conformity with the Divine order.

But death can be regarded with complacency
only when it is looked upon, — as Cicero represents
it, — as not an end, but a way, — as not a ceasing to
live, but a beginning to live. The jubilant strains
in which the assurance of immortality is here
voiced are hardly surpassed in grandeur by St.
Paul's words of triumph when the crown of mar-
tyrdom hung close within his reach. Yet there is
a difference. Cicero's faith transcended, and in
great part created, his reasons for it, and it failed

him in the very crises in which he most needed it; St. Paul "knew in whom he had believed," and his faith was sightlike when death seemed nearest. It is of no little worth to us that Socrates and Plato, Cicero and Plutarch, felt so intensely the pulse-beat of the undying life within. Of inestimably greater evidential value is it, that he whose peerless beauty of holiness made his humanity divine ever spoke of the eternal life as the one reality of human being. But there are for us emergencies of sore need and of heavy trial, times when we go down to the margin of the death-river with those dear to us as our own souls, critical moments when we ourselves are passing under the shadow of death; and at such seasons we can rest on no reasoning, we can be satisfied with no unbuttressed testimony; but our faith can repose in undoubting security on the broken sepulchre, on the risen Saviour, on those words spoken for all time, "Because I live, ye shall live also."

# ATTICUS.

Titus Pomponius, as he was originally named, on his adoption by his uncle prefixed that uncle's name, Quintus Caecilius, to his own, and subsequently, in consequence of his long residence in Athens, assumed, or received and accepted, the surname of Atticus, by which he is known in history. He was born in Rome, 109 B. C., and was Cicero's senior by three years. He belonged to an old Equestrian family, not eminent, but of high respectability. His father was a man of culture and of literary tastes, and gave his son a liberal education. The civil war between the factions of Marius and Sulla broke out in the son's early manhood, and he hardly escaped being a victim of Sulla's proscription. He determined to insure safety by voluntary exile, and, his father being dead, he betook himself with the movable portion of his ample patrimony to Athens, where he lived for twenty years.

He called himself an Epicurean, and, though not deeply versed in philosophy, he probably realized more nearly than any man whose history we know the ethical ideal of Epicurus himself. Supremely, but judiciously selfish; covetous of pleasure, yet with an aesthetic sense which found pleasure only in things decent, tasteful, and becoming; a persist-

ent and loyal friend, so far as friendship demanded
neither conflict nor sacrifice; sedulously avoiding
pain, annoyance, and trouble; plucking roses all
along his lifeway so carefully as never to incur a
thorn-prick, — he must have derived as large a
revenue of enjoyment from his seventy-seven years
in this world as ever accrued to any man whose
aims were all self-centred and self-terminated.

He was fond of money, frugal while elegant in
his mode of living, with no vices so far as we know,
certainly with no costly vices. He was married
only late in life, and had but one child to provide
for. His uncle — a usurer of ignoble reputation —
left him an estate five times as large as that received from his father. This he increased by the
remunerative purchase of extensive tracts of land in
Epeirus and elsewhere, by loans to individuals, corporations, and cities, by traffic in slaves and gladiators, and, as a publisher, by multiplying, for high
prices, through the numerous copyists whom he
owned, transcripts of Cicero's works and of other
writings of friends who sought to reach the public
by his agency. At the same time, he made a judicious investment of charities far within his income,
in loans without interest and public benefactions to
the city of Athens, in loans and gifts to those within
the circle of his intimacy, and in gratuities to persons straitened or suffering through stress of political
convulsions and perils.

He belonged, by sympathy and in his private

*b*

correspondence, to the Marian, and then to the Pompeian party, and had a strong antipathy to the course and policy of Julius Caesar, his race and kind; but he publicly identified himself with no party, refrained from political activity of every sort, and refused contributions in aid even of movements that had his full approval and his best wishes. He was always ready to relieve the distressed members of both and of all parties. He held friendly relations equally with Julius Caesar and Pompey, Cassius and Antony, Brutus and Caesar Augustus.

He had the most winning and attractive manners, a voice of rare sweetness and melody, and conversational powers unsurpassed, if equalled, by any man of his time. He was hospitable, yet without extravagance or ostentation, and his entertainments, first in Athens, and then in Rome, were remarkable as reunions of all that there was of learning, genius, wit, and grace. He loved to maintain peaceful and harmonious relations among his wonted guests, and was persevering in his endeavors to reconcile differences, soothe jealousies, and prevent rivals from becoming enemies. It was wholly due to their common friend and host that Cicero and Hortensius, as alike candidates for the palm of eloquence, preserved at least the show of friendship.

Atticus was also a man of large and varied learning, was equally versed in Greek and in Roman literature, and used either tongue in speech and in writing as if he had never known any other.

He was a thorough grammarian and a careful critic. His friends were in the habit of sending their works to him for a last revision, and it is by no means improbable that some of the delicate touches of Cicero's rhetoric may be due to his consummate taste and skill. He was himself an author, and wrote among other things an epitome of Roman history from the earliest time to his own. He was a ready and fluent letter-writer. But none of his writings are extant, except such few scraps of his epistles as are preserved in Cicero's answers to them.

The friendship between Cicero and Atticus began in their early boyhood. When Cicero first went to Athens — shortly after his defence of Roscius, and not improbably to escape the vengeance of Sulla — he found Atticus already established there, and for six months they, with Cicero's brother Quintus, who married the sister of Atticus, were constantly associated in study and in recreation. From that time Atticus was Cicero's closest and dearest friend, entering with the most vivid interest into all his plans and pursuits, lending him money, advising him in business, taking care of his property during his absences, and rendering counsel and aid in connection with the successive divorces of Terentia and Publilia. The correspondence between them now extant commenced only three years before Atticus returned to Rome, though it is hardly possible that they should not have exchanged letters previously.

On Cicero's side the epistles are of the most familiar character, giving us a minute narrative of incident, occupation, thought, and sentiment, day by day, and furnishing more ample and more authentic materials for his biography than are derived from all other sources. They include equally such references to the details of the life of Atticus, and to all his peculiarities of habit, opinion, and taste, that we feel hardly less intimately acquainted with him than with his illustrious correspondent. He became to Cicero as another self, an admirer of his genius, a participant in all his ambitions, and in many matters of practical life by far the wiser of the two. That he knew the worth, prized the privilege, and undoubtedly anticipated the enduring fame of such a friendship, is the best title that remains on record to the place which he would have claimed in the list of genuine philosophers.

# CATO.

Marcus Porcius Cato Censorius was born at Tusculum in Latium, probably B. C. 234, and died at the age of at least eighty-five years. Livy and Plutarch both say that he passed his ninetieth year. He was of plebeian birth, and the founder of his own illustrious family. Porcius was the family name, and Cato was a name either given to him in childhood with foresight of his shrewdness and practical wisdom, or else bestowed on him and accepted by him after his peculiar traits of character were well known and distinctly recognized. It denotes wisdom of an entirely terrestrial, and even feline type, and is on the whole more appropriate to him than the surname Sapiens, which attached itself to him in his later years. He had great virtues, but defects as great. In not one of the beatitudes in the Sermon on the Mount could he have claimed a part, nor would he have deigned to claim it, unless, in the almost numberless suits at law in which he was his own advocate, he might have regarded himself as " persecuted for righteousness' sake." He was rigidly truthful, sternly and ferociously upright, intensely courageous, and devotedly patriotic, — kind, too, to his wives and children. But he was mean and miserly, an exacting and tyrannical master, an implacable enemy, and his lower appetites were not governed by principle, but kept in check only so far as prudence required. He probably seemed a better man in Cicero's time than in his own, and this for two reasons; namely, that his peculiar virtues had almost died out of the Roman commonwealth, and that, when a man transmits to posterity any valid title to fame, time enhances his merits and extenuates his faults, so that the generation which "builds the sepulchres of the prophets" always idealizes the busts that surmount them.

As regards versatility of endowment, number and diversity of official trusts, ability and faithfulness as a servant of the public, and influence — unspent by death — over the Senate and the people, Cato had no equal in the history of Rome. The impress of his life and character on the ages that looked back on his career from the interval of centuries, may best be seen from Livy's panegyric, of which we give a literal translation. After enumerating the long list of competitors for the office of Censor, he says : —

"Marcus Porcius [Cato] stood in the canvass far before all the patricians and plebeians of the most noble families. In this man there was so great force of mind and genius, that, whatever might have been his position by birth, he seemed destined to be the artificer of his own fortune. He lacked no skill in the management of either private or public interests. He was equally versed in the affairs of the city and of the country.

Some have attained the highest honors by virtue of legal science, some by eloquence, some by military fame; he had a genius so capable of excelling in all, that whatever he had in hand you would say that he was expressly born for it. In war he was the bravest of soldiers, renowned in many signal conflicts; after he rose to high honors, a consummate general; in peace, if you asked legal advice, the wisest of counsellors; if you had a cause to be argued, the most eloquent of advocates. Nor was he one whose fame as an orator, flourishing while he lived, left no memorial of itself behind him. His eloquence still lives, consecrated by writings of every description. There are extant many of his speeches for himself, and for others, and against others; for he harassed his opponents equally by accusing them and by pleading his own cause. An excessive number of enmities were cherished against him, and cherished by him; nor was it easy to say whether the nobles were the more earnest to put him down, or he to annoy them. He was, undoubtedly, of a harsh temper, and of a bitter and an inordinately free tongue, but of a soul unconquered by sensual appetites, of rigid integrity, a despiser of adulation and of bribes. In frugal living, in endurance of labor and of danger, he was of an iron constitution of body and mind; nor could old age, which enfeebles all things, break him. In his eighty-sixth year he had a case in court, pleaded his own cause, and continued to write, and in his ninetieth year he brought Servius Galba to trial before the people."

Cato inherited a small farm in the Sabine territory, where he spent his boyhood and such portions

of his subsequent life as were free from public service.   Here he lived with the utmost simplicity,
worked on his farm, and associated on familiar
terms with his rustic neighbors.   At the age of
seventeen he made his first campaign as a soldier,
and three years later reached the dignity of a military Tribune under Fabius Maximus, whose friendship he enjoyed.   B. C. 205, he went to Sicily as
military Quaestor under the elder Africanus.   In due
time he became Aedile, and the next year Praetor,
having Sardinia for his province, with a considerable military command.   In this office he renounced
the wonted pomp of his predecessors, walked on his
circuits, cut down to the lowest point all public
expenses, waged war against usury, and visited
usurers with condign punishment.   Chosen Consul
B. C. 195, he sustained during his term of office the
only signal defeat in his whole career.   Twenty
years previously, in the stress of the Punic war, a
severe sumptuary law had been passed, limiting the
amount of gold which women might possess, forbidding them to wear many-colored garments, and
prohibiting their use of carriages for short distances
in the city.   The women absolutely mobbed the
Senators, imploring the repeal of restrictions no
longer needed.   Cato opposed them to the last;
but they by importunity won the day, and celebrated their victory by a procession, in which they
made ample show of the late-proscribed finery.   As
soon as this domestic war was over, Cato set sail for

his allotted province, Hither Spain (*Hispania Cite-rior*).   Here there were rebel and recalcitrant tribes to be reduced to submission, and Cato in the con-duct of this campaign displayed at once the highest military ability and the most wanton and savage cruelty.   He was rewarded with a triumph ; but returned to encounter the enmity of the elder Scipio Africanus, toward whom he had previously stood in unfriendly relations.   He successfully de-fended himself against the charges urged against him, which seem to have related, in part at least, to the pecuniary administration of his province, in which Cato was able, by producing his accounts, to show himself, as in these matters he always was, not only above suspicion, but minutely exact, and as parsimonious in public office as he was in his own private affairs.   He subsequently served under Glabrio, probably as *Legatus*, or lieutenant-general, in the war with Antiochus the Great, and the battle of Thermopylae, which crippled Antiochus, was brought to a successful issue confessedly by the prowess, energy, and strategic skill of Cato.

B. C. 184, Cato was chosen Censor, and applied himself at once with characteristic vigor and acri-mony to the duties of his office.   He made the most stringent provisions against luxury.   He put the aqueducts, sewers, and other public works in order, and arrested all the modes in which public property had been perverted to private uses, such as the drawing off of water from the reservoirs for the special supply of houses and gardens. He brought farmers of the revenue and contractors of every class to strict account, and regulated all contracts by his own perhaps too low estimate of the actual worth of the work done or the service rendered. He degraded from the Senate and from their Equestrian privileges a very considerable number of men of previously high standing, most of them for grave and sufficient reasons, — some, it must be confessed, on very frivolous pretexts. He laid up by his censorial career a stock of enmities which lasted him for the rest of his life, during which he held no public office, but appeared constantly in the courts, in the Senate, and before the people, retaining to the last his clearness and vigor of intellect, and much of his oratorical power. He was during his lifetime prosecuted before the tribunals forty-four times, and failed of successful defence but once. He was still oftener a public accuser, and generally procured the conviction of the defendant. In the case of Servius Galba, recorded by Livy as his last, he lost the cause, though a righteous one, by the wonted resource of an appeal by weeping children to the pity of the judges.

Cato, though not a profligate or a sot, was not consistently pure nor uniformly temperate. He dealt with his slaves as with cattle, treating them as merchantable chattels, punishing them with wanton severity, and sometimes condemning them to death for trivial offences. His whole life must have been coarse, in many aspects even brutal, and the aesthetic faculty seems to have been entirely wanting in him.

Yet his literary culture must have been of a high order. He learned Greek in his old age, after despising the language and its writers during the whole of his earlier life. He was a friend and patron of the poet Ennius, and brought him to Rome, though manifestly without any generous provision for his subsistence; for Ennius led in Rome as poor and straitened a life as he could have left in Sardinia, where Cato found him. Of Cato's orations, letters, and great historical work, we have only fragments extant. His *De Re Rustica* exists, probably unchanged in substance, though modernized in form. It is not so much a treatise as a miscellaneous compend of materials relating to agriculture and rural affairs, and it undoubtedly presents the most genuine picture that has been preserved to our time of rustic life in Italy two thousand years ago.

# LAELIUS.

Caius Laelius Sapiens, of a distinguished patrician family, was born in Rome, B. C. 186. His surname was given to him for his prudence in retracting certain agrarian measures in which he would have shared with the Gracchi the intensest enmity of the whole patrician body. He was vacillating in his political opinions and proclivities, feeling strong sympathy with the popular cause, yet unwilling to forfeit the friendship and esteem of his own native caste. Though he was not a great man, he filled reputably several high public trusts, both civil and military, and was regarded as the most learned and acute of jurists in augural law, which was largely made up of authority and precedent, and abounded in intricacies and subtilties, while yet it constantly had grave complications with the most important affairs of state.

He was a man of large and varied erudition, was well versed in philosophy, and as a pupil of Diogenes of Babylon, and then of Panaetius, was among the earliest Roman disciples of the Stoic school.

His social qualities won for him many and warm friends. He had an even temper, genial manners, fine conversational powers, ready wit and affluent humor. In the *De Senectute* he is fitly associated with the younger Scipio Africanus, with whom he lived in the closest intimacy, as his father had with the elder Africanus. Thoroughly amiable in his domestic relations, he seems to have almost antici- pated the home life of modern Christendom, and we have accounts of games not unlike our blind- man's-buff, in which he and Scipio dropped all dignity and became boys again. Many of his face- tious sayings lingered long in the popular memory, and some still survive. The best of them is his reply to an impertinent man, who reproached him with not being worthy of his ancestors, — " But you are worthy of yours."

Of his writings — chiefly orations — nothing re- mains except a few titles. He was regarded as singularly smooth and elegant in his style ; but the Latin tongue was by no means in his day the subtle and flexible organ of thought which Cicero both found and made it, and some of the later gramma- rians resorted to Laelius for specimens of archaic words and idioms.

# SCIPIO.

Publius Cornelius Scipio Aemilianus Africanus
Minor was a son of Lucius Aemilius Paullus, and
was adopted by his cousin, Publius Cornelius Scipio
Africanus, the son of the elder Africanus. He was
born in the same year with Laelius. He has his
place in history as the most able and successful
military commander of his age. He first gained
celebrity in Spain as military Tribune under Lucius
Lucullus, whom he eclipsed in fame, equally as to
courage, integrity, and humanity. At the beginning
of the third Punic war he still served as Tribune;
but by his valor and skill he so won the suffrages
of the army and the confidence of the people, that
he was made Consul before the legal age, and was
thus placed in supreme command. The war, under
his energetic conduct, issued in the capture and
destruction of Carthage. He was subsequently
chosen Consul a second time, with a view to his
service as commander in Spain, where the war had
been prolonged for many years, and with repeated
disasters for the Roman army. Scipio laid siege to
Numantia, and, after the most obstinate resistance
on the part of the Spaniards, took the city, levelled
it with the ground, reserved fifty of its inhabitants
to grace his triumph, and sold the rest of them as
slaves.

He was Censor for a year in the interval between his two consulships, and in that office he chose Cato for his model, employed the utmost severity in the repression of extravagance, luxury, and licentiousness, and made some strong and bitter enemies. He was always and consistently an aristocrat, and an opposer of all agrarian measures, and of the self-constituted leaders of the popular or plebeian party; and as his death occurred suddenly and mysteriously, it was supposed that he had been murdered by some one of his political antagonists, probably by Papirius Carbo, who had been unsparing in denunciations and invectives against him as the enemy of the Roman people.

Scipio was one of the most learned and accomplished men of his age, a friend of Polybius and Panaetius, a patron of the poets Lucilius and Terence, and, it was said, — probably on no sufficient evidence, — a collaborator with Terence, or at least a reviser of some of his comedies.

In my translation I have uniformly followed the text of Otto. Few of the various readings are of any importance; and where there is a difference worthy of notice, I find that, so far as I can remember without an exception, Lahmeyer and Sommerbrodt, whose editions I have constantly consulted, coincide with Otto.

# CICERO DE SENECTUTE.

I.   " Titus, if I can lift or ease the care
      That ceaseless burns and rankles in your breast,
      What guerdon shall be mine ? "

For I may be permitted to address you, Atticus, in the very verses in which Flamininus [1] is addressed by

    " That man so rich in probity, not gold," [2]

[1] Titus Quintius Flamininus, who was a coeval of Ennius. His was an eminently successful career. The " care " pressing so constantly upon him may have been that of the war with Philip of Macedonia, in which he showed eminent ability as a commander and a strategist, and which he closed by a peace of which he seems to have dictated the terms. But it more probably may have been a strong and lasting sense of the disgrace brought upon the family by the flagitious conduct of his brother Lucius Quintius Flamininus, who was ignominiously expelled from the Senate, by Cato the Elder, during his Censorship.

[2] Ennius, who spent the last years of his life in Rome, and maintained himself as a preceptor to youths of patrician families. He was born in a small village near Brundusium, and was induced to come to Rome by Cato the Elder. He was held in the highest esteem, affection, and reverence by the best men of his time.

although I feel assured that it is by no means true, as of Flamininus, that

" You, Titus, pass but anxious nights and days " ;

for I know the moderation and evenness of your temperament, and am aware that you brought away from Athens, not only your surname, but also liberal culture and practical wisdom.  Yet I am inclined to think that you are sometimes seriously disturbed by the same things[1] that weigh heavily on my mind, under which such comfort as may be had is a matter of graver moment, and must be deferred to some other time.  But my present purpose is to write to you something about Old Age.  For I desire that you and I may be lightened of this burden, which we have in common, of old age already pressing upon us or drawing close at hand,[2] though I am certain that you indeed bear and will bear it, as all things else, serenely and wisely.  But when it came into my mind to write something about old age, you occurred to me as worthy to receive in this essay an offering of which you and I may in common enjoy the benefit.  Indeed, the composition of this book has been so pleasant to me, that it has not only brushed away all the vexations of old age, but has made it even easy and agreeable.  In truth, sufficiently worthy praise can

[1] By the condition of public affairs, as to which Atticus professed an indifference which he can hardly have felt.

[2] Atticus was three years older than Cicero, who was in his sixty-second year when this treatise was written.

never be given to philosophy, whose votaries can pass every period of life without annoyance. But on other philosophical subjects I have said much, and hope to revert to them often; this book, on Old Age, I send specially to you. I put what I have to say, not, like Aristo of Chios,[1] into the mouth of Tithonus[2] (for a fictitious character cannot speak with authority), but into that of the aged Cato, that the discourse may gain authority from his name. With him I introduce Laelius and Scipio, admiring the ease with which he bears old age, and I give his answers to them. If I make him talk more learnedly than he was wont to do in his books, you may ascribe it to the Greek literature and philosophy, of which, as is well known, he was very studious in his latter years. But what need is there of a longer preface? For, as it were in Cato's own words, you shall forthwith hear all that I think and feel about old age.

[1] Latin, *Chius.* Aristo, or Ariston, of Chios, was a Stoic philosopher, and an immediate disciple of Zeno. Some authorities read *Ceus,* and there was an Ariston, a Peripatetic philosopher, of Ceos, of whose many writings only a few fragments have been preserved. The two are often confounded, even by ancient writers, and either of them may have written the treatise or dialogue on old age here referred to.

[2] The son of Eos, or Aurora, who obtained for him, from Zeus, the gift of immortality, but forgot to stipulate for that of eternal youth. He shrivelled in old age by slow degrees; his voice became a mere chirp, and he at length dwindled into a cricket. Can this myth mean that the son of the morning, the early riser, has the promise of long life?

II. SCIPIO. I often express, Marcus Cato, in conversation with Caius Laelius, now present, my admiration of your surpassing and consummate wisdom, in other matters indeed, but especially because I have never perceived that old age was grievous to you, though to old men in general it is so hateful that they account themselves as bearing a burden heavier than Aetna.[1]

CATO. You seem, Scipio and Laelius, to admire what has been to me by no means difficult. For those who have in themselves no resources for a good and happy life, every period of life is burdensome; but to those who seek all goods from within, nothing which comes in the course of nature can seem evil. Under this head a place especially belongs to old age, which all desire to attain, yet find fault with it when they have reached it. Such is the inconsistency and perverseness of human folly. They say that age creeps upon them faster than they had thought possible. In the first place, who forced them to make this false estimate? In the next place, how could old age be less burdensome to them if it came on their eight-hundredth year than it is in their eightieth? For the time past, however long, when it had elapsed, could furnish no comfort to soothe a foolish old age. If, then, you are wont to admire my wisdom; — would that it

---

[1] Briareus, Enceladus, and Typhoeus, giants, who made war against the gods, were said, in Grecian fable, to have been buried alive by Zeus under Mount Aetna. See the *Aeneid*, iii. 578.

were worthy of your appreciation and of my own surname,[1] — I am wise in this respect, that I follow and obey Nature, the surest guide, as if she were a god, and it is utterly improbable that she has well arranged the other parts of life, and yet, like an unskilled poet, slighted the last act of the drama. There must, however, of necessity, be some end, and, as in the case of berries on the trees and the fruits of the earth, there must be that which in its season of full ripeness is, so to speak, ready to wither and fall, — which a wise man ought to bear patiently. For to rebel against Nature is but to repeat the war of the Giants with the Gods.

LAELIUS. Indeed, Cato, you will have rendered us a most welcome service — I will answer for Scipio — if, since we hope, indeed wish, at all events, to become old, we can learn of you, far in advance, in what ways we can most easily bear the encroachment of age.

CATO. I will render this service, Laelius, if, as you say, it will be agreeable to both of you.

LAELIUS. We do indeed desire, Cato, unless it will give you too much trouble, since you have

---

[1] The reference may here be to *Cato*, which name he seems to have been the first to bear, and which may have been given him in childhood for the promise of the qualities fully developed in later years. The term denotes shrewdness and cunning, rather than wisdom, — in fine, the feline attributes which have given name both in the Latin (*catus*) and in the English to the cat. Reference may, however, be had to *Sapiens*, — a surname currently given to Cato in his later years.

taken a long journey which we must begin, that you will show us the goal which you have reached.

III. CATO. I will do so, Laelius, to the best of my ability. I have, indeed, often been a listener to complaints of men of my own age, — for, as the old proverb says, "Like best mates with like," [1] — such complaints, for instance, as those which Caius Salinator and Spurius Albinus, men of consular dignity, nearly my coevals, used to make, because they were deprived of the sensual gratifications without which life appeared to them a blank, and because they were neglected by those by whom they were wont to be held in reverence. They seemed to me to lay the blame where it did not belong. For if old age had been at fault, I and all other persons of advanced years would have the same experience; while I have known many old men who have made no complaint, who did not regret their release from the slavery of sensual appetite, and were not despised by their fellow-citizens. But all complaints of this kind are chargeable to character, not to age. Old men who are moderate in their desires, and are neither testy nor morose, find old age endurable; but rudeness and incivility are offensive at any age.

LAELIUS. You are right, Cato; yet some one may perhaps say that old age seems to you less

---

[1] Latin, *Pares cum paribus facillime congregantur.* In Plato's *Symposium,* Ὅμοιον ὁμοίῳ ἀεὶ πελάζει is quoted as an old proverb (παλαιὸς λόγος).

burdensome on account of your wealth, your large resources, your high rank, but that these advantages fall to the lot of very few.

CATO. There is, indeed, Laelius, something in this; but it by no means gives the full explanation. It is somewhat as in the case of Themistocles in an altercation with a certain native of Seriphos,[1] who told him that he owed his illustrious fame, not to his own greatness, but to that of his country; and Themistocles is said to have answered, "If I had been born in Seriphos, I should not have been renowned, nor, by Hercules, would you have been eminent had you been an Athenian." Very much the same may be said about old age, which cannot be easy in extreme poverty, even to a wise man, nor can it be otherwise than burdensome to one destitute of wisdom, even with abundant resources of every kind. The best-fitting defensive armor of old age, Scipio and Laelius, consists in the knowledge and practice of the virtues, which, assiduously cultivated, after the varied experiences of a long life, are wonderfully fruitful, not only because they never take flight, not even at the last moment, —

[1] One of the Cyclades, known in mythology, as the island on which Perseus was driven on shore and brought up, and whose inhabitants he turned to stone with the Gorgon's head; and in history, for its insignificance and poverty, — the reason why under the Roman emperors it was a frequent place of banishment for state criminals; celebrated also (probably in myth rather than fact) for a race of voiceless frogs. — Herodotus tells this story of Themistocles.

although this is a consideration of prime importance, — but because the consciousness of a well-spent life and a memory rich in good deeds afford supreme happiness.

IV. In my youth I loved Quintus Maximus,[1] the one who recovered possession of Tarentum, then an elderly man, as if he had been of my own age; for in him gravity was seasoned by an affable deportment, nor had time made his manners less agreeable. When I first became intimate with him, he was not, indeed, so very old, though advanced in years. I was born the year after his first consulate.[2] In my early youth I served as a soldier under him at Capua, and five years afterward at Tarentum. Four years later I was made Quaestor, and held that office in the consulship of Tuditanus and Cethegus, at the time when he, then quite old, urged the passage of the Cincian law concerning gifts and fees.[3] He in his age showed in military command all the vigor of youth, and by his perseverance put a check to Hannibal's youth-

---

[1] The fourth of the name.

[2] Quintus Maximus must, then, have been forty-four years older than Cato.

[3] This law not only prohibited the payment of fees or offering of gifts to advocates; but it limited the amount of gifts that could be made in any case, except with certain legal formalities. The object of this last provision was, undoubtedly, to prevent the wheedling of men out of valuable property by taking advantage of their illnesses, their temporary loss of disposing mind, or their apprehension of approaching death.

ful enthusiasm. My friend Ennius well said of
him, —

> " One man by slow delays restored our fortunes,
>     Preferring not the people's praise to safety,
>     And thus his after-glory shines the more."

How much vigilance, how much wisdom, did he
show in the retaking of Tarentum! In my hearing, indeed, when Salinator, who, after the town was
taken, had retreated to the citadel, boastfully said,
" You recovered Tarentum, Quintus Fabius, by my
aid," he replied, laughing, " Very true, for, if you
had not lost it, I should never have recovered it." [1]
Nor had he more eminence as a soldier than he won
as a civilian, when, in his second consulate, unsup-
ported by his colleague, Carvilius, he resisted to the
utmost of his ability Caius Flaminius, tribune of the
people, in his division in equal portions, to the plebeians, of conquered territory in Picenum and Gaul;
and when, holding the office of augur, he dared to
say that whatever was done for the well-being of
the republic was done under the most favorable
auspices, but that whatever measures were passed
to the injury of the republic were passed under

---

[1] The retaking of Tarentum was the fatal stroke on Hannibal
as to the possession of Southern Italy. But in this anecdote,
Cicero, or some early transcriber, made a mistake as to the name
of the unsuccessful commander. Marcus Livius Salinator was a
distinguished general; but it was Marcus Livius Macatus that
lost the town of Tarentum, and then did good service from the
citadel toward its retaking. It is strange, but true, that Cicero
was not well versed in the history of the Punic wars.

adverse auspices. In him I knew many things worthy of renown, but nothing more admirable than the way in which he bore the death of his son, an illustrious man and of consular dignity. We have in our hands his eulogy on his son, and in reading it we feel that he surpassed in this vein even trained philosophers. Nor was he great only in public and in the eyes of the community; but he was even more excellent in private and domestic life. How rich in conversation! How wise in precept! How ample his knowledge of early times! How thorough his legal science in everything appertaining to his office as an augur![1] He had, too, for a Roman, a large amount of. literary culture. He retained in his memory, also, all the details of our wars, whether in Italy or in regions more remote. I indeed availed myself as eagerly of my opportunities of conversing with him as if I had already divined, what proved to be true, that, when he should pass away, no man of equal intelligence and information would be left.

V. To what purpose have I said so much about Maximus? That you may be assured by his exam-

---

[1] The augurs acquired great power in the age when the signs which it was their office to interpret were still implicitly believed in. From the nice distinctions then deemed of importance there grew up a minute formalism, which by degrees constituted a body of augural law. The augurs at first had unlimited authority in their sphere ; but as faith in auspices declined, the magistrates, and even patricians not in office, usurped and maintained certain augural rights, so that there was sometimes a conflict of jurisdiction, giving rise to nice questions of law.

ple that one has no right to pronounce an old age
like his wretched. Yet it is not every one that can
be a Scipio or a Maximus, so that he can recall the
memory of cities taken, of battles by land and sea,
of wars conducted, of triumphs won. There is,
however, a calm and serene old age, which belongs
to a life passed peacefully, purely, and gracefully,
such as we learn was the old age of Plato, who died
while writing in his eighty-first year; or that of
Isocrates, who says that he wrote the book entitled
*Panathenaicus* [1] in his ninety-fourth year, and who
lived five years afterwards, and whose preceptor,
Leontinus Gorgias, filled out one hundred and seven
years without suspending his study and his labor.
When he was asked why he was willing to live so
long, he replied, "I have no fault to find with old
age," — a noble answer, worthy of a learned man.
Unwise men, indeed, charge their vices and their
faults upon old age. So did not Ennius, of whom I
have just spoken, who writes,

> "As the brave steed, oft on th' Olympian course
> Foremost, now worn with years, seeks quiet rest,"

comparing his own age to that of the brave horse
that had been wont to win the race. You can distinctly remember him. The present Consuls, Titus
Flamininus and Manius Acilius, were chosen nineteen years after his death, which took place in the

---

[1] A discourse commemorative of the Athenian patriots held in
special honor by their fellow-countrymen.

consulship of Caepio and the second consulship of
Philippus, when I, being sixty-five years old, with a
strong voice and sound lungs, spoke in favor of the
Voconian law.[1]　At the age of seventy years — for
so many did Ennius live — he bore the two burdens
which are esteemed the heaviest, poverty and old
age, in such a way that he almost seemed to take
delight in them.　To enter into particulars, I find
on reflection four reasons why old age seems
wretched; — one, that it calls us away from the
management of affairs; another, that it impairs
bodily vigor; the third, that it deprives us to a
great degree of sensual gratifications; the fourth,
that it brings one to the verge of death.　Let us
see, if you please, how much force and justice there
is in each of these reasons.

VI. Old age cuts one off from the management
of affairs.　Of what affairs?　Of those which are
managed in youth and by strength of body?　But
are there not affairs properly belonging to the later
years of life, which may be administered by the
mind, even though the body be infirm?　Did Quintus Maximus then do nothing?　Did Lucius Paullus,

---

[1] A law restricting, and in the case of large estates prohibiting,
the bequest of property to women, perhaps with the view of pre-
venting the alienation of estates from the families in which they
had been transmitted.　But an extract from Cato's speech, given
by Aulus Gellius, charges wives who had separate estates of their
own with first lending money to their husbands in their stress of
need, and then becoming their most relentless and annoying
creditors.

your father, Scipio, the father-in-law of that excellent man, my son, do nothing? Did other old men that I might name — the Fabricii, the Curii, the Coruncanii — do nothing, when they defended the republic by their counsel and influence? Blindness came upon Appius Claudius[1] in his old age; yet he, when the sentiment of the Senate leaned toward the conclusion of peace and a treaty with Pyrrhus, did not hesitate to say to them what Ennius has fully expressed in verse, —

> "Wont to stand firm, upon what devious way
> Demented rush ye now?"

and more, most forcibly, to the same purpose. You know the poem, and the speech that Appius actually made is still extant. This took place seventeen years after his second consulship, ten years having

---

[1] Appius Claudius was undoubtedly the greatest statesman and the most useful citizen of his time. His name still lives and some vestiges of his public spirit remain in the *Appia Via,* Rome's first great military road, and the *Aqua Appia,* the earliest aqueduct by which water from the mountains was brought into the city. Livy tells a curious story of his blindness. The patrician *gens* of the Potitii were hereditary priests of Hercules, whom they worshipped by rites which were their family secret. Appius, probably apprehensive, as so many modern statesmen have been, of potential mischief from secret societies, hired these men to divulge the mysteries of their worship to certain public slaves or servants. The consequence was that the whole *gens,* including twelve families and thirty young men, perished in a single year, and some years afterward (*post aliquot annos*) by the persistent anger of the gods Appius was deprived of sight. *Post, ergo propter.*

intervened between his two consulates, his censorship having preceded the first, — so that you may infer that he was far advanced in age at the time of the war with Pyrrhus, and such is the tradition that has come to us from our fathers. Those, therefore, who deny that old age has any place in the management of affairs, are as unreasonable as those would be who should say that the pilot takes no part in sailing a ship because others climb the masts, others go to and fro in the gangways, others bail the hold, while he sits still in the stern and holds the helm. The old man does not do what the young men do; but he does greater and better things. Great things are accomplished, not by strength, or swiftness, or suppleness of body, but by counsel, influence, deliberate opinion, of which old age is not wont to be bereft, but, on the other hand, to possess them more abundantly. This you will grant, unless I, having been soldier, and military Tribune, and second in command, and as Consul at the head of the army, seem to you now idle and useless, because I am no longer actively engaged in war. I now prescribe to the Senate what ought to be done, and how. I declare war far in advance against Carthage,[1] which has long been plotting to our detriment, and whose hostility I shall never cease to fear, till I know that the city is utterly swept out

---

[1] *Delenda est Carthago*, Carthage must be destroyed, was the close of all Cato's speeches in the Senate, whatever the subject of discussion.

of being. O that the immortal gods may reserve
for you, Scipio, this honor, that you may fully accomplish what your grandfather[1] left to be yet
done! This is the thirty-third year since his
death; but the memory of such a man all coming
years will hold in special honor. He died the year
before my censorship, nine years after my consulate,
during which he was chosen Consul for the second
time. If he had lived till his hundredth year,
would he have had reason to regret his old age?
He would not, indeed, have sought added distinction by running, or leaping, or hurling the spear, or
handling the sword, but by counsel, reason, judgment. Unless these were the characteristics of
seniors in age, our ancestors would not have called
the supreme council the Senate. Among the Lacedaemonians, too, the corresponding name is given
to the magistrates of the highest grade, who are
really old men.[2] But if you see fit to read or hear
the history of foreign nations, you will find that
states have been undermined by young men, maintained and restored by old men.

"Say, how lost you so great a state so soon?"

For this men ask, as it is asked in Naevius's play of
*The School*, and with other answers this is among
the first: —

"A brood came of new leaders, foolish striplings."

[1] By adoption. See Introduction.
[2] Γερουσία. None of the members of this body were less than
sixty years of age.

Rashness, indeed, belongs to youth; prudence, to age.

VII. But memory is impaired by age. I have no doubt that it is, in persons who do not exercise their memory, and in those who are naturally slow-minded. But Themistocles knew by name all the citizens of Athens, and do you suppose that, at an advanced age, when he met Aristides he called him Lysimachus? I not only know the men who are now living; but I have a clear remembrance of their fathers and their grandfathers. Nor am I afraid to read sepulchral inscriptions, an occupation which is said to destroy the memory;[1] on the other hand, my recollection of the dead is thus made more vivid. Then, too, I never heard of an old man's forgetting where he had buried his money. Old men remember everything that they care about,[2] —the bonds they have given, what is due to them, what they owe. What shall we say of lawyers?

---

[1] Evidently the reference is here to a popular superstition, of which, however, I know of no other vestige.

[2] The converse of this proposition is, probably, the best statement of the causes of what is termed the failure of memory in old age. Lasting memory and prompt recollection are the result of attention, and attention springs from interest. Old men have a vivid recollection of early events, because their interest in them was vivid; while in advanced life strong impressions are more rarely made, most of its scenes and incidents being little else than the repetition, with slight change, of previous experiences. Yet the instances are not infrequent in which, after one has reached the condition in which yesterday's life is a blank, a novel and striking event remains unforgotten.

Of priests ?[1] Of augurs ? Of philosophers ? How many things do they retain in their memory! Old men have their powers of mind unimpaired, when they do not suspend their usual pursuits and their habits of industry. Nor is this the case only with those in conspicuous stations and in public office ; it is equally true in private and retired life. Sophocles in extreme old age still wrote tragedies. Because in his close application he seemed to neglect his property, his sons instituted judicial proceedings to deprive him, as mentally incompetent, of the custody of his estate, in like manner as by our law fathers of families who mismanage their property have its administration taken from them. The old man is said to have then recited to the judges the *Oedipus at Colonus*, the play which he had in hand and had just written, and to have asked them whether that poem seemed the work of a failing intellect.[2] On hearing this, the judges dismissed the case. Did old age then impose silence, in their several modes of utterance, on him, on Homer, on Hesiod, on Simonides, on Stesichorus, on Isocrates and Gorgias of whom I have just spoken, on those

[1] There was a considerable body of pontifical law, — corresponding to the canon law of Christendom, — consisting, in part, of immemorial usage or prescription, and, in part, even of legislative enactments, of which the members of the pontifical college were the judges and administrators, so that, like the augurs, they needed officially unimpaired powers of mind and retentive memory.

[2] He was at this time nearly ninety years of age.

foremost of philosophers, Pythagoras and Democritus, on Plato, on Xenocrates, in later time, on Zeno and Cleanthes, or on that Diogenes the Stoic whom you saw when he was in Rome?[1] Or with all these men was not activity in their life-work coextensive with their lives? But leaving out of the account these pursuits, which have in them a divine element, I can name old Romans who are farmers in what was the Sabine territory, my neighbors and friends,[2] without whose oversight hardly any important work is ever done on their land, whether in sowing, or harvesting, or storing their crops. This, however, is not so surprising in them; for no one is so old that he does not expect to live a year longer. But the same persons bestow great pains in labor from which they know that they shall never derive any benefit.

> "He plants
> Trees to bear fruit when he shall be no more,"

as our poet Statius says in his *Synephebi.*[3] Nor, indeed can the farmer, though he be an old man, if asked for whom he is planting, hesitate to answer, "For the immortal gods, whose will it was, not only

---

[1] We know not how long Homer or Hesiod lived; but they are always spoken of as old men. The reputed age of the others on the list ranged from Plato, at eighty-one, to Democritus, who was said to have reached his hundredth year.

[2] Cato generally lived on his Sabine farm when public duty did not require his presence in Rome.

[3] *Young Friends*, probably the name of a play. None of the works of Caecilius Statius, its author, are extant.

that I should receive this estate from my ancestors, but that I should also transmit it in undiminished value to my posterity."

VIII. What I have just quoted from Caecilius [1] about the old man's providing for a coming generation, is very far preferable to what he says elsewhere, —

> "Old Age, forsooth, if other ill thou bring not,
>   This will suffice, that with one's lengthened years
>   So much he sees he fain would leave unseen," —

and much, it may be, that he is glad to see; while youth, too, often encounters what it would willingly shun. Still worse, that same Caecilius writes, —

> "The utmost misery of age I count it,
>   To feel that it is hateful to the young."

Agreeable rather than hateful; for as wise old men are charmed with well-disposed youth, so do young men delight in the counsels of the old, by which they are led to the cultivation of the virtues. I do not feel that I am less agreeable to you than you are to me. — To return to our subject, you see that old age is not listless and inert, but is even laborious, with work and plans of work always in hand, generally, indeed, with employments corresponding to the pursuits of earlier life. But what shall we say of those who even make new acquisitions?

[1] Caecilius Statius. There can hardly be need of discriminating him from Publius Papinius Statius, whose poems are extant, and familiarly known to classical scholars.

Thus we see Solon, in one of his poems, boasting that, as he grows old, he widens the range of his knowledge every day. I have done the like, having learned Greek in my old age, and have taken hold of the study so eagerly — as if to quench a long thirst — that I have already become familiar with the topics from Greek authors which I have been using, as I have talked with you, by way of illustration. When I read that Socrates in his old age learned to play on the lyre, I could have wished to do the same, had the old custom been still rife; but I certainly have worked hard on my Greek.

IX. To pass to the next charge against old age, I do not now desire the bodily strength of youth, any more than when I was a young man I desired the strength of a bull or an elephant. It is becoming to make use of what one has, and whatever you do, to do in proportion to your strength. What language can be more contemptible than that reported of Milon of Crotona,[1] when in his old age he saw athletes taking exercise on the race-ground, and is said to have cast his eyes on his own arms, and to have exclaimed, weeping, "But these are dead now"? Not these, indeed, simpleton, so much as you yourself; for you never gained any fame from your own self, but only from your lungs and arms. You hear nothing like this from Sextus

---

[1] Six times victor in wrestling in the Olympic games, and six times in the Pythian.

Aelius,[1] nothing at a much earlier time from Titus Coruncanius,[2] nor yet from Publius Crassus,[3] who expounded the laws to their fellow-citizens, and whose wisdom grew to their last breath. There is reason, indeed, to fear that a mere orator may lose something of his power with age; for he needs not mind alone, but strong lungs and bodily vigor. Yet there is a certain musical quality of the voice which becomes — I know not how — even more melodious in old age. This, indeed, I have not yet lost, and you see how old I am. But the eloquence that becomes one of advanced years is calm and gentle, and not infrequently a clear-headed old man commands special attention by the simple, quiet elegance of his style. If, however, you cannot attain this merit, you may be able at least to give wholesome advice to Scipio and Laelius. You can at least help others by your counsel; and what is more pleasant than old age surrounded by young disciples? Must we not, indeed, admit that old age has sufficient strength to teach young men, to educate them, to train them for the discharge of every duty? And what can be more worthy of re-

[1] The most distinguished jurist of his time, and not many years Cato's senior.

[2] Said to have been the earliest jurist who received pupils. He was undoubtedly second in learning and in practical wisdom, as in reputation and official honor, to no man of his age. He flourished about a century before Cato's time.

[3] Said to have been equally learned and skilled in civil and in pontifical law. He was not many years older than Cato.

nown than work like this ?   I used to think Cneius
and Publius Scipio, and, Scipio, your two grandfathers, Lucius Aemilius and Publius Africanus,
truly fortunate in being surrounded by noble youth ;
nor are there any masters of liberal culture who
are not to be regarded as happy, even though their
strength may have failed with lengthened years.
This failure of strength, however, is due oftener to
the vices of youth than to the necessary infirmity
of age ; for a licentious and profligate youth transmits to one's later years a worn-out bodily constitution.   Cyrus indeed, in his dying speech which
Xenophon records, though somewhat advanced in
years, says that he has never felt that his old age
was more feeble than his youth.   I remember in my
boyhood Lucius Metellus, who, having been made
high-priest four years after his second consulate,
served in that office twenty-two years,[1] and was to
the very last in such full strength that he did not
even feel the loss of youth.   There is no need of

---

[1] He was Consul in 251 and 247 B. C.   The earliest age at
which he was eligible to the consulship was forty-three ; but he
probably must have reached that dignity at a later age, if he was
so very old a man thirty years afterward.   The *pontifex maximus*
(for which we have no better English rendering than *high-priest*),
like the other *pontifices*, held his office by life tenure.   At some
epochs, he was chosen by popular vote ; at others, appointed by
the college.   He and the *pontifices* were not priests of any special
divinity, but the legal trustees of the national religion, its rites
and its laws.   The *pontifex maximus* was, oftener than not, a
jurist of eminence, and most of the early Roman jurists attained
that dignity.

my speaking of myself, though that is an old man's habit, and is conceded as a privilege of age.

X. Do you not know how very often Homer introduces Nestor as talking largely of his own merits ? Nor was there any fear that, while he told the truth about himself, he would incur the reproach of oddity or garrulity ; for, as Homer says, " words sweeter than honey flowed from his tongue." For this suavity of utterance he had no need of bodily strength ; yet for this alone the leader of the Greeks,[1] while not craving ten like Ajax, says that with ten like Nestor he should be sure of the speedy fall of Troy. — But to return to my own case, I am now in my eighty-fourth year. I should be glad if I could make precisely the same boast with Cyrus ; yet, in default of it, I can say this at least, that, while I am not so strong as I was when a soldier in the Punic war, or a Quaestor in the same war, or Consul in Spain, or when, four years afterward, I fought as military Tribune [2] at Thermopylae, in the consulate of Manius Acilius Glabrio, still, as you see, old age has not wholly unstrung my nerves

[1] Agamemnon, who craves ten συμφράδμονες, equally wise in counsel, with Nestor.

[2] According to Livy, Cato was *legatus*, or second in command, at this time, and it is hardly possible that an ex-consul should have served as a military tribune. We have here, perhaps, an oversight of Cicero, or, possibly, an over-acting of the old man's treacherous memory in Cato, whose extreme old age Cicero evidently personates with marvellous dramatic skill throughout this dialogue.

or broken me down. Neither the Senate, nor the rostrum, nor my friends, nor my clients, nor my guests miss the strength that I have lost. Nor did I ever give assent to that ancient and much-lauded proverbial saying, that you must become an old man early if you wish to be an old man long. I should, indeed, prefer a shorter old age to being old before my time. Thus no one has wanted to meet me to whom I have denied myself on the plea of age. Yet I have less strength than either of you. Nor have you indeed the strength of Titus Pontius the centurion.[1] Is he therefore any better than you? Provided one husbands his strength, and does not attempt to go beyond it, he will not be hindered in his work by any lack of the requisite strength. It is said that Milo walked the whole length of the Olympian race-ground with a living ox on his shoulders;[2] but which would you prefer, —this amount of bodily strength, or the strength of mind that Pythagoras had?[3] In fine, I would

---

[1] Nothing else is known of Pontius than this reference to his extraordinary strength. He may be the centurion of that name, whose name alone occurs in some verses of Lucilius quoted by Cicero in the *De Finibus*.

[2] He is said to have commenced by lifting and carrying a calf daily, and to have continued so doing till the calf had attained full growth.

[3] There was a tradition that Milo was a pupil of Pythagoras, and that on one occasion the roof of the building in which Pythagoras was lecturing gave way, and was sustained by the single might of Milo.

have you use strength of body while you have it; when it fails, I would not have you complain of its loss, unless you think it fitting for young men to regret their boyhood, or for those who have passed on a little farther in life to want their youth back again. Life has its fixed course, and nature one unvarying way; each age has assigned to it what best suits it, so that the fickleness of boyhood, the sanguine temper of youth, the soberness of riper years, and the maturity of old age, equally have something in harmony with nature, which ought to be made availing in its season. You, Scipio, must have heard what your grandfather's host Masinissa [1] does now that he is ninety years old. When he starts on a journey on foot, he never mounts a horse ; when he starts on horseback, he never relieves himself by walking ; he is never induced by rain or cold to cover his head ; he has the utmost power of bodily endurance ; and so he performs in full all the offices and functions of a king. Exercise and temperance, then, can preserve even in old age something of one's pristine vigor.

XI. Old age lacks strength, it is said. But strength is not demanded of old age. My period of life is exempted by law and custom from offices

---

[1] King of the Numidians, and for the most part a faithful, though not a disinterested, ally of the Romans, in the Punic wars. He was eulogized by Roman writers generally ; yet with the rude strength he probably combined no little of the rude ethics of a barbarian chieftan.

which cannot be borne without strength.[1] Therefore we are compelled to do, not what we are unable
to do, but even less than we can do.  Is it said that
many old men are so feeble that they are incapable
of any duty or charge whatsoever?  This, I answer,
is not an inability peculiar to old age, but common
to bodily infirmity at whatever period of life.  How
feeble, Scipio, was that son of Africanus who adopted
you![2]  But for this, he would have shone second in
his family as a luminary of the state, adding to his
father's greatness a more ample intellectual culture.
What wonder, then, is it that old men are sometimes feeble, when it is a misfortune which even the
young cannot always escape?  Old age, Laelius and
Scipio, should be resisted, and its deficiencies should
be supplied by faithful effort.  Old age, like disease,
should be fought against.  Care must be bestowed
upon the health; moderate exercise must be taken;
the food and drink should be sufficient to recruit
the strength, and not in such excess as to become
oppressive.  Nor yet should the body alone be sustained in vigor, but much more the powers of mind;
for these too, unless you pour oil into the lamp,

[1] By law no one over forty-six years of age was required to
render military service, and Senators above sixty years of age were
not summoned to the sessions of the Senate, but attended them
or were absent from them at their own option.

[2] Publius Cornelius Scipio Africanus Minor, undoubtedly in
genius, learning, and ability the foremost of the Scipio family,
but never able to fill any other offices than those — involving
little labor — of Augur and *Flamen Dialis.*

are extinguished by old age. Indeed, while over-
exertion tends by fatigue to weigh down the body,
exercise makes the mind elastic. For, when Caecilius speaks of

"Foolish old men, fit sport for comedy," [1]

he means those who are credulous, forgetful, weak-
minded,[2] and these are the faults, not of old age,
but of lazy, indolent, drowsy old age. As wanton-
ness and licentiousness are the faults of the young
rather than of the old, yet not of all young men,
but only of such of them as are depraved, so the
senile folly which is commonly called dotage[3] belongs not to all, but only to frivolous old men.
Appius, when both blind and old, governed four
grown-up sons, five daughters, a very large household, a numerous body of clients; for he had his
mind on the alert, like a bent bow, nor did he, as
he became feeble, succumb to old age. He maintained, not only authority, but absolute command
over all who belonged to him. His servants feared
him; his children held him in awe; all loved him.
In that family the manners and discipline of the
earlier time were still in the ascendant. Old age,

---

[1] A foolish old man, the butt of ridicule and the victim of
fraud, trickery, and knavery, was a favorite character in Roman
comedy, having a part in almost every comic drama extant.

[2] Latin, *dissolutos*, which might be not unaptly rendered *out
of joint*, or *at loose ends*.

[3] Latin, *deliratio*, which is here much better expressed by
*dotage* than by *delirium*.

indeed, is worthy of honor only when it defends itself, when it asserts its rights, when it comes into bondage to no one, when even to the last breath it maintains its sway over those of its own family. Still farther, as I hold in high esteem the youth who has in him some of the qualities of age, I have like esteem for the old man in whom there is something of the youth, which he who cultivates may be old in body, but will never be so in mind. I have now in hand the seventh Book of my *History.*[1] I am collecting all the memorials of earlier times. I am just now writing out, as my memory serves me, my speeches in the celebrated cases that I have defended. I am treating of augural, pontifical, civil law. I read a good deal of Greek. At the same time, in order to exercise my memory in the method prescribed by Pythagoras,[2] I recall every evening whatever I have said, heard, or done during the day. These are the exercises of the mind; these, the race-ground of the intellect. In these pursuits while I labor vigorously, I hardly feel my loss of bodily strength. I appear in court in behalf of my friends. I often take my place in the Senate,

---

[1] Latin, *Origines.* This was an historical work in seven Books, some fragments of which are extant. It purported to give the history of Rome from its foundation to the author's own time. In the seventh Book his own speeches had their proper place. The second and third Books gave the history of the origin of the Italian towns. Hence the name of the entire work.

[2] Prescribed by him, however, not for mnemonic, but for moral uses.

and I there introduce of my own motion[1] subjects
on which I have thought much and long, and I
defend my opinious with strength of mind, not of
body. If I were too feeble to pursue this course
of life, I still on my bed should find pleasure in
thinking out what I could no longer do; but that I
am able still to do, as well as to think, is the result
of my past life. One who is always occupied in
these studies and labors is unaware when age creeps
upon him. Thus one grows old gradually and un-
consciously, and life is not suddenly extinguished,
but closes when by length of time it is burned out.

XII. I come now to the third charge against
old age, that, as it is alleged, it lacks the pleasures
of sense. O admirable service of old age, if indeed it takes from us what in youth is more harmful than all things else! For I would have you
hear, young men, an ancient discourse of Archytas
of Tarentum,[2] a man of great distinction and celeb-

---

[1] While in the Roman Senate individual Senators could not
introduce resolutions without previous formalities, there was the
same liberty of debate that exists in our Congress, and a Senator
could give free utterance to his views on any subject, however
remote from the business in hand.

[2] Archytas was equally distinguished as a philosopher, mathematician, statesman, and general. He is believed to have been
coeval with Plato, though there is some discrepancy of authorities
as to the precise period when he lived. Certain letters that purport to have passed between him and Plato are preserved; but
their genuineness is open to question. He was represented as
having been singularly pure, kind, and generous in his private
life.

rity, as it was repeated to me when in my youth I
was at Tarentum with Quintus' Maximus. " Man
has received from nature," said he, " no more fatal
scourge than bodily pleasure, by which the passions
in their eagerness for gratification are made reckless
and are released from all restraint. Hence spring
treasons against one's country ; hence, overthrows of
states; hence, clandestine plottings with enemies.
In fine, there is no form of guilt, no atrocity of
evil, to the accomplishment of which men are not
driven by lust for pleasure. Debaucheries, adulte-
ries, and all enormities of that kind have no other
inducing cause than the allurements of pleasure.
Still more, while neither Nature nor any god has
bestowed upon man aught more noble than mind,
nothing is so hostile as pleasure to this divine endowment and gift. Nor while lust bears sway can
self-restraint find place, nor under the reign of
pleasure can virtue have any foothold whatever."
That this might be better understood, Archytas
asked his hearers to imagine a person under the
excitement of the highest amount of bodily pleasure that could possibly be enjoyed, and maintained
that it was perfectly obvious to every one that so
long as such enjoyment lasted it was impossible for
the mind to act, or for anything to be determined by
reason or reflection. Hence he concluded that nothing was so execrable and baneful as pleasure, since,
when intense and prolonged, it extinguishes all the
light of intellect. That Archytas discoursed thus

with Caius Pontius the Samnite, father of the Pontius who defeated the consuls Spurius Postumius and Titus Veturius at the Caudine Forks, I learned from Nearchus of Tarentum, my host, a persistent friend of the Roman people, who said that he had heard it from his elders, Plato having been present when it was uttered, who, I find, came to Tarentum in the consulate of Lucius Camillus and Appius Claudius. To what purpose do I speak thus? That you may understand that, were we indeed unable by reason and wisdom to spurn pleasure, we ought to feel the warmest gratitude to old age for making what is opposed to our duty no longer a source of delight. For pleasure thwarts good counsel, is the enemy of reason, and, if I may so speak, blindfolds the eyes of the mind, nor has it anything in common with virtue. It was, indeed, with great reluctance that, seven years after his consulate, I expelled from the Senate Lucius Flamininus, the brother of that eminently brave man Titus Flamininus; but I thought that such vile conduct as his ought to be branded. For he, during his consulship in Gaul, was persuaded by the companion of his lust, at a banquet, himself to kill with an axe one of the prisoners in chains and under sentence of death.[1] He escaped during the censorship of

[1] Livy's story is even worse than this. He says that a Boian noble came with his children to cast himself upon the protection of the Consul, who, because his infamous associate complained of having never seen a gladiator die, first struck the Boian's head

his brother, my immediate predecessor; but I and my colleague Flaccus could not by any possibility give our implied sanction to lust so infamous, so abandoned, which blended with private ignominy disgrace to the office of supreme commander of our army.

XIII. I have often heard from my seniors in age, who said that they when they were boys had so heard from the old men of their time, that Caius Fabricius was wont to express his amazement when, while he was ambassador to King Pyrrhus, Cineas the Thessalonian told him that there was a certain man in Athens,[1] professing to be a philosopher, who taught that all that we do ought to be referred to pleasure as a standard. Fabricius having told this to Manius Curius and Titus Coruncanius, they used to wish that the Samnites and Pyrrhus himself might become converts to this doctrine, so that, giving themselves up to pleasure, they might be the more easily conquered. Manius Curius had lived in intimacy with Publius Decius, who, five years before Curius was Consul, had in his fourth

with a sword, and when he attempted to retreat, invoking the good faith of the Roman people, stabbed him to the heart.

[1] Epicurus, undoubtedly. Cineas was his contemporary, though probably not his disciple. He was the intimate friend and favorite minister of Pyrrhus, king of Epeirus, who used to say that Cineas had taken more cities by his words than he himself had taken by his sword. This sentence — almost overdone — is evidently framed expressly in imitation of an old man's rambling way of telling a story.

consulate devoted his own life for the safety of the state.[1]  Fabricius had known Publius Decius, Coruncanius had known him, and from that act of self-sacrifice, as well as from his whole life, they inferred that there is that which in its very nature is beautiful and excellent, which is chosen of one's own free will, and which every truly good man pursues, spurning and despising pleasure.  But to what purpose am I saying so much about pleasure?  Because it is not only no reproach to old age, but even its highest merit, that it does not severely feel the loss of bodily pleasures.  But, you may say, it must dispense with sumptuous feasts, and loaded tables, and oft-drained cups.  True, but it equally dispenses with sottishness, and indigestion, and troubled dreams.[2]  But if any license is to be given to pleasure, seeing that we do not easily resist its allurements, — insomuch that Plato calls pleasure the bait of evil, because, forsooth, men are caught by it as fishes by the hook, — old age, while it dispenses with excessive feasting, yet can find delight in moderate conviviality.  When I was a boy I

---

[1] In the battle of Sentinum, Decius, finding that his soldiers were giving way before the fierce onslaught of the Gauls, called one of the *pontifices*, and asked him to dictate the proper form of self-devotion, with imprecation upon the enemy.  Then, repeating the sacred words, he rushed into the ranks of the enemy and was slain.  His army, inspirited by his self-sacrifice, won a splendid victory.  His father had, on a previous occasion, devoted himself in like form and manner.

[2] Latin, *insomniis*, which literally means *sleeplessness*.

often saw Caius Duilius, the son of Marcus, who first gained a naval victory over the Carthaginians, returning home from supper. He took delight in the frequent escort of a torch-bearer and a flute-player, — the first person not actually in office who ventured on such display, — a liberty assumed on the score of his military fame.[1] But why am I talking about others? I now return to my own case. In the first place, I have for many years belonged to a guild.[2] Indeed, guilds were established when I was Quaestor, at the time when the Idaean rites in honor of the Great Mother were adopted in Rome. I then used to feast with my guild fellows, moderately on the whole, yet with something of the joviality that belonged to my earlier years; but with advancing age, day by day, everything is tempered down. Nor did I ever measure my delight

[1] Dr. Schmitz, in Smith's Dictionary, says, undoubtedly on competent authority, though I can find none, that the torch-bearer and the flute-player were permitted to Duilius as a reward for his victory. Livy says, in almost the same words with those in our text, that Duilius assumed these marks of distinction.

[2] *Club* would perhaps be a better rendering. The Roman clubs were formed nominally in honor of some divinity, but grew naturally into associations for convivial enjoyment, by the same tendencies which in Christendom have converted *holy days* into *holidays*. Whenever a new worship was introduced, a new club was formed to take it in charge. Cato's club was formed at the time when a shapeless stone, probably meteoric, — said to have fallen from heaven on Mount Ida, and worshipped under the name of *Magna Mater*, or Cybele, — was brought to Rome, in accordance with counsels said to have been derived from the Sibylline oracles.

at these entertainments by the amount of bodily pleasure more than by the intercourse and conversation of friends. In this feeling, our ancestors fitly called the festive meeting of friends at table, as implying union in life, a convivial meeting, — a much better name than that of the Greeks, who call such an occasion sometimes a compotation, sometimes a social supper,[1] evidently attaching the chief importance to that which is of the least moment in an entertainment.

XIV. I, indeed, for the pleasure of conversation, enjoy festive entertainments, even when they begin early and end late,[2] and that, not only in the company of my coevals, of whom very few remain, but with those of your age and with you; and I am heartily thankful to my advanced years for increasing my appetency for conversation, and diminishing my craving for food and drink. But if any one takes delight in the mere pleasures of the table, lest I may seem utterly hostile to appetites which

[1] The following is a more literal rendering of this passage : "Our ancestors appropriately named the reclining together of frends at a banquet *convivium* [*cum* and *vivo*, living together], because it implied a community of life. Better they than the Greeks, who called the same thing sometimes *compotatio* [*cum* and *poto*, drinking together], and sometimes *concoenatio* [*con* and *coeno*, supping together]." *Compotatio* and *concoenatio* are both Latin words. The corresponding Greek words are συμπόσιον (whence *symposium*) and σύνδειπνον.

[2] Latin, *tempestivis conviviis*. *Tempestivus* originally meant *seasonable*, thence *over early*. It is often used to designate at the same time the *over early* and the *over late*.

perhaps spring from a natural impulse, I would not
have it understood that old age is not susceptible of
them. I, indeed enjoy the ancestral fashion of appointing a master of ceremonies for the feast,[1] and
the rules for drinking announced from the head of
the table, and cups, as in Xenophon's *Symposium*,[2]
not over large, and slowly drunk, and the cool breeze
for the dining-hall in summer, and the winter's sun
or fire.[3] Even on my Sabine farm I keep up these
customs, and daily fill my table with my neighbors,
prolonging our varied talk to the latest possible
hour. But it is said that old men have less inten-
sity of sensual enjoyment. So I believe; but there
is no craving for it. You do not miss what you
do not want. Sophocles very aptly replied, when

---

[1] The Roman arrangements for a festive occasion were not
unlike our own. A presiding officer — the host, or some one
appointed by him, or chosen by the throw of dice — called upon
the guests in turn, that on subjects of conversation no opinion
might be lost, and no guest slighted. He also, in the fashion
maintained in England among convivialists till a comparatively
recent time, announced the rules to be observed in drinking, and
closed his speech with the words, *Aut bibe, aut abi*, "Either
drink or go."

[2] Συμπόσιον, a dialogue specially designed to bring out the
leading traits in the character of Socrates, who is the chief
speaker, and of value, also, as grouping the interlocutors at a
banquet, and thus incidentally presenting a picture of the eti-
quette and arrangements of an Athenian supper-table.

[3] It was not uncommon for rich Romans to have both summer
and winter banqueting-rooms, — the winter room, if possible,
open to the full heating power of the sun, which in that climate
supersedes the necessity of artificial heat.

asked in his old age whether he indulged in sensual pleasure, " May the gods do better for me! I
rejoice in my escape from a savage and ferocious
tyrant." To those who desire such pleasures it
may be offensive and grievous to be debarred from
them; but to those already filled and satiated it is
more pleasant to lack them than to have them.
Though he does not lack who does not want them,
I maintain that it is more for one's happiness not
to want them. But if young men take special
delight in these pleasures, in the first place, they
are very paltry sources of enjoyment, and, in the
second place, they are not wholly out of the reach
of old men, though it be in a restricted measure.
As the spectator in the front seat gets the greater
enjoyment from the acting of Turpio Ambivius,[1]
yet those on the farthest seat are delighted to be
there; so youth, having a closer view of the pleasures of sense, derives, it may be, more joy from
them, while old age has as much enjoyment as it
wants in seeing them at a distance. But of what
immense worth is it for the soul to be with itself,
to live, as the phrase is, with itself, discharged from
the service of lust, ambition, strife, enmities, desires
of every kind! If one has some provision laid up,
as it were, of study and learning, nothing is more
enjoyable than the leisure of old age. We saw
Caius Gallus, your father's friend, Scipio, almost to

---

[1] The most celebrated actor of his time, contemporary with
Terence, and taking leading parts in some of his plays.

the last moment occupied in measuring heaven and earth. How often did the morning light overtake him when he had begun some problem [1] by night, and the night when he had begun in the early morning! How did he delight to predict to us far in advance the eclipses of the sun and moon! What pleasure have old men taken in pursuits less recondite, yet demanding keenness and vigor of mind! How did Naevius rejoice in his *Punic War !* [2] Plautus in his *Truculentus,* — in his *Pseudolus !* [3] I saw also Livius [4] in his old age, who, having brought out a play [5] six years before I was born, in the consulship of Cento and Tuditanus, continued before the public till I was almost a man. What shall I say of the devotion of Publius Licinius Crassus [6] to the study of pontifical and civil law? What of the similar diligence of this

---

[1] Latin, *aliquid describere,* probably denoting *to draw a diagram.* Gallus undoubtedly employed geometrical methods in his astronomical studies.

[2] Naevius was the earliest Roman poet of enduring reputation. He wrote both comedies and tragedies, and in his old age, banished to Utica for libels contained in his plays, he produced an epic poem on the first Punic war, in which he had served as a soldier.

[3] Both of these plays are extant. They were probably the latest that he wrote.

[4] Livius Andronicus, earlier than Naevius. His plays were in ruder Latin, and in Cicero's time were no longer read.

[5] Latin, *fabulam docuisset,* i. e. taught the actors their parts, and presided at the rehearsal.

[6] He was both Consul and *pontifex maximus.*

Publius Scipio,[1] who has just been put at the head
of the pontifical college? We have seen all these
whom I have named ardently engaged in their old
age in their several departments of mental labor.
Marcus Cethegus,[2] too, whom Ennius rightly called
the "Marrow of Persuasion," — how zealously did
we see him exercise himself when an old man in
the art of speaking! What, then, are the pleasures of feasts, and games, and sensual indulgence,
compared with these pleasures? Indeed, it is these
intellectual pursuits that for wise and well-nurtured
men grow with years, so that it is to Solon's honor
that he says, in the verse which I just now quoted,
that as he advanced in age he learned something
every day, — a pleasure of the mind than which
there can be none greater.

XV. I pass now to the pleasures of agriculture,
which give me inconceivable delight, to which age
is no impediment, and in which one makes the
nearest approach to the life of the true philosopher.
For the farmer keeps an open account with the

[1] Publius Cornelius Scipio Corculum, twice Consul, also Censor and *pontifex maximus,* a man of superior integrity as well as
learning, and a strong conservative as to manners and morals.
The surname of *Corculum,* a diminutive of *cor,* was given him, it
is said, for his wisdom, but more probably for the combined qualities of mind and heart that won for him the confidence of the
people.

[2] He filled successively the highest offices in the republic, and
was for many years *pontifex maximus.* Horace refers to him as
valid authority for the use of words that were obsolescent when
he wrote.

earth, which never refuses a draft, nor ever returns
what has been committed to it without interest,
and if sometimes at a small, generally at an ample
rate of increase. Yet I am charmed not only with
the revenue, but with the very nature and properties of the soil. When it has received the seed into
its softened and prepared bosom, it keeps it buried [1]
(whence our word for the harrowing [2] which buries
the seed is derived), then by its pressure and by
the moisture which it yields it cleaves the seed and
draws out from it the green shoot, which, sustained
by its rootlet-fibres, grows till it stands erect on its
jointed stalk, enclosed in sheaths, as if to protect
the down of its youth, till, emerging from them, it
yields the grain, with its orderly arrangement in the
ear, defended against predatory birds by its bearded
rampart. What can I say of the planting, up-
springing, and growth of vines? It is with insa-
tiable delight that I thus make known to you the
repose and enjoyment of my old age. Not to speak
of the vital power of all things that grow directly
from the earth, — which from so tiny a fig or grape
seed, or from the very smallest seeds of other
fruits or plants, produces such massive trunks and

[1] Latin, *occaecatum*, literally *blinded*, from *ob* and *caecus.*

[2] Latin, *occatio*, from the verb *occo*. There seems no reason for
deriving this from *occaeco*. Cicero is very apt to infer derivation
from similarity, and there are not a few tokens of his carelessness
in this regard. Thus in different works of his he derives *religio*
from *religo* and *relego*, giving from each derivation the definition
that serves his turn at the time.

branches, — do not shoots, scions, quicksets, layers,
accomplish results which no one can behold without delighted admiration ? The vine, indeed, droop-
ing by nature, unless supported, is weighed down to
the ground; but to raise itself it embraces with its
hand-like tendrils whatever it can lay hold upon;
and then, as it twines with multifold and diffusive
growth, the art of the vine-dresser trims it close
with the pruning-knife, that it may not run unto
useless wood and spread too far. Thus in the early
spring, in what remains after the pruning, the gem
(so called) starts out at the joints of the twigs, from
which the incipient cluster of grapes makes its appearance; and this, growing by the moisture of the
earth and the heat of the sun, is at first very sour
to the taste ; then, as it ripens, it becomes sweet,
while, clothed with leaves, it lacks not moderate
warmth, and at the same time escapes the sun's
intenser beams. What can be more gladdening
than the fruit of the vine; what more beautiful, as
it hangs ungathered ? I am charmed, as I have said,
not only with the utility of the vine, but equally
with the whole process of its cultivation and with
its very nature, — with its rows of stakes, the lat-
eral supports from stake to stake, the tying up and
training of the vines, the amputation of some of
the twigs, of which I have spoken, and the planting
of others. What can I tell you of irrigation, and
of the repeated digging of the soil to make the
ground more fertile ? What shall I say of the

efficacy of manuring ? of which I have written in
my book on *Farm Life*,[1] but of which the learned
Hesiod, in writing about agriculture, says not a
word, — though Homer, who, I think, lived many
generations before him, introduces Laertes as reliev-
ing his solicitude for his son by tilling and manuring his field.   Nor is rural life made cheerful by
grainfields, meadows, vineyards, and shrubberies
alone, but also by gardens and orchards ; then
again, by the feeding of sheep, by swarms of bees,
by a vast variety of flowers.   Nor does one take
pleasure merely in the various modes of planting,
but equally in those of grafting, than which no
agricultural invention shows greater skill.

XVI.   I could enumerate many other charms of
rural life ; but I feel that those which I have named
have occupied fully enough of your time.   Pardon
me ; for I am thoroughly versed in everything belonging to country life, and old age is naturally
prolix, nor can I pretend to acquit it of all the

---

[1] *De Re Rustica,* — a work much less sentimental than a
"Farmer's Almanac."   The Cato who has such an æsthetic appreciation of the charms of rural life, is a myth of Cicero.   Cato's
own book is a manual of hard, stern, sometimes brutal economy,
advising the sale of worn-out cattle, and of old or sick slaves.
*Vendat boves vetulos . . . . servum senem, servum morbosum, et
siquid aliud supersit, vendat.*   He even carries his niggardliness
so far as to recommend that, when a slave has a new garment
given him, the old shall be taken from him, to be used for
patches.   But Cicero is right in representing Cato as wise on the
subject of manure, on which, if I am not mistaken, he was in
advance, not only of his own time, but even of ours.

weaknesses laid to its charge. With your leave I would add, then, that Manius Curius, after winning triumphs over the Samnites, over the Sabines, over Pyrrhus, spent the close of his life in the country; and when I look at his house, which is not far from mine, I cannot sufficiently admire either the self-denying integrity of the man himself or the high moral standard of his time. As Curius was sitting by his hearth the Samnites brought him a large amount of gold, and he spurned the bribe, saying that he thought it better than having gold to bear sway over those who have gold. Such a mind cannot fail to make a happy old age. — But to return to my subject, and not to wander from my own mode of life, there were in those days Senators, that is, as the name implies, old men, living on farms, if indeed Lucius Quinctius Cincinnatus received when ploughing the announcement that he had been made Dictator, under whose dictatorship it was that Caius Servilius Ahala, the Master of Horse, by his order, slew Spurius Maelius, who was aspiring after royalty.[1] Curius, too, and other old men, were wont to be summoned from their farms to the Senate, giving thus to the messengers who summoned them a special name[2] derived from the highways

---

[1] Cincinnatus was twice Dictator. It was to his first dictatorship that he was called from the plough; in his second, that he ordered the killing of Spurius Maelius.

[2] *Viatores*, from *via*, a public highway. This name was given from early time to messengers of the magistrates and of the courts,

on which they travelled. Was then the old age of
these men who found delight in tilling the ground
unhappy? I indeed doubt whether there can be
any happier old age, taking into account not only
the occupation of agriculture which is healthy for
every one, but also the enjoyment of which I have
spoken, and the bountiful supply of everything that
can be desired for the food of man and the worship
of the gods, so that, if any persons have such cravings, we may come again into friendly terms with
the pleasures of sense. For a thrifty and industri-
ous farmer has a full wine-cellar, oil-cellar, and
larder, and the whole estate is rich, abounding in
swine, kids, lambs, fowls, milk, cheese, honey. The
farmers themselves are wont to call their garden a
second stock of the winter's relishing food.[1] All
else has the richer zest from the work of leisure
time in fowling and hunting. Why should I say
more about the green of the meadows, or the rows
of trees, or the beauty of the vineyards and the
olive groves? To cut the subject short, nothing

---

whether their office was performed within or beyond the city
limits. There may be other authorities than Cicero's for the
derivation of the word from the summoning of Senators resident
in the country : I know of none.

[1] Latin, *succidiam alteram. Succidia* means *bacon,* and I can
find no other probable meaning for it. My interpretation of the
passage is this. Farmers laid in a stock of bacon, or strongly
salted meats, for winter, to give a relish to other food. They
looked to their gardens to furnish a corresponding relish for
summer.

can be more bountiful for use, or more ornate to the eye, than a well-cultivated farm, to the enjoyment of which advanced years not only interpose no hindrance, but hold forth invitation and allurement; for where can old age find more genial warmth of sunshine or fire, or, on the other hand, more cooling shade or more refreshing waters? Let others take for their own delight arms, horses, spears, clubs, balls, swimming-bouts, and foot-races. From their many diversions let them leave for us old men knuckle-bones and dice.[1] Either will serve our turn; but without them old age can hardly be contented.

XVII. Xenophon's books are in many ways very useful, and I beg you to continue, to read them. With what a flow of eloquence does he praise agriculture in that book of his about the care of one's estate, called *Oeconomicus!* [2] Still more, to show that there is nothing so worthy of a king as the pursuits of agriculture, he introduces in that book Socrates as telling this story to Critobolus. Cyrus

---

[1] Latin, *talos et tesseras.* *Talus* means an ankle- or knuckle-bone. The *tali* used by the Romans were either the actual bones of animals, or imitations of them in ivory, bronze, or stone. They were employed sometimes as jack-stones or dib-stones are now, in games of skill, and sometimes with the numbers I., II., III., and IV. on their four plane surfaces, in games of chance. The *tesserae* were cubes of ivory, bone, or wood, like our dice, numbered from one to six.

[2] Οἰκονομικός, a work wholly devoted to the care of property.

the younger, king of Persia,[1] of surpassing genius and renown, when Lysander, the Lacedaemonian, a man of the highest military reputation,[2] came to him at Sardis to bring presents from the confederate states, having treated Lysander in other ways with familiar courtesy, showed him an enclosed field planted with the utmost care. Lysander, marvelling at the great height of the trees, their arrangement in ornamental groups,[3] the ground thoroughly tilled and free from weeds, and the delicious odors breathing from the flowers, said that he admired, not only the care, but also the skill of him who had planned and laid out these grounds. Cyrus answered, "I myself laid out all this field. The plan is mine; the arrangement is mine, and many of these trees I planted with my own hand." Then Lysander, looking at his purple robe, his elegance of person,[4] and his Persian ornaments rich in gold and precious stones, said, "Men may well call

---

[1] This Cyrus was not a king, but a viceroy under his brother, Artaxerxes Mnemon.

[2] Latin, *vir summae virtutis.* I have given to *virtus* its primitive military signification. He was a brave man and an able commander, but cruel and treacherous; and it is hardly possible that Cicero could have meant to ascribe to him *virtus* in the ethical sense in which he often uses the word.

[3] Latin, *directos in quincuncem ordines.* The *quincunx* was a favorite mode of planting with the Roman gardeners. The name is derived from the numeral V, every three trees being so arranged as to form a V.

[4] Latin, *nitorem corporis.* Perhaps, but I think not, his body shining with oil.

you happy, Cyrus, since your fortune corresponds to your merit." This fortune, then, old men can enjoy, nor does age preclude our interest in other things indeed, but least of all in agriculture, to the very last moment of life. We have heard that Marcus Valerius Corvus lived to his hundredth year, passing the close of his life in the country, and engaged to the last in labors of the field. There were forty-six years between his first and his sixth consulship. Thus his term of public life lasted the full number of years which our ancestors accounted as the beginning of old age,[1] and his old age was happier than middle life, having more authority with less labor. Indeed, the crowning glory of old age is authority. How great was this in Lucius Caecilius Metellus! How great in Atilius Calatinus! whose eulogy is, —

> " Him first of men all tribes and nations own
> With one consent."

This, you know, is the inscription on his tomb. He was rightly held, then, in the highest esteem, since all were unanimous in his praise. How great a man did we see in Publius Crassus, the chief priest, of whom I have just spoken, and afterward in Marcus Lepidus, invested with the same priesthood! What shall I say of Paullus or of Africanus? Or of Maximus,[2] if I may name him again?

---

[1] In their forty-sixth year Roman citizens were exempted on the score of age from liability to military service.

[2] Quintus Fabius Maximus. See Sect. X.

These were men, not only in whose uttered opinion, but in whose very nod, dwelt authority. Old age, especially when it has filled offices of high public trust, has so much authority, that for this alone it is worth all the pleasures of youth.

XVIII. But remember that in all that I say I am praising the old age that has laid its foundations in youth. Hence follows the maxim to which I once gave utterance with the assent of all who heard me : " Wretched is the old age which has to speak in its own defence." White hairs or wrinkles cannot usurp authority ; but an early life well spent reaps authority as the fruit of its age. Indeed, attentions which seem trivial and conventional are honorable when merited; for instance, being saluted in the morning, grasped by the hand, received by the rising of those present, escorted to the Forum, escorted home, asked for advice, — customs carefully observed with us, and in other states so far as good manners prevail. It is related that Lysander the Lacedaemonian, of whom I just made mention, used to say that Lacedaemon was the best home for an old man, insomuch as nowhere else was such deference paid to length of years, or age held in such honor. There is, indeed, a tradition that once in Athens, at a public festival, when an old Athenian entered the crowded theatre, no one of his fellow-citizens made room for him, but that, as he approached the place assigned to the delegates from Lacedaemon, they all rose and remained standing till the old man was seated. When they were applauded for this in every possible way by the whole assembly, one of them said, "The Athenians know what is right, but will not do it." Of many excellent usages in our college of Augurs none deserves higher commendation than this, — that the members give their opinions in the order of age, the elder members taking precedence, not only of those who have held higher official rank, but even of those who for the time being are at the head of the state.[1] What pleasures of body are then to be compared with the prerogatives of authority ? Those who have borne these honors with due dignity seem to me to have thoroughly performed their part in the drama of life, and not, like untrained players, to have broken down in the last act. — But it is said that old men are morose, and uneasy, and irritable, and hard to please ; and were we to make the inquiry, we might be told that they are avaricious. But these are faults of character, not of age. Yet moroseness and the faults that I named with it have some excuse, sufficient, not indeed to justify, but to extenuate them. Old men imagine that they are scorned, despised, mocked. Then, too, with a frail body, any cause of vexation is felt more keenly. But such infirmities of temper are

---

[1] The Augurs were chosen for life, and did not lose their official rank and title, even in case of disgraceful punishment. It was, therefore, possible for a Consul or Censor to be at the same time an Augur.

corrected by good manners and liberal culture, as
we may see in actual life, as well as on the stage in
the brothers in the play of the *Adelphi.* What
grimness do we see in one of these brothers; what a
genial disposition in the other! So it is in society;
for as it is not wine of every vintage, so it is not
every temper that grows sour with age. I approve
of gravity in old age, so it be not excessive; for
moderation in all things is becoming : but for bitterness I have no tolerance. As for senile avarice,
I do not understand what it means; for can anything be more foolish than, in proportion as there
is less of the way to travel, to seek the more
provision for it ?

XIX. There remains a fourth reason for depre-
cating old age, that it is liable to excessive solicitude
and distress, because death is so near; and it certainly cannot be very far off. O wretched old man,
not to have learned in so long a life that death is
to be despised ! which manifestly ought to be regarded with indifference if it really puts an end to
the soul, or to be even desired if at length it leads
the soul where it will be immortal; and certainly
there is no third possibility that can be imagined.[1]
Why then should I fear if after death I shall be

---

[1] Cicero seems to have forgotten that the Stoics of the earlier
school believed in the survival of the soul after death, but not in
its immortality. The soul was, at the consummation of the present order of the universe, to be reabsorbed into the divine essence
from which it emanated, and thus in the new creation that would
ensue to have no separate existence.

either not miserable, or even happy ? Moreover,
who is so foolish, however young he may be, as to
feel sure on any day that he will live till nightfall ?
Youth has many more chances of death than those
of my age. Young men are more liable to illnesses ; they are more severely attacked by disease ;
they are cured with more difficulty. Thus few
reach old age. Were it otherwise, affairs would be
better and more discreetly managed ; for old men
have mind and reason and practical wisdom ; and
if there were none of them, communities could not
hold together. But to return to impending death,
— can this be urged as a charge against old age,
when you see that it belongs to it in common with
youth ? I felt in the death of my most excellent
son,[1] and equally, Scipio, in that of your brothers,[2]
who were born to the expectation of the highest
honors, that death is common to all ages. But, it
is said, the young man hopes to live long, while the

[1] Marcus Porcius Cato Licinianus. He was Cato's only son by
his first marriage. He had reached middle life, and died but a
few years before his father. He was a man of high character, had
become eminent as a jurist, and was praetor elect at the time of
his death. His father pronounced his eulogy at his funeral, which
was conducted at the lowest possible rate of expense, on the plea
of poverty, which the father's miserly disposition probably justified to his own consciousness.

[2] Two sons of Aemilius Paullus, who died at the ages of twelve
and fifteen, one just before, the other shortly after their father's
triumph over Perseus. As his two elder sons had become by
adoption members of other families, he was left without legal
heir or successor.

old man can have no such hope. The hope, at any
rate, is unwise; for what is more foolish than to
take things uncertain for certain, false for true? Is
it urged that the old man has absolutely nothing
to hope? For that very reason he is in a better
condition than the young man, because what the
youth hopes he has already obtained. The one
wishes to live long; the other has lived long.
Yet, ye good gods, what is there in man's life that
is long? Grant the very latest term of life; suppose that we expect to reach the age of the king
of Tartessus.[1] For it is on record that a certain
Arganthonius, who reigned eighty years in Gades,
lived to the age of a hundred and twenty. But to
me no life seems long that has any end. For when
the end comes, then that which has passed has
flowed away; that alone remains which you have
won by virtue and by a good life. Hours, indeed,
and days, and months, and years, glide by, nor does
the past ever return, nor yet can it be known what
is to come. Each one should be content with such
time as it is allotted to him to live. In order to give
pleasure to the audience, the actor need not finish

---

[1] A region in the southwest corner of Spain, supposed, not un-
reasonably, to be the Tarshish of the Hebrew Scriptures. Its
chief city was Gades (a plural form, including adjacent islands),
or Gadis, known in modern geography by the slightly altered
name of Cadiz. This city was the seat of a very ancient Phoeni-
cian colony. The longevity of Arganthonius is mentioned by
several writers, who do not agree as to his age. Pliny says that
he lived a hundred and thirty years.

the play; he may win approval in whatever act he
takes part in; nor need the wise man remain on
the stage till the closing plaudit. A brief time is
long enough to live well and honorably;[1] but if
you live on, you have no more reason to mourn
over your advancing years, than the farmers have,
when the sweet days of spring are past, to lament
the coming of summer and of autumn. Spring
typifies youth, and shows the fruit that will be;
the rest of life is fitted for reaping and gathering
the fruit. Moreover, the fruit of old age is, as I
have often said, the memory and abundance of
goods previously obtained. But all things that occur according to nature are to be reckoned as goods;
and what is so fully according to nature as for old
men to die? while the same thing happens to the
young with the opposition and repugnancy of nature. Thus young men seem to me to die as when
a fierce flame is extinguished by a stream of water;
while old men die as when a spent fire goes out of
its own accord, without force employed to quench
it. Or, as apples, if unripe, are violently wrenched
from the tree, while, mature and ripened, they fall,
so force takes life from the young, maturity from
the old; and this ripeness of old age is to me so

---

[1] "Honorable age is not that which standeth in length of
time, or that is measured by number of years. But wisdom is the
gray hair unto men, and an unspotted life is old age..... He,
being made perfect in a short time, fulfilled a long time." — *Wisdom of Solomon*, iv. 8, 9, 14.

pleasant, that, in proportion as I draw near to death, I seem to see land, and after a long voyage to be on the point of entering the harbor.

XX. The close of other ages is definitely fixed;[1] but old age has no fixed term, and one may fitly live in it so long as he can observe and discharge the duties of his station, and yet despise death. Old age, fearless of death, may transcend youth in courage and in fortitude. Such is the meaning of Solon's answer to the tyrant Pisistratus, who asked him what was his ground of confidence in resisting him so boldly, and Solon replied, "Old age." But the most desirable end of life is when — the understanding and the other faculties unimpaired — Nature, who put together, takes apart her own work. As he who built a ship or a house can take it to pieces the most easily, so Nature, who compacted the human frame, is the best agent for its dissolution. Then, again, whatever has been recently put together is torn apart with difficulty; old fabrics, easily. Thus what brief remainder there may be of life ought to be neither greedily sought by old men, nor yet abandoned without cause,[2] and Pythagoras forbids one to desert the garrison and post of life without the order of the commander, that is,

---

[1] Childhood legally terminated at seventeen, youth at forty-six; then old age began.

[2] The Stoics generally maintained the lawfulness of suicide *for sufficient cause*, and Cicero more than intimates this as his opinion. Pythagoras, and Socrates, as reported by Plato, utterly condemned it.

God. There are extant, indeed, verses of Solon the Wise,[1] in which he says that he does not want to die without the grief and lamentation of his friends, desiring, as I suppose, to be held dear by those in intimate relation with him; but I am inclined to prefer what Ennius writes,—

> " Let no one honor me with tears, or make
>  A lamentation at my funeral."

He thinks that death is not to be mourned, since it is followed by immortality. There may be, indeed, some painful sensation in dying, yet for only a little while, especially for the old; after death there is either desirable sensation or none at all. But such thoughts as this ought to be familiar to us from youth, that we may make no account of death. Without such habits of thought one cannot be of a tranquil mind; for it is certain that we must die, and it is uncertain whether it be not this very passing day. How then can one be composed in mind while he fears death, which impends over him every hour? On this subject there seems no need of a long discussion, when I recall to memory,—not Lucius Brutus, who was slain in setting his country free; not the two Decii, spurring their horses to a death of their own choice; not Marcus Atilius, returning to the punishment of death that he might keep faith with an enemy; not the two Scipios, who wanted to block the way for the Carthaginians even

---

[1] Solon was one of the Seven Wise Men of Greece.

with their own bodies; not your grandfather, Lucius Paullus, who yielded up his life to expiate his
colleague's rashness in the ignominious battle of
Cannae; not Marcus Marcellus, whose body not
even the most cruel of enemies would suffer to
lack the honor of a funeral,[1] — but our legions,
often going, as I have said in my *History*,[2] with a
firm and cheerful mind, to scenes of peril whence
they expected never to return.  Shall well-trained
old men, then, fear what youth, and they not only
untrained, but even fresh from the country, despise ? — In fine, satiety of life, as it seems to me,
creates satiety of pursuits of every kind.  There are
certain pursuits belonging to boyhood; do grown-
up young men therefore long for them ?  There are
others appertaining to early youth; are they required in the sedate period of life which we call
middle age ?  This, too, has its own pursuits, and
they are not sought in old age.  As the pursuits of
earlier periods of life fail, so in like manner do
those of old age.  When this period is reached,
satiety of life brings a season ripe for death.

XXI.  I see, indeed, no reason why I should
hesitate to tell you how I myself feel about death ;
for I seem to have a clearer view of it, the nearer
I approach it.  My belief is that your father, Pub-

---

[1] The names and incidents here enumerated and referred to are
too familiar to the readers of Roman history to require special
notice.

[2] *Origines.*

lius Scipio, and yours, Caius Laelius, men of the highest renown and my very dear friends, are living, and are living the only life that truly deserves to be called life. Indeed, while we are shut up in this prison of the body, we are performing a heavy task laid upon us by necessity; for the soul, of celestial birth, is forced down from its supremely high abode, and, as it were, plunged into the earth, a place uncongenial with its divine nature and its eternity. I believe, indeed, that the gods disseminated souls, and planted them in human bodies, that there might be those who should hold the earth in charge, and contemplating the order of celestial beings, should copy it in symmetry and harmony of life. I was led to this belief, not only by reason and argument, but by the pre-eminent authority of the greatest philosophers. I learned that Pythagoras and the Pythagoreans, almost our fellow-countrymen,[1] who used to be called Italian philosophers, never doubted that we had souls that emanated from the universal divine mind. I was impressed, also, by what Socrates, whom the oracle of Apollo pronounced the wisest of men, taught with regard to the immortality of souls, on the last

[1] Pythagoras was probably a native of Samos, but after extensive travel in the East established himself and gathered disciples at Crotona, a city founded by Greek colonists in Magna Graecia, or Southern Italy. Hence his followers bore the name of the Italian or Italic school, the only school of philosophy, it is believed, that ever seemed indigenous — though this not native — in Italian soil.

day of his life. Why should I say more ? So have
I convinced myself, so I feel, that since such is the
rapid movement of souls, such their memory of
the past and foresight of the future, so many are
the arts, so profound the sciences, so numerous the
inventions to which they have given birth, the nature which contains all these things cannot be mortal; that as the soul is always active, and has no
prime cause of motion inasmuch as it puts itself in
motion, so it can have no end of motion, because
it can never abandon itself; moreover, that since
the nature of the soul is uncompounded, and has in
itself no admixture of aught that is unequal to or
unlike itself, it is indivisible, and if so, is imperish-
able; and that there is strong reason for believing
that men know a great deal before they are born in
the ease with which boys learn difficult arts, and
the rapidity with which they seize upon innumerable things, so that they seem not to be receiving
them for the first time, but to be recalling and re-
membering them. This is the sum of what I have
from Plato.[1]

XXII. In Xenophon's narrative,[2] the elder Cyrus says in dying: "Do not imagine, my beloved
sons, that when I go from you I shall be nowhere,
or shall cease to be. For while I was with you,
you did not see my soul; but you inferred its exist-

[1] A synopsis of the argument for immortality given, as in the
words of Socrates, in Plato's *Phaedon.*
[2] The *Cyropaedia.*

ence from the things which I did in this body.
Believe then that I am the same being, even though
you do not see me at all. The fame of illustrious
men would not remain after their death, if the souls
of those men did nothing to perpetuate their memory. Indeed, I never could be persuaded that souls
live while they are in mortal bodies and die when
they depart from them, nor yet that the soul becomes void of wisdom on leaving a senseless body ;
but I have believed that when, freed from all corpo-
real mixture, it begins to be pure and entire, it then
is wise. Moreover, when the constitution of man
is dissolved by death, it is obvious what becomes of
each of the other parts; for they all go whence
they came: but the soul alone is invisible, alike
when it is present in the body and when it departs.
You see nothing so nearly resembling death as
sleep. Now in sleep souls most clearly show their
divineness;[1] for when they are thus relaxed and
free, they foresee the future. From this we may
understand what they will be when they have entirely released themselves from the bonds of the
body. Therefore, if these things are so, reverence
me as a divine being.[2] If, however, the soul is
going to perish with the body, you still, revering

---

[1] Latin, *divinitatem suam.*

[2] Latin, *sic me colitote, ut deum,* referring, as I suppose, not
to an apotheosis after the manner of the Roman Emperors, but to
the divineness (*divinitas*) ascribed to the soul in prescient dreams,
which, as has just been said, prefigure what the soul will become
in dying.

the gods who protect and govern all this beautiful
universe, will keep my memory in pious and inviolate regard." [1]

XXIII. Such were the last words of Cyrus.
Let me now, if it seem good to you, express my
own opinion and feeling. No one will ever con-
vince me, Scipio, that your father Paullus, or your
two grandfathers, Paullus and Africanus, or the
father or the uncle of Africanus, or many men of
surpassing excellence whom I need not name,
undertook such noble enterprises which were to
belong to the grateful remembrance of posterity,
without a clear perception that posterity belonged
to them. Or think you, — if after the manner of
old men I may boast a little on my own account, —
think you that I would have taken upon myself
such a vast amount of labor, by day and by night,
at home and in military service, if I had been going
to put the same limits to my fame that belong to
my earthly life? Would it not have been much
better to pass my time in leisure and quiet, remote
from toil and strife? But somehow my soul, raising itself [2] above the present, was always looking
onward to posterity, as if, when it departed from
life, then at length it would truly live. But unless

---

[1] This is not a literal translation from Xenophon, nor can it
have been intended for one. Cicero meant to give it in the form
in which Cato might have been supposed to quote it from
memory.

[2] Latin, *sese erigens . . . . prospiciebat.* The figure implies
standing, as it were, on tiptoe, to get a clearer distant view.

souls were indeed immortal, men's souls would not
strive for undying fame in proportion to their tran-
scending merit. What ? . Since men of the highest
wisdom die with perfect calmness, those who are
the most foolish with extreme disquiet, can you
doubt that the soul which sees more and farther
perceives that it is going to a better state, while
the soul of obtuser vision has no view beyond
death ?  For my part, I am transported with desire
to see your fathers whom I revered and loved;
nor yet do I long to meet those only whom I have
known, but also those of whom I have heard and
read, and about whom I myself have written.
Therefore one could not easily turn me back on
my lifeway, nor would I willingly, like Pelias,[1] be
plunged in the rejuvenating caldron.  Indeed, were
any god to grant that from my present age I might
go back to boyhood, or become a crying child in the
cradle, I should steadfastly refuse; nor would I be
willing, as from a finished race, to be summoned
back from the goal to the starting-point.  For what
advantage is there in life ?  Or rather, what is there
of arduous toil that is wanting to it ?  But grant
all that you may in its favor, it still certainly has
either its excess or its fit measure of duration.  I
am not, indeed, inclined to speak ill of life, as many
and even wise men have often done, nor am I sorry

---

[1] The myth, as it has come down to us, represents Aeson as
the old man whom magic arts made young again, while the like
experiment on Pelias was a disastrous failure.

to have lived; for I have so lived that I do not think that I was born to no purpose. Yet I depart from life, as from an inn, not as from a home; for nature has given us here a lodging for a sojourn, not a place of habitation. O glorious day, when I shall go to that divine company and assembly of souls, and when I shall depart from this crowd and tumult! I shall go, not only to the men of whom I have already spoken, but also to my Cato, than whom no better man was ever born, nor one who surpassed him in filial piety, whose funeral pile I lighted, — the office which he should have performed for me, — but whose soul, not leaving me, but looking back upon me, has certainly gone into those regions whither he saw that I should come to him. This my calamity I seemed to bear bravely. Not that I endured it with an untroubled mind; but I was consoled by the thought that there would be between us no long parting of the way and divided life. For these reasons, Scipio, as you have said that you and Laelius have observed with wonder, old age sits lightly upon me. Not only is it not burdensome; it is even pleasant. But if I err in believing that the souls of men are immortal, I am glad thus to err, nor am I willing that this error in which I delight shall be wrested from me so long as I live; while if in death, as some paltry philosophers[1] think, I shall have no consciousness, the

---

[1] The Epicureans, whose grovelling philosophy Cicero never loses an opportunity of assailing or decrying. This essay, it will

dead philosophers cannot ridicule this delusion of mine. But if we are not going to be immortal, it is yet desirable for man to cease living in his due time; for nature has its measure, as of all other things, so of life. Old age is the closing act of life, as of a drama, and we ought in this to avoid utter weariness, especially if the act has been prolonged beyond its due length. — I had these things to say about old age, which I earnestly hope that you may reach, so that you can verify by experience what you have heard from me.

be remembered, is dedicated to Atticus, who professed to belong to the Epicurean school, but whose opinions sat so lightly upon him that he was not likely to take offence at their being impugned or ridiculed.

# INDEX.

———•———

# CICERO DE AMICITIA

(ON FRIENDSHIP)

AND

# SCIPIO'S DREAM.

TRANSLATED

WITH

AN INTRODUCTION AND NOTES.

By ANDREW P. PEABODY.

BOSTON:
LITTLE, BROWN, AND COMPANY.
1887.

University Press:
JOHN WILSON AND SON, CAMBRIDGE.

# SYNOPSIS.

## DE AMICITIA.

§ 1. Introduction.
2. Reputation of Laelius for wisdom. The curiosity to know how he bore the death of Scipio.
3. His grounds of consolation in his bereavement.
4. He expresses his faith in immortality. Desires perpetual memory in this world of the friendship between himself and Scipio.
5. True friendship can exist only among good men.
6. Friendship defined.
7. Benefits derived from friendship.
8. Friendship founded not on need, but on nature.
9. The relation of utility to friendship.
10. Causes for the separation of friends.
11. How far love for friends may go.
12. Wrong never to be done at a friend's request.
13. Theories that degrade friendship.
14. How friendships are formed.
15. Friendlessness wretched.
16. The limits of friendship.
17. In what sense and to what degree friends are united. How friends are to be chosen and tested.
18. The qualities to be sought in a friend.
19. Old friends not to be forsaken for new.
20. The duties of friendship between persons differing in ability, rank, or position.

## SCIPIO'S DREAM.

# INTRODUCTION.

## DE AMICITIA.

THE *De Amicitia*, inscribed, like the *De Senectute*, to Atticus, was probably written early in the year 44 B. C., during Cicero's retirement, after the death of Julius Caesar and before the conflict with Antony. The subject had been a favorite one with Greek philosophers, from whom Cicero always borrowed largely, or rather, whose materials he made fairly his own by the skill, richness, and beauty of his elaboration. Some passages of this treatise were evidently suggested by Plato; and Aulus Gellius says that Cicero made no little use of a now lost essay of Theophrastus on Friendship.

In this work I am especially impressed by Cicero's dramatic power. But for the mediocrity of his poetic genius, he might have won pre-eminent honor from the Muse of Tragedy. He here so thoroughly enters into the feelings of Laelius with reference to Scipio's death, that as we read we forget that it is not Laelius himself who is speaking. We find ourselves in close sympathy with him, as if he were telling us the story of his bereavement, giving utterance

to his manly fortitude and resignation, and portray-
ing his friend's virtues from the unfading image
phototyped on his own loving memory.   In other
matters, too, Cicero goes back to the time of Laelius,
and assumes his point of view, assigning to him just
the degree of foresight which he probably possessed,
and making not the slightest reference to the very
different aspect in which he himself had learned to
regard and was wont to represent the personages and
events of that earlier period.   Thus, while Cicero
traced the downfall of the republic to changes in the
body politic that had taken place or were imminent
and inevitable when Scipio died, he makes Laelius
perceive only a slight though threatening deflection
from what had been in the earlier time.[1]   So too,
though Cicero was annoyed more than by almost
any other characteristic of his age by the prevalence
of the Epicurean philosophy, and ascribed to it in a
very large degree the demoralization of men in public life, with Laelius the doctrines of this school are
represented, as they must have been in fact, as new
and unfamiliar.   In fine, Laelius is here made to
say not a word which he, being the man that he
was, and at the date assumed for this dialogue,
might not have said himself; and it may be doubted
whether a report of one of his actual conversations
would have seemed more truly genuine.

This is a rare gift, often sought indeed, yet sought
in vain, not only by dramatists, who have very

---

[1] *Deflexit jam aliquantulum.*

seldom attained it, but by authors of a very great diversity of type and culture. One who undertakes to personate a character belonging to an age not his own hardly ever fails of manifest anachronisms. The author finds it utterly impossible to fit the antique mask so closely as not now and then to show through its chinks his own more modern features; while this form of internal evidence never fails to betray an intended forgery, however skilfully wrought. On the other hand, there is no surer proof of the genuineness of a work purporting to be of an earlier, but alleged to be of a later origin, than the absence of all tokens of a time subsequent to the earliest date claimed for it.[1]

In connection with this work it should be borne in mind that the special duties of friendship constituted an essential department of ethics in the ancient world, and that the relation of friend to friend was regarded as on the same plane with that of brother to brother. No treatise on morals would have been thought complete, had this subject been omitted. Not a few modern writers have attempted the formal treatment of friendship; but while the relation

---

[1] Thus among the many proofs of the genuineness of our canonical Gospels, perhaps none is more conclusive than the fact that, though evidently written by unskilled men, they contain not a trace or token of certain opinions known to have been rife even before the close of the first Christian century; while the (so-called) apocryphal Gospels bear, throughout, such vestiges of their later origin as would neutralize the strongest testimony imaginable in behalf of their primitive antiquity.

of kindred minds and souls has lost none of its sacredness and value, the establishment of a code of rules for it ignores, on the one hand, the spontaneity of this relation, and, on the other hand, its entire amenableness to the laws and principles that should restrict and govern all human intercourse and conduct.

Shaftesbury, in his " Characteristics," in his exquisite vein of irony, sneers at Christianity for taking no cognizance of friendship either in its precepts or in its promises. Jeremy Taylor, however, speaks of this feature of Christianity as among the manifest tokens of its divine origin; and Soame Jenyns takes the same ground in a treatise expressly designed to meet the objections and cavils of Shaftesbury and other deistical writers of his time. These authors are all in the right, and all in the wrong, as to the matter of fact. There is no reason why Christianity should prescribe friendship, which is a privilege, not a duty, or should essay to regulate it; for its only ethical rule of strict obligation is the negative rule, which would lay out for it a track that shall never interfere with any positive duty selfward, manward, or Godward. But in the life of the Founder of Christianity, who teaches, most of all, by example, friendship has its apogee, — its supreme pre-eminence and honor. He treats his apostles, and speaks of and to them, not as mere disciples, but as intimate and dearly beloved friends ; among these there are three with whom he stands in peculiarly near relations; and one of the three was singled out by him in dying for the most sacred charge that he left on the earth; while at the same time that disciple shows in his Gospel that he had obtained an inside view, so to speak, of his Master's spiritual life and of the profounder sense of his teachings, which is distinguished by contrast rather than by comparison from the more superficial narratives of the other evangelists.

But Christianity has done even more than this for friendship. It has superseded its name by fulfilling its offices to a degree of perfectness which had never entered into the ante-Christian mind. Man shrinks from solitude. He feels inadequate to bear the burdens, meet the trials, and wage the conflicts of this mortal life, alone. Orestes always needed and craved a Pylades, but often failed to find one. This inevitable yearning, when it met no human response, found still less to satisfy it in the objects of worship. Its gods, though in great part deified men, could not be relied on for sympathy, support, or help. The stronger spirits did not believe in them; the feebler looked upon them only with awe and dread. But Christianity, in its anthropomorphism, which is its strongest hold on faith and trust, insures for the individual man in a Divine Humanity precisely what friends might essay to do, yet could do but imperfectly, for him. It proffers the tender sympathy and helpfulness of Him who bears the griefs and carries the sorrows of

each and all; while the near view that it presents
of the life beyond death inspires the sense of unbroken union with friends in heaven, and of the
fellow-feeling of "a cloud of witnesses" beside.
Thus while friendship in ordinary life is never to
be spurned when it may be had without sacrifice
of principle, it is less a necessity than when man's
relations with the unseen world gave no promise
of strength, aid, or comfort.

Experience has deepened my conviction that
what is called a free translation is the only fit rendering of Latin into English; that is, the only way
of giving to the English reader the actual sense of
the Latin writer. This last has been my endeavor.
The comparison is, indeed, exaggerated; but it often
seems to me, in unrolling a compact Latin sentence,
as if I were writing out in words the meaning of
an algebraic formula. A single word often requires
three or four as its English equivalent. Yet the language is not made obscure by compression. On the
contrary, there is no other language in which it is
so hard to bury thought or to conceal its absence by
superfluous verbiage.

I have used Beier's edition of the *De Amicitia*,
adhering to it in the very few cases in which other
good editions have a different reading. There are
no instances in which the various readings involve
any considerable diversity of meaning.

## LAELIUS.

Caius Laelius Sapiens, the son of Caius Laelius, who was the life-long friend of Scipio Africanus the Elder, was born B. C. 186, a little earlier in the same year with his friend Africanus the Younger. He was not undistinguished as a military commander, as was proved by his successful campaign against Viriathus, the Lusitanian chieftain, who had long held the Roman armies at bay, and had repeatedly gained signal advantages over them. He was known in the State, at first as leaning, though moderately and guardedly, to the popular side, but after the disturbances created by the Gracchi, as a strong conservative. He was a learned and accomplished man, was an elegant writer, — though while the Latin tongue retained no little of its archaic rudeness, — and was possessed of some reputation as an orator. Though bearing his part in public affairs, holding at intervals the offices of Tribune, Praetor, and Consul, and in his latter years attending with exemplary fidelity to such duties as belonged to him as a member of the college of Augurs, he yet loved retirement, and cultivated, so far as he was able, studious and contemplative habits. He was noted for his wise economy of time. To an idle man who said to him, "I have sixty years "[1] (that is, I am sixty years old), he replied, "Do you mean the sixty years which you have not ?" His private life was worthy of all praise for the virtues that enriched and adorned it; and its memory was so fresh after the lapse of more than two centuries, that Seneca, who well knew the better way which he had not always strength to tread, advises his young friend Lucilius to "live with Laelius;"[2] that is, to take his life as a model.

The friendship of Laelius and the younger Scipio Africanus well deserves the commemoration which it has in this dialogue of Cicero. It began in their boyhood, and continued without interruption till Scipio's death. Laelius served in Africa, mainly that he might not be separated from his friend. To each the other's home was as his own. They were of one mind as to public men and measures, and in all probability the more pliant nature of Laelius yielded in great measure to the stern and uncompromising adherence of Scipio to the cause of the aristocracy. While they were united in grave pursuits and weighty interests, we have the most charming pictures of their rural and seaside life together, even of their gathering shells on the shore, and of fireside frolics in which they forgot the cares of the republic, ceased to be stately old Romans, and played like children in vacation-time.

[1] *Sexaginta annos habeo.*
[2] *Vive cum Laelio.*

## FANNIUS.

Caius Fannius Strabo in early life served with high reputation in Africa, under the younger Africanus, and afterward in Spain, in the war with Viriathus. Like his father-in-law, he was versed in the philosophy of the Stoic school, under the tuition of Panaetius. He was an orator, as were almost all the Romans who aimed at distinction; but we have no reason to suppose that he in this respect rose above mediocrity. He wrote a history, of which Cicero speaks well, and which Sallust commends for its accuracy; but it is entirely lost, and we have no direct information even as to the ground which it covered. It seems probable, however, that it was a history either of the third of the Punic wars, or of all of them; for Plutarch quotes from him — probably from his History — the statement that he, Fannius, and Tiberius Gracchus were the first to mount the walls of Carthage when the city was taken.

## SCAEVOLA.

Quintus Mucius Scaevola filled successively most of the important offices of the State, and was for many years, and until death, a member of the college of Augurs. He was eminent for his legal learning, and to a late and infirm old age was still consulted in questions of law, never refusing to receive clients at any moment after daylight. But while he was regarded as foremost among the jurists of his time, he professed himself less thoroughly versed in the laws relating to mortgages than two of his coevals, to whom he was wont to send those who brought cases of this class for his opinion or advice. He was remarkable for early rising, constant industry, and undeviating punctuality, — at the meetings of the Senate being always the first on the ground.

No man held a higher reputation than Scaevola for rigid and scrupulous integrity. It is related of him that when as a witness in court he had given testimony full, clear, strong, and of the most damnatory character against the person on trial, he protested against the conviction of the defendant on his testimony, if not corroborated, on the principle held sacred in the Jewish law, that it would be a dangerous precedent to suffer the issue of any case to depend on the intelligence and veracity of a single witness. When, after Marius had been driven from the city, Sulla asked the Senate to declare him by their vote a public enemy, Scaevola stood in a minority of one; and when Sulla urged him to give his vote in the affirmative, his reply was: " Although you show me the military guard with which you have surrounded the Senate-house, although you threaten me with death, you will never induce me, for the little blood still in an old man's veins, to pronounce Marius — who has been the preserver of the city and of Italy — an enemy."

His daughter married Lucius Licinius Crassus, who had such reverence for his father-in-law, that, when a candidate for the consulship, he could not persuade himself in the presence of Scaevola to cringe to the people, or to adopt any of the usual self-humiliating methods of canvassing for the popular vote.

## SCIPIO'S DREAM.

PALIMPSESTS [1] — the name and the thing — are at least as old as Cicero. In one of his letters he banters his friend Trebatius for writing to him on a palimpsest,[2] and marvels what there could have been on the parchment which he wanted to erase. This was a device probably resorted to in that age only in the way in which rigid economists of our day sometimes utilize envelopes and handbills. But in the dark ages, when classical literature was under a cloud and a ban, and when the scanty demand for writing materials made the supply both scanty and precarious, such manuscripts of profane authors as fell into the hands of ecclesiastical copyists were not unusually employed for transcribing the works of the Christian Fathers or the lives of saints. In such cases the erasion was so clumsily performed as often to leave distinct traces of the previous letters. The possibility of recovering lost writings from these palimpsests was first suggested by Montfaucon in the seventeenth century; but the earliest successful

---

[1] *Rubbed again,* — the parchment, or papyrus, having been first polished for use, and then rubbed as clean as possible, to be used a second time.

[2] *In palimpsesto.*

experiment of the kind was made by Bruns, a German scholar, in the latter part of the eighteenth century. The most distinguished laborer in this field has been Angelo Mai, who commenced his work in 1814 on manuscripts in the Ambrosian Library at Milan, of which he was then custodian. Transferred to the Vatican Library at Rome, he discovered there, in 1821, a considerable portion of Cicero's *De Republica*, which had been obliterated, and replaced by Saint Augustine's Commentary on the Psalms. This latter being removed by appropriate chemical applications, large portions of the original writing remained legible, and were promptly given to the public.

This treatise Cicero evidently considered, and not without reason, as his master-work. It was written in the prime of his mental vigor, in the fifty-fourth year of his age, after ample experience in the affairs of State, and while he still hoped more than he feared for the future of Rome. His object was to discuss in detail the principles and forms of civil government, to define the grounds of preference for a republic like that of Rome in its best days, and to describe the duties and responsibilities of a good citizen, whether in public office or in private life. He regarded this treatise, in its ethics, as his own directory in the government of his province of Cilicia, and as binding him, by the law of self-consistency, to unswerving uprightness and faithfulness. He refers to these six books on the Republic as so

many hostages[1] for his uncorrupt integrity and un-
tarnished honor, and makes them his apology to
Atticus for declining to urge an extortionate demand
on the city of Salamis.

The work is in the form of Dialogues, in which,
with several interlocutors beside, the younger Africanus and Laelius are the chief speakers; and it is
characterized by the same traits of dramatic genius
to which I have referred in connection with the *De
Amicitia.*

The *De Republica* was probably under interdict
during the reigns of the Augustan dynasty; men
did not dare to copy it, or to have it known that
they possessed it; and when it might have safely
reappeared, the republic had faded even from regret-
ful memory, and there was no desire to perpetuate
a work devoted to its service and honor. Thus the
world had lost the very one of all Cicero's writings
for which he most craved immortality. The portions of it which Mai has brought to light fully
confirm Cicero's own estimate of its value, and feed
the earnest — it is to be feared the vain — desire
for the recovery of the entire work.

Scipio's Dream, which is nearly all that remains
of the Sixth Book of the *De Republica,* had survived
during the interval for which the rest of the treatise
was lost to the world. Macrobius, a grammarian
of the fifth century, made it the text of a commentary of little present interest or value, but much

---

[1] *Praedibus.*

prized and read in the Middle Ages. The Dream, independently of the commentary, has in more recent times passed through unnumbered editions, sometimes by itself, sometimes with Cicero's ethical writings, sometimes with the other fragments of the *De Republica.*

In the closing Dialogue of the *De Republica* the younger Africanus says : " Although to the wise the consciousness of noble deeds is a most ample reward of virtue, yet this divine virtue craves, not indeed statues that need lead to hold them to their pedestals, nor yet triumphs graced by withering laurels, but rewards of firmer structure and more enduring green." " What are these ? " says Laelius. Scipio replies by telling his dream. The time of the vision was near the beginning of the Third Punic War, when Scipio, no longer in his early youth, was just entering upon the career in which he gained pre-eminent fame, thenceforward to know neither shadow nor decline.

I have used for Scipio's Dream, Creuzer and Moser's edition of the *De Republica.*

# CICERO DE AMICITIA.

———◆———

1. QUINTUS MUCIUS, the Augur, used to repeat from memory, and in the most pleasant way, many of the sayings of his father-in-law, Caius Laelius, never hesitating to apply to him in all that he said his surname of The Wise. When I first put on the robe of manhood,[1] my father took me to Scaevola, and so commended me to his kind offices, that thenceforward, so far as was possible and fitting, I kept my place at the old man's side.[2] I thus laid

[1] In the earliest time a boy put on the *toga virilis* when he had completed his sixteenth year; in Cicero's time pupilage ceased a year earlier; and by Justinian's code the period at which it legally ceased was the commencement of the fifteenth year. The Scaevola to whom Cicero was thus taken was Quintus Mucius (Scaevola), the Augur, already named.

[2] It was customary for youth in training for honorable positions in the State to attach themselves especially to men of established character and reputation, to attend them to public places, and to remain near them whenever anything was to be learned from their conversation, their legal opinions, their public harangues, or their pleas before the courts. Distinguished citizens deemed themselves honored by a retinue of such attendants. Cicero, in the *De Officiis*, says that a young man may best commend himself to the early esteem and confidence of the community by such an intimacy.

1

up in my memory many of his elaborate discussions of important subjects, as well as many of his utterances that had both brevity and point, and my endeavor was to grow more learned by his wisdom. After his death I stood in a similar relation to the high-priest Scaevola,[1] whom I venture to call the foremost man of our city both in ability and in uprightness. But of him I will speak elsewhere. I return to the Augur. While I recall many similar occasions, I remember in particular that at a certain time when I and a few of his more intimate associates were sitting with him in the semicircular apartment[2] in his house where he was wont to receive his friends, the conversation turned on a subject about which almost every one was then talking, and which you, Atticus, certainly recollect, as you were much in the society of Publius Sulpicius; namely, the intense hatred with which Sulpicius, when Tribune of the people, opposed Quintus Pompeius, then Consul,[3] with whom he had lived

---

[1] As Cicero says, the most eloquent of jurists, and the most learned jurist among the eloquent. He was at the same time preeminent for moral purity and integrity. It was he, who, as Cicero (*De Officiis*, iii. 15) relates, insisted on paying for an estate that he bought a much larger sum than was asked for it, because its price had been fixed far below its actual value.

[2] Latin, *hemicyclio*, perhaps, a semicircular seat.

[3] The quarrel arose from the zealous espousal of the Marian faction by Sulpicius, who resorted to arms, in order to effect the incorporation of the new citizens from without the city among the previously existing tribes. Hence a series of tumults and conflicts, in one of which a son of Pompeius lost his life.

in the closest and most loving union, — a subject of general surprise and regret. Having incidentally mentioned this affair, Scaevola proceeded to give us the substance of a conversation on friendship, which Laelius had with him and his other son-in-law, Caius Fannius, the son of Marcus, a few days after the death of Africanus. I committed to memory the sentiments expressed in that discussion, and I bring them out in the book which I now send you. I have put them into the form of a dialogue, to avoid the too frequent repetition of "said I" and "says he," and that the discussion may seem as if it were held in the hearing of those who read it. While you, indeed, have often urged me to write something about friendship, the subject seems to me one of universal interest, and at the same time specially appropriate to our intimacy. I have therefore been very ready to seek the profit of many by complying with your request. But as in the *Cato Major*, the work on Old Age inscribed to you, I introduced the old man Cato as leading the discussion, because there seemed to be no other person better fitted to talk about old age than one who had been an aged man so long, and in his age had been so exceptionally vigorous, so, as we had heard from our fathers of the peculiarly memorable intimacy of Caius Laelius and Publius Scipio, it appeared appropriate to put into the mouth of Laelius what Scaevola remembered as having been said by him when friendship was the subject in hand. Moreover, this method of treatment, resting on the authority of men of an earlier generation, and illustrious in their time, seems somehow to be of specially commanding influence on the reader's mind. Thus, as I read my own book on Old Age, I am sometimes so affected that I feel as if not I, but Cato, were talking. But as I then wrote as an old man to an old man about old age, so in this book I write as the most loving of friends to a friend about friendship.[1] Then Cato was the chief speaker, than whom there was in his time scarcely any one older, and no one his superior in intellect; now Laelius shall hold the first place, both as a wise man (for so he was regarded), and as excelling in all that can do honor to friendship. I want you for the while to turn your mind away from me, and to imagine that it is Laelius who is speaking. Caius Fannius and Quintus Mucius come to their father-in-law after the death of Africanus. They commence the conversation; Laelius answers them. In reading all that he says about friendship, you will recognize the picture of your own friendship for me.

2. FANNIUS. It is as you say,[2] Laelius; for there never was a better man, or one more justly re-

---

[1] In the Latin we have here two remarkable series of assonances, rhythmical to the ear, and though translatable in sense, not so in euphony. "Ut tum *senex* ad *senem* de *senectute,* sic hoc libro ad *amicum amicissimus* de *amicitia* scripsi."

[2] The reference is to what Laelius is supposed to have said already. The dialogue, as given here, is made to commence in the midst of a conversation.

nowned, than Africanus. But you ought to bear it
in mind that the eyes of all are turned upon you
at this time; for they both call you and think you
wise. This distinction has been latterly given to
Cato, and you know that in the days of our fathers
Lucius Atilius [1] was in like manner surnamed The
Wise; but both of them were so called for other
reasons than those which have given you this
name, — Atilius, for his reputation as an adept
in municipal law; Cato, for the versatility of his
endowments: for there were reported to his honor
many measures wisely planned and vigorously carried through in the Senate, and many cases skilfully defended in the courts, so that in his old age
The Wise was generally applied to him as a surname. But you are regarded as wise on somewhat
different grounds, not only for your disposition and
your moral worth, but also for your knowledge and
learning; and not in the estimation of the common
people, but in that of men of advanced culture,
you are deemed wise in a sense in which there is
reason to suppose that in Greece — where those
who look into these things most discriminatingly
do not reckon the seven who bear the name as on
the list of wise men — no one was so regarded except the man in Athens whom the oracle of Apollo
designated as the wisest of men.[2] In fine, you are

---

[1] The first Roman known to have borne the surname of Sapiens.
He was one of the earliest of the jurisconsults who took pupils.

[2] Socrates.

thought to be wise in this sense, that you regard all that appertains to your happiness as within your own soul, and consider the calamities to which man is liable as of no consequence in comparison with virtue. I am therefore asked, and so, I believe, is Scaevola, who is now with us, how you bear the death of Africanus; and the question is put to us the more eagerly, because on the fifth day of the month next following,[1] when we met, as usual, in the garden of Decimus Brutus the Augur, to discuss our official business, you were absent, though it was your habit always on that day to give your most careful attendance to the duties of your office.

SCAEVOLA. As Fannius says, Caius Laelius, many have asked me this question. But I answered in accordance with what I have seen, that you were bearing with due moderation your sorrow for the death of this your most intimate friend, though you, with your kindly nature, could not fail to be moved by it; but that your absence from the monthly meeting of the Augurs was due to illness, not to grief.

LAELIUS. You were in the right, Scaevola, and spoke the truth; for it was not fitting, had I been in good health, for me to be detained by my own

[1] Latin, *proxumis nonis.* The *nones*, the ninth day before the *ides*, fell on the fifth of the month, except in March, May, July, and October, when the *ides* were two days later. We have elsewhere intimation that the Augurs held a meeting for business on the *nones* of each month.

sad feeling from this duty, which I have never failed to discharge; nor do I think that a man of firm mind can be so affected by any calamity as to neglect his duty. It is, indeed, friendly in you, Fannius, to tell me that better things are said of me than I feel worthy of or desire to have said; but it seems to me that you underrate Cato. For either there never was a wise man (and so I am inclined to think), or if there has been such a man, Cato deserves the name. To omit other things, how nobly did he bear his son's death! I remembered Paulus,[1] I had seen Gallus,[2] in their bereavements. But they lost boys; Cato, a man in his prime and respected by all.[3] Beware how you place in higher esteem than Cato even the man whom Apollo, as you say, pronounced superlatively wise; for it is the deeds of Cato, the sayings of Socrates, that are held in honor. Thus far in reply to Fannius. As regards myself, I will now answer both of you.

3. Were I to deny that I feel the loss of Scipio, while I leave it to those who profess themselves wise in such matters to say whether I ought to feel

---

[1] Paulus Aemilius, who lost two sons, one a few days before, the other shortly after, the triumph decreed to him for the conquest of the Macedonian King Perseus.

[2] Çaius Sulpicius Gallus, mentioned as an astronomer by Cicero, *De Officiis*, i. 6, and *De Senectute*, 14.

[3] The younger Cato had won fame as a soldier and distinguished eminence as a jurist. At the time of his death he was prætor elect.

it, I certainly should be uttering a falsehood. I do indeed feel my bereavement of such a friend as I do not expect ever to have again, and as I am sure I never had beside. But I need no comfort from without; I console myself, and, chief of all, I find comfort in my freedom from the apprehension that oppresses most men when their friends die; for I do not think that any evil has befallen Scipio. If evil has befallen, it is to me. But to be severely afflicted by one's own misfortunes is the token of self-love, not of friendship. As for him, indeed, who can deny that the issue has been to his pre-eminent glory? Unless he had wished — what never entered into his mind — an endless life on earth, what was there within human desire that did not accrue to the man who in his very earliest youth by his incredible ability and prowess surpassed the highest expectations that all had formed of his boyhood; who never sought the consulship, yet was made consul twice, the first time before the legal age,[1] the second time in due season as to himself, but almost too late for his country;[2] who by the

----

[1] He left the army in Africa, B. C. 147, for Rome, to offer himself as a candidate for the aedileship, for which he had just reached the legal age of thirty-seven; but such accounts of his ability, efficiency, and courage had preceded him and followed him from the army, that he was chosen Consul, virtually by popular acclamation.

[2] The war in Spain had been continued for several years, with frequent disaster and disgrace to the Roman army, when Scipio, B. C. 134, was chosen Consul with a special view to this war,

overthrow of two cities implacably hostile to the Roman empire put a period, not only to the wars that were, but to wars that else must have been? What shall I say of the singular affability of his manners, of his filial piety to his mother,[1] of his generosity to his sisters,[2] of his integrity in his relations with all men? How dear he was to the community was shown by the grief at his funeral. What benefit, then, could he have derived from a few more years? For, although old age be not burdensome,— as I remember that Cato, the year before he died, maintained in a conversation with me and Scipio,[3] — it yet impairs the fresh vigor which Scipio had not begun to lose. Thus his life was such that nothing either in fortune or in fame could be added to it; while the suddenness of his death must have taken away the pain of dying. Of the mode of his death it is hard to speak with certainty; you are aware

which he closed by the capture and destruction of Numantia, in connection with which, it must be confessed, his record is rather that of a relentless and sanguinary enemy than of a generous and placable antagonist.

[1] He was the son of Paulus Aemilius, and the adopted son of Publius Cornelius Scipio Africanus. His mother, divorced for no assignable reason, was left very poor, and her son, on the death of the widow of his adopting father, gave her the entire patrimony that then came into his possession.

[2] After his mother's death, law and custom authorized him to resume what he had given her; but he bestowed it on his sisters, thus affording them the means of living comfortably and respectably.

[3] The *De Senectute.*

what suspicions are abroad.[1] But this may be said with truth, that of the many days of surpassing fame and happiness which Publius Scipio saw in his lifetime, the most glorious was the day before his death, when, on the adjournment of the Senate, he was escorted home by the Conscript Fathers, the Roman people, the men of Latium, and the allies,[2] — so that from so high a grade of honor he seems to have passed on into the assembly of the gods rather than to have gone down into the underworld.

---

[1] He retired to his sleeping apartment apparently in perfect health, and was found dead on his couch in the morning, — as was rumored, with marks of violence on his neck. His wife was Sempronia, the sister of the Gracchi whose agrarian schemes he had vehemently opposed. She was suspected of having at least given admission to the assassin, and even her mother, the Cornelia who has been regarded as unparalleled among Roman women for the virtues appertaining to a wife and mother, did not escape the charge of complicity. Her son Caius was also among those suspected ; but the more probable opinion is that Papirius Carbo was alone answerable for the crime. Carbo had been Scipio's most bitter enemy, and had endeavored to inflame the people against him as their enemy.

[2] Scipio had at that session of the senate proposed a measure in the utmost degree offensive to Caius Gracchus and his party. The law of Tiberius Gracchus would have disposed, at the hands of the commissioners appointed under it, of large tracts of land belonging to the Italian allies. Scipio's plan provided that such lands should be taken out of the jurisdiction of the commissioners, and that matters relating to them should be adjudged by a different board to be specially appointed, — a measure which would have been a virtual abrogation of the agrarian law. On this account he had his honorable escort home ; and on this account, in all probability, he was murdered.

4. For I am far from agreeing with those who have of late promulgated the opinion that the soul perishes with the body, and that death blots out the whole being.[1] I, on the other hand, attach superior value to the authority of the ancients, whether that of our ancestors who established religious rites for the dead, which they certainly would not have done if they had thought the dead wholly unconcerned in such observances ;[2] or that of the former Greek colonists in this country, who by their schools and teaching made Southern Italy[3]

[1] The reference here is, of course, to the Epicureans. This school of philosophy had grown very rapidly, and numbered many disciples when this essay was written ; but in the time of Laelius it had but recently invaded Rome, and Amafanius, who must have been his contemporary, was the earliest Roman writer who expounded its doctrines.

[2] This is sound reasoning, as these rites were annually renewed, and consisted in great part of the invocation of ancestors, — a custom which could not have originated if those ancestors were supposed to be utterly dead. This passage may remind the reader of the answer of Jesus Christ to the Sadducees, who denied that the Pentateuch contained any intimation of immortality. He quotes the passage in which God is represented as saying, " I am the God of Abraham, and the God of Isaac, and the God of Jacob," and adds, "God is not the God of the dead, but of the living," implying that ancestors whom the writer of that record supposed to be dead could not have been thus mentioned.

[3] Latin *Magnam Graeciam,* — the name given to the cluster of Greek colonies that were scattered thick along the shore of Southern Italy. At Crotona, in Magna Graecia, Pythagoras established his school, and these colonies were the chief seat and seminary of his philosophy, which taught the immortality of the soul.

— now in its decline, then flourishing — a seat of
learning ; or that of him whom the oracle of Apollo
pronounced the wisest of men, who said not one
thing to-day, another to-morrow, as many do, but
the same thing always, maintaining that the souls
of men are divine, and that when they go out
from the body, the return to heaven is open to
them, and direct and easy in proportion to their
integrity and excellence. This was also the opinion
of Scipio, who seemed prescient of the event so
near, when, a very short time before his death, he
discoursed for three successive days about the
republic in the presence of Philus, Manilius, and
several others, — you, Scaevola, having gone with me
to the conferences, — and near the close of the discussion he told us what he said that he had heard
from Africanus in a vision during sleep.[1] If it is
true that the soul of every man of surpassing excellence takes flight, as it were, from the custody and
bondage of the body, to whom can we imagine the
way to the gods more easy than to Scipio ? I
therefore fear to mourn for this his departure, lest
in such grief there be more of envy than of friendship. But if truth incline to the opinion that soul

---

[1] The *De Republica* consists of dialogues on three successive
days in Scipio's garden, and Scipio is the chief speaker. The
work was supposed to be irrecoverably lost, with the exception
of this Dream of Scipio, and a few fragments ; but considerable
portions of it were discovered in a palimpsest in 1822. The
Dream of Scipio will be found in the latter part of this volume.

and body have the same end, and that there is no remaining consciousness, then, as there is nothing good in death, there certainly is nothing of evil. For if consciousness be lost, the case is the same with Scipio as if he had never been born, though that he was born I have so ample reason to rejoice, and this city will be glad so long as it shall stand. Thus in either event, with him, as I have said, all has issued well, though with great discomfort for me, who more fittingly, as I entered into life before him, ought to have left it before him. But I so enjoy the memory of our friendship, that I seem to have owed the happiness of my life to my having lived with Scipio, with whom I was united in the care of public interests and of private affairs, who was my companion at home and served by my side in the army,[1] and with whom — and therein lies the special virtue of friendship — I was in perfect harmony of purpose, taste, and sentiment. Thus I am now not so much delighted by the reputation for wisdom of which Fannius has just spoken, especially as I do not deserve it, as by the hope that our friendship will live in eternal remembrance; and this I have the more at heart because from all ages scarce three or four pairs of friends are on record,[2]

---

[1] Laelius went with Scipio on the campaign which resulted in the destruction of Carthage.

[2] Those referred to are probably Theseus and Peirithous, Achilles and Patroclus, Orestes and Pylades, Damon and Phintias, — all but the last, perhaps the last also, mythical.

on which list I cannot but hope that the friendship of Scipio and Laelius will be known to posterity.

FANNIUS. It cannot fail, Laelius, to be as you desire. But since you have made mention of friendship, and we are at leisure, you will confer on me a very great favor, and, I trust, on Scaevola too, if, as you are wont to do on other subjects when your opinion is asked, you will discourse to us on friendship, and tell us what you think about it, in what estimation you hold it, and what rules you would give for it.

SCAEVOLA. This will indeed be very gratifying to me, and had not Fannius anticipated me, I was about to make the same request. You thus will bestow a great kindness on both of us.

5. LAELIUS. I certainly would not hesitate, if I had confidence in my own powers; for the subject is one of the highest importance, and, as Fannius says, we are at leisure. It is the custom of philosophers, especially among the Greeks, to have subjects assigned to them which they discuss even without premeditation.[1] This is a great accomplishment, and requires no small amount of exercise. I therefore think that you ought to seek the treatment of friendship by those who profess this art. I can only advise you to prefer friendship to all things else within human attainment, insomuch as nothing beside is so well fitted to nature, — so well adapted to our needs whether in prosperous

---

[1] This was the boast and pride of the Greek sophists.

or in adverse circumstances. But I consider this as a first principle, — that friendship can exist only between good men. In thus saying, I would not be so rigid in definition [1] as those who establish specially subtle distinctions,[2] with literal truth it may be, but with little benefit to the common mind; for they will not admit that any man who is not wise is a good man. This may indeed be true. But they understand by wisdom a state which no mortal has yet attained; while we ought to look at those qualities which are to be found in actual exercise and in common life, not at those which exist only in fancy or in aspiration. Caius Fabricius, Manius Curius, Tiberius Coruncanius, wise as they were in the judgment of our fathers, I will consent not to call wise by the standard of these philosophers. Let them keep for themselves the name of wisdom, which is invidious and of doubtful meaning, if they will only admit that these may have been good men. But they will not grant even this; they insist on denying the name of good to any but the wise. I therefore adopt the standard of common sense.[3] Those who

[1] Latin, *Neque id ad vivum reseco*, literally, nor in this matter do I cut to the quick.

[2] The Stoics of the more rigid type, who maintained that the wise man alone is good, but denied that the truly wise man had yet made his appearance on the earth.

[3] Latin, *agamus igitur pingui (ut aiunt) Minerva ;* that is, with a less refined, a grosser wisdom, — a wisdom more nearly conformed to the sound, if somewhat crass, common-sense of the majority.

so conduct themselves, so live, that their good faith, integrity, equity, and kindness win approval, who are entirely free from avarice, lust, and the infirmities of a hasty temper, and in whom there is perfect consistency of character; in fine, men like those whom I have named, while they are regarded as good, ought to be so called, because to the utmost of human capacity they follow Nature, who is the best guide in living well. Indeed, it seems to me thoroughly evident that there should be a certain measure of fellowship among all, but more intimate the nearer we approach one another. Thus this feeling has more power between fellow-citizens than toward foreigners, between kindred than between those of different families. Toward our kindred, Nature herself produces a certain kind of friendship. But this lacks strength; and indeed friendship, in its full sense, has precedence of kinship in this particular, that good-will may be taken away from kinship, not from friendship; for when good-will is removed, friendship loses its name, while that of kinship remains. How great is the force of friendship we may best understand from this, — that out of the boundless society of the human race which Nature has constituted, the sense of fellowship is so contracted and narrowed that the whole power of loving is bestowed on the union of two or a very few friends.

6. Friendship is nothing else than entire fellow-feeling as to all things, human and divine, with

mutual good-will and affection;[1] and I doubt whether anything better than this, wisdom alone excepted, has been given to man by the immortal gods. Some prefer riches to it; some, sound health; some, power; some, posts of honor; many, even sensual gratification. This last properly belongs to beasts; the others are precarious and uncertain, dependent not on our own choice so much as on the caprice of Fortune. Those, indeed, who regard virtue as the supreme good are entirely in the right; but it is virtue itself that produces and sustains friendship, nor without virtue can friendship by any possibility exist. In saying this, however, I would interpret virtue in accordance with our habits of speech and of life; not defining it, as some philosophers do, by high-sounding words, but numbering on the list of good men those who are commonly so regarded, — the Pauli, the Catos, the Galli, the Scipios, the Phili. Mankind in general

---

[1] It may be doubted whether this close conformity of opinion and feeling is essential, or even favorable, to friendship. The amicable comparison and collision of thought and sentiment are certainly consistent with, and often conducive to, the most friendly intimacy. Friends are not infrequently the complements, rather than the likenesses, of each other. Cicero and Atticus were as close friends as Scipio and Laelius; but they were at many points exceedingly unlike. Atticus had the tact and skill in worldly matters which Cicero lacked. Atticus kept aloof from public affairs, while Cicero was unhappy whenever he could not imagine himself as taking a leading part in them. Atticus was an Epicurean, and Cicero never loses an opportunity of attacking the Epicurean philosophy.

are content with these. Let us then leave out of the
account such good men as are nowhere to be found.
Among such good men as there really are, friendship has more advantages than I can easily name.
In the first place, as Ennius says : —

> " How can life be worth living, if devoid
> Of the calm trust reposed by friend in friend ?
> What sweeter joy than in the kindred soul,
> Whose converse differs not from self-communion ? "

How could you have full enjoyment of prosperity,
unless with one whose pleasure in it was equal to
your own ?  Nor would it be easy to bear adversity, unless with the sympathy of one on whom it
rested more heavily than on your own soul.  Then,
too, other objects of desire are, in general, adapted,
each to some specific purpose, — wealth, that you
may use it ; power, that you may receive the homage of those around you ; posts of honor, that you
may obtain reputation ; sensual gratification, that
you may live in pleasure ; health, that you may be
free from pain, and may have full exercise of your
bodily powers and faculties.  But friendship com-
bines the largest number of utilities.  Wherever
you turn, it is at hand.  No place shuts it out.  It
is never unseasonable, never annoying.  Thus, as
the proverb says, "You cannot put water or fire
to more uses than friendship serves."  I am not
now speaking of the common and moderate type
of friendship, which yet yields both pleasure and
profit, but of true and perfect friendship, like that

which existed in the few instances that are held in special remembrance. Such friendship at once enhances the lustre of prosperity, and by dividing and sharing adversity lessens its burden.

7. Moreover, while friendship comprises the greatest number and variety of beneficent offices, it certainly has this special prerogative, that it lights up a good hope for the time to come, and thus preserves the minds that it sustains from imbecility or prostration in misfortune. For he, indeed, who looks into the face of a friend beholds, as it were, a copy of himself. Thus the absent are present, and the poor are rich, and the weak are strong, and — what seems stranger still[1] — the dead are alive, such is the honor, the enduring remembrance, the longing love, with which the dying are followed by the living; so that the death of the dying seems happy, the life of the living full of praise.[2] But if from the condition of human life you were to exclude all kindly union, no house, no city, could stand, nor, indeed, could the tillage of the field

---

[1] Literally, *what is harder to say.*

[2] The sense of this sentence is somewhat overlaid by the rhetoric; yet it undoubtedly means that an absent friend is esteemed and honored in the person of the friend who not only loves him, but is regarded as representing him; that a poor friend enjoys the prosperity of his rich friend as if it were his own; that a weak friend feels his feebleness energized by the friend who in need will fight his battles for him; and that no man is suffered to lapse from the kind and reverent remembrance of those who see his likeness in the friend who keeps his memory green.

survive. If it is not perfectly understood what virtue there is in friendship and concord, it may be learned from dissension and discord. For what house is so stable, what state so firm, that it cannot be utterly overturned by hatred and strife? Hence it may be ascertained how much good there is in friendship. It is said that a certain philosopher of Agrigentum [1] sang in Greek verse that it is friendship that draws together and discord that parts all things which subsist in harmony, and which have their various movements in nature and in the whole universe. The worth and power of friendship, too, all mortals understand, and attest by their approval in actual instances. Thus, if there comes into conspicuous notice an occasion on which a friend incurs or shares the perils of his friend, who can fail to extol the deed with the highest praise? What shouts filled the whole theatre at the performance of the new play of my guest [2] and friend Marcus Pacuvius, when — the king not knowing

---

[1] Empedocles. Only a few fragments of his great poem are extant. His theory seems like a poetical version of Newton's law of universal gravitation. The analogy between physical attraction and the mutual attraction of congenial minds and souls has its record in the French word *aimant*, denoting *loadstone* or *magnet*.

[2] Or *host;* for the word *hospes* may have either meaning. It denotes not the fact of giving or receiving hospitality, but the permanent and sacred relation established between host and guest. This relation has lost much of its character in modern civilization, and I doubt whether it has a name in any modern European language.

which of the two was Orestes — Pylades said that he was Orestes, while Orestes persisted in asserting that he was, as in fact he was, Orestes![1] The whole assembly rose in applause at this mere fictitious representation. What may we suppose that they would have done, had the same thing occurred in real life ? In that case Nature herself displayed her power, when men recognized that as rightly done by another, which they would not have had the courage to do themselves. Thus far, to the utmost of my ability as it seems to me, I have given you my sentiments concerning friendship. If there is more to be said, as I think that there is, endeavor to obtain it, if you see fit, of those who are wont to discuss such subjects.

FANNIUS. But we would rather have it from you. Although I have often consulted those philosophers also, and have listened to them not unwillingly, yet the thread of your discourse differs somewhat from that of theirs.

---

[1] Among the many and conflicting legends about Orestes is that which seems to have been the theme of the lost tragedy of Pacuvius. Orestes, after avenging on his mother and her paramour the murder of his father, in order to expiate the guilt of matricide, was directed by the Delphian oracle to go to Tauris, and to steal and transport to Athens an image of Artemis that had fallen from heaven. His friend Pylades accompanied him on this expedition. They were seized by Thoas the king, and Orestes, as principal offender, was to be sacrificed to Artemis. His sister, Iphigeneia, priestess of Artemis, contrived their escape, and the three arrived safe at Athens with the sacred image.

SCAEVOLA. You would say so all the more, Fannius, had you been present in Scipio's garden at
that discussion about the republic, and heard what
an advocate of justice he showed himself in answer
to the elaborate speech of Philus.[1]

FANNIUS. It was indeed easy for the man pre-
eminently just to defend justice.

SCAEVOLA. As to friendship, then, is not its defence easy for him who has won the highest celebrity on the ground of friendship maintained with
pre-eminent faithfulness, consistency, and probity?

8. LAELIUS. This is, indeed, the employing of
force; for what matters the way in which you

[1] Carneades, when on an embassy to Rome, for the entertainment of his Roman hosts, on one day delivered a discourse in
behalf of justice as the true policy for the State, and on the next
day delivered an equally subtile and eloquent discourse maintaining the opposite thesis. In the third Book of the *De Republica*
Philus is made a "devil's advocate," and has assigned to him the
championship of what we are wont to call a Machiavelian policy,
and, in general, of the morally wrong as the politically right. He
is represented as taking the part reluctantly, saying that one con-
sents to soil his hands in order to find gold, and he professes to
give the substance of the famous discourse of Carneades. Laelius
answers him, and, so far as we can judge from the fragments of his
reply that are extant, with the preponderance of reason, which
Cicero intended should incline on the better side. There was
perhaps a sublatent irony in making Philus play this part; for
he was an eminently upright man. Valerius Maximus eulogizes
him for his rigid integrity and impartiality, and relates that when
at the expiration of his consulship he was sent to take command
of the army against Numantia, he chose for his lieutenants
Metellus and Pompeius, both his intensely bitter enemies, but
the men best fitted for the service.

compel me? You at any rate do compel me; for
it is both hard and unfair not to comply with the
wishes of one's sons-in-law, especially in a case that
merits favorable consideration.

In reflecting, then, very frequently on friendship,
the foremost question that is wont to present itself
is, whether friendship is craved on account of conscious infirmity and need, so that in bestowing and
receiving the kind offices that belong to it each
may have that done for him by the other which
he is least able to do for himself, reciprocating services in like manner; or whether, though this relation of mutual benefit is the property of friendship,
it has yet another cause, more sacred and more
noble, and derived more genuinely from the very
nature of man. Love, which in our language gives
name to friendship,[1] bears a chief part in unions
of mutual benefit; for a revenue of service is levied even on those who are cherished in pretended
friendship, and are treated with regard from interested motives. But in friendship there is nothing
feigned, nothing pretended, and whatever there is
in it is both genuine and spontaneous. Friendship, therefore, springs from nature rather than
from need, — from an inclination of the mind with
a certain consciousness of love rather than from
calculation of the benefit to be derived from it.
Its real quality may be discerned even in some
classes of animals, which up to a certain time so

_____
[1] *Amor, — amicitia.*

love their offspring, and are so loved by them, that
the mutual feeling is plainly seen, — a feeling which
is much more clearly manifest in man, first, in the
affection which exists between children and parents,
and which can be dissolved only by atrocious guilt;
and in the next place, in the springing up of a like
feeling of love, when we find some one of manners
and character congenial with our own, who becomes
dear to us because we seem to see in him an illustrious example of probity and virtue.   For there is
nothing more lovable than virtue, — nothing which
more surely wins affectionate regard, insomuch that
on the score of virtue and probity we love even
those whom we have never seen.   Who is there
that does not recall the memory of Caius Fabricius,
of Manius Curius, of Tiberius Coruncanius, whom
he never saw, with some good measure of kindly
feeling?   On the other hand, who is there that can
fail to hate Tarquinius Superbus, Spurius Cassius,
Spurius Maelius?   Our dominion in Italy was at
stake in wars under two commanders, Pyrrhus and
Hannibal.   On account of the good faith of the
one, we hold him in no unfriendly remembrance;[1]
the other because of his cruelty our people must
always hate.[2]

[1] Pyrrhus, after the only victory that he obtained over the
Romans, treated his prisoners with signal humanity, and restored
them without ransom.   See *De Officiis*, i. 12.

[2] It may be doubted whether Hannibal deserved the reproach
here implied.   The Roman historians ascribe to him acts of cruelty no worse than their own generals were chargeable with; while

9. But if good faith has such attractive power that we love it in those whom we have never seen, or — what means still more — in an enemy, what wonder is it if the minds of men are moved to affection when they behold the virtue and goodness of those with whom they can become intimately united?

Love is, indeed, strengthened by favors received, by witnessing assiduity in one's service, and by habitual intercourse; and when these are added to the first impulse of the mind toward love, there flames forth a marvellously rich glow of affectionate feeling. If there are any who think that this proceeds from conscious weakness and the desire to have some person through whom one can obtain what he lacks, they assign, indeed, to friendship a mean and utterly ignoble origin, born, as they would have it, of poverty and neediness. If this were true, then the less of resource one was conscious of having in himself, the better fitted would he be for friendship. The contrary is the case; for the more confidence a man has in himself, and the more thoroughly he is fortified by virtue and wisdom, so

---

nothing of the kind is related by either Polybius or Plutarch. It is certain that after the battle of Cannae he checked the needless slaughter of the Roman fugitives, and Livy relates several instances in which he paid funeral honors to distinguished Romans slain in battle. The intense hostility of the Romans to Carthage may have led to an unfair estimate of the great general's character, and to the invention or exaggeration of reports to his discredit.

that he is in need of no one, and regards all that
concerns him as in his own keeping, the more note-
worthy is he for the friendships which he seeks and
cherishes. What? Did Africanus need me? Not
in the least, by Hercules. As little did I need
him. But I was drawn to him by admiration of
his virtue, while he, in turn, loved me, perhaps,
from some favorable estimate of my character;
and intimacy increased our mutual affection. But
though utilities many and great resulted from our
friendship, the cause of our mutual love did not
proceed from the hope of what it might bring.
For as we are beneficent and generous, not in
order to exact kindnesses in return (for we do not
put our kind offices to interest), but are by nature inclined to be generous, so, in my opinion, friendship
is not to be sought, for its wages, but because its
revenue consists entirely in the love which it implies. Those, however, who, after the manner of
beasts, refer everything to pleasure,[1] think very
differently. Nor is it wonderful that they do; for
men who have degraded all their thoughts to so
mean and contemptible an end can rise to the
contemplation of nothing lofty, nothing magnificent and divine. We may, therefore, leave them
out of this discussion. But let us have it well
understood that the feeling of love and the en-
dearments of mutual affection spring from nature,
in case there is a well-established assurance of

---

[1] The Epicureans.

moral worth in the person thus loved. Those who
desire to become friends approach each other, and
enter into relation with each other, that each may
enjoy the society and the character of him whom
he has begun to love; and they are equal in love,
and on either side are more inclined to bestow
obligations than to claim a return, so that in this
matter there is an honorable rivalry between them.
Thus will the greatest benefits be derived from
friendship, and it will have a more solid and genuine foundation as tracing its origin to nature than
if it proceeded from human weakness. For if it
were utility that cemented friendships, an altered
aspect of utility would dissolve them. But because nature cannot be changed, therefore true
friendships are eternal. This may suffice for the
origin of friendship, unless you have, perchance,
some objection to what I have said.

FANNIUS. Go on, Laelius. I answer by the right
of seniority for Scaevola, who is younger than I am.

SCAEVOLA. I am of the same mind with you.
Let us, then, hear farther.

10. LAELIUS. Hear, then, my excellent friends,
the substance of the frequent discussions on friendship between Scipio and me. He, indeed, said[1]

----

[1] The construction of this entire section is in the subjunctive
imperfect, depending on the *dicebat* in the second sentence. It
has seemed to me that the direct form of construction which
I have adopted is more consonant with the genius of our
language.

that nothing is more difficult than for friendship to last through life ; for friends happen to have conflicting interests, or different political opinions. Then, again, as he often said, characters change, sometimes under adverse conditions, sometimes with growing years. He cited also the analogy of what takes place in early youth, the most ardent loves of boyhood being often laid aside with its robe. But if friendships last on into opening manhood, they are not infrequently broken up by rivalry in quest of a wife, or in the pursuit of some advantage which only one can obtain.[1] Then, if friendships are of longer duration, they yet, as Scipio said, are liable to be undermined by competition for office ; and indeed there is nothing more fatal to friendship than, in very many cases, the greed of gain, and among some of the best of men the contest for place and fame, which has often engendered the most intense enmity between those

---

[1] Had Cicero not been personating Laelius, who died long before the quarrel occurred, he would undoubtedly have cited the case of Servilius Caepio and Livius Drusus. They married each other's sisters, and were united in the closest intimacy, and seemingly in the dearest mutual love ; but as rivals in bidding for a ring at an auction-sale they had their first quarrel, which grew into intense mutual hatred, led almost to a civil war between their respective partisans, and bore no small part in starting the series of dissensions which issued in the Social War, and the destruction of not far from three hundred thousand lives. I refer to this in a note, because it must have been fresh in Cicero's memory, and had annotation been the habit of his time, he would most assuredly have given it the place which I now give it.

who had been the closest friends. Strong and generally just aversion, also, springs up when anything morally wrong is required of a friend; as
when he is asked to aid in the gratification of
impure desire, or to render his assistance in some
unrighteous act, — in which case those who refuse,
although their conduct is highly honorable, are yet
charged by the persons whom they will not serve
with being false to the claims of friendship, while
those who dare to make such a demand of a friend
profess, by the very demand, that they are ready
to do anything and everything for a friend's sake.
By such quarrels, not only are old intimacies often
dissolved, but undying hatreds generated. So many
of these perils hang like so many fates over friendship, that to escape them all seemed to Scipio, as
he said, to indicate not wisdom alone, but equally
a rare felicity of fortune.

11. Let us then, first, if you please, consider
how far the love of friends ought to go. If Coriolanus had friends, ought they to have helped
him in fighting against his country, or should
the friends of Viscellinus[1] or those of Spurius

---

[1] Spurius Cassius Viscellinus, the author of the earliest agrarian law, passed, but never carried into execution. He was condemned to death, — probably a victim to the rancorous opposition
of the patrician order, of which he was regarded as a recreant
member by virtue of his advocacy of the rights or just claims of
the *plebs*. Cicero in early life was by no means so hostile to the
principle underlying the agrarian laws and to the memory of the
Gracchi, as he was after he had reached the highest offices in
the gift of the people.

Maelius [1] have aided them in the endeavor to usurp regal power? We saw, indeed, Tiberius Gracchus, when he was disturbing the peace of the State, deserted by Quintus Tubero and others with whom he had been on terms of intimacy. But Caius Blossius, of Cumae, the guest,[2] Scaevola, of your family, coming to me, when I was in conference with the Consuls Laenas and Rupilius, to implore pardon, urged the plea that he held Tiberius Gracchus in so dear esteem that he felt bound to do whatever he desired. I then asked him, "Even if he had wanted you to set fire to the Capitol, would you have done it?" He replied, "He never would have made such a request." "But if he had?" said I. "I would have obeyed him," was the answer. And, by Hercules, he did as he said, or even more; for he did not so much yield obedience to the audacious schemes of Tiberius Gracchus, as he was foremost in them; he was not so much the companion of his madness, as its leader. Therefore, in consequence of this folly, alarmed by the appointment of special judges for his trial, he fled to Asia, entered the service of

---

[1] Maelius, of the equestrian order, but of a plebeian family, obtained unbounded popularity with the *plebs* by selling corn at a low price, and giving away large quantities of it, in a time of famine. He was charged with seeking kingly power, and, on account of his alleged movements with that purpose, Cincinnatus was appointed dictator, and Maelius, resisting a summons to his tribunal, was killed by Ahala, his master of the horse. There seems to have been little evidence of his actual guilt.

[2] *Hospes*, guest, host, or both.

our enemies, and finally met the heavy and just
punishment for his disloyalty to his country.[1]  It
is, then, no excuse for wrong-doing that you do
wrong for the sake of a friend.  Indeed, since it
may have been a belief in your virtue that has
made one your friend, it is hard for friendship to
last if you fall away from virtue.  But if we should
determine either to concede to friends whatever
they may ask, or to exact from them whatever we
may desire, we and they must be endowed with
perfect wisdom, in order for our friendship to be
blameless.  We are speaking, however, of such
friends as we have before our eyes, or as we have
seen or have known by report, — of such as are
found in common life.  It is from these that we
must take our examples, especially from such of
them as make the nearest approach to perfect
wisdom.  We have learned from our fathers that
Papus Aemilius was very intimate with Caius
Luscinus, they having twice been consuls together,
as well as colleagues in the censorship; and it is
said also that Manius Curius and Tiberius Coruncanius lived in the closest friendship both with
them and with each other.  Now we cannot suspect that either of these men would have asked of
one of his friends anything inconsistent with good
faith, or with an engagement sanctioned by oath, or

---

[1] He took refuge with Aristonicus, King of Pergamus, then at
war with Rome ; and when Aristonicus was conquered, Blossius
committed suicide for fear of being captured by the Roman army.

with his duty to the State. Indeed, to what purpose is it to say that among such men if one had
asked anything wrong, he would not have obtained .
it ? For they were men of the most sacred integrity ; while to ask anything wrong of a friend and
to do it when asked are alike tokens of deep de-
pravity. But Caius Carbo and Caius Cato were
the followers of Tiberius Gracchus, as was his
brother Caius, at first with little ardor, but now[1]
most zealously.

12. As to friendship, then, let this law be enacted,
that we neither ask of a friend what is wrong, nor
do what is wrong at a friend's request. The plea
that it was for a friend's sake is a base apology, —
one that should never be admitted with regard to
other forms of guilt, and certainly not as to crimes
against the State. We, indeed, Fannius and Scaevola, are so situated that we ought to look far in
advance for the perils that our country may incur. Already has our public policy deviated somewhat from the method and course of our ancestors.
Tiberius Gracchus attempted to exercise supreme
power ; nay, he really reigned for a few months.
What like this had the Roman people ever heard or
seen before ? What, after his death, the friends
and kindred who followed him did in their revenge

---

[1] *Now;* that is, at the time at which this dialogue has its
assumed date, immediately after Scipio's death. At that time
Caius Gracchus was acting as a commissioner under his brother's
agrarian law.

on Publius Scipio[1] I cannot say without tears. We put up with Carbo[2] as well as we could in consideration of the recent punishment of Tiberius Gracchus; but I am in no mood to predict what is to be expected from the tribuneship of Caius.Gracchus. Meanwhile the evil is creeping upon us, from its very beginning fraught with threats of ruin. Before recent events,[3] you perceive how much degen-. eracy was indicated in the legalizing of the ballot, first by the Gabinian,[4] then two years later by the Cassian law.[5] I seem already to see the people

[1] Publius Cornelius Scipio Nasica, who took the lead of the Senate in the assassination of Tiberius Gracchus, and incurred such popular odium that he could not safely stay in Rome. He was sent on a fictitious mission to Asia to get him out of the way of the people, and, not daring to return, wandered with no settled habitation till his death at Pergamum not long before the assumed date of this dialogue.

[2] Carbo succeeded Tiberius Gracchus on the commission for carrying the agrarian law into execution, and was shortly afterward chosen Tribune. He then proposed a law, permitting a tribune to be re-elected for an indefinite number of years. This law was vehemently opposed by Scipio Africanus the Younger, and if he was really killed by Carbo, it was probably on account of his hostility to Carbo's ambitious schemes.

[3] The reference undoubtedly here is to the Papirian law which had been passed just before the assumed date of this dialogue, having been proposed and carried through by (Caius *Papirius*) Carbo. By this law the use of the ballot was established in all matters of popular legislation.

[4] By which magistrates were to be chosen by ballot.

[5] By which the judges were to be chosen by ballot. With reference to the use of the ballot the parties in Rome were prototypes of like parties in England. The voice of the people

utterly alienated from the Senate, and the most important affairs determined by the will of the multitude; for more persons will learn how these things are brought about than how they may be resisted. To what purpose am I saying this? Because no one makes such attempts without associates. It is therefore to be enjoined on good men that they must not think themselves so bound that they cannot renounce their friends when they are guilty of crimes against the State. But punishment must be inflicted on all who are implicated in such guilt, — on those who follow, no less than on those who lead. Who in Greece was more renowned than Themistocles'? Who had greater influence than he had? When as commander in the Persian war he had freed Greece from bondage, and for envy of his fame was driven into exile, he did not bear as he ought the ill treatment of his ungrateful country. He did what Coriolanus had done with us twenty years before. Neither of these men found any helper against his country;[1] they therefore both

was for the ballot, on the ground that it made suffrage free, as it could not be when employers or patrons could dictate to their dependents and make them suffer for failure to vote in favor of their own candidates or measures. The aristocratic party opposed the ballot as fatal to their controlling influence, which many sincere patriots, like Cicero, regarded as essential to the public safety, while patrician demagogues, intriguers, and office-seekers made it subservient to their own selfish or partisan interests.

[1] No one of his own fellow-countrymen.

committed suicide.[1] Association with depraved men for such an end is not, then, to be shielded by the plea of friendship, but rather to be avenged by punishment of the utmost severity, so that no one may ever think himself authorized to follow a friend to the extent of making war upon his country, — an extremity which, indeed, considering the course that our public affairs have begun to take, may, for aught I know, be reached at some future time. I speak thus because I feel no less concern for the fortunes of the State after my death than as to its present condition.

13. Let this, then, be enacted as the first law of friendship, that we demand of friends only what is right, and that we do for the sake of friends only what is right.[2] This understood, let us not wait to be asked. Let there be constant assiduity and no loitering in a friend's service. Let us also dare to give advice freely; for in friendship the authority of friends who give good counsel may be of the

[1] If the story of Coriolanus be not a myth, as Niebuhr supposes it to be, his suicide forms no part of the story as Livy tells it. The suicide of Themistocles is related as a supposition, not as an established fact. If he died by poison, as was said, it may have been administered by a rival in the favor of Artaxerxes.

[2] This is a virtual repetition of the law of friendship announced at the beginning of the previous section, and Cicero probably so intended it. He states the rule, then demonstrates its validity, then repeats it in an almost identical form, implying what the mathematician expresses when he puts at the end of a demonstration *Quod erat demonstrandum.*

greatest value. Let admonition be administered, too, not only in plain terms, but even with severity, if need be, and let heed be given to such admonition.

On this subject some things that appear to me strange have, as I am told, been maintained by certain Greeks who are accounted as philosophers, and are so skilled in sophistry that there is nothing which they cannot seem to prove. Some of them hold that very intimate friendships are to be avoided; that there is no need that one feel solicitude for others; that it is enough and more than enough to take care of your own concerns, and annoying to be involved to any considerable extent in affairs not belonging to you; that the best way is to have the reins of friendship as loose as possible, so that you can tighten them or let them go at pleasure; for, according to them, ease is the chief essential to happy living, and this the mind cannot enjoy, if it bears, as it were, the pains of travail in behalf of a larger or smaller circle of friends.[1]

---

[1] This passage seems to be a paraphrase of a passage in the *Hippolytus* of Euripides, in which the Nurse says: "It behooves mortals to form moderate friendships with one another, and not to the very marrow of the soul; and the affections of the mind should be held loosely, so that we may slacken or tighten them. That one soul should be in travail for two is a heavy burden." Euripides was regarded, and rightly, as no less a philosopher than a tragedian, and was not infrequently styled σοφός. Cicero here veils his thorough conversance with Greek literature and philosophy, and assumes the part of Laelius, in whose time, though

Others,[1] I am told, with even much less of true human feeling, teach what I touched upon briefly a a little while ago, that friendships are to be sought for defence and help, not on account of good-will and affection. The less of self-confidence and the less of strength one has, the more is he inclined to make friends. Thus it is that women[2] seek the support of friendship more than men do, the poor more than the rich, the unfortunate more than those who seem happy. Oh, pre-eminent wisdom! It is like taking the sun out of the world, to bereave human life of friendship, than which the immortal gods have given man nothing better, nothing more gladdening. What is the ease of which they speak? It is indeed pleasing in aspect, but on many occasions it is to be renounced; for it is not fitting, in order to avoid solicitude, either to refuse to undertake any right cause or act, or to drop it after it is undertaken. If we flee from care, we must flee from virtue, which of necessity with no little care spurns and abhors its opposites, as goodness spurns and abhors wickedness; temperance, excess; courage, cowardice. Thus you

Greek was not omitted in the education of cultivated men, the study was comparatively new, and was not carried to any great extent.

[1] The Epicureans.

[2] Latin, *mulierculae*, a diminutive, meaning, however, not *little women*, but denoting the feebleness and dependence of women in comparison with men. It must be confessed, too, that the term is sometimes used, and perhaps here, semi-contemptuously; for the Roman man felt an overweening pride in mere manhood.

may see that honest men are excessively grieved
by the dishonest, the brave by the pusillanimous,
those who lead sober lives by the dissolute.   It is
indeed characteristic of a well-ordered mind to rejoice in what is good and to be grieved by the opposite.   If, then, pain of mind fall to the lot of a wise
man, as it must of necessity unless we imagine his
mind divested of its humanity, why should we take
friendship wholly out of life, lest we experience
some little trouble on account of it?   Yet more; if
emotion be eliminated, what difference is there, I
say not between a man and a brute, but between a
man and a rock, or the trunk of a tree, or any inanimate object?   Nor are those to be listened to, who
regard virtue as something hard and iron-like.[1]   As
in many other matters, so in friendship, it is tender
and flexible, so that it expands, as it were, with a
friend's well-being, and shrinks when his peace is
disturbed.   Therefore the pain which must often be
incurred on a friend's account is not of sufficient
moment to banish friendship from human life, any
more than the occasional care and trouble which
the virtues bring should be a reason for renouncing
them.

14. Since virtue attracts friendship, as I have
said, if there shines forth any manifestation of vir-

---

[1] Here, undoubtedly, Cicero refers to the sterner type of Stoicism, which in his time was already obsolescent, and was yielding
place to the milder, while no less rigid, ethics of which the *De
Officiis* may be regarded as the manual.

tue with which a mind similarly disposed can come
into contact and union, from such intercourse love
must of necessity spring. For what is so absurd as
to be charmed with many things that have no substantial worth, as with office, fame, architecture,
dress, and genteel appearance, but not to be in any
wise charmed by a mind endowed with virtue, and
capable of either loving, or — if I may use the
word — re-loving ?[1] Nothing indeed yields a richer
revenue than kind affections; nothing gives more
delight than the interchange of friendly cares and
offices. Then if we add, as we rightly may, that
there is nothing which so allures and attracts aught
else to itself as the likeness of character does to
friendship, it will certainly be admitted that good
men love good men and adopt them into fellowship,
as if united with them by kindred and by nature.
By nature, I say; for nothing is more craving or
greedy of its like than nature. This, then, as I
think, is evident, Fannius and Scaevola, that among
the good toward the good there cannot but be mutual kind feeling, and in this we have a fountain of
friendship established by nature.

But the same kind feeling extends to the community at large. For virtue is not unsympathetic, nor
unserviceable,[2] nor proud. It is wont even to watch
over the well-being of whole nations, and to give

---

[1] Latin, *redamare*, a word coined by Cicero, and used with the
apology, *ut ita dicam*.

[2] Latin, *immunis*, literally, without office.

them the wisest counsel, which it would not do if
it had no love for the people.

Now those who maintain that friendships are
formed from motives of utility annul, as it seems to
me, the most endearing bond of friendship; for it
is not so much benefit obtained through a friend as
it is the very love of the friend that gives delight.
What comes from a friend confers pleasure, only in
case it bears tokens of his interest in us; and so
far is it from the truth that friendships are cultivated from a sense of need, that those fully endowed
with wealth and resources, especially with virtue,
which is the surest safeguard, and thus in no need
of friends, are the very persons who are the most
generous and munificent. Indeed, I hardly know
whether it may not be desirable that our friends
should never have need of our services. Yet in the
case of Scipio and myself, what room would there
have been for the active exercise of my zeal in his
behalf, had he never needed my counsel or help at
home or in the field ? In this instance, however,
the service came after the friendship, not the friendship after the service.

15. If these things are so, men who are given up
to pleasure are not to be listened to when they
express their opinions about friendship, of which
they can have no knowledge either by experience or
by reflection. For, by the faith of gods and men,
who is there that would be willing to have a super-
abundance of all objects of desire and to live in the

utmost fulness of wealth and what wealth can bring, on condition of neither loving any one nor being loved by any one? This, indeed, is the life of tyrants, in which there is no good faith, no affection, no fixed confidence in kindly feeling, perpetual suspicion and anxiety, and no room for friendship; for who can love either him whom he fears, or him by whom he thinks that he is feared? Yet they receive the show of homage, but only while the occasion for it lasts.[1] If they chance to fall, as they commonly have fallen, they then ascertain how destitute of friends they have been, as Tarquin is reported to have said that he learned what faithful and what unfaithful friends he had, when he could no longer render back favors to those of either class, — although I wonder whether pride and insolence like his could have had any friends. Moreover, as his character could not have won real friends, so is the good fortune of many who occupy foremost places of influence so held as to preclude faithful friendships. Not only is Fortune blind, but she generally makes those blind whom she embraces. Thus they are almost always beside themselves under the influence of haughtiness and waywardness; nor can there be created anything more utterly insupportable than a fortune-favored fool. There are to be seen those who previously behaved

---

[1] Latin, *dum taxat ad tempus;* that is, while the homage rendered is in close contact with the occasion, — with the immunity or profit to be purchased by it.

with propriety who are changed by station, power,
or prosperity, and who spurn their old friendships
and lavish indulgence on the new. But what is
more foolish than when men have resources, means,
wealth at their fullest command, and can obtain
horses, servants, splendid raiment, costly vases,
whatever money can buy, for them not to procure
friends, who are, if I may so speak, the best and
the most beautiful furniture of human life? Other
things which a man may procure know not him who
procures them, nor do they labor for his sake, —
indeed, they belong to him who can make them his
by the right of superior strength. But every one
has his own firm and sure possession of his friendships; while even if those things which seem the
gifts of fortune remain, still life unadorned and
deserted by friends cannot be happy. But enough
has been said on this branch of our subject.

16. We must now determine the limits or bounds
of friendship. On this subject I find three opinions
proposed, neither of which has my approval, — the
first, that we should do for our friends just what we
would do for ourselves; the second, that our good
offices to our friends should correspond in quantity
and quality to those which they perform for us;
the third, that one's friends should value him
according to his own self-estimate. I cannot give
unqualified assent to either of these opinions. The
first — that one should be ready to do for his
friends precisely what he would do for himself — is

inadmissible. How many things there are that we do for our friends which we should never do on our own account! — such as making a request, even an entreaty, of a man unworthy of respect, or inveighing against some person with a degree of bitterness, nay, in terms of vehement reproach. In fine, we are perfectly right in doing in behalf of a friend things that in our own case would be decidedly unbecoming. There are also many ways in which good men detract largely from their own comfort, or suffer it to be impaired, that a friend may have the enjoyment which they sacrifice. The second opinion is that which limits kind offices and good-will by the rule of equality. This is simply making friendship a matter of calculation, with the view of keeping a debtor and creditor account evenly balanced. To me friendship seems more affluent and generous, and not disposed to keep strict watch lest it may give more than it receives, and to fear that a part of its due may be spilled over or suffered to leak out, or that it may heap up its own measure over-full in return.[1] But worst of all is the third limit, which prescribes that friends shall take a man's opinion of himself as a measure for their estimate and treatment of him. There are some per-

---

[1] We have here, first, a figure drawn from pecuniary accounts, then one from liquid measure, then one from dry measure, — all designed to affix the brand of the most petty meanness on the (so-called) friendship which makes it a point neither to leave nor to brook a preponderance of obligation on either side.

sons who are liable to fits of depression, or who have little hope of better fortune than the present. In such a case, it is the part of a friend, not to hold the position toward his friend which he holds toward himself, but to make the efficient endeavor to rouse him from his despondency, and to lead him to better hope and a more cheerful train of thought. It remains for me, then, to establish another limit of friendship. But first let me tell you what Scipio was wont to speak of with the severest censure. He maintained that no utterance could have been invented more inimical to friendship [1] than that of him who said that one ought to love as if he were going at some future time to hate; nor could he be brought to believe that this maxim came, as was reported, from Bias, who was one of the seven wise men, but he regarded it as having proceeded from some sordid person, who was either inordinately ambitious, or desirous of bringing everything under his own control. For how can one be a friend to him to whom he thinks that he may possibly become an enemy? In this case one would of necessity desire and choose that his friend should commit offences very frequently, so as to give him, so to speak, the more numerous handles for fault-finding; and on the other hand one would be vexed, pained, aggrieved by all the right and fitting things that friends do. This precept, then, from whomsoever it came, amounts to the annulling of friendship. The

---

[1] Latin, *inimiciorem* (that is, *in-amiciorem*) *amicitiae.*

proper rule should be, that we exercise so much caution in forming friendships, that we should never begin to love a friend whom it is possible that we should ever hate; but even in case we should have been unfortunate in our choice, Scipio thought that it would be wiser to bear the disappointment when it comes than to keep the contingency of future alienation in view.

17. I would then define the terms of friendship by saying that, where friends are of blameless character, there may fittingly be between them a community of all interests, plans, and purposes, without any exception, even so far that, if perchance there be occasion for furthering the not entirely right wishes of friends when life or reputation is at stake, one may in their behalf deviate somewhat from a perfectly straight course,[1] yet not so far as to

---

[1] This at first sight appears like a license to yield up moral considerations to friendship, though the qualification, in the sequel, "not so far as to incur absolute dishonor," and "virtue is by no means to be sacrificed," seem saving clauses. But Cicero certainly has a right to be his own interpreter, since in the *De Officiis*, as I think, he explains in full, and in accordance with the highest moral principle, what he means here; and we have a double right to insist on this interpretation, first, because the *De Officiis* was written so very little while after the *De Amicitia*, and both at so ripe an age, that a change of opinion on important matters was improbable, and, secondly, because in the later treatise he expressly refers to the former as giving in full his views on friendship, and thus virtually sanctions that treatise. Now in the *De Officiis* he says: "A good man will do nothing against the State, or in violation of his oath or of good faith, for the sake of his

incur absolute dishonor.  There is a point up to
which a concession made to friendship is venial.
But we are not bound to be careless of our own
reputation, nor ought we to regard the esteem of
our fellow-citizens as an instrument of small importance in the management of such affairs as devolve
upon us, — an esteem which it is base to conciliate [1]
by flattery and fawning.  Virtue, which has the
sincere regard of the people as its consequence, is
by no means to be sacrificed to friendship.

friend, not even if he were a judge in his friend's case. . . . He
will yield so far to friendship as to wish his friend's case to be
worthy of succeeding, and to accommodate him as to the time of
trial, within legal limits.   But inasmuch as he must give sentence
upon his oath, he will bear it in mind that he has God for a witness."   In another passage of the *De Officiis,* Cicero asserts, somewhat hesitatingly, yet on the authority of Panaetius as the
strictest of Stoics, the moral rightfulness of "defending on some
occasions a guilty man, if he be not utterly depraved and false to
all human relations."   As in the passage on which I am comment-
ing special reference is made to the peril of life or reputation, what
Cicero contends for, as it seems to me, is the right of defending a
guilty friend as an advocate, or of favoring him as to time and
mode of trial as a judge.   Aulus Gellius, in connection with this
passage in the *De Amicitia,* tells the following story of Chilo, who
was on some of the lists of the seven wise men.   Chilo, on the
last day of his life, said that the only thing that gave him uneasy
thought, and was burdensome to his conscience, was that once
when he and two other men were judges in a case in which a friend
of his was on trial for a capital crime, he, in accordance with his own
conviction, voted his friend guilty, but so influenced the minds of
his two associates that they gave their voice for his acquittal.

[1] Latin, *colligere,* to collect, or gather up, one by one, the good-
will of each individual citizen.

But, to return to Scipio, who was all the time talking about friendship, he often complained that men exercised greater care about all other matters; that one could always tell how many goats and sheep he had, but could not tell how many friends he had ; and that men were careful in selecting their beasts, but were negligent in the choice of friends, and had nothing like marks and tokens[1] by which to determine the fitness of friends.

Firm, steadfast, self-consistent men are to be chosen as friends, and of this kind of men there is a great dearth. It is very difficult to judge of character before we have tested it; but we can test it only after friendship is begun. Thus friendship is prone to outrun judgment, and to render a fair trial impossible. It is therefore the part of a wise man to arrest the impulse of kindly feeling, as we check a carriage in its course, that, as we use only horses that have been tried, so we may avail ourselves of friendships in which the characters of our friends have been somehow put to the test. Some readily show how fickle their friendship is in paltry pecuniary matters ; others, whom a slight consideration of that kind cannot influence, betray themselves when a large amount is involved. But if some can be found who think it mean to prefer money to friendship, where shall we come upon those who do not put honors, civic offices, military commands, places

---

[1] Latin, *signa et notas*, the marks and tokens by which the quality and worth of goats and sheep were estimated.

of power and trust, before friendship, so that when these are offered on the one hand, and the claims of friendship on the other, they will much rather make choice of the objects of ambition? For nature is too feeble to despise a commanding station; and even though it be obtained by the violation of friendship, men think that this fault will be thrown into obscurity, because it was not without a weighty motive that they held friendship in abeyance. Thus true friendships are rare among those who are in public office, and concerned in the affairs of the State. For where will you find him who prefers a friend's promotion to his own? What more shall I say? Not to dwell longer on the influence of ambition upon friendship, how burdensome, how difficult does it seem to most men to share misfortunes! to which it is not easy to find those who are willing to stoop. Although Ennius is right in saying,

"In unsure fortune a sure friend is seen,"

yet one of these two things convicts most persons of fickleness and weakness, — either their despising their friends when they themselves are prosperous, or deserting their friends in adversity.

18. Him, then, who alike in either event shall have shown himself unwavering, constant, firm in friendship, we ought to regard as of an exceedingly rare and almost divine order of men.

Still further, good faith is essential to the maintenance of the stability and constancy which we demand in friendship; for nothing that is unfaithful is stable. It is, moreover, fitting to choose for a friend one who is frank, affable, accommodating, interested in the same things with ourselves, — all which qualities come under the head of fidelity; for a changeful and wily disposition cannot be faithful, nor can he who has not like interests and a kindred nature with his friend be either faithful or stable. I ought to add that a friend should neither take pleasure in finding fault with his friend, nor give credit to the charges which others may bring against him, — all which is implied in the constancy of which I have been speaking. Thus we come back to the truth which I announced at the beginning of our conversation, that friendship can exist only between the good. It is, indeed, the part of a good or — what is the same thing — a wise man[1] to adhere to these two principles in friendship, — first, that he tolerate no feigning or dissembling (for an ingenuous man will rather show even open hatred than hide his feeling by his face); and, secondly, that he not only repel charges made against his friend by others, but that he be not himself suspicious, and always thinking that his friend has done something unfriendly.

To these requisites there may well be added suavity of speech and manners, which is of no little worth as giving a relish to the intercourse of friendship. Rigidness and austerity of demeanor on every

---

[1] Wisdom and goodness were identical with the Stoics.

4

occasion indeed carry weight with them ; but friendship ought to be more gentle and mild, and more inclined to all that is genial and affable.

19. There occurs here a question by no means difficult,[1] whether at any time new friends worthy of our love are to be preferred to the old, as we are wont to prefer young horses to those that have passed their prime. Shame that there should be hesitation as to the answer! There ought to be no satiety of friendships, as there is rightly of many other things. The older a friendship is, the more precious should it be, as is the case with wines that will bear keeping ;[2] and there is truth in the proverb, that many pecks of salt must be eaten together to bring friendship to perfection.[3] If new friendships offer the hope of fruit, like the young shoots in the grain-field that give promise of harvest, they are not indeed to be spurned ; yet the old are to be kept in their place. There

---

[1] Latin, *subdifficilis*, which I should render *somewhat difficult*, did not Cicero treat the question as one that presents no difficulty. In the ancient tongues, as in our own, or even more than in our own, a word is often better defined by its use than in the dictionary.

[2] Some of the best Italian wines will not " bear keeping," and it was probably true of more of them in Cicero's time than now that wines are so often vitiated by strong alcoholic mixtures in order to preserve them. Cato, in his *De Re Rustica*, prescribes a method of determining whether the wine of any given vintage will " keep."

[3] Aristotle quotes this as a proverbial saying, so that it must be of very great antiquity.

is very great power in long habit. To recur to
the horse, there is no one who would not rather
use the horse to which he has become accustomed, if he is still sound, than one unbroken
and new. Nor has habit this power merely as
to the movements of an animal; it prevails no
less as to inanimate objects. We are charmed
with the places, though mountainous and woody,[1]
where we have made a long sojourn. But what is
most remarkable in friendship is that it puts a
man on an equality with his inferior. For there
often are in a circle of friends those who excel the
rest, as was the case with Scipio in our flock, if I
may use the word. He never assumed superiority
over Philus, never over Rupilius, never over Mummius, never over friends of an order lower than his
own. Indeed he always reverenced as a superior,
because older than himself, his brother Quintus
Maximus,[2] a thoroughly worthy man, but by no
means his equal; and in fact he wanted to make all
his friends of the more consequence by whatever
advantages he himself possessed. This example all
ought to imitate, that if they have attained any superiority of virtue, genius, fortune, they may impart

[1] Therefore uninviting; for mountain and forest had not in
early time the charm which we find in them. Indeed, the love
of nature uncultivated and unadorned is, for the most part, of
modern growth.

[2] Quintus Fabius Maximus Aemilianus, the eldest son of
Aemilius Paulus, and the adopted son of Fabius Maximus.

it to and share it with those with whom they are the most closely connected; and that if they are of humble parentage, and have kindred of slender ability or fortune, they may increase their means of well-being, and reflect honor and worth upon them, — as in fable those who were long in servile condition through ignorance of their parentage and race, when they were recognized and found to be sons either of gods or of kings, retained their love for the shepherds whom for many years they supposed to be their fathers. Much more ought the like to be done in the case of real and well-known fathers; for the best fruit of genius, and virtue, and every kind of excellence is reaped when it is thus bestowed on near kindred and friends.

20. Moreover, as among persons bound by ties of friendship and intimacy those who hold the higher place ought to bring themselves down to the same plane with their inferiors, so ought these last not to feel aggrieved because they are surpassed in ability, or fortune, or rank by their friends. Most of them, however, are always finding some ground of complaint, or even of reproach, especially if they can plead any service that they have rendered faithfully, in a friendly way, and with a certain amount of painstaking on their part. Such men, indeed, are hateful when they reproach their friends on the score of services which he on whom they were bestowed ought to bear in mind, but which it is unbecoming for him who conferred them to recount.

Those who are superior ought, undoubtedly, not only to waive all pretension in friendly intercourse, but to do what they can to raise their humbler friends to their own level.[1] There are some who give their friends trouble by imagining that they are held in low esteem, which, however, is not apt to be the case except with those who think meanly of themselves. Those who feel thus ought to be raised to a just self-esteem, not only by kind words, but by substantial service. But what you do for any one must be measured, first by your own ability, and then by the capacity of him whom you would favor and help. For, however great your influence may be, you cannot raise all your friends to the highest positions. Thus Scipio could effect the election of Publius Rupilius to the consulship ; but he could not do the same for his brother Lucius.[2] In general, friendships that are properly so called are formed between persons of mature years and established character; nor if young men have been fond of hunting or of ball-playing, is there any need of permanent attachment to those whom they then liked as associates in the same sport. On this principle our nurses and the slaves that led us to school will demand by right of priority the highest grade

---

[1] Or, as it might be rendered by supplying a *se*, "so ought the humbler to do what they can to raise themselves." Some of the commentators prefer this sense ; but if Cicero meant *se*, I think that he would have written it.

[2] The brother of Publius Rupilius, not his own brother.

of affectionate regard, — persons, indeed, who are not to be neglected, but who are on a somewhat different footing from that of friends. Friendships formed solely from early associations cannot last; for differences of character grow out of a diversity of pursuits, and unlikeness of character dissolves friendships. Nor is there any reason why good men cannot be the friends of bad men, or bad men of good, except that the dissiliency of pursuits and of character between them is as great as it can be.

It is also a counsel worthy of heed, that excessive fondness be not suffered to interfere, as it does too often, with important services that a friend can render. To resort again to fable, Neoptolemus could not have taken Troy[1] if he had chosen to comply with the wishes of Lycomedes, who brought him up, and who with many tears attempted to dissuade him from his expedition. Equally in actual life there are not infrequently important occasions on which the society of friends must be for a time abandoned; and he who would prevent this because he cannot easily bear the separation, is of a weak and unmanly nature, and for that very reason unfit to fill the place of a friend. In fine, in all matters you should take into consideration both what you may reasonably demand of your friend, and what you can fitly suffer him to obtain from you.

[1] Or rather, could not have borne the indispensable part which it was predicted that he should bear in the taking of Troy.

21. The misfortune involved in the dissolution of friendships is sometimes unavoidable; for I am now coming down from the intimacies of wise men to common friendships. Faults of friends often betray themselves openly — whether to the injury of their friends themselves, or of strangers — in such a way that the disgrace falls back upon their friends. Such friendships are to be effaced by the suspension of intercourse, and, as I have heard Cato say, to be unstitched rather than cut asunder, unless some quite intolerable offence flames out to full view, so that it can be neither right nor honorable not to effect an immediate separation and dissevering. But if there shall have been some change either in character or in the habits of life, or if there have sprung up some difference of opinion as to public affairs, — I am speaking, as I have just said, of common friendships, not of those between wise men, — care should be taken lest there be the appearance, not only of friendship dropped, but of enmity taken up; for nothing is more unbecoming than to wage war with a man with whom you have lived on terms of intimacy. Scipio, as you know, had withdrawn from the friendship of Quintus Pompeius [1] on my

---

[1] Laelius intending to present himself as a candidate for the consulship, Scipio asked Pompeius whether he was going to be a candidate, and when he replied in the negative, asked him to use his influence in behalf of Laelius. This Pompeius promised, and then, instead of being true to his word, offered himself for the consulship, and was elected.

account; he became alienated from Metellus[1] because of their different views as to the administration of the State. In both cases he conducted himself with gravity and dignity, and without any feeling of bitterness. The endeavor, then, must first be, to prevent discord from taking place among friends, and if anything of the kind occurs, to see that the friendship may seem to be extinguished rather than crushed out. Care must thus be taken lest friendships lapse into violent enmities, whence are generated quarrels, slanders, insults, which yet, if not utterly intolerable, are to be endured, and this honor rendered to old friendship, that the blame may rest with him who does, not with him who suffers, the wrong.

The one surety and preventive against these mistakes and misfortunes is, not to form attachments too soon, nor for those unworthy of such regard.

But it is those in whose very selves there is reason why they should be loved, that are worthy of friendship. A rare class of men! Indeed, superlatively excellent objects of every sort are rare, nor is anything more difficult than to discover that which is in all respects perfect in its kind. But most persons have acquired the habit of recognizing

[1] Scipio and Metellus, though their intimacy was suspended for political reasons, held each other in the highest regard ; and no person in Rome expressed profounder sorrow than Metellus for Scipio's death, or was more warm in his praise as a man of unparalleled ability, worth, and patriotism.

nothing as good in human relations and affairs that
does not produce some revenue, and they most love
those friends, as they do those cattle, that will yield
them the greatest gain. Thus they lack that most
beautiful and most natural friendship, which is to
be sought in itself and for its own sake; nor can
they know from experience what and how great is
the power of such friendship. One loves himself,
not in order to exact from himself any wages for
such love, but because he is in himself dear to himself. Now, unless this same property be transferred
to friendship, a true friend will never be found; for
such a friend is, as it were, another self. But if it
is seen in beasts, birds, fishes, animals tame and
wild, that they first love themselves (for self-love is
born with everything that lives), and that they then
require and seek those of their kind to whom they
may attach themselves, and do so with desire and
with a certain semblance of human love, how much
more is this natural in man, who both loves himself, and craves another whose soul he may so blend
with his own as almost to make one out of two!

22. But men in general are so perverse, not to
say shameless, as to wish a friend to be in character
what they themselves could not be, and they expect
of friends what they do not give them in return.
The proper course, however, is for one first to be
himself a good man, and then to seek another
like himself. In such persons the stability of
friendship, of which I have been speaking, can be

made sure, since, united in mutual love, they will, in the first place, hold in subjection the desires to which others are enslaved; then they will find delight in whatever is equitable and just, and each will take upon himself any labor or burden in the other's stead, while neither will ever ask of the other aught that is not honorable and right. Nor will they merely cherish and love, they will even reverence each other. But he who bereaves friendship of mutual respect[1] takes from it its greatest ornament. Therefore those are in fatal error who think that in friendship there is free license for all lusts and evil practices. Friendship is given by nature, not as a companion of the vices, but as a helper of the virtues, that, as solitary virtue might not be able to attain the summit of excellence, united and associated with another it might reach that eminence. As to those between whom there is, or has been, or shall be such an alliance, the fellowship is to be regarded as the best and happiest possible, inasmuch as it leads to the highest good that nature can bestow. This is the alliance, I say, in which are included all things that men think worthy their endeavor,—honor, fame, peace of mind, and pleasure, so that if these be present life is happy, and cannot be happy without them. Such a life being the best

---

[1] Latin, *verecundia*, an indefinite word; for it may have almost any good meaning. I have rendered it *respect*, because I have no doubt that it derives its meaning here from *verebuntur*, which I have rendered *reverence*, in the preceding sentence.

and greatest boon, if we wish to make it ours, we must devote ourselves to the cultivation of virtue, without which we can attain neither friendship nor anything else desirable. But if virtue be left out of the account, those who think that they have friends perceive that they are mistaken when some important crisis compels them to put their friends to the test. Therefore — for it is worth reiterating — you ought to love after having exercised your judgment on your friends, instead of forming your judgment of them after you have begun to love them. But while in many things we are chargeable with carelessness, we are most so in choosing and keeping our friends. We reverse the old proverb,[1] take counsel after acting, and attempt to do over again what we have done ; for after having become closely connected by long habit and even by mutual services, some occasion of offence springs up, and we suddenly break in sunder a friendship in full career.

23. The more blameworthy are they who are so very careless in a matter of so essential importance. Indeed, among things appertaining to human life, it is friendship alone that has the unanimous voice

---

[1] What this proverb may have been we cannot determine with precision from its opposite ; but the caution based upon it might remind one of our proverb about shutting the barn-door after the horse is stolen. The words, *acta agimus,* so terse that they can be translated only by a paraphrase, are probably the converse of the proverb, which may have been something like *non agenda sunt acta.*

of all men as to its capacity of service. By many even virtue is scorned, and is said to be a mere matter of display and ostentation. Many despise wealth, and, contented with little, take pleasure in slender diet and inexpensive living. Though some are inflamed with desire for office, many there are who hold it in so low esteem that they can imagine nothing more inane or worthless. Other things, too, which seem to some admirable, very many regard as of no value. But all have the same feeling as to friendship, — alike those who devote themselves to the public service, those who take delight in learning and philosophy, those who manage their own affairs in a quiet way, and, lastly, those who are wholly given up to sensual pleasure. They all agree that without friendship life cannot be, if one only means to live in some form or measure respectably.[1] For friendship somehow twines through all lives, and leaves no mode of being without its presence. Even if one be of so rude and savage a nature as to shun and hate the society of men, as we have learned was the case with that Timon of Athens,[2] if there ever was such a man,[3] he yet

---

[1] Latin, *liberaliter;* that is, worthily of a free man.

[2] Plutarch says that Timon had an associate, virtually a friend, not unlike himself, Apemantus, on whom he freely vented his spite and scorn for all the world beside, and that he also took a special liking to Alcibiades in his youth, perhaps as to one fitted and destined to do an untold amount of mischief.

[3] Latin, *nescio, quem,* I know not whom, or, of whom I am ignorant ; that is, there may or may not have been such a man.

cannot help seeking some one in whose presence he may vomit the venom of his bitterness. The need of friendship would be best shown, were such a thing possible, if some god should take us away from this human crowd, and place us anywhere in solitude, giving us there an abundant supply of all things that nature craves, but depriving us utterly of the sight of a human countenance. Who could be found of so iron make that he could endure[1] such a life, and whom solitude would not render incapable of enjoying any kind of pleasure? That is true then which, if I remember aright, our elders used to say that they had heard from their seniors in age as having come from Archytas of Tarentum,—"If one had ascended to heaven, and had obtained a full view of the nature of the universe and the beauty of the stars, yet his admiration would be without delight, if there were no one to whom he could tell what he had seen." Thus Nature has no love for solitude, and always leans, as it were, on some support; and the sweetest support is found in the most intimate friendship.

24. But while Nature declares by so many tokens what she desires, craves, needs, we — I know not how — grow deaf, and fail to hear her counsel.

Intercourse among friends assumes many different forms and modes, and there frequently arise causes

---

[1] Latin, tam . . . *ferreus*, qui . . . *ferre* posset, — an assonance which cannot be represented by corresponding English words.

of suspicion and offence, which it is the part of a wise man sometimes to avoid, sometimes to remove, sometimes to bear. One ground of offence, namely, freedom in telling the truth, must be put entirely away, in order that friendship may retain its serviceableness and its good faith; for friends often need to be admonished and reproved, and such offices, when kindly performed, ought to be received in a friendly way. Yet somehow we witness in actual life what my friend[1] says in his play of *Andria :* —

" Complacency[2] wins friends; but truth gives birth to hatred."

Truth is offensive, if hatred, the bane of friendship, is indeed born of it ; but much more offensive is complacency, when in its indulgence for wrong-doing it suffers a friend to go headlong to ruin. The greatest blame, however, rests on him who both spurns the truth when it is told him, and is driven by the complacency of friends to self-deception. In this matter, therefore, there should be the utmost discretion and care, first, that admonition be without bitterness, then, that reproof be without invective. But in complacency — for I am ready to use the word which Terence furnishes — let pleasing truth be told ; let flattery, the handmaid of the

---

[1] Terence, with whom Laelius was so intimate that he was reported, probably on no sufficient ground, to have aided in the composition of some of the plays that bear Terence's name. This verse is from the *Andria.*

[2] *Obsequium.*

vices, be put far away, as unworthy, not only of
a friend, but of any man above the condition of
a slave; for there is one way of living with a
tyrant, another with a friend. We may well despair of saving him whose ears are so closed to the
truth that he cannot hear what is true from a
friend. Among the many pithy sayings of Cato
was this: "There are some who owe more to their
bitter enemies than to the friends that seem sweet;
for those often tell the truth, these never." It is
indeed ridiculous for those who are admonished
not to be annoyed by what ought to trouble them,
and to be annoyed by what ought to give them no
offence. Their faults give them no pain; they take
it hard that they are reproved; — while they ought,
on the contrary, to be grieved for their wrong-doing,
to rejoice in their correction.

25. As, then, it belongs to friendship both to
admonish and to be admonished, and to do the
former freely, yet not harshly, to receive the latter
patiently, not resentfully, so it is to be maintained
that friendship has no greater pest than adulation,
flattery, subserviency; for under its many names [1]
a brand should be put on this vice of fickle and

---

[1] Latin, *multis nominibus*, which some commentators render
"on many accounts," *nomen* being used familiarly in the sense of
"account" with reference to matters of purchase and sale, debt
and credit. But I think that Cicero brings in *adulatio, blanditia,*
and *assentatio,* as so many synonyms of *obsequium,* intending to
comprehend in his indictment whatever *alias* the one vice may
assume.

deceitful men, who say everything with the view of
giving pleasure, without any reference to the truth.
While simulation is bad on every account, inasmuch as it renders the discernment of the truth
which it defaces impossible, it is most of all inimical to friendship; for it is fatal to sincerity, without which the name of friendship ceases to have
any meaning. For since the essence of friendship
consists in this, that one mind is, as it were, made
out of several, how can this be, if in one of the
several there shall be not always one and the same
mind, but a mind varying, changeful, manifold?
And what can be so flexible, so far out of its rightful course, as the mind of him who adapts himself,
not only to the feelings and wishes, but even to the
look and gesture, of another?

> "Does one say No or Yes? I say so too.
> My rule is to assent to everything,"

as Terence, whom I have just quoted, says; but he
says it in the person of Gnatho,[1] — a sort of friend
which only a frivolous mind can tolerate. But as
there are many like Gnatho, who stand higher
than he did in place, fortune, and reputation, their
subserviency is the more offensive, because their
position gives weight to their falsehood.

But a flattering friend may be distinguished and
discriminated from a true friend by proper care, as
easily as everything disguised and feigned is seen to

---

[1] A parasite, in Terence's play of *Eunuchus*, from which these
verses are quoted.

differ from what is genuine and real. The assembly of the people, though consisting of persons who have the least skill in judgment, yet always knows the difference between him who, merely seeking popularity, is sycophantic and fickle, and a firm, inflexible, and substantial citizen. With what soft words did Caius Papirius [1] steal [2] into the ears of the assembly a little while ago, when he brought forward the law about the re-election of the tribunes of the people! [3] I opposed the law. But, to say nothing of myself, I will rather speak of Scipio. How great, ye immortal gods, was his dignity of bearing! What majesty of address! So that you might easily call him the leader of the Roman people, rather than one of their number. But you were there, and you have copies of his speech. Thus the law was rejected by vote of the people. But, to return to myself, you remember, when Quintus Maximus, Scipio's brother, and Lucius Mancinus were Consuls, how much the people seemed to favor the law of Caius Licinius Crassus about the priests. The law proposed to transfer the election of priests

---

[1] Caius Papirius Carbo, the suspected murderer of Scipio.

[2] Latin, *influebat*, flowed in, a figure beautifully appropriate, but hardly translatable.

[3] There was an old law, which prohibited the re-election of a citizen to the same office till after an interval of ten years. In the law here referred to, Carbo — then Tribune — sought to provide for the re-election of tribunes as soon and as often as the people might choose, thus undoubtedly hoping to secure for himself a permanent tenure of office.

from their own respective colleges to the suffrage of the people;[1] and he on that occasion introduced the custom of facing the people in addressing them.[2] Yet under my advocacy the religion of the immortal gods obtained the ascendency over his plausible speech. That was during my praetorship, five years before I was chosen Consul. Thus the cause was gained by its own merits rather than by official authority.

26. But if on the stage, or — what is the same thing — in the assembly of the people, in which there is ample scope for false and distorted representations, the truth only needs to be made plain and clear in order for it to prevail, what ought to be the case in friendship, which is entirely dependent for its value on truth, — in which unless, as the phrase is, you see an open bosom and show your own, you can have nothing worthy of confidence, nothing of which you can feel certain, not even the fact of your loving or being loved, since you are ignorant of what either really is? Yet this flattery of which I have spoken, harmful as it is, can injure only him who takes it in and is delighted with it. Thus it is the case that he is most ready to open his ear to flattery, who flatters himself and finds supreme

---

[1] The several pontifical colleges had been close corporations, filling their own vacancies. The law which Laelius defeated proposed transferring the election of priests to the people.

[2] It had been customary, when the Senate was in session, for him who harangued the people to face the temple where the Senate sat, thus virtually recognizing the supreme authority of that body.

delight in himself. Virtue indeed loves itself; for it has thorough knowledge of itself, and understands how worthy of love it is. But it is reputed, not real, virtue of which I am now speaking; for there are not so many possessed of virtue as there are that desire to seem virtuous. These last are delighted with flattery, and when false statements are framed purposely to satisfy and please them, they take the falsehood as valid testimony to their merit. That, however, is no friendship, in which one of the (so-called) friends does not want to hear the truth, and the other is ready to lie. The flattery of parasites on the stage would not seem amusing, were there not in the play braggart soldiers[1] to be flattered.

" Great thanks indeed did Thais render to me ?"

" Great " was a sufficient answer ; but the answer in the play is " Prodigious." The flatterer always magnifies what he whom he is aiming to please wishes to have great. But while this smooth falsehood takes effect only with those who themselves attract and invite it, even persons of a more substantial and

---

[1] Latin, *milites gloriosi*. *Miles Gloriosus* is the title of one of the comedies of Plautus ; and one of the stock characters of the ancient comedy is a conceited, swaggering, brainless soldier, who is perpetually boasting of his own valor and exploits, and who takes the most fulsome and ridiculous flattery as the due recognition of his transcendent merit. The verse here quoted is from Terence's *Eunuchus*. Thraso, a *miles gloriosus* (from whom is derived our adjective *thrasonical*), asks this question of Gnatho, the parasite, one of whose speeches is quoted in § 25. *Magnas* is the word in the question ; *ingentes*, in the answer.

solid character need to be warned to be on their
guard, lest they be ensnared by flattery of a more
cunning type.   No one who has a moderate share
of common-sense fails to detect the open flatterer ;
but great care must be taken lest the wily and cov-
ert flatterer may insinuate himself; for he is not
very easily recognized, since he often assents by
opposing, plays the game of disputing in a smooth,
caressing way, and at length submits, and suffers
himself to be outreasoned, so as to make him on
whom he is practising his arts appear to have had
the deeper insight.   But what is more disgraceful
than to be made game of ?   One must take heed
not to put himself in the condition of the character
in the play of *The Heiress :* [1] —

> " Of an old fool one never made such sport
>    As you have made of me this very day ; "

for there is no character on the stage so foolish as
that of these unwary and credulous old men.   But
I know not how my discourse has digressed from
the friendships of perfect, that is, of wise men, —
wise, I mean, so far as wisdom can fall to the lot
of man, — to friendships of a lighter sort.   Let us
then return to our original subject, and bring it to
a speedy conclusion.

---

[1] *Epicleros,* a comedy by Caecilius Statius, of whose works
only a few fragments, like this, are extant.   Next to the braggart
soldier, a credulous old man — generally a father — who could
have all manner of tricks played upon him without detecting their
import, was the favorite butt for ridicule in the ancient comedy.

27. Virtue, I say to you, Caius Fannius, and to you, Quintus Mucius, — virtue both forms and preserves friendships. In it is mutual agreement; in it is stability; in it is consistency of conduct and character. When it has put itself forth and shown its light, and has seen and recognized the same light in another, it draws near to that light, and receives in return what the other has to give; and from this intercourse love, or friendship, — call it which you may, — is kindled. These terms are equally derived in our language from loving;[1] and to love is nothing else than to cherish affection for him whom you love, with no felt need of his service, with no quest of benefit to be obtained from him; while, nevertheless, serviceableness blooms out from friendship, however little you may have had it in view.' With this affection I in my youth loved those old men, — Lucius Paulus, Marcus Cato, Caius Gallus, Publius Nasica, Tiberius Gracchus, the father-in-law of my friend Scipio. This relation is more conspicuous among those of the same age, as between myself and Scipio, Lucius Furius, Publius Rupilius, Spurius Mummius. But in my turn, as an old man, I find repose in the attachment of young men, as in yours, and in that of Quintus Tubero, and I am delighted with the intimacy of Publius Rutilius and Aulus Virginius, who are just emerging from boyhood. While the order of human life and of nature is such that another generation

---

[1] *Amor . . . amicitia . . . ab amando.*

must come upon the stage, it would be most desirable, could such a thing be, to reach the goal, so to speak, with those of our own age with whom we started on the race; but since man's life is frail and precarious, we ought always to be in quest of some younger persons whom we may love, and who will love us in return; for when love and kindness cease all enjoyment is taken out of life.

For me indeed, Scipio, though suddenly snatched away, still lives and will always live; for I loved the virtue of the man, which is not extinguished. Nor does it float before my eyes only, as I have always had it at hand; it will also be renowned and illustrious with generations to come. No one will ever enter with courage and hope on a high and noble career, without proposing to himself as a standard the memory and image of his virtue. Indeed, of all things which fortune or nature ever gave me, I have nothing that I can compare with the friendship of Scipio. In this there was a common feeling as to the affairs of the State; in this, mutual counsel as to our private concerns; in this, too, a repose full of delight. Never, so far as I know, did I offend him in the least thing; never did I hear from him a word which I would not wish to hear. We had one home;[1] the same diet, and that sim-

---

[1] This may refer to their living together on their campaigns, journeys, and rural sojourns; but more probably to the fact that each felt as much at home in the other's house as in his own.

ple ;[1] we were together, not only in military service,
but also in journeying and in our rural sojourns.
And what shall I say of our unflagging zeal in the
pursuit of knowledge, and in learning everything
new within our reach, — an employment in which,
when not under the eyes of the public, we passed all
our leisure time together? Had the recollection and
remembrance of these things died with him, I could
not anyhow bear the loss of a man, thus bound to
me in the closest intimacy and holding me in the
dearest love. But they are not blotted out, they are
rather nourished and increased by reflection and
memory; and were I entirely bereft of them, my
advanced age would still be my great comfort , for
I can miss his society but for a brief season, and all
sorrows, however heavy, if they can last but a little
while, ought to be endured.

I had these things to say to you about friendship;
and I exhort you that you so give the foremost
place to virtue without which friendship cannot
be, that with the sole exception of virtue, you may
think nothing to be preferred to friendship.

---

[1] Latin, *communis.* I do not find that this word has in Latin
the sense of *cheap* and *mean* which our word *common* has. But
here it cannot mean that Laelius and Scipio fed together, which
is sufficiently said in the preceding *idem victus*. It must therefore denote such fare as was common to them with their fellow-
citizens in general, and that is simple and not luxurious fare.

# SCIPIO'S DREAM.

1. WHEN I arrived in Africa, to serve, as you know, in the office of military Tribune of the fourth Legion, under Manius [1] Manilius as consul, I desired nothing so much as to meet Masinissa [2] the king, who for sufficient reasons [3] stood in the most friendly relation to our family. When I came to him, the old man embraced me with tears, and shortly afterward looked up to heaven and said: " I thank thee, sovereign Sun,[4] and all of you lesser

---

[1] The praenomen *Marcus* is given to Manilius in the manuscript of the *De Republica* discovered by Angelo Mai; but Manius is the reading in all previous authorities as to this special fragment.

[2] King of Numidia, — a country nearly identical in extent with the present province of Algeria. Its name defines its people, being derived from νομάδες, *nomads*. Its inhabitants were a wild, semi-savage cluster of tribes, black and white. Masinissa, though faithful to the Romans after he had convinced himself that theirs must be the ascendant star, was a crafty, treacherous, cruel prince, probably with enough of civilization to have acquired some of its vices, while he had not lost those of the savage.

[3] The elder Africanus had confirmed him in the possession of his own Numidia, and had added to it the adjoining kingdom of Cirta.

[4] The Numidians worshipped the heavenly bodies.

lights of heaven, that before I pass away from this
life I behold in my kingdom and beneath this roof
Publius Cornelius Scipio, whose very name renews
my strength, so utterly inseparable from my thought
is the memory of that best and most invincible of
men who first bore it." Then I questioned him
about his kingdom, and he asked me about our
republic; and with the many things that we had to
communicate to each other, the day wore away.

At a later hour, after an entertainment of royal
magnificence, we prolonged our conversation far
into the night, while the old man talked to me
about nothing else but Africanus, rehearsing not
only all that he had done, but all that he had said.
When we parted to go to our rest, sleep took a
stronger hold on me than usual, on account both of
the fatigue of my journey and of the lateness of
the hour. In my sleep, I suppose in consequence
of our conversation (for generally our thoughts and
utterances by day have in our sleep an effect like
that which Ennius describes in his own case as to
Homer,[1] about whom in his waking hours he was
perpetually thinking and talking), Africanus appeared to me, with an aspect that reminded me
more of his bust than of his real face. I shuddered
when I saw him. But he said: "Preserve your
presence of mind, Scipio; be not afraid, and commit to memory what I shall say to you.

[1] The first verse of the *Annales* of Ennius was : —
" In somnis mihi visus Homerus adesse poeta."

2. "Do you see that city, which was brought through me into subjection to the Roman people, but now renews its old hostility, and cannot remain quiet,"—and he showed me Carthage from a high place full of stars, shining and splendid, — "against which you, being little more than a common soldier, are coming to fight? In two years from now you as Consul will overthrow this city, and you will obtain of your own right the surname which up to this time you hold as inherited from me. When you shall have destroyed Carthage, shall have celebrated your triumph over it, shall have been Censor, and shall have traversed, as an ambassador, Egypt, Syria, Asia, and Greece, you will be chosen a second time Consul in your absence, and will put an end to one of the greatest of wars by extirpating Numantia. But when you shall be borne to the Capitol in your triumphal chariot after this war, you will find the State disturbed by the machinations of my grandson.[1]

"In this emergency, Africanus, it will behoove you to show your country the light of your energy, genius, and wisdom. But I see at that time, as it were, a double way of destiny. For when your age shall have followed the sun for eight times seven revolutions, and these two numbers[2] — each perfect,

---

[1] Tiberius Gracchus, whose mother, Cornelia, was the daughter of the elder Africanus.

[2] The Pythagoreans regarded seven as the number representing light, and eight as representing love. Seven was also a perfect

though for different reasons — shall have completed for you in the course of nature the destined period, to you alone and to your name the whole city will turn ; on you the Senate will look, on you all good citizens, on you the allies, on you the Latini. You will be the one man on whom the safety of the city will rest ; and, to say no more, you, as Dictator, must re-establish the State, if you escape the impious hands of your kindred." [1] Here, when Laelius had cried out, and the rest of the company had breathed deep sighs, Scipio, smiling pleasantly upon them, said, "I beg you not to rouse me from sleep and break up my vision. Hear the remainder of it."

3. "But that you, Africanus, may be the more prompt in the defence of the State, know that for all who shall have preserved, succored, enlarged their country, there is a certain and determined place in heaven where they enjoy eternal happiness ; for to the Supreme God who governs this whole universe nothing is more pleasing than those companies and unions of men that are called cities. Of

number, as corresponding to the number of celestial orbits (including the sun, the moon, and the five known planets), the number of days in the quarter of the moon's revolution, and the number of the gates of sense (so to speak), mouth, eyes, ears, and nostrils. Eight was a perfect number, as being first after unity on the list of cubes ; and Plato in the *Timaeus* speaks of eight celestial revolutions — including that of the earth — as unequal in duration and velocity, but as forming, in some unexplained way, a cycle synchronous with the year.

[1] See *De Amicitia* § 3, note.

these the rulers and preservers, going hence, return hither."

Here I, although I had been alarmed, not indeed so much by the fear of death as by that of the treachery of my own kindred, yet asked whether Paulus, my father, and others whom we supposed to be dead were living. "Yes, indeed," he replied, "those who have fled from the bonds of the body, like runners from the goal, live; while what is called your life is death. But do you see your father Paulus coming to you?" When I saw him, I shed a flood of tears; but he, embracing and kissing me, forbade my weeping.

Then as soon as my tears would suffer me to speak, I began by saying, "Most sacred and excellent father, since this is life, as Africanus tells me, why do I remain on the earth, and not rather hasten to come to you?" "Not so," said he; "for unless the God who has for his temple all that you now behold, shall have freed you from this prison of the body, there can be no entrance for you hither. Men have indeed been brought into being on this condition, that they should guard the globe which you see in the midst of this temple, which is called the earth; and a soul has been given to them from those eternal fires which you call constellations and stars, which, globed and round, animated with god-derived minds, complete their courses and move through their orbits with amazing speed. You, therefore, Publius, and all rightly disposed men are

bound to retain the soul in the body's keeping, nor
without the command of him who gave it to you
to depart from the life appointed for man, lest you
may seem to have taken flight from human duty as
assigned by God.   But, Scipio, like this your grandfather,[1] like me, your father, cherish justice and
that sacred observance of duty to your kind, which,
while of great worth toward parents and family, is
of supreme value toward your country.   Such a life
is the way to heaven, and to this assembly of those
who have already lived, and, released from the body,
inhabit the place which you now see," — it was that
circle that shines forth among the stars in the most
dazzling white,— "which you have learned from
the Greeks to call the Milky Way."   And as I
looked on every side I saw other things transcen-
dently glorious and wonderful.   There were stars
which we never see from here below, and all the
stars were vast far beyond what we have ever imagined.   The least of them was that which, farthest
from heaven, nearest to the earth, shone with a
borrowed light.   But the starry globes very far surpassed the earth in magnitude.   The earth itself indeed looked to me so small as to make me ashamed of
our empire, which was a mere point on its surface.

4. While I was gazing more intently on the
earth, Africanus said : " How long, I pray you, will
your mind be fastened on the ground ?   Do you not

---

[1] By adoption.   The younger Africanus was adopted by a son
of the elder.

see into the midst of what temples you have come ?
In your sight are nine orbs, or rather globes, by
which all things are held together. One is the
celestial, the outermost, embracing all the rest, —
the Supreme God himself,[1] who governs and keeps
in their places the other spheres. In this are
fixed those stars which ever roll in an unchanging
course. Beneath this are seven spheres which have
a retrograde movement, opposite to that of the
heavens. One of these is the domain of the star
which on earth they call Saturn. Next is the luminary which bears the name of Jupiter, of prosperous and healthful omen to the human race ; then,
the star of fiery red which you call Mars, and which
men regard with terror. Beneath, the Sun holds
nearly the midway space,[2] leader, prince, and ruler
of the other lights, the mind and regulating power
of the universe, so vast as to illuminate and flood
all things with his light. Him, as his companions,
Venus and Mercury follow on their different courses ;
and in a sphere still lower the moon revolves,
lighted by the rays of the sun. Beneath this there
is nothing that is not mortal and perishable, except the souls bestowed upon the human race by
the gift of the gods. Above the moon all things are

---

[1] Here crops out the Pantheism — the non-detachment or
semi-detachment of God from nature — which casts a penumbra
around monotheism and the approaches to it, almost always,
except under Hebrew and Christian auspices.

[2] The middle, as the fifth of the nine spheres, enclosed by four,
and enclosing four.

eternal. The earth, which is the central and ninth sphere, has no motion, and is the lowest[1] of all, and all heavy bodies gravitate spontaneously toward it."

5. When I had recovered from my amazement at these things I asked, "What is this sound so strong and so sweet that fills my ears?" "This," he replied, "is the melody which, at intervals unequal, yet differing in exact proportions, is made by the impulse and motion of the spheres themselves, which, softening shriller by deeper tones, produce a diversity of regular harmonies. Nor can such vast movements be urged on in silence; and by the order of nature the shriller notes sound from one extreme of the universe, the deeper from the other. Thus yonder supreme celestial sphere with its clustered stars, as it revolves more rapidly, moves with a shrill and quick strain; this lower sphere of the moon sends forth deeper notes; while the earth, the ninth sphere, remaining motionless,[2] always stands fixed in the lowest place, occupying the centre of the universe. But these eight revolutions, of which two, those of Mercury and Venus, are in unison, make seven distinct tones, with measured intervals between, and almost all things are arranged in sevens.[3] Skilled men, copying this harmony with

---

[1] The lowest because central, and therefore farthest from the outermost or celestial sphere.

[2] Therefore without sound.

[3] Latin, *qui numerus* (that is, *septem*) *rerum omnium fere nodus est.* Literally, "which number is the knot of almost everything." The more intelligible form in which I have rendered these words

strings and voice, have opened for themselves a way
back to this place, as have others who with excelling
genius have cultivated divine sciences in human
life. But the ears of men are deafened by being
filled with this melody; nor is there in you mortals
a duller sense than that of hearing. As where
the Nile at the Falls of Catadupa pours down from
the loftiest mountains, the people who live hard
by lack the sense of hearing because of the loud-
ness of the cataract, so this harmony of the whole
universe in its intensely rapid movement is so loud
that men's ears cannot take it in, even as you cannot look directly at the sun, and the keenness and
visual power of the eye are overwhelmed by its
rays." While I marvelled at these things, I ever
and anon cast my eyes again upon the earth.

6. Then Africanus said: "I perceive that you are
now fixing your eyes on the abode and home of men,
and if it seems to you small, as it really is, then
look always at these heavenly things, and despise
those earthly. For what reputation from the speech
of men, or what fame worth seeking, can you obtain?
You see that the inhabited places of the earth are
scattered and of small extent, that in the spots [1] —
so to speak — where men dwell there are vast soli-

seems to me to convey their true meaning, and my belief to that
effect is confirmed by reading what several commentators say
about the passage.

[1] Latin, *maculis*, — a figure so bold in Cicero's time as to need
an apology for its use, but now employed with no consciousness of
its being otherwise than strictly literal.

tary tracts interposed, and that those who live on
the earth are not only so separated that no com-
munication can pass from place to place, but stand,
in part at an oblique angle, in part at a right angle
with you, in part even in an opposite direction;[1]
and from these you certainly can anticipate no
fame.

"You perceive also that this same earth is girded
and surrounded by belts, two of which — the farthest from each other, and each resting at one extremity on the very pole of the heavens — you see
entirely frost-bound; while the middle and largest
of them burns under the sun's intensest heat.
Two of them are habitable, of which the southern,
whose inhabitants are your antipodes, bears no relation to your people; and see how small a part
they occupy in this other northern zone, in which
you dwell. For all of the earth with which you
have any concern — narrow at the north and south,
broader in its central portion — is a mere little
island, surrounded by that sea which you on earth
call the Atlantic, the Great Sea, the Ocean, while
yet, with such a name, you see how small it is.
To speak only of these cultivated and well-known
regions, could your name even cross this Caucasus
which you have in view, or swim beyond that

---

[1] It hardly needs to be said, that the reference here is to the
convex surface of the earth, on which those remote from one
another may hold all the various angles to each other that are
borne by the spokes of a wheel.

Ganges? Who, in what other lands may lie in the extreme east or west, or under northern or southern skies, will ever hear your name? All these cut off, you surely see within what narrow bounds your fame can seek to spread. Then, too, as regards the very persons who tell of your renown, how long will they speak of it?

7. "But even if successive generations should desire to transmit the praise of every one of us from father to son in unbroken succession, yet because of devastations by flood and fire, which will of necessity take place at a determined time, we must fail of attaining not only eternal fame, but even that of very long duration. Now of what concern is it that those who shall be born hereafter should speak of you, when you were spoken of by none who were born before you, who were not fewer, and certainly were better men? — especially, too, when among those who might hear our names there is not one that can retain the memories of a single year. Men, indeed, ordinarily measure the year only by the return of the sun, that is, one star, to its place; but when all the stars, after long intervals, shall resume their original places in the heavens, then that completed revolution may be truly called a year. As of old the sun seemed to be eclipsed and blotted out when the soul of Romulus entered these temples, so when the sun shall be again eclipsed in the same part of his course, and at the same period of the year and day, with all the

constellations and stars recalled to the point from which they started on their revolutions, then count the year as brought to a close.[1] But be assured that the twentieth part of this year has not yet come round.

"Therefore, should you renounce the hope of returning to this place in which are all things that great and excellent men can desire, of what worth is that human glory which can scarcely extend to a small part of a single year? If, then, you shall determine to look high up, and to behold continuously this dwelling and eternal home, you will neither give yourself to the flattery of the people, nor place your hope of well-being on rewards that man can bestow. Let Virtue herself by her own charms draw you to true honor. What others may say of you, regard as their concern, not yours. They will doubtless talk about you, but all that they say is confined within the narrow limits of the regions which you now see; nor did such speech as to any one ever last on into eternity, — it is buried with those who die, and lost in oblivion for those who may come afterward."

8. When he had spoken thus, I said, "O Africanus, if indeed for those who have deserved well

---

1 The Stoics maintained that the visible universe would last through such a cycle as is here described, which in their conjectural astronomy comprehended many thousands of years, and then would be consumed by fire, or somehow be reduced to chaos, and a new universe take its place.

of their country there is, as it were, an open road
by which they may enter heaven, though from boyhood treading in my father's steps and yours, I have
done no discredit to your fame, I yet shall now
strive to that end with a more watchful diligence."
And he replied: "Strive [1] indeed, and bear this in
mind, that it is not you that are mortal, but your
body only. Nor is it you whom this outward form
makes manifest; but every man's mind is he, — not
the bodily shape which can be pointed at by the
finger. Know also that you are a god, if he indeed
is a god who lives, who perceives, who remembers,
who foresees, who governs and restrains and moves
the body over which he is made ruler even as the
Supreme God holds the universe under his sway;
and in truth as the eternal God himself moves the
universe which is mortal in every part, so does the
everlasting soul move the corruptible body.

"That, indeed, which is in perpetual movement is
eternal; but that which, while imparting motion
to some other substance, derives its own movement
from some other source, must of necessity cease to
live when it ceases to move. Then that alone
which is the cause of its own motion, because it
is never deserted by itself, never has its movement suspended. But for other substances that are
moved this is the source, the first cause,[2] of movement. But the first cause has no origin; for all

---

[1] Or, you will strive indeed.
[2] Latin, *principium.*

things spring from the first cause: itself, from nothing. That indeed would not be a first cause which derived its beginning from anything else; and if it has no beginning, it never ceases to be. For the first cause, if extinct, will neither itself be born again from aught else, nor will it create aught else from itself, if indeed all things must of necessity originate from the first cause. Thus it is that the first cause of motion is derived from that which is in its nature self-moving; but this can neither be born nor die. Were it to die, the whole heaven would of necessity collapse, and all nature would stand still, nor could it find any force which could be set in movement anew from a primitive impulse.[1]

9. "Since, then, that which is the source of its own movement is manifestly eternal, who is there that can deny that this nature has been given to the soul? For whatever is moved by external impulse is soulless;[2] but whatever has a soul[3] is stirred to action by movement inward and its own; for this is the peculiar nature and virtue of the soul. Moreover, if it is this alone of all things that is the source of its own movement, it certainly did not begin to be, and is eternal.

[1] From a first cause; the first cause, by hypothesis, having ceased to be.

[2] Latin, *inanimum*.

[3] Latin, *animal*. My renderings of *inanimum* and *animal* here, if not justified by any parallel instances (and I know not whether they are), are required by the obvious meaning of the sentence.

"This soul I bid you to exercise in the best pursuits, and the best are your cares for your country's safety, by which if your soul be kept in constant action and exercise, it will have the more rapid flight to this its abode and home. This end it will attain the more readily, if, while it shall be shut up in the body, it shall peer forth, and, contemplating those things that are beyond, abstract itself as far as possible from the body. For the souls of those who have surrendered themselves to the pleasures of the body, have yielded themselves to their service, and, obeying them under the impulse of sensual lusts, have transgressed the laws of gods and men, when they pass out of their bodies are tossed to and fro around the earth, nor return to this place till they have wandered in banishment for many ages."

He departed ; I awoke from sleep.

# INDEX.

AUGUSTINE, SAINT, a work of, written on a palimpsest over a copy
    of the *De Republica,* xvi.

Carneades, sophistry of, 29 n.
Christianity, relation of, to friendship, viii.
Cicero, dramatic power of, v.
        liable to be misjudged as to the moral bearing of a pas-
        sage in the *De Amicitia,* 45 n.

*De Amicitia,* the, when written, v.
*De Republica,* discovery of the, xvii.
        form of the, xviii.

Empedocles, poem of, anticipating the theory of universal gravi-
    tation, 20 n.
Euripides, paraphrase of a passage in the *Hippolytus* of, 36 n.

Fannius, Caius, life of, xiii.
Friendship, place of, in ancient systems of ethics, vii.
        how replaced under Christian auspices, viii.
        defined, 16.
        power of, 19.
        source of, 23.
        how far dependent on mutual benefits, 25.
        how formed between individuals, 26.
        how broken, 28.
        limits of, 29.
        duties of, 32.

University Press: John Wilson & Son, Cambridge.